LOW
RIDER

Books by Philip Reed

FICTION

Bird Dog
Low Rider

NONFICTION

Free Throw
Candidly, Alan Funt

LOW RIDER

PHILIP REED

POCKET BOOKS
New York   London   Toronto   Sydney   Tokyo   Singapore

POCKET BOOKS, a division of Simon & Schuster Inc.
1230 Avenue of the Americas, New York, NY 10020

Copyright © 1998 by Philip Reed

All rights reserved, including the right to reproduce
this book or portions thereof in any form whatsoever.
For information address Pocket Books, 1230 Avenue
of the Americas, New York, NY 10020

Library of Congress Cataloging-in-Publication Data

Reed, Philip.
    Low rider / Philip Reed.
        p.   cm.
    ISBN: 0-671-00166-3
    I. Title.
PS3568.E3693L69   1998   98–15898
813'.54—dc21   CIP

First Pocket Books hardcover printing July 1998

10 9 8 7 6 5 4 3 2 1

POCKET and colophon are registered trademarks of
Simon & Schuster Inc.

Printed in the U.S.A.

To my Grandfather,
Kenneth Vaux Reed,
the first and most important
writer in my early years.

Acknowledgments

Once again I want to express my thanks to my agent, John Hawkins, for his keen eye, his terrific sense of humor and his enthusiasm for the creative process. Dudley Frasier, as always, was not only honest but unfailingly accurate in his assessment of the early drafts; he helped me in more ways than I can name. Luis Rios helped me rediscover the right title at the right time. Irv Schwartz, a film agent who actually understands books, provided exceptional feedback and support with both books.

At Pocket Books, I was very fortunate to work with Dave Stern, who provided patient assistance throughout the process and provided one of the best notes about *Low Rider*. Max Greenhut deserves credit for helping to pull the pieces together. Jeff Theis did a great job letting reviewers and readers alike know about Harold Dodge. I can't say enough about the wonderful cover illustration by Eric Peterson, the jacket design by Brigid Pearson, the cover copy by Catherine Ritzinger, and the help provided by other staff members at Pocket Books. Amelia Sheldon is a former Pocket Books editor and current friend who was very helpful during this process.

In England, I want to thank Philippa Pride, my editor at Hodder & Stoughton, and Sara J. Menguc at David Higham Associates.

ACKNOWLEDGMENTS

Opera singer, Louis Lebherz, Basso Profondo, helped me pick the aria sung in this story by Fabian Skura and provided me with the lyrics in Italian. He also made me see that even a thug such as Fabian could have music in his heart.

Sgt. Dennis L. Prescott, at the County Coroner's Office in Santa Barbara, generously took the time to discuss his difficult job with me and show me the coroner's offices which are given a fictional representation in this book.

Jackie Green's expert assistance publicizing *Bird Dog* has paved the way for this continuing story. Bill Wade, a gifted photographer, has my thanks for the moody photograph on this book.

I also want to thank the many bookstore owners, and book collectors I met last summer while promoting *Bird Dog* for their thoughts about the character of Harold Dodge who returns in *Low Rider*.

Finally, I offer my sincere thanks for the support and understanding given to me by my family and friends. No one deserves more thanks than my wife, Vivian, and our two sons, Andrew and Tony.

LOW
RIDER

Harold was on the 405 Freeway in the South Bay Curve when he looked in his rearview mirror and saw the Buick Riviera moving up behind him. It pulled even with him in the fast lane and he looked over and saw there were four of them, black hair slicked back, Dago T's showing the tattoos on their muscled shoulders. *Gangbangers*. What the hell did they want? He half expected them to pull out guns and start blasting.

But no, they were smiling. Smiling and nodding, checking out his car and liking what they saw: a Bahama green '64 Chevy Impala SS with a 340-horse engine. The last of the muscle machines. The Buick's driver gave Harold thumbs-up, put his foot down, and disappeared in traffic, glasspacks rumbling. *That's life in* LA, Harold thought, realizing all over again how bizarre this city was.

He had lived here his whole life until he was forced to leave the country last year because of a couple of murders he didn't commit. Now, he was back to straighten things out. Repair the damage he had done to Vikki's life, and his own, and—who knows?—make some nice money in the process. He'd planned it out while living in Chile and, from there, it seemed like it'd be a piece of cake. But now that he was back on the restless streets of LA, he had that edgy feeling again, the feeling that here, nothing was a done deal. Everything was up for grabs.

He took the Hawthorne Exit and began the climb into the Palos Verdes Hills to Vikki's house. Twenty minutes later he parked next to the gates to the big house, under the jacaranda trees dropping purple flowers on the quiet street.

Vikki was in the garage, bending over the engine of an Austin Healey Mark III with a FOR SALE sign in the windshield. He was tempted to stand there and admire this view of her, but the last thing he needed was to have her turn and catch him at it so he cleared his throat and said, "Don't see many of those anymore. What is it? A '62?"

Her face came out from under the hood and she stood up, staring at him, realizing who he was and not liking it at all, and finally said, "The hell do you want?"

"I'm Harold Dodge. I met you—"

"I know who you are."

She held a 12 millimeter box-end wrench, her muscled forearms smeared black to the elbow. There was nothing, he thought, quite as sexy as a woman with grease on her hands and a chip on her shoulder.

"Problem with those"—Harold nodded at the Healey—"you could never balance those S.U. carburetors. Thing runs okay, but it won't idle."

"That's why I swapped them out for Webers," she said. "Only an asshole would run one of these with S.U.s. And it's not a '62, it's a '63."

He realized that she thought he was testing her, seeing if she really did know cars—and obviously she did—so he let that subject die, paused, laughed apologetically, and said, "You've changed since I saw you in Chile last year."

"I guess I had to, didn't I?" she said, pushing back a strand of blond hair with an ungreased patch on the back of her wrist.

Harold could see her breath coming fast, chest rising and

falling under the denim shirt, blue eyes shining like polished chrome. She reached into her breast pocket and lifted an unfiltered cigarette out of the pack and straight up into her mouth. The cigarette, with one small grease mark, bobbed unlit, as she talked.

"One day I'm leading the good life—your basic high-maintenance woman. I mean, hey, my husband owns the biggest car dealership in LA, so I'm loaded, right? Then my husband disappears—I don't know if he's dead or alive. Suddenly, it's up to me to provide for this mansion on the hill. Four grand a month in mortgage. Plus I find out my husband was up to his ass in debt, and it looks like I might lose everything—I mean *everything*—so, yeah, I guess maybe I have changed."

Harold felt this scene wasn't going well, not at all like he pictured it, so he said, "Maybe I can help."

Her hands stopped, lighter halfway to the unlit cigarette: "There's only one thing you can tell me that will help. Where's my husband?"

He paused, wanting to make it easier, but finally just said, "In the morgue, up in Santa Barbara."

That stopped her cold and he could almost hear her thinking, *So he really is dead then. He really is dead,* and in that moment he saw the attitude fall away like a mask and she was fresh and vulnerable and very beautiful.

A phone began ringing inside the big house and she said, "I'm sorry," and pushed past him and disappeared inside. Through the door he could hear her voice, unsteady as she said, "Yeah, it's still for sale—a '63 Mark III with a rebuilt engine. I'm asking seven grand, but make me an offer."

Harold stood there in the silent garage, smelling the gasoline and carburetor cleaner and thinking how, when he had last seen her, she was a California blonde—a bimbo,

3

really—not his type at all. But she wasn't perfect anymore. She was angry and banged up and even aged a little bit. And that changed everything. A woman like this he could go for.

Besides that, it was great to find a woman he could talk cars with.

From the outside, Vikki's house looked like a damn palace. But as Harold moved inside from the garage he saw the rooms were empty, the furniture sold for cash, he assumed. Even the chandelier in the dining room was gone, the wires taped off and dangling. Blocks of mismatched paint on the walls showed where pictures had been, depressions in the carpet where furniture had stood. Room after room, stripped and abandoned like a stolen car.

He found Vikki in a room at the top of the stairs. The shelves lining the walls were bare except for a few framed photos that had fallen facedown in the dust. She was leaning against the window frame, finally smoking the cigarette, looking out at the ocean, wind blowing the tops off the waves and the mountains of Catalina like ghosts over the horizon of the Pacific. Harold noticed that little lines were appearing around her eyes now that she was, what, maybe thirty, thirty-three. But she still looked great. Hell, she'd probably look great for about another two decades.

She turned away from the window and straightened, her eyes raking him. "So okay. So you're after the money, right?"

"Money?"

"You want money for telling me about Joe. You're like those private detectives, or those lawyers that keep calling. You're after a cut of the insurance money."

"I—look, I'm no lawyer—i.e., I hate those bloodsuckers."

"Then why'd you come back?"

"I have some family problems to take care of. My dad's sick and . . . well, I figured it was time to tell you."

She was staring at him, maybe wondering whether to believe him, so he continued the little speech he'd heard in his head so many times: "Lot of crazy stuff happened last year. I screwed things up pretty bad. So what I want to do is straighten things out."

"*Straighten things out*? Excuse me, but I don't really think you can *straighten things out*. And for you to even propose it is the most asinine thing I've ever heard."

Harold knew she had to say those things. So he took it, listening to wind outside and watching the anger in her face. Then he softly said, "I can't explain why it happened. My *ex* used to say, 'You've got a storm around you.' She's right. But I'm doing my best to put that behind me now. And I don't know where else to start but here, with you, telling you what I know."

It probably wasn't his words, but it might have been the feeling behind them that dissolved the anger in her eyes. He took a step toward the door.

"You gotta understand—it screwed up my life too. Hell, I almost wound up in prison. So I had to let things cool off first. So now you know. Sorry I couldn't say anything sooner."

When she didn't speak, he said, "Well, good luck," and slowly walked out the door.

He was in the hallway when he heard her voice, without the anger now, say, "Harold?" He paused, stepped back inside the room.

"I need your help." It hurt her to say it.

"Help?"

"You know, don't you? You know what happened to Joe. How he was killed and . . ."

"Not everything—"

5

"But enough. So if there's a problem, with the insurance, with the police, you could help. See, I don't have time for problems now because I'm very close to the end."

Don't jump at it, he told himself, trying to look like the offer took him by surprise.

"I'll make it worth your while."

"How could I take money for something like this?" Man, he was really pushing it now. But the offer should come from her. He had figured she'd never go for it otherwise.

"I could give you a percentage of the insurance money— say, five percent."

He had been hoping for ten. But what were we talking here? Five percent of a half mill? That was still a nice chunk of change.

"And I'll give you another five percent on everything else."

"What else is there?" Harold said, trying to keep his face blank as he thought, *This could be better than I thought.*

"I want Joe's dealership. Way I figure it, what belonged to Joe belongs to me now. Eddie Fallon, he was Joe's general manager. After Joe disappeared Fallon filed suit claiming he and Joe were actually partners. He's running the dealership now."

"And?"

"I countersued saying it was willed to me. Now it's stuck in the courts. But I found out that Fallon and Joe were into something, before he was killed."

She took down the one picture still hanging on the wall. Behind it was a small safe, unlocked. She reached in and took out a folder stuffed with computer printouts, handwritten notes.

"I found this after he—he left. He was moving cars all over the place. Money too. I can't figure it out. And he had this." She took out a small pistol, a Saturday night special by the looks of it, the light reflecting dully off the blue steel. "He never told me he had this. So he must have been in some kind of danger."

"Okay," Harold said, stepping aside so the gun didn't point at him. Christ, he hated guns.

"And now I'm getting calls."

"What kind of calls?"

"A voice telling me to drop the suit. Or else. And I'm being followed, I think. I've seen a big man, driving a black Suburban."

"Jesus."

"Yeah. So maybe you can figure out what Joe was into."

She held out the folder with the papers from the safe. Harold reached for them, but she didn't let go. And he found her intense blue eyes holding his, energy flowing between them.

"These are the only copies. Lose them and we're screwed."

"I'll eyeball them, give them back to you *mañana*."

She nodded, finally releasing the folder, saying, "So you'll help me then?"

"You have to understand, I'm not like a bodyguard or anything. I just know cars."

"And you know what happened to Joe."

"Not everything. . . . But, yeah, I'll do what I can."

"For five percent."

"Five percent."

"Okay then." She almost smiled, and in her eyes, Harold saw a trace of relief. "But priority number one is the insurance. We've got to prove he's dead. If we can't do that, everything else is moot, right?"

Harold didn't quite know what she meant by *moot* and he had always been intimidated by people who could use the word with confidence, so he nodded noncommittally, then quickly added: "Who insured Joe?"

7

"TransPacific. Dash Schaffner's the agent. He's got an office off Harbor just south of the 405 in Huntington."

"Tell you what. I got to run an errand first, but I'll meet you there in, say, hour and a half." He thought of something. "Wait till I get there. We better do this together."

It went well, Harold thought, climbing up the slope of the Vincent Thomas Bridge, rising above the LA Harbor. Vikki went for his offer and even teased him with a nice little bonus. But he'd have to prioritize, get his cut of the insurance, then, when he had a little operating money, go after the gravy, poke around at Joe's dealership, see what he was into. *Prioritize.* Yeah, that was the way to go.

Harold was still climbing, higher on the broad back of the bridge, impressed with the way the Impala's big V-8 performed. *There's no replacement for displacement.* That's what his old man always said. And he was right. They built cars to last back then, out of steel. Like this horn ring, he thought, glancing down at the words *Super Sport* stamped into the gleaming chrome. Nice touch.

Looking north, through bridge cables flashing by, Harold saw the incredible sprawl of the LA Basin, the houses and freeways with power lines stretching over the whole damn mess. To the south: Terminal Island, the shipyards, jagged necks of hammerhead cranes looming over docked freighters, cargo containers stacked everywhere like building blocks.

That reminded him . . . Once he got some operating money he was going to rent one of those cargo containers for a little export deal he'd cooked up. He knew a place he could get TVs and CD players at cost. Load up the container and ship it down to Chile. Sure, they were last year's model. But they didn't know that in Chile. And he could probably move them at a nice profit, make maybe a grand or two for his trouble.

Operating money, he thought, glancing at the folder on the car seat, the one Vikki loaned him with documents about Joe's dealership. What a wonderful sound that had to it. Truth of the matter was, he was in desperate need of operating money (and every other kind of money for that matter). He had just enough dough left for a one-way ticket up here, and a month's rent on a one-room dump over the Club Cheri. That left him about five hundred bucks until he scored. If he struck out he couldn't get back to Chile, back to Marianna and the life they were building together. He had to do it all *and* keep his ass out of prison for past misdeeds. Talk about putting your back to the wall.

On top of the bridge now, he got that coming-over-the-top feeling you get on roller-coasters, like you were going to sail off into space. And in that moment, with thoughts of money and dreams and women, and all the foolish hope he so often felt, he realized the weather was changing. Far below, the marine layer was creeping back in from the ocean, hazy fingers of fog like a giant hand, reaching over the land. *June Gloom* they called it. The sight chilled him and made him discard all thoughts of bonus money or cargo containers filled with electronic crap. He was here to help Vikki get the insurance money. Once he got his cut of the money, he'd beat it back to Chile on the first flight out. Yeah, he thought, gliding down the bridge to Terminal Island. For once in his life, he'd take the smart play. The sure thing.

Seconds later he was down into the fog.

"**You** must be the son from Brazil."

"Ah, Chile. I live there now," Harold told the nurse as he followed her down the long corridor at St. Mary's Hospital, smelling of the awful food left over from lunch and other smells he really didn't want to identify.

"How interesting!" the nurse said in a way that struck Harold as being well intended but basically phony. "Your brother's with him now."

"What?" Harold stopped walking.

"Your brother, Randy. He's been so good about visiting. Here every day."

"Probably trying to borrow money."

The nurse laughed, then was suddenly quiet, knowing how deep these things are with families.

"In here," she said, gesturing toward a doorway.

"Look, I'm just going to stand out here for a second. Okay?" Harold said, not knowing how to explain it.

The nurse nodded looking at him sadly. "Your dad talks about you all the time," she said, and left.

Harold looked in the door, past a pulled curtain, and saw his father in a bed by the window. It was almost dark in the room, the only light coming from the flickering TV. He saw Randy there with him, dirty T-shirt and sagging jeans, long hair pulled back. He was spinning a ring of keys around one finger and nodding as he motormouthed, telling his dad about his new job, mechanic at a GM dealership, how he was really going to stick to it this time. Yeah, sure. We've heard that one before.

Harold stepped back out of sight. Damn. He didn't have time for this, he thought, checking his watch, hoping Vikki didn't get down to Huntington first. Maybe he should come back later, once he had some good news for his dad. . . .

Movement. Harold looked up as Randy emerged from the room and walked past without seeing him but close enough so he could smell cigarette smoke on his clothes. He watched his brother move away with that sloppy walk of his. Harold turned into the room and approached his father. In the white light from the TV his father looked like he was already dead. Harold felt a rush of emptiness and despair fill him that he hoped wouldn't show on his face.

"You're here," his father said, and sighed.

Harold took his father's hand, finding it alarmingly cool, like a plastic bag filled with ice water and bones. It was hard to see his face with the oxygen being pumped into his nostrils. He'd been a two-pack-a-day man for fifty years and now the bill was due: His heart was so weak it just couldn't keep up.

"Got your letter," Harold started. "Thought I'd come up and see how they're treating you."

"You doin' okay down there, Harry?"

"Fine."

"Where is Brazil, anyway?"

"It's Chile, Dad. I live in Chile."

"You married again?"

"Living with a lady. . . . We want to get hitched. But we gotta work things out first."

"What things?"

"She needs an operation. . . . We don't have the money for it and—Look, it's too complicated to go into."

"You makin' a buck? Gettin' by?"

"Things are pretty tight. But I'm workin' a little deal now. . . . It pans out, I'll have plenty of cash couple days from now."

"That's nice." Maybe neither of them really believed it.

Harold had only seen his father in the hospital once before. When he was a kid, his dad took a night job in a filling station. The place got robbed and he was hurt pretty bad. But when Harold got to the hospital he found his bandaged father ecstatic.

"Two of them came at me, Harry! With hatchets. Hatchets! But they couldn't put me down. You hear what I'm saying? Two guys—and they couldn't put me down."

Now, the fight was gone; he lay there without the energy to turn up the sound on the TV.

"Dad."

"Yeah?"

"I borrowed the Chevy. I hope it's all right."

"The Chevy? My Chevy?"

"Yeah, the Impala. I went by the house and picked it up. I'm just in town a few days. I need something to rat around in so . . . Don't worry, I'll take good care of it."

"It's a cream puff, Harry. They don't make cars like that anymore."

Harold was thinking of that time again, his father bragging about how he had survived the hatchet attack, when he said, "Dad, I'm gonna get you out of here. Couple days from now, everything goes okay, I'll come back and get you."

"Get me?"

"I'm gonna take you with me, Dad. You'll like it down there."

His father thought about that for a moment.

"Where is Brazil, anyway?"

"A long way away from here."

Harold sat there, holding his father's hand in his, thinking maybe somehow he could warm it up.

"**Death** certificate," Dash Schaffner said, looking across the desk at Vikki Covo and this guy she brought in with her.

"Death certificate? That's all I need?" Vikki asked.

"Actually, the claims department will issue you a settlement kit. It's got a lot of forms and papers for you to fill out. But the death certificate—signed, with the cause of death—that's the main thing."

Vikki turned to look at the guy (what did he say his name was? Dodge?) older guy, pushing fifty maybe, heavyset, short graying hair. And that suit. Jesus, where'd he get that thing? And he just sat there, taking it all in with his steady gray-green eyes.

Dash leaned back, hearing his leather chair creak, smoothing back his long blond hair. "Vikki, you come to me, say, 'Dash, I need to settle this.' But I gotta tell you, I don't do that here. We have a claims department that will handle all that for you."

"Then what do you do?" Vikki asked, blood rising in her face.

Dash wanted to laugh. He liked a woman that could zing you like that. He knew he was in for a treat when he saw her drive up ten minutes ago and step out wearing that black dress. Nothing fancy. Just a simple black dress riding up on those tanned legs. She was older than him—tad past her prime maybe—but hey, so what? He'd had older women before and they could be better than the young 'uns. I mean, they all knew *all* the moves. He should have known Vikki would be first class. He'd known Joe and Joe always went first class.

But then this guy pulls up in that old Impala and they came up together. That changed the dynamics of the situation.

Where the hell did he fit in? In that baggy suit, he sure didn't look the type to be hanging with a killer blonde like Vikki Covo.

"What do I do? As little as possible. No, just kidding. Basically, I'm your contact. We've got the claims department, over here, and you, our customer, over here. I'm in between. I make sure you get what you need to be very comfortable in your time of need."

Vikki looked at the guy again as if she wanted him to say something. But he just sat there looking around, checking out the computer humming at Dash's elbow, the claims books, the photos spread out on his desk, even his golf clubs leaning in the corner.

That reminded him. With Vikki dropping in like this, he had to cancel his match with Bobby Skura. He was going to give Bobby two strokes a side, play him for half of what he owed the Skura brothers. Dash planned to be losing on the seventeenth hole, offer a double-or-nothing press, and make a few lucky shots to close out the match. But no. Vikki had to see him that afternoon. And now they were talking about a half-million-dollar policy with the offices silent around them, and the sky outside turning the color of lead as fog blew in from the ocean.

"Vikki said you knew Joe?" Dash said to Harold.

"That's right."

"Your name again?"

Pause, then: "Harold Dodge," slow, like each word cost him a hundred bucks.

"Dodge, as in cars?" He laughed. "Like Dodge Charger? Remember that old car?"

Harold nodded. His eyes didn't move.

Dash picked up his Mont Blanc and unscrewed the cap. The fat pen looked like a little bomb. But Dash liked the way it felt in his hand. Heavy, like money. He slowly wrote *Harold Dodge* on his note pad next to the facts that Vikki had given him.

"How'd you know Joe?"

It was like he hadn't even heard the question. Just the eyes looking back at him. It was very quiet in here.

"From a long time ago, okay? I was in the car business."

"Sales?"

"I was a closer for Joe."

"And Vikki said you knew what—where Joe was killed?"

Harold nodded minimally.

"How do you know all this?"

"You said you don't handle claims."

"That's right."

"Then you don't need to know."

Dash felt his anger rising. But he wouldn't show it. He knew how to handle guys like this. He'd lower his voice, that made people lean forward. Get the old body language flowing in his favor. And he'd use his *client voice*: sincere, reassuring while saying basically nothing at all.

"Vik, I want you to understand—I'm sorry. Do you prefer Vik, Vikki?"

"Vikki."

"Vikki, I considered Joe to be a very close personal friend. We used to go down to Baja, play golf all weekend, party a little—margaritas—the whole bit." He laughed, then continued earnestly. "So, when I ask a question like this, I'm not asking as an insurance agent. I'm asking as a friend, because I care."

Dodge shifted in his seat, cleared his throat. "Since this claim is going to be settled soon, Vikki needs an advance on the settlement."

Just like that. Guy comes in here and asks for money up

front. Very slick. Dash held his eyes, letting it go quiet again. That drove most people nuts. But this guy didn't seem to care.

Vikki picked up the ball and ran with it. "Harold's right. Things are very tight for me right now. And Joe paid a hell of a lot of money for this policy. It's not like we're asking you for your money."

"I know what you're saying, Vikki, it's just that—" *Just that I've already run through the agency's fund long ago*, Dash thought. That reminded him of the way Bobby was turning up the heat on him, saying, *Pay up or Fabian's coming after you*. Every time he heard the front office door open he thought that monster was coming for him. That's why he wanted to get Fabian's brother, Bobby, out on the golf course, work on that macho ego of his.

He cleared his mind and continued: "You come to me, say, 'Dash, I want to settle this claim.' Fine. But at this point, you don't have proof of Joe's death."

"You have my word." Dodge's voice was firm in the quiet room.

"But a lot of things can go wrong. You don't have a death certificate."

Vikki shook her head.

"An obituary?"

She shook her head again.

"Okay. So all we have is the statement of"—he made a big show of referring to his handwritten note—"Mr. Dodge."

Harold tapped the desk with a thick finger. "I guarantee we'll be back tomorrow with a death certificate."

"Then we're talking about twenty-four hours." Dash leaned back, opening his hands as if to say, *What's the problem?* "Tell you what I'm going to do. I'm going to handle this case personally, because Joe was a very close personal friend. I'm going to call claims, cut the red tape, get them to expedite this case. Then, when you get back with the death certificate, I'll cut a check to cover your immediate needs until the policy settles. How's that sound?''

"You can do that here?'' Dodge asked.

"Right here on my trusty computer. Tomorrow, this time, you'll be all set.''

Dash took his business card and wrote a number on it.

"Here's my beeper number. Call me anytime—literally. You have a question in the middle of the night—call me, say, 'Dash, I've got a problem.'" He handed the card to Vikki, ignoring Dodge, sort of a minor little *fuck you*. That's the way he'd deal with this guy—treat him like he wasn't even there. Because he knew that pretty soon, he wouldn't be.

Dash stood at the office window, smoothing his tie down the front of his crisp white shirt, watching Vikki and the guy emerge into the parking lot below and stand next to the entrance of the Denny's across the way. They agreed on something, got into her Healey, and drove off, leaving the Impala parked in the lot as dirty strands of fog blew in from the ocean.

Harold Dodge. Joe never mentioned that name to him. With a half million bucks at stake, guys like this Dodge character came out of the woodwork. For Vikki's sake it might be wise to split them up. Give Dodge a little trouble of his own to deal with. He would do it for Joe, because Joe had been a very close personal friend. He wouldn't want Vikki hanging out with some old loser in a dumpy suit, some hard luck case sniffing around for easy money.

Once Dodge was out of the picture, he'd work closely with

Vikki, help her settle the claim, then tactfully explain that Joe owed him a little debt, ten grand for arranging a night of gentleman's entertainment for some out-of-town clients. The very night, in fact, that Joe disappeared. Then he'd pay off the Skura brothers and be back in business. Ten grand would be chump change once Vikki was holding a check for a half million.

But how could he get Dodge out of the picture?

Still staring out the window, he found the answer right in front of him. He picked up his phone and punched a button on his speed dialer.

The first thing he heard was the machine-gun rattle of the power wrench echoing in the Skuras' body shop. Then Bobby's voice was in his ear, like he was pissed off or something, saying: "Dent Doctor Auto Body."

"Bob, hey, it's Dash. Wanted to let you know, I'm getting your money together."

"When?"

"Cut a check for you first of next week."

"Fabian wants it now."

"Next week's as soon as I can get it, man." Dash quickly added, "Reason for the call. Who's that *cholo* you got working for you? The homeboy."

"Neto?"

"Neto, right. He's into that lowrider shit, isn't he?"

"So what?"

"So I got one for him—a Chevy Impala. That's what lowriders go for, right?"

Dash imagined Bobby, stroking that skeevy goatee of his and smiling. "Kind of shape's it in?"

"It's good for parts. And you know what? I bet he could pick it up for almost nothing."

There. That would take care of the Dodge Charger, he

thought, setting the phone down. Dash imagined him returning to find his car gone. That would get him out of the picture. Because, in LA, stealing a guy's car was like cutting him off at the knees.

They decided to take the Healey up to Santa Barbara, so Harold climbed into the two-seater and Vikki blasted off into traffic, working the short stick as they headed up the 405 with the top down. Harold was quiet, feeling the torque of the engine and finally he said, "The Brits get a lot out of these little four-cylinder jobs."

"It's a six," she said, downshifting and hitting the fast lane in the South Bay Curve.

"What's the top end?"

"Had it up to one-twenty once, but there was still some pedal left."

"One-twenty on a factory engine?"

"No way. Joe had it bored out, high-performance cams and straight pipes. He modified every car he owned. He had this mechanic—I mean, this guy was an amazing wrench—used to work pit crews at Indy."

She stopped herself—why was she talking so much? She looked over at Harold. He was different now, relaxed, out of his negotiating mode. He was quiet as they passed LAX, looking up at the jets coming in low with their gear and flaps down, engines whining, vapor tailing off the wingtips as the jet went in and out of low clouds.

It felt good to be with someone who was moving her toward the truth, going to bat for her. She liked how Harold had dealt with Dash. She liked to watch him, the way he leaned forward and tapped the desk, asking for her money.

Didn't even blink. Just laid it out there like it was cold fact. For a second she thought Dash would fork over some cash. What a relief that would be. Enough for a house payment, enough so she wouldn't have to sell the Healey. Maybe Harold would come through for her. But maybe he'd be like the others, the sleazy P.I.'s and the shyster lawyers, wanting a retainer and a third of the settlement. Leaving her in the lurch. Out of answers—shit out of luck.

Traffic thinned out as they came over the pass into the Simi Valley and she saw it was clear ahead, no fog now that they were inland, the sun setting over mountains to the west. She looked at the fields on the valley floor, with the neat rows of low plants and, on the hilltops around, the encroaching subdivisions of some newly discovered community that was—as the realtors would promise—"commuter-close to LA." *Commuter-close.* Vikki laughed to herself. Try two hours grinding your gears in stop-and-go traffic.

She heard Harold beside her say, "Man, you really know how to drive."

"Joe taught me," she yelled back to him, her hair whipping her face. "He'd take me down to the mountains above San Diego, tell me he'd pay for any tickets I got."

The mention of Joe's name quieted Harold. What she didn't tell Harold about their little forays into the mountains was how Joe taught her to drive *death-fast.*

"Take it up to the red line, where you think you're going to crash and burn," Joe told her. "When you go into the turn, you'll want to hit the brakes—*but don't.* You have to power out of it. Okay? Accelerate in the curve. Lemme show you."

Joe had thrown the Healey into a turn she thought would be her last. But as they came out of the corner and accelerated hard, a raw thrill swept through her body. Deep in the next curve, she looked at Joe's strong face as he drove, his black hair flying, and felt that for that one second she saw him as he really was and knew why she loved him.

Then there was the motel.

It was a shitty little place in the mountains near Julian. But that was the whole idea. It was along a country road and it shared a parking lot with the fried chicken restaurant next door. After two hours of taking turns at the wheel, stinking up their clothes with fear-sweat, he nosed the Healey into the gravel lot and told the manager, "Gimme some keys," threw a few twenties at him, and didn't wait for change.

A moment later they were facing each other in the shabby room with the depressing furniture, their tangled hair and faces reddened from the wind, and all they could hear was the rush of blood in their ears.

"Hit me," Joe said, his voice thick.

His request sounded strange to her mind, but her mind had been detached for some time now so she slapped him.

"Harder," he said, and she smashed him again with all her might, turning her shoulder into the punch and feeling how heavy and strong he was and how hard it would be to do any real damage.

"Again." Her arm lashed out again but he caught it, throwing her on the dingy bed with a faded brown spread. He stood over her, dropping his pants, and she wondered if they were going to lose control. There was losing control but keeping just a little bit of control somewhere in the back of your mind. And then there was getting completely and totally out of control and not knowing what would happen.

When they left the hotel she had to hold her clothes together where he'd ripped them off her. And for days she remembered the things he called her, things that made sense then, but she hated later. She wasn't like that. Joe made her like that. *The bastard used me*, she thought, realizing with disgust that the incredible excitement still burned inside her.

They never did it that way at home. And they didn't do it in the motel very often. Maybe twice a year Joe came home on a Friday and say, "We're going driving this weekend."

She didn't say yes or no. But right off it started building— even though she hated herself for it. And when she got behind the wheel again, she was ready to drive death-fast. It was her revenge against him. Scare the shit out of the bastard. Maybe that would make him respect her.

"We're not going to make Santa Barbara tonight."

She turned and looked at Harold, where Joe had sat, and all sorts of mixed-up things went through her head. He smiled and said, "Maybe we should find a place to stay, get a bite to eat. I know a greasy spoon up here makes a good patty melt."

Why was she remembering all this? Because that agent, Dash, reminded her of Joe? Thinner. Taller. Blond, not dark. Or was it because Harold was sitting where Joe sat? He had known him too, years ago. They hated each other. That was something they had in common, Vikki thought.

The old life was calling to her, that life that had been turned off, like someone hit the light switch the night Joe disappeared. She would never be like that again. Never let a man make her lose control.

She downshifted and took the exit.

Neto was in front of the mirror in his bedroom, listening to his sister's salsa music blasting in the living room, trying to see if the bulge under his shirt was visible, when he felt his beeper move and he saw Bobby Skura's number on the display. That meant Bobby had a job for him so he dialed the number and waited.

Neto boosted his first car for Bobby about three months ago and the money came through a week later when the insurance paid off. He gave a few bills to his mother, saying he earned it doing day labor for a body shop in Wilmington, blew a couple hundred on a new sound system for his lowrider, and then went shopping for some hardware. A hundred up front, a hundred on delivery. This morning he got the call and picked it up.

Bobby answered, "Dent Doctor Auto Body."

"It's Neto. Whassup?"

"Want you to pick up a car. But you gotta understand, it's not for us." He was talking in that slow way of his. "What I'm saying is we're not gonna pass papers on it. I knew you're into that lowrider rider shit so I'm passing it along to you to do as you please."

"Gotcha," Neto said, feeling let down at first, but when Bobby gave him the make and model his disappointment lifted.

Neto heard his father's voice in the living room, home from work, so he double-checked his shirt. In the mirror he noticed the wall behind him plastered with drawings he had made when he was younger, in colorful Magic Markers, copies of comic book superheroes and sexy ladies with big titties firing laser guns. He had talent, everyone said so, even that white guy that used to tutor him at the church down the street. But he didn't have time for that kid shit now. Besides, his artistic expression had taken a different outlet.

When he walked through the living room, his father was sitting on the plastic-covered sofa watching Veronica dance around the room. Neto moved slowly, so as not to create suspicion, but his father's dark eyes followed him closely and Neto felt relieved when he stepped out onto the cement front porch of the aging bungalow on Gaviota in the shadow of Signal Hill and smelled the sticky sweet jacaranda tree that was dropping purple flowers all over the tiny yard. He kicked the ball around with Stevie until Oscar rolled up in the big

Econoline van and he jumped in, saying, "Whassup, homes? Whassup?" and they took off south until they hit the light at Pacific Coast Highway. A hooker crossed in front of them and Oscar slid down in the seat, put his hands behind his head, and said, "Man, look at the *chichis* on her!"

Rolling again, Oscar said, "Where we headin'?"

"Parking lot near off Harbor in Huntington," Neto said, reaching into the waistband of his baggy pants, pulling out the 9 millimeter AA Arms assault pistol, and pointing it at Oscar's head, saying, "Check it out, fool."

Oscar looked over, then ducked, cutting the wheel. He straightened out the big van as horns blared around them. "Crazy fucker!" he screamed.

Neto's insane laughter filled the van as he pointed the gun at some white guy in a Blazer driving next to them. Before the guy could look over, Oscar yelled, "Oh man!" reached across, and knocked Neto's arm down.

"Someone cuts you off, I'm ready," Neto said laughing.

"Put that fuckin' thing away, man. Some cop sees that they'll send me back to Chino."

"You want, I can get you one."

"Lemme see," Oscar said, smiling as he took the weight of the pistol in his hand. "Sweet. What'd you pay for it?"

"One ninety-nine. And the man threw in a box of hollow points."

Neto took the gun back and rammed it down into his pants. He looked around at the six lanes of rush hour traffic finally breaking up, sweeping them south past the Long Beach Airport and the tangle of oil refineries and auto malls and down into Orange County, where he looked out over the tops of houses to baseball diamonds and miniature golf amusement parks. Seeing all the nice clean houses and the bright stores, Neto felt the familiar hatred deep in his gut.

"Here! Here!" Neto shouted, pointing to the Harbor Exit coming up fast.

"Give me some warning, man." Oscar craned his neck, fighting across three lanes, catching the ramp, circling a field of ice plant and low bushes. Neto caught a flash of a man camped among the brush next to a shopping cart filled with clothes. A second later they were southbound on the wide street flanked by strip malls and burger joints and gas stations, with a river of glass and chrome restlessly flowing through it.

"Left into the—yeah, right here," Neto said, pointing to the parking lot next to a Denny's and a sporting goods store. An office complex ran along the other side of the lot, with blank second-story windows looking down on the parked cars. Neto could see a white pillar of water rising in a fountain in the courtyard, deserted now in the evening.

Oscar cruised through the lot as Neto eyeballed the parked cars, sorting them in his mind, noting the hot prospects— dark green Range Rover . . . Toyota Avalon . . . a couple of Accords . . . Any one, man. He could take any car in the whole damn lot. But today he wasn't shopping. He was after one car and one car only.

"There it is, man!" Neto pointed at the green '64 Impala.

"Oh, man, it's cherry," Oscar said.

"*Firme*," Neto agreed.

It was just like the one Neto had in the garage at the back of his lot, a slammed-to-the-ground Impala, chopped and channeled, with a trunk full of hydraulic lifters that could make the thing leap, make it fly. He pictured it doing a spider crawl across an intersection while traffic stopped, drivers watching with their mouths hangin' open. Only problem was, finding parts for a car like this was a real bitch. He needed a new driver's side door, horn rim, rear bumper, taillight bracket, and . . .

Oscar eased the Econoline into a nearby slot where they could see the Impala and the entrance of Denny's, slow now after the dinner rush.

"It's got a Club," Oscar said.

"Piece of cake." Neto rummaged in a metal toolbox, lifting out the battery-operated Makita Saws-all with the hacksaw blade.

Neto dropped the Saws-all in a backpack like he was some high school kid with a load of books. He slid the Slim Jim up under his shirt and pocketed the wire cutters and needle-nosed pliers.

"I'm gonna go take a leak, then come out like I'm heading for my car. Wait till I get it rollin', then I'll see you back at home."

Neto strolled into Denny's and along the counter, where the manager, a fat white guy in a shirt and tie, was talking to a Mexican cook flipping burgers on the grill. The fried food smelled good but his stomach was too tight for anything now. In the men's room he pissed, checked himself in the mirror, then walked back along the counter. He felt the manager's eyes on him, but, fuck it, he was out the door and moving to the Impala now.

Neto thought of the time Oscar helped him pick up his first G-Ride, a brand-new Montero. *Your attitude's gotta be, 'This is my car.' Anyone watching'll just go, 'Hey, the man's getting in his car.'*

Good advice, Neto thought. Then people won't even notice you sliding the Slim Jim down inside the door panel and yanking up hard. Inside the car now, Neto saw the interior was super clean. On the seat next to him was a folder filled with papers. Check it out later.

He got the Makita cranked up, cut a gap in the steering wheel, and slid the Club off. He reached below the dash, working by feel with the wire cutters, picturing the tuck and roll upholstery you could put in one of these things, fuzzy dash and a sound system that could really move air. Then you'd go out *bumpin'*.

Neto heard the van's horn, turned to look, and saw the window filled by a big face, the manager from Denny's, frowning and saying, "What're you doing?"

Neto came out of the car fast and had the gun barrel right in the guy's face.

"On the ground, bitch!"

The manager dropped to the pavement.

"Under the car!" Neto said, jamming the gun barrel into the guy's head, noticing the name tag that read *Gordon*. "Under the car, bitch! Don't ya see the gun?"

"I'm tryin'!" the guy whined, trying to roll under the car next to the Impala, a low-slung Acura, but he was too fat and couldn't do it. Neto started kicking him, bounced his head off the car door like a soccer ball and saw the blood start down his face and onto the white shirt.

The van's horn was going again as Neto shifted the gun to his left hand and reached under the dash and crossed the leads with his right. The engine cranked and caught, then settled to smooth idle.

Neto crouched next to Gordon and pointed the gun right into his eye socket, the guy saying, *Please . . . ,* over and over. But Neto was listening to a voice in his head saying, *Do it! Do it!* and felt something rising inside him, but then for no reason at all he didn't pull the trigger, just slid into the Impala and backed out and headed for the exit.

Just before he pulled out onto Harbor he took one more look around and happened to notice a guy up in an office window, a big blond guy, which wasn't strange at all, but what was weird was the huge smile spreading across his face.

"I have a right to know," Vikki said, standing beside his booth in the back of the restaurant next to the motel where they stopped for the night just south of Santa Barbara. Harold had been relaxing into his second beer, waiting for his dinner to arrive, feeling the alcohol glow in his system and round off the edges of the day, when he saw her come through the door and make for him like a homing missile.

"I go into my room, I'm about to go to bed," she said, "then it hits me, *Jesus, I don't know yet.* And you do. So I want you to tell me what happened to him. And I want you to tell it without making the facts easier to protect me. Just tell it flat out like it happened."

She sat down across from him, anger behind her face, and Harold saw that she'd changed out of the black dress and was wearing jeans and a white T-shirt now. Just jeans and a T-shirt and she had brushed her thick blond hair until it lay smooth on her shoulders.

The waitress set a plate down in front of Harold with an omelet and hash browns and he realized how glad he was to have the interruption. Maybe he could figure out how to tell it. And how much of it to tell her.

"Want something?" he said to Vikki.

"Shot of tequila with a chaser," she said, without looking away from Harold.

The waitress nodded, tired. Harold added, "And my water? Two glasses—one with just ice and one with water. Extra napkins and a little salsa on the side."

When the waitress left he found Vikki watching him and he laughed in his embarrassed way. "I guess I have some strange habits." He pointed at his wristwatch that he had taken off and placed next to his beer. "Like that. In Chile I park the watch. Time doesn't exist there," he explained, laughing again. But she wasn't with him on this. Just sitting there waiting for answers.

Harold wrapped his hand around the sweating mug and realized there would be little pleasure in drinking the beer now. He would tell her the story and his stomach would shrink down to the size of a fist. The only up side to this was, it might make it go easier tomorrow. The cops would drag him over the same territory again, that's for sure. This would be a helpful review. Say it out loud and see how it sounded.

The waitress brought Harold's salsa and water glasses along with Vikki's shot and beer.

"Heineken on tap," Harold said, hoisting his beer mug. "Heinie's a decent brew. But in Chile these old Krauts came over after the war, they make the best damn beer. It's so good you can even drink it when it's—"

"I have a right to know." Her voice was husky with dread. "I mean, he was my husband."

A skinny guy in a striped delivery shirt was feeding the jukebox. Just as Harold started talking, a country western song filled the barroom and he felt like it was movie music, making the story more dramatic. But then he looked up into her icy blue eyes and wiped the thought from his mind.

"What I'm about to tell you, I've never told to anyone else—i.e., it could get me put away for life. So I'm taking a big flyer here, telling you."

She was absolutely still, watching him closely. He took a long pull on his beer.

"I guess you already know I once worked for Joe, years ago."

"A bird dog, right? You sent suckers in so Joe could sell them cars."

"And later I was a salesman and a closer too. But anyway, nine months ago I was working at Aerodyne—a chemical engineer, for Christ's sake—thinking I'd be stuck there the rest of my life. One day, this girl—woman, sorry—Marianna Perado, she worked in my department, she comes to me and says she got ripped off while she was buying a car. At Joe Covo Matsura, okay?"

Vikki downed the shot, then began sipping the beer.

"I'd written this book, *How to Buy a Cream Puff*, so, like an idiot, I say, sure, I'll help you unwind the deal. We go down there and the salesman, Vito, jacks us around, pisses Marianna off big time. Next thing I know she steals back her trade-in and runs down Vito in the process."

The story was taking ahold of them both and he looked down at his white knuckles around the empty beer mug. Harold continued, describing how Joe was drawn into their feud. As he got closer to the death of her husband, Vikki's eyes were dark points of energy. He paused, then softly told her how Vito planned to retaliate by shooting Marianna. When Joe unexpectedly appeared, he was killed in a case of mistaken identity.

"Oh, my God!" she gasped. "Oh my God!" Then, a moment later she asked, "But how did Joe's body wind up in Santa Barbara?"

This would be harder to tell, because it involved Harold directly. He would try to tell it without bringing the dark images into his mind, the thought of jail cells he had been in, the bloody car trunk, the face of the corpse he found beside the stream near Santa Barbara.

"The cops were gonna pin Joe's murder on me. I figured they couldn't get me if they didn't have a body. So I found where Joe's body had been dumped and I was going to move it. But before I could, the cops came and—how could I explain what I was doing?" He paused, thinking how sometimes things happened you couldn't explain. But they still happened. "On the spur of the moment, I told them Joe's body was actually my brother and that he'd committed suicide."

"So all this time Joe's body has been up in Santa Barbara identified as your brother," she said, acid in her voice. "While my life went to hell."

He waited. Finally she said, "Unbelievable. So it all happened because that bitch, Marianna, didn't *like* the deal she got."

"It happened because Joe ripped her off and she decided she wasn't gonna take it." He instantly felt he had been too harsh, so he added, "Hey, it screwed up my life too. But it's done now. And—like I keep saying—I'm going to straighten things out. I mean, I don't know why these things happen to me."

"Part of that storm that's around you," she said, her voice softer now.

They were silent a moment, during which Harold listened to the jukebox and hoped like hell the waitress would come so he could order another beer.

"I know Vito was killed up by the airport. So what happened to her?"

"Her?"

"Yeah, you know . . ."

"Marianna?"

"Yeah, you must have been really stuck on her, to do what you did."

Harold laughed, *ah-ah-ah*, stalling, realizing this is where he would have to lie a little. Vikki knew he was hiding something so Harold felt she'd never accept a flat denial. So he said, "I didn't want to say anything this afternoon but—that's part of why I'm here."

"You mean—?"

"Right. To find her."

"So you're still stuck on her."

"I feel I owe her something."

Vikki's laughed harshly. "Like what?"

"She asked for my help. I let her down."

"But you had no idea she was psycho."

"She's not a psycho." Harold was surprised by the tone in his voice.

"Well, excuse me. Running down a car salesman—that's perfectly normal behavior?"

"Look, I—One thing led to the next. It got out of hand."

"I guess so."

She was quiet, blue eyes boring into him.

Harold shrugged. "Anything else you want to know?"

"You're not gonna give me a straight answer, so what's the point?" But she smiled a little, pulling his chain, standing and saying, "*Mañana*," over her shoulder, using his word.

"*Mañana*," he said, and watched her all the way across the barroom and out the door.

Marianna had been sitting on the edge of the bed, taking her braces off, when the phone began ringing. By the end of the day her legs hurt like hell so she always enjoyed this moment when she could step out of the leather and steel "instruments of torture." But now the phone was interrupting her ritual. She let it ring three times before answering and, before she even knew for sure who was calling, she heard background voices, laughter, music from a jukebox maybe.

"*Hola.*"

"It's me," she heard Harold say. He sighed and added, "Good to hear your voice. Two days back here and I'm already stressed out. Man, this place . . ."

"You said you weren't going to call."

"Yeah, well, I got a deal on one of those calling cards. And, hell, I miss you. This place is really getting to me. You wouldn't believe what it's like here now. The economy's in the toilet. Everyone's gettin' pink slips. I went back to Aerodyne—they closed our division. The whole damn division—gone."

His voice was thick and had that edge she hadn't heard since they wound up together here in Chile nine months ago. She realized he was probably drinking again.

"Where are you calling from?"

"Motel in Oxnard."

"A motel? You're in a motel?"

"Bar next to a motel. I'm on my way to Santa Barbara. Get that taken care of."

"Oh."

"Anyway, it's looking good. I met with her today and she went for it."

"She did?"

"Yeah. She got me down on the commission. But she went for it."

"She get you down on anything else?"

"Say again?"

"She get you down on the bed maybe?"

Pause, then, "Come on. It was strictly business. Besides, there wasn't even a bed in the house. She's hawked everything in the whole damn place to cover the mortgage."

"Poor baby."

"Yeah, well."

"So how is she?"

"Who?"

"The bimbo with the fake tits."

"I don't think they're—" He paused. "I told you it was business. Everything's cut and dried. We make the identification tomorrow. Then I get my cut, I'll send for you, find a good doctor. Couple of weeks from now you'll be good as new."

They were quiet for a moment, as only people who are very close can do on the phone. He began thinking about his dad back in that hospital bed, wondering whether to tell her about it, pave the way for his arrival, but thinking, no, let that slide for now.

"She with you there? At the motel?"

"Who, Vikki?"

"Yes."

"We're in separate rooms."

"Well, I should hope so! Why did you have to stay in a motel?"

"We got a late start and—Look, it's complicated. I'll tell you when I see you."

"Tell me now."

"It's no biggie. I mean, anything I say will be moot in a few days, anyway."

"*Moot*?" She laughed. "Harold, what the hell're you talking about?"

"Nothin'. I told you. Couple of days and I'll probably be ready to send for you. Okay?"

He laughed, flustered, like he often was around her, and then they were silent again. She worked her way into the wheelchair and got her hairbrush from the bureau. Harold brushed her raven hair every night until it seemed to shine. But he wasn't here to do it now and Marianna was realizing how far away he was.

She put on her pouty voice, knowing he loved it, and said, "I hate it here without you."

"I know. . . ."

"I'm lonely."

"Tina's still coming, isn't she?"

"Big deal. I get to talk to the maid." Then, she lowered her voice. "I want to touch your secret places."

"Don't do this to me. Only two days back here and I'm already a basket case." Then: "Gotta go."

"Why?"

"Someone wants the phone.

"So what?"

"Don't do this to me. I'll call you *mañana*. Okay?"

"Harold."

"What?"

"I'll think about them as I go to sleep."

"What?"

"Your secret places."

"*Jesus.*"

"Remember, Harold. You belong to me."

"Bye."

She hung up and stared at the phone, trying to picture the bar he was in, and for the first time in a while it all came back to her how crazy it got in LA last year. The thousands of streets and millions of people spread out in the basin and mountainsides and canyons, all colliding in ways that would never happen anywhere else. What was it about the place that made people do those things? And what was happening to Harold? One thing was for damn sure. She wasn't hanging around here alone much longer with him on the loose in LA.

Walking across the parking lot at the coroner's office in Santa Barbara the next day, Harold looked at the small brick building and the hazy mountains beyond it, remembering how it had been when he followed the ambulance in here last fall. Then, the clouds were low and purple, like facial lacerations, and the sky hemorrhaged rain. He had watched as the tinted sliding doors with *Authorized Personnel Only* rolled open and the ambulance driver wheeled Joe's body into what looked like a big meat locker. As the heavy door opened, he saw still forms lying on metal shelves, draped in blue plastic sheets. When the steel door slammed shut, cutting off his view, the cold of that room went deep into Harold's bones.

But now it was a beautiful morning; the sunlight was like golden syrup poured over the trees and purple flowers surrounding the coroner's office and dotting the little cemetery on the nearby hill with neat white headstones. Here he was, back again with the ridiculous hope of straightening out the mess he had created. Yes, *straightening things out*, he thought, mocking himself, feeling suddenly shaky as he wondered how in hell he ever expected to pull this off.

They were at the front door now, Vikki beside him, wearing the simple black dress again, hair pulled back, taking it all in, emotions hypersensitive. Harold had the urge to protect her from what she would see here and what it might do to her. They moved into the reception area, where a middle-aged woman looked up from papers on a desk. There were nice pictures on the wall and that sunlight was pouring in the windows. Christ, it was all so damn ordinary, Harold felt like he was going to a dentist appointment instead of ID-ing a body.

"May I help you?" the woman asked.

Harold took the lead because this was why he was here—to earn his money. And to confess his sins.

"We want to make an identification."

"What's the decedent's name?"

"This is a little complicated," Harold began, unable to suppress a nervous laugh (and hoping it didn't seem inappropriate). "The ah—the person—the body we want to identify is probably under the wrong name. We want to straighten things out and, you know, make arrangements."

There was an uncomfortable pause. Finally the woman said, "What name is it currently under?"

"Dodge. Randell Dodge."

The receptionist seemed to jump back in her chair. Then she looked through a door to her right. A man appeared and Harold knew right off he was a cop. He didn't wear a gun or a badge but he was a cop all right, and Harold thought, *Here we go again.*

"I'm Sergeant Wycoff. Can I help you?" His voice was soft but firm. It was all so polite that Harold felt like saying, *I'm just here for a checkup.* Wycoff had a heavy shapeless body and a drooping mustache that gave him a sad look. His eyes were strangely liquid, but never seemed to blink, examining Harold with unnatural intensity.

"I was just trying to explain," Harold began, laughing again (*he had to stop doing that!*). "It's kind of complicated really but . . . Last winter my brother disappeared. He was . . . he had been acting weird—depressed—and I, well, I thought he took his own life. A body you had here seemed to fit the description and, well, I can't explain it really but, I identified it as my brother."

Wycoff was very still, watching Harold closely. Then his watery eyes seemed to dry out and harden. Rules had been broken, lies told, and he would have to find out how this happened. Before he could speak Harold began again, piling up the words to stall the inevitable.

"Like I said, it's very complicated because I've since found out that the body I identified as my brother is actually her husband," he pointed at Vikki to clarify the point. "Now you'd probably like to know how all this could happen. Well, I—"

"Yes. Yes, I would like to know that," Wycoff said, stopping

Harold. "In here, please," he gestured to the door he had come through.

They moved into an open room with several gray steel desks and windows high on the wall, through which they could see the cemetery and the blue mountains in the distance. Harold noticed that Vikki was looking at a television and VCR in the corner. Wycoff gestured toward two chairs and they sat. He suddenly thought of something and walked out of the room. Harold heard him saying to the receptionist, "Get ahold of—" and then, "—tell him to get down here—" and then more words that he couldn't quite catch but that gave him a hot, panicky feeling.

Wycoff returned with a folder and a tape recorder. "It would be a good idea if we get this on tape."

"On *tape*?" Harold felt idiotic as soon as he said it.

"You have a problem with that?"

Shit! Things were getting legal now, Harold thought, his breath coming fast and his thoughts starting to whirl.

"Eventually, I guess it will come to that," Harold said. "But the main reason I'm—we're here is, Mrs. Covo doesn't know if her husband is dead or alive. I.e., it seems like the first step is to find out if the—the body is actually her husband. If not, this whole thing is moot."

"*Moot*? I don't think it's moot at all," Wycoff said, eyes hardening still further. Harold instantly regretted trying to get fancy with words he didn't know. "Whether intentional or not, false statements were made leading to a serious—"

"But he's right," Vikki said, giving Harold a burst of pride for backing him up. "I've waited nine months to find out what happened to my husband. Can't we settle that first? I mean, if it's not him, then this is between you two."

Thanks a lot, Harold thought as he watched Wycoff consider her request. In the silence Harold found himself thinking of the cemetery on the hill.

"Mrs. Covo, we have every intention of making a positive identification. . . ."

"Now. I really want to get this over with now." Vikki leaned forward, touching the edge of the sergeant's desk.

"The person in question—whether it's Mr. Dodge's brother or your husband—can't be viewed, if that's what you're thinking."

"I have to know."

"I understand. Let me finish."

"Where is he?" She was getting close to an answer now and she wouldn't be stopped.

"Here. But—"

"Why can't I see him?"

Wycoff paused. Then, without turning, he pointed at the TV behind him. "That television is connected to a video camera in our examination room. Before we did the autopsy we took pictures of the body, for evidentiary purposes."

"You want to show me a video?"

"Believe me, when it's on TV it's easier."

"I don't care about *easy*, Sergeant."

"Mrs. Covo, I want to make one thing very clear. For you to see what we have in our refrigerator won't bring you any closer to the truth about your husband."

Harold saw the impact of these words on Vikki and softly added, "Why don't you take a look at the video, then see how you feel?"

She looked at Harold as if he had betrayed her, sat back, and said, "Okay, show me the damn video."

Wycoff got up, crossed the room, and opened a drawer holding rows of videotapes. As he searched through them, Harold sat next to Vikki feeling like he should do something. Like what? Hold her hand? Put his arm around her? But he didn't want her to think he was hitting on her while she was in a jam. So he just sat there with a sense of dread building in the room, until Wycoff located a tape, moved to the TV, and turned it on.

The screen went to snow and then was replaced with a close-up of a piece of paper reading *Santa Barbara County Sheriff's Department Evidence*. A voice offscreen was saying, ". . . male Caucasian found at oh-thirteen hundred near the rest area off Highway 101 at mile twenty-seven." Then, the face of what was obviously a corpse filled the screen, irregularly framed and partially turned in profile. Harold heard Vikki make a low moaning noise.

The corpse's skin was a waxy yellow, the flesh torn and covered with specks of dirt; the hair was thick and black and the eyes were partially open. It was the face Harold had seen beside the swollen stream that rainy day, the day when, Harold realized now, he really had been out of his mind.

Vikki was leaning forward, staring at the screen, arms wrapped around herself, nails digging into her bare arms.

The view suddenly widened to show the head and shoulders and they could see the man was wearing a white shirt, torn open, a tie still knotted around his neck. A gloved hand reached into view and pointed at a small red mark just under the chin, saying, ". . . the entry wound of a small-caliber gun . . . powder burns are partially visible surrounding the area. A probe inserted in the wound shows the angle of entry is approximately—" The hand inserted a small rod into the opening and a protractor was held beside it.

"Okay." Vikki stood up abruptly.

Wycoff turned, looked at her, then cut off the TV.

Vikki stood up and began pacing and Harold again felt that he should do something. He stood and moved toward her but she held up her hands, as if to shove him away, saying, "I'm okay. Okay?"

"Was that your husband?" Wycoff asked.

"Yes."

"Were there identifying marks that indicated—"

"Everything. Everything. When you're married to someone for seven years you can't say, well, it was this or that. It was just everything." She paused a minute and added: "It was him."

Harold looked at Vikki's face and felt the turbulence under the surface, the breaking and shifting of memories and large sections of the future too. It was all happening at an unnatural pace, like those time-lapse shots of clouds sweeping over the landscape bringing sunlight and rain almost simultaneously.

Harold turned to find Wycoff staring at him with eyes that were not sad at all now. They were pissed off, probably because he was thinking how he was in this uncomfortable position now because of Harold.

"Shall we?" Wycoff said, indicating the two chairs again.

"No!" Vikki said, as if touched by an electric shock. "Just give me the death certificate. I want to leave."

"Mrs. Covo, it would be best if we clear all this up right now."

Vikki couldn't seem to look at Wycoff, so Harold said, "Give her the death certificate. She has a right to that."

"Really? I don't think she wants it."

"Why?"

"Cause of death is listed as suicide."

"I don't understand."

"You're after the insurance, aren't you?" he asked bluntly.

"Yes."

"I'm surprised your agent didn't tell you—most policies don't pay anything on a suicide."

Vikki shook her head, trying to understand. "Wait a second, this was not a suicide."

"Based on what Mr. Dodge told us, cause of death is listed as suicide." Harold thought Wycoff enjoyed saying that, driving a wedge between him and Vikki.

Silence. She turned to Harold and looked him full in the face. She said, "Oh, Jesus." Then she said it again, "Oh, Jesus." She turned back to Wycoff. "Let me get this straight. As of now, I can't collect *anything* on the insurance?"

"You'll have to talk to your agent. But that's my understanding."

"But if it's proved to be murder, it will pay?"

"Actually, homicide usually pays double."

"Then you've got to change it. My husband was murdered."

"That will be determined by an investigation."

She was livid. She looked at Harold once more, then headed for the door. Harold started after her.

"Sir, you can't leave," Wycoff said. "You have to give us your statement." He was walking beside Harold and took his arm. Harold shuddered at his touch and shook off his hand.

"Look, let me get her settled somewhere and I'll come right back."

"Where are you staying?" They were in the outer office now, moving past the receptionist.

Harold looked across the parking lot and saw Vikki was already in the car, starting it up, so he said, "I'll be back," kept going, feeling that, under the circumstances, it looked like he was doing the right thing, going to the aid of a distraught woman. What else could he do?

But then he heard Wycoff behind him, barking at the receptionist, "I told you to get Homicide." Then, "Have dispatch radio them again!"

A moment later Harold was in the Healey, Vikki revving the engine, the exhaust pipes snarling, and he knew he was in for one hell of a ride.

Fabian Skura was at Auto Export Salvage & Dismantling doing some bodywork on his buddy's Deuce, and singing an aria from *La Traviata*, when he saw the canary yellow Camero roll into the dirt parking lot. It wasn't unusual to see a car like that come in. Hell, you drive a car that old you're always looking for parts. But when the short, bald guy stepped out of the car carrying a briefcase, wearing a coat and tie, Fabian got a bad feeling. Fifteen minutes later, when the Camero rolled out of the lot again, Fabian went into the cramped office and asked Cookie what the guy wanted.

"Estimates for insurance claims," Cookie said, handing Fabian the guy's card. It read James P. Shields, TransPacific, Insurance, Claims.

"You're *not* gonna tell me you showed him our records?" Cookie looked up at Fabian, whose six-foot six-inch bulk towered above him.

"He was some insurance guy, wanted to see the estimates we wrote, see if they jived with what they got billed for. Guy had a little card, said I hadda show him what he wanted."

"You're not gonna tell me you actually showed him our records?"

Cookie nodded slowly, cowering. "What could I do? It said right on the card I had to show it to him. Said it was the law."

Fabian saw the frightened look in the old man's eyes so he tried to take his anger down a notch as he said, "What could you do? You could call Bobby. Or call me. I'd deal with the guy."

Fact of the matter was, he liked dealing with guys like that. Guys who thought they could come in here, throw their weight around, show some bogus card and trick a feeble-minded old fart into opening their files. He imagined standing over the guy, looking down at him, just *looking* at the guy and seeing the smart-ass expression drop off his face.

Shit, here he was getting worked up, probably over nothing. He promised himself he'd stop doing this. But it was hard. His anger was always there. He got it from the old man. Like most Armenians he was a hot-tempered son-of-a-bitch. He tried hard to control himself, and he had even shortened their name from Skurosjian, like that would change anything. But he still had a hair-trigger temper and beat hell out of anyone that crossed him.

Fabian grabbed the phone and sat in the metal folding chair next to Cookie's desk, feeling it flex under his bulk. As he dialed he said, "You been working too hard, Cookie. Take a break. Go over to Angel's and get me some coffee." As the old man shuffled out the door he yelled after him, "And don't forget—four sugars!"

Seconds later, his older brother's voice came on the phone, saying, "Dent Doctor Auto Body."

"Listen, Bobby, no one's gonna take me down. Understand?"

"What're you shoutin' about? You're always shoutin' at me."

"Well, if you'd listen to me I wouldn't have to shout. Okay? Now look, a insurance guy was just here—"

"Guy drives a piece of shit Camero?"

"How'd you know?"

"He's over here now."

"*There?*"

"Downstairs. Tanya's pullin' copies for him."

"Oh, man."

"Oh, man, is right. And Victor just called me. The guy was over there too, this morning."

"You think Dash sent the guy? Get us off his back for the money he owes?"

"Why would Dash send him? Dash wrote the policies, for Christ's sake. Listen, you don't have to get involved in this end of the business. All you gotta do is . . ."

Cookie walked back into the office and handed Fabian a steaming cup of coffee. He sipped the coffee, then sank his stubby teeth in the rim, tearing away pieces of the paper as he listened to his brother. Finally he interrupted saying, "I'm not goin' down. You got me into this. Now you get me out of it."

"I got you into this? Into what? Making money? Driving a good car and owning your own house? Yeah, I guess I did get you into this. If it hadn't been for me, you know what you'd be doing?"

"Making an honest living as a butcher."

"Don't tell me you forgot? Did you really forget?"

"Forget what?" His voice was sullen.

"Hell, you'd be wearing tights and tippy-toeing around on stage."

"That's *ballet*, you dumb shit. I sing opera. They're two different things."

"Whatever. It was a stupid idea and I saved your ass from major embarrassment."

"I don't know, Bobby. Something like this happens, I wish I was still in that meat locker."

Actually, the meat locker was a good place to sing. Fabian loved to fill the frozen space with his big voice, seeing the heat from his lungs shoot out in white clouds. The guys he worked with loved his singing. But when he told Bobby he was going to take voice lessons and try out for local productions, his big brother said, "Wanna know what I think?"

"Yeah."

"Keep cuttin' that meat."

A while later Bobby asked Fabian to collect two grand from

a contractor who wouldn't pay for a custom paint job they did on his pickup. Fabian didn't have to do much. Just showed up at the guy's house while he was flippin' burgers in the backyard. Guy tried to get smart with him, show off in front of his old lady. Fabian snatched him off his feet, held him up over his head until he shut his smart mouth. Together they went to his bank and got a cashier's check. Since then he quit his job as a butcher and left a string of broken bodies across the South Bay. Fabian was good at his new job because he had an animal ferocity that people immediately sensed. But when he was done, standing over a man he'd dropped, breathing hard, coming out of that frightening place he always went, he hated what he'd become.

"Bobby, I'm going to make this clear. This guy ain't gonna take me down. Understand what I'm telling you?"

"Will you relax?"

"No, I won't. I'm concerned about this, Bobby. And I think you should be too. When the guy was here he knew everything. *Everything.* Okay? And if he went to Victor's that means he's hitting all our shops. And he's got our quotes. Dash gave him our quotes."

"Sometimes I think your brain is the size of a pea. Dash didn't give him our quotes. The guy got copies from his, you know, home office or whatever you call it."

"Oh, so you're defending Dash now?"

"*Right.*" He paused, then chuckled softly. "You know, there might be a way we could use this to our advantage."

"Use it? For what?"

"Fabian, try using your brain for once, okay? Dash owes us, what? Ten grand?"

"Yeah."

"What if we use this insurance guy to squeeze Dash?"

"What if I go to Dash's office, drag him into the garage by his hair, and beat his brains out with a pipe wrench."

"Then we don't get the money."

Fabian had finished the coffee and was shredding the last of the paper cup with his teeth, swallowing some of it, spitting the rest onto the concrete floor around his chair. Into the phone he said: "So what're you gonna do?"

"Play it by ear," Bobby said. "Call you back. Okay?"

Bobby's office was right over the reception area of the auto body shop, where customers came in for estimates, to check the paint books, drop off their keys, and whatnot. In between the whir of the power wrenches and the hiss of the spray gun Bobby could hear Tanya dealing with the insurance guy, trying to act dumb like they told her to do if anyone showed up asking questions. But this guy kept right on coming, asking the same thing over and over again like he hadn't heard what she said.

When Bobby came downstairs he almost wanted to laugh. Here they were all worked up about this guy, he turns out to be a real wuss. Thick glasses, bald as a coot, narrow shoulders, and a blue sports coat that looked like he bought the thing in a thrift shop for a buck.

Tanya looked up and seemed surprised to see Bobby coming down, but she kept her mouth shut and sat there on the stool behind the counter with her long legs crossed. Bobby met Tanya while eating lunch over at Angel's and thought it wouldn't be a bad idea to have a girl with a rack like that dealing with his customers. They look down to make out a check, see that cleavage staring them in the face, it might take some of the sting out of the bill. Not only that, but when things got slow she came up to his office and helped him pass the lonely hours. So what if his wife was getting a little hot about the whole thing? The kind of money he brought home gave him the right.

"Bobby Skura. Can I help you?"

The guy looked up from the estimate he was reading and Bobby noticed his eyes behind the thick glasses. Cop eyes.

"Jim Shields. TransPacific Insurance." They shook. Then, in a way that told Bobby nothing, the guy said, "As you know, we ask for estimates from three shops, then we usually take the lowest bid. I'm just trying to verify the estimates that were submitted to us. It's a routine audit."

"Audit? Like investigation?"

The guy blinked once behind the trifocals. "Audit only means we're trying to see if the estimates and claims submitted to us were an accurate representation of the actual work that was done."

"Yeah, an investigation."

Tanya was turning her head back and forth like she was watching a tennis game.

"Hey, Tanya, get Mr. Shields a cappuccino."

"No, thanks."

"You'll love it. Tanya gets the milk really foamy." Bobby pumped his fist in and out and winked at Shields.

"I'm not a coffee drinker, thanks. This will only take a—"

"Coke then? Diet Pepsi. Tanya, get him a—"

"Nothing, really."

The phone started ringing. Tanya's hand was on the phone when Bobby covered it with his, saying, "Honey, whyn't you work the phones from my desk." She jumped off the stool and hurried up the stairs as they both watched. Bobby turned back to Shields, smiling. "A real piece of work, no?"

Shields said: "I'd like to see a copy of your paperwork on this job you did on"—he craned his neck around— "November 21."

Bobby saw that the guy had a Xerox of the customer's

carbon copy with *Dent Doctor Auto Body* on top and their slogan, *We take the dent out of accident.* He remembered that job. Remembered it well. So he moved to the file cabinet and began flipping through files without any intention of locating it.

"I want you to know, Mr. Shields, that I've always cooperated with you guys. I mean, you hear so much about insurance rip-offs and whatnot. And the taxpayers are the ones that take a big hit on it. Am I right?"

The guy waited patiently, eyes steady behind the thick glasses.

"Now, say the guy's driving down the road and he has a little wangus, scrapes his fender or something. Okay, so he brings his car in here for an estimate. And he might want me to put it down as a four-point collision. But I say, 'Look, the insurance guys aren't stupid. You play fair with them, they'll play fair with you.' That's why we've always kept our shops as clean as is realistically possible."

"Do you own other body shops in this area?"

"No."

"Then why did you say *shops*?"

"Listen, I want you to know that I never bullshit people. Especially a smart guy like you. I can tell you probably went to college and everything. Right?"

"I'm a CPA."

"Bean counter, huh? But no offense. Someone's gotta do it. Anyway, Mr. Shields, I just want you to know that I'm not gonna bullshit you. Okay?"

"Okay."

"In my line of work, I hear things."

"What things?"

"Well, before I get into that I want to know how this whole thing works."

"I'm not following you."

"This investigation."

"I told you, this is an audit. An internal audit."

"But it's not really that *internal* if you're out here asking me questions. Right? What I'm saying is, in theory, say you find out something ain't kosher. What then? I mean, do I go to jail?" He laughed as if that was absurd.

"Let me first of all make it clear that I'm not here investigating you or your shop."

"Right, of course not."

"The purpose is to benefit TransPacific by controlling its branch offices. But—" Here it comes, Bobby thought, still bent over the filing cabinet. "But if we were to find evidence of a criminal offense it would be turned over to the State Insurance Commissioner for review."

"Okay."

"They have a fraud division to follow up on leads we provide."

"Naturally. But what I need you to understand is, word gets out I've talked to some bean counter—no offense—my business goes in the toilet. 'Cause let's face it, insurance claims are my bread and butter. What if I could give you some information to help your investigation? Could you *not* divulge where you got that information?"

The guy was quiet for a long time as he plugged this into whatever he already knew. Finally he said, "At this point, all sources of information are confidential."

Bobby smiled and rolled the file door closed. He stood up and folded his thick arms across his chest. He was a head shorter than his younger brother, but he was built the same—chest like a steamer trunk, arms roped with muscle.

"The only thing that worries me is how do I know I can trust you."

"I give you my word."

"I appreciate that. I appreciate that. But I'm a cautious guy.

Maybe we should take this one step at a time. I'm gonna tell you part of what I know, and see what you do with it. If it works out, I'll tell you everything. Now, is that fair?''

"I'm really not in a position to bargain. If you want to tell me something, tell me.''

"There's this guy, an agent I've, well, come in contact with. I've always felt there's something not quite on the up and up about him.''

"What's his name?''

Bobby paused, smiling, stroking his goatee, in no hurry to answer. He was surprised to find how much he enjoyed this.

Vikki had the Healey in a four-wheel drift on a blind mountain curve. If someone was coming the other way, it was checkout time for them all. This was, Harold realized, one of those times when his chances of getting killed were excellent, and he couldn't do a damn thing about it. They were roaring into the mountains above Santa Barbara, live oaks stretching out overhead, sudden patches of sunlight exploding like muzzle flashes in Harold's brain, the wind tearing his thoughts to pieces and leaving his mind empty and raw.

Seconds later, the road leveled out and turned into a straightaway ahead of them, with a white rail fence on one side and the mountain falling away on the other, and Harold knew she would give it everything here. Pedal to the metal time. He felt her urge growing next to him and looked over to see the wind snatching the black dress off her long legs, angled up as she worked the pedals, her hair swirling around her like golden smoke. The engine swelled and the speed flowed through them like a white-hot light. Harold saw the needle touching 120 mph and he suddenly understood that she was punishing him for what he had done to her life.

They were running out of straightaway now, the road dropping away, and Harold knew the turn was coming up too fast, way too fast, and he felt that deep biological resistance to the speed, knowing they couldn't possibly make the turn, it was against all the laws of nature. But on the other side of this realization Harold found a strange freedom, a sense of letting go, and he turned to watch Vikki, thinking he would finally come to know her in this moment, and saw her face lit from inside as if she were consuming years of her life in a few seconds.

Later, Harold tried to put together what had happened, how they could possibly have survived. There was the truck, appearing in front of them, which they passed on the wrong side. Then the Healey was airborne as the road dropped away and when they hit they began spinning on the dirt shoulder, slamming into the guardrail at an angle so Harold was thrown sideways and hit his head on the door. And when they finally stopped moving Harold knew they were connected in a way that would change everything.

Vikki was breathing hard, her chest surging under the black dress, amazed to be alive. She slowly turned to him, eyes drugged with speed, then clearing as if coming out of a trance.

"Oh, my God!" she said, and touched the cut on Harold's forehead where blood had trickled down and was soaking a round wet spot on his collar. She drew her finger back and stared at the shiny redness.

She climbed out of the car to check the damage and Harold could feel the grit of dust between his teeth. He looked over the edge of the guardrail and saw the ocean in the distance and the homes of Santa Barbara climbing the flanks of the blue mountains.

He heard her say, *Damn*, as she saw that the taillight was smashed and the trunk lid sprung. A moment later the trunk slammed and she was beside him again in the seat. He waited for it all to begin again but she pulled out saying, "We have to find a place to talk."

"You want a beer or something?" he said. Then, when she didn't answer, he added, "I could really use a drink."

She laughed at that and said, "Yeah. That was close. Joe would've liked it." Her comment seemed to jolt her and she looked at Harold strangely, then back at the road.

A mountain town appeared around the corner with bungalows on the outskirts and shops around a fountain in the square. Two field-workers with sweat-soaked straw hats were sprawled on the grass sharing a twelve-pack of Bud Lite, the empties scattered around them, glinting in the sun. The Healey slowly rolled through town and then out along a strip with fast-food restaurants and cheap motels.

Vikki nosed the car into a dirt lot in front of a bar, liquor store, and a motel. As they got out Harold could almost taste the beer. But first he would have to make the call. He entered the bar and found a pay phone next to the kitchen that smelled like ammonia and roach powder.

"Sergeant Wycoff?"

"Who's calling, please?"

"Harold Dodge." That would get him on the line, Harold thought, looking around and thinking, Hey, where's Vikki?

"Wycoff."

"I want to go over something with you."

"Good, because I'd like to go over a lot of things with you."

"Covo's death was no suicide. He was murdered." Wycoff was silent. "You've got to change that death certificate."

"Do I?"

"It's what happened." He wished Vikki was hearing him be so assertive on her behalf.

"Why don't you come back in and tell us all about it."

"Us?"

53

"You're saying it was a murder, we'll get Homicide in here to take your statement."

Harold hesitated, not quite so assertive, as he asked, "Are you going to arrest me?"

"Have you done anything wrong?"

"Well, I sure as hell didn't murder him, if that's what you think."

"I don't *think* anything, Harold. Because I don't know anything. If you want this death certificate changed, you're going to have to give us your statement. And we're not going to take it over the phone. Is that clear?"

"I'll come back in."

"When?"

"I don't know. Okay? But I'll be back."

He hung up and moved into the barroom thinking he'd find Vikki there. As he slid onto a stool in the dark room, with guns and stuffed animals hanging from the walls, he looked out the window and finally saw Vikki, across the parking lot, through the glass office window of the Tally Ho Motor Court, and he knew what she wanted. And he knew what he would do. But first he would drink the tall cold beer the bartender put in front of him while that familiar feeling rose inside him, completely beyond his control.

The first thing he noticed when she stepped from the bathroom was that she was completely naked, holding a cigarette in one hand and a bottle of Jose Cuervo Tequila in the other. The second thing he noticed was that her body, undressed, surpassed even the promise of her body when it was clothed.

She extended the bottle to him saying, "One tequila, two tequila, three tequila, floor."

"There's something I really should tell you about myself." Harold hated the way his voice sounded. He accepted the bottle thinking maybe he could get drunk enough, fast enough, to do what he had to do.

"Confession time," she said, still standing in the doorway, drawing on the cigarette. The smoke seemed to seep out of her pores and cling to her body like gauze. "I have something to tell you about myself, too."

"What's that?"

"I'm a real slut."

He looked at her a long time, so classy, so beautiful, so utterly sexy, and felt she was trying to play a role—a role that no longer fit her.

"Don't say that about yourself."

He sat on a chair beside the bed, took another hit off the bottle.

"The way I like it, the things I've done, with people or persons unnamed, would shock the living hell out of you."

"Tell me about it."

She stood in front of him.

"How about I show you?"

She lowered herself onto him, spreading her legs around him, lacing her fingers behind his neck and staring into his eyes. He could smell her sweat, her breath, and the moist animal smell that rose up from below—and as if in response, he suddenly was aware of the smell of his own body.

He put the bottle on the floor and wrapped his arms around her, feeling her muscled back with his hands under a glaze of sweat. He crushed her to him and she began working herself against his belly and, as he rose hard and demanding, she worked against that too.

"Fuck me now, before it all goes to hell."

One more hit of the tequila. One more hit and he could do it. He swung the bottle up to his mouth and found hers there too, so they drank what they could, and the rest flowed over their mouths and tongues down onto her breasts and his white shirt, pasting them both together. The room was spinning around him from the sex rush and alcohol and he stood with her still around him, and he was as strong and stupid as a bull who wanted to gore her so hard it hurt them both. He fell on top of her on the bed and felt her ripping at his clothes, her nails raking his chest and his hands in her hair yanking her head back so he could get at her face and neck and breasts. Everything was so damn wet and confused he didn't know where he was or what he was doing, and especially what he would do next. But he heard their sounds, like tortured animals, and found her moans forming into foul words that tore at herself. *Use me*, she was saying. Then, her voice saying, *Down on your knees, bitch*, and again: *Use me . . . Keep using me, you bastard, Use me like you did today.*

The words began reaching that rational place in his brain that he just couldn't turn off and they fit with the whole insane ride up the mountain.

"What'd you say?" He stopped her as she descended his body.

Pause. Then she came back from a long way. "I don't know."

"I'm not *using* you." He sat up. She was kneeling in front of him, breathing like she had just escaped with her life.

"The hell you're not. You tried to use me to clear your deal with the cops. You knew they wouldn't move on you with the grieving widow there. So you go in, tell your story, and get the hell out, think that's gonna solve something."

He was stunned, for a moment seeing it all from her point of view and hating himself for it.

"But, hey, what else is new? I've been used so much they should put me in a swap meet."

She lay her head on his leg, waiting for him to recover, then stroking his thighs, trying to get him back to where they had been. He wanted it to start again but the room was filling up with the faces of dead men: Joe and Vito and the unnamed man who had fallen under the trees in the park. And finally, the dead men gave way to the face of Marianna, who had escaped it all and controlled him now, although she was thousands of miles away in Chile. He saw her shadowy beauty, her black hair and eyes that he could never really know. If she were here now she would kill Vikki with her bare hands. Then she would turn to Harold and calmly say, "You belong to me, Harold."

Vikki felt him going cold on her and pulled back. "What happened?"

"I'm thinking."

"Oh, Christ. Don't do that."

She kissed him once more and found that it was all gone now, so she dumped herself on the bed and curled away from him and was frighteningly still. Harold turned and rubbed her shoulder. As lame as it was, it was the only thing he did that felt honest.

"I think there's a way out of all this."

She made a noise that lacked all hope. "They'll take my car. They'll take my house. And I'll be back to zero. All the way back to zero."

He looked at her beautiful back, so suddenly still now, and at her tangled hair on the pillow and found no sex there anymore. There was something childlike about her position that made him see how alone she was and how she needed his help more than she could say. But first he needed to do some thinking. He could do that and at the same time quench the thirst that had come roaring back.

"I'm gonna go get a beer. Wanna come?"

No answer.

"I'll be in the bar." He was heading for the door when she spoke without turning: "You said you want to straighten things out."

"I do. I really do."

"Tell the cops what you told me."

"They'll lock me up," he said, remembering the cell he'd been in last fall, the faces of cops interrogating him, the judge who frowned down at him, ordering him back to his cell. He promised himself he'd never go back to that. Never.

"You should have thought of that before you started this."

"I'm going to figure something out," he said, and left her, returning to the dark barroom next door with the guns and stuffed animals on the walls and a tall cold beer. And as he went over the three-by-five cards and returned an hour later to talk to her about it, he found the room empty. The only clue that they had ever been there was the bed with its stained sheets looking like someone had been murdered on them.

Torres never came into the detective bureau on Wednesdays because that was his day off and he usually spent his days off testifying in court. But he happened to stop by on this particular day to pick up a file, so lo and behold, he was there when the call came in.

It was coincidences like this that led to arrests; and it was coincidences like this that kept him going to Mass on Sundays even though he didn't believe in God. Another reason he went to Mass was because his mother used to make him go every Sunday while he was growing up in Boyle Heights, where every other kid wound up gangbanging or in prison or dead by the time they were twenty. Still, coincidences like this made you wonder.

The caller had been switched around to about five divisions when Diaz held up the receiver and yelled across to Torres, "This one's for you, Richard!"

"I'm in court," Torres said, and kept moving across the big open room, filled with desks, mounded with files.

"It might be about that double at the airport last year."

Torres stopped, paused, then returned to his desk. He picked up the phone.

"Detective Torres. Can I help you?"

"I sure hope so. I'm tired of getting bounced all over. This is Sergeant Wycoff in the Santa Barbara coroner's office. Did you work a case last year involving Joe Covo?"

Torres ran the name through his memory.

Wycoff added: "It might have been a missing person."

"Okay. I remember it now. Yeah, I had that case."

"Well, he's not missing any longer. He's in our cooler. He's been there for the last nine months."

Torres sighed. "We called you—a couple of times. Didn't get a match."

Wycoff's laugh was breathy over the phone. "Here's why: The body was under the wrong name."

"Oh, yeah?"

"Guy came in today with Covo's wife, selling me a story how he thought the body was his brother who blew his brains out in a rest area on the 101. This guy's name is—" He paused and the name flashed into Torres's mind at the same time as Wycoff said, "Harold Dodge. Ring a bell?"

"Bird Dog."

"Sorry?"

"That's what we call him. He used to bird dog for a car dealer. Is Dodge still there?"

"He was in and out before I could put it together. He came on like—almost like a Fed or something, wearing a suit, very respectable, like it was all a big mistake."

"That's his style."

"What's he done?"

"He was connected to a double homicide up by LAX last year. Then he disappeared."

"You still want him?"

"Most definitely. Know where can we pick him up?"

"No. But here's the thing. It looks like he's helping the widow Covo go after the insurance money. But right now, cause of death is suicide." He paused, letting it sink in.

"I like where this is going."

"Yeah. I told Dodge he was going to have to give us a statement to get the cause of death changed. So I expect to hear from him again."

"I expect you will."

"Yeah."

Torres thought it over. "One thing you've got to know, this Dodge is not your typical deadbeat. He's liable to try to pull something."

"Pull something?"

"Yeah, so when he calls, set up a meeting. Then call me. Me or my partner, Detective Gammon. We'll be there—any time, any place."

"He's likely to show up in our office again."

"We'll make the drive. You just call us—any time, any place. Meantime, I'll send you our paperwork on him, you can see what we got so far."

After he hung up, Torres made a note to check if the Remy warrant they got last fall had expired or could they use it to pick him up. If they could find him. With Dodge, that was always the problem.

Torres leaned back in his chair thinking how Gammon

would be very pleased with this development and would start fixating on how to nail Dodge. "You're my number one," Gammon told Dodge as he walked out of the interrogation room that rainy day back in October. Torres enjoyed the way Gammon had said that. He enjoyed working with the big man. So he wrote a note and left it in Gammon's message box, where he would see it as soon as he walked in. It said: "Bird Dog's back."

Vikki watched as Dash emerged from the bar carrying two glasses of beer and moved toward her across the deserted patio of the Mardi Gras in Huntington Beach. Tall, blond, crisp white shirt tucked into pleated pants, beeper clipped to his belt. It was like a uniform guys wore these days—sort of *corporate cool*. But she found herself thinking how she liked the way he moved, liked the way he looked, like a clean-cut life guard except for that off-kilter smile that could mean anything.

They had stopped serving out here on the patio now but that was okay. It would make it easier for what she had to do. So he fetched a pair of fresh beers from the bar and they continued to sit here under the heat lamps with the surf booming in the darkness off across the beach.

He set the beers down in front of her and said, "Bulls are getting their fannies spanked. You a Lakers fan?"

"Joe had season tickets—for clients, of course. We never went."

Where to begin, she thought, *where to begin* . . . Time to put the small talk about sports and cars aside and get down to it. She felt dreamy, two beers on an empty stomach already glowing in her system, disconnecting her from the nightmarish images of the day: Joe dead on the TV screen, racking up the Healey, her close encounter with Harold. What a mess. What she needed was a fresh approach, a new tack. So she had called Dash, set up this little meeting. It almost seemed like he had been waiting for her call.

"Yesterday," she began, seeing him detach his eyes from the TV over the bar and the all-important Lakers game. "Yesterday you said if I had any problems—"

"To call me. Sure, I remember."

"Well, we ran into a little trouble. . . ."

"Uh-huh."

"It comes down to a matter of timing, really."

"Timing?"

"Yeah. See, we found out that Joe's death is listed as—as a suicide."

Dash frowned.

"I know. But it wasn't a suicide. He was shot through the neck and no gun was found near him, his car was parked back in LA. But the cops want a statement from Harold—Harold Dodge, the guy who was with me—and he's already in trouble so he doesn't want to give a statement. But I really believe he will and the cause of death will be changed and the policy will eventually pay out. But you see, I can't wait any longer for the money."

Dash nodded seriously. She reached across the table and touched his arm. *Time to turn it on now*, she thought. "So, you see, it's not a big problem. It's more a matter of timing."

He paused thoughtfully, then said, "What exactly do you need, Vikki?"

"Got a pencil?" She laughed, then looked around, saw the patio was empty. "Hell, I'm going to smoke." She shook out a cigarette from the nearly empty pack.

Dash waited as she lit up, then blew out smoke saying, "I need money. Oh, man, do I need money."

"And—? What else do you need?" He waited, smiling, confident, playing with her. They both knew where this was going.

She laughed, tonguing off a bit of tobacco from her lip, then removing it with a fingertip. "It doesn't show?" They both laughed and he took her hand and she didn't pull away because she realized they had just reached an agreement.

"Vikki, before we get to that, I do want to help with the money, but I don't know what I can do."

"If you wanted to, you could give me an advance, like Harold said, since the policy will settle soon anyway."

"Problem with that—I'm going through a little cash flow crisis of my own. I got an inside tip on a junk bond and lost ten grand that didn't belong to me."

"Oh-oh."

"No big deal. But it came at a time when things were a little tight. So what I'm thinking here is maybe we could collaborate."

"I've heard it called a lot of things, but never that."

He smiled, then: "Life insurance policies take a while to pay out. Other policies settle faster. If you're up for a little adventure, I could get you, say, ten grand a week from now. Make a house payment, have a few bucks left over for fun and games."

She felt a tingle of excitement as the unknown drifted closer, like a cold wind off the dark ocean. Here she was trying to hustle him for some quick bucks, and now it looked like he was working a hustle of his own.

"What do I have to do?"

"Buy a new car."

"Buying a car's going to get me money?"

"Insurance is a beautiful thing." He winked at her, seeing her understand all of it—or almost all of it.

"But I don't have the money to buy a car."

"Got any plastic?"

"Of course. But it's maxed out."

"We've got a dealership we work with where that doesn't matter."

Now she understood all of it. "Let me guess: Joe Covo Matsura."

"You're quick," he said, wagging a finger at her, "very quick."

"Dash, I still don't see how—"

"Babe, let me put it this way . . ." He paused as she thought, *babe*? but realized that it fit somehow, his low voice, his smooth style. Some guys could pull it off. But Dash seemed too smart for that—like he was just playing a role, waiting for you to say, "Oh, please . . ."

"Let me put it this way," he repeated. "The less you know the better."

She thought of the papers she'd found in the safe in Joe's study, the ones she gave to Harold saying, *Joe was into something, he was moving money and cars around.* Maybe this was the *something* Joe was into. Maybe it was time to get that folder back from Harold now that she was done with him. Or was she? It might not be smart to go into Joe Covo Matsura unescorted. She read somewhere that you should never go car shopping alone. Come to think of it, she'd read that in Harold's book.

Dash had just checked the score (Lakers up by ten with four minutes on the clock) when he happened to see Fabian Skura crossing from the parking lot and heading toward the restaurant. He lumbered forward like a destroyer ready to crush anything in his path, shirt stretched tight across his gut, straining at the buttons, then tenting down over the tops of his pants, his arms swinging like heavy machinery, palms turned out and the swollen fingers obscenely thick and etched with grease. His head jutted forward on a stump of a neck between enormous shoulders and his eyes were dark and filled with rage, a rage that, unfortunately, Dash understood. It was caused by people owing him money they wouldn't pay.

"Vik," Dash said quickly. "A client of mine will be stopping by in a few minutes."

"A client?"

"Yeah, and he needs some delicate handling."

Fabian was at the bar now, a beer in his thick hand. He drank it off, slammed it down, and began scanning the restaurant, looking for them. Dash thought of the stories he'd heard about Fabian that drifted through the auto body shops of Wilmington and the docks of Los Angeles Harbor. Stories of how Fabian caught a falling steel beam that would have crushed his brother, Bobby; how he once lifted a V-8 engine block out of a Buick to win a bet. How he killed an Iranian taxi driver who tried to cheat him and threw his body off a fishing boat on the back side of Catalina before dawn.

"I need to stall this guy a little. So do me a favor and roll with what I say," Dash said. "And make sure you ask him about his singing."

"Singing?"

"Yeah, he's some kind of an opera wanna-be."

Moving across the patio, Dash thought how lucky it was he saw Fabian first. He was ready with a line and a plan before the dark eyes caught him in their sights.

"Fabian!" Dash waved to him. "Hey, we're out here!"

Fabian started toward them. Dash met him halfway saying, "Where you been, man?"

"Where've I been?" Fabian's anger was rising.

"You got my message, right? I called Bobby's girl—Tanya. Told her I got a check for you if you wanted it."

"If I *wanted* it."

"I got a check in the car for you. Lemme buy you a beer, then we'll take care of business."

"I want the money now, Dash, no bullshit."

"Sure. But, hey, I got someone you gotta meet." He gestured toward Vikki, and watched as the rage in Fabian's eyes receded. "Fabian Skura. Vikki Covo."

Fabian took her hand, looking at her like she was something he might want to eat. She realized this but held his eyes anyway, staring at him like she was trying to place him. Dash admired that; Fabian scared the shit out of most men, and here she was staring him down.

"Pleasure to meet you," Fabian said, lowering himself into a patio chair that looked like it was made of soda straws.

"Be right back with a couple of fresh ones," Dash said, and left for the bar, hearing Vikki behind him saying, "I understand you have a terrific voice."

And Fabian saying, "I sing a little—not professionally, but—"

Then Dash was into the noisy restaurant, moving toward the bar, seeing the bartender and yelling, "Hey, Jerr!"

"Hey, Dash. What d'ya been up to, man?"

"Oh, you know, just maintaining my lifestyle."

"I hear ya."

"Three dark ones, okay?"

A heavyset guy in a Hawaiian shirt was watching the game. Waiting, Dash asked: "What's the score?"

"Lakers're up by six. But Jordan's gettin' hot."

"Shit. I got two hundred bucks on this game."

"You took the Lakers over Chicago?" The guy laughed.

Dash ignored him, paying for the beers. He scooped them

up and started for the patio, then stopped halfway and set the beers on an empty table. Reaching into his pocket he found the tiny pills. *Try this sometime*, a buddy of his said, a college kid who knew about all sorts of weird new shit. *But try it on someone else. When they wake up they don't remember a thing.* Later he read about them in the newspaper. *Roofies*, they called it, *the date-rape drug*. It might be just the ticket for dealing with the big gorilla, Dash thought, dropping two pills in the dark foamy liquid.

He picked up the three beers and headed out onto the patio as a funny thought hit him: Better keep these beers straight now, or I might be the one to wind up on my ass.

Shoving the patio door open he heard Fabian's massive voice, his singing filling the great outdoors and pushing back even the sound of the surf. When it ended he heard Vikki's sparkling voice say, "*Wonderful!*" and she began applauding. As he set the beer down in front of Fabian, he realized that Vikki had probably just saved his life.

Fabian slammed down the last of his beer, swiped his sausage lips with a napkin, his mood changing as his big head swiveled to face Dash: "You have something for me. No?"

Dash watched him closely, looking for signs the pills were taking effect. But Fabian looked unchanged, the pig eyes hooded with anger as he bit down on the wadded napkin, grinding back and forth with his yellowed front teeth.

"One for the road?" Dash asked, stalling, hoping to hear slurred speech, or see the eyes go dull.

Fabian jabbed a finger at him. "You puttin' me off?"

Vikki jumped in. "How about a curtain call?"

Fabian's expression softened. He said to Dash, "I like her."

But then he stood, yanked up on his pants trying to cover his massive gut, which was hanging out now like a hairy water-melon. He stabbed Dash with his finger. "You and me. Let's go. Now."

"I shall return," Dash said to Vikki, thinking, *That is, if the roofies work. If not, look for a bloody heap in the parking lot.*

Vikki nodded, almost like she understood what was at stake and, at that moment, Dash felt something stirring inside him, something he hadn't felt for a long time. But he was leaving her now, walking beside this monster, through the bar (stopping to check the final score and, *Yes!* The Lakers pulled it out—where was that asshole in the Hawaiian shirt?) then feeling a big hand on his back, shoving him out into the night.

They walked across a courtyard filled with tropical-looking plants, palm fronds overhead rustling in the night wind. During the day this place was packed with joggers, kids lugging Boogie boards, girls on Rollerblades. Now it was deserted and Dash heard the surf in the distance.

The parking lot was ahead, across the foot of the pier and down a short flight of steps. At the far end Dash saw Vikki's Healey next to his Range Rover 4.0 SE with the blackout windows.

Dash realized his senses were heightened, ready for what he might have to do, and he felt the adrenaline flowing, heart pumping, pumping, like it had that night in the park in Atlanta. He had set up a meeting with a private investigator, telling him he had information on who was embezzling money from the company Dash was working for. Actually, what he really wanted to do was put a stop to the investigation, buy some time to leave the state. So he arranged to meet the investigator in the shadows under the trees. Ten minutes later, he walked out of the park alone.

The Rover loomed ahead. Dash took out his keys with the attached car alarm remote control. He turned off the alarm with a chirp that echoed off a nearby apartment building. As they covered the last twenty feet Dash listened to Fabian's footsteps, trying to see if they were dragging, unsteady.

Fabian suddenly stopped. Dash saw that he was looking at lights out in the ocean, a deep sea fishing boat leaving the pier.

Fabian's voice was different as he said, "They'll be off Mexico by dawn."

"You like to fish?" Dash wanted to prolong the delay.

"Them yellowtails fight like bastards. I hooked one last year off San Felipe, fought it for an hour. I was done, I felt like I'd gone ten rounds with Mike Tyson. And me at three hundred twenty pounds." He laughed. Then the memory left him and he turned to Dash. "Move it."

They reached the car. Dash slowly swung open the rear gate of the Rover, the heavy door opening to the right, not lifting up like other models. Good thing, too. That was part of his plan. He took out his briefcase and held it in his right hand. He turned to face Fabian, whose face now seemed blank and loose.

Dash watched the big man carefully, his weight balanced.

"Well? You have the money or not?"

"No."

Fabian bared his teeth and charged, growling. Dash knew he'd come in low, try to get him off his feet, like he'd seen him do with other men. Dash sidestepped and slammed the briefcase into his head. Fabian dropped between the open rear door and the tailgate of the car. He started to rise and Dash swung the heavy door into his head. The door shuddered on its hinges and Fabian dropped to his knees. He tried to rise but dropped back down again, his cannonball head turning back and forth, blood dripping from his temple. He looked like a rhino shot with a tranquilizer gun.

"Get in the car, Fabian." Dash stood over him, feeling a thrill of power.

Fabian looked up; the anger was tiny in his hooded eyes. "What'd you do to me?"

"Get in the car, Fabian."

Fabian turned and looked where Dash was pointing.

"Get in the car, Fabian, or I'll hit you again."

Fabian struggled to his feet, then rolled into the cargo area, the Rover rocking on its springs. Dash picked up Fabian's legs and bent them into the small space, then pulled the vinyl covering over the cargo area so no one could see inside. A moment later he returned with a piece of newspaper, which he put under Fabian's head to catch the blood. As he began walking back to the restaurant, he thought of how Vikki gave him the time he needed to deal with Fabian. He owed her one for that and now, with the danger under control (at least for now) he had a pretty good idea how he'd repay her.

It was pushing midnight when Dash pulled the Rover into the garage under his building and cut the ignition. He sat there in the sudden silence for a moment, Vikki beside him, as if he was listening for something. They got out and crossed to the elevator. As the elevator doors closed, sealing them in the small space, he stared at her challengingly, then leaned down and kissed her. In her glory days, waiting tables in sports bars, trying anything once, before she met Joe and settled into seven years of monogamy, she would have called it an expert kiss. It made her want more, a lot more.

When they broke and the doors opened, she said to him, "You think you're smarter than most people, don't you?"

He looked at her, a half-smile twisting his mouth, trying to figure out why she said that, and finally said, "I am smarter than most people."

They stepped out of the elevator, crossed the hallway, and entered his apartment. Right off she saw that she wouldn't learn anything about him by being in his place. In fact, it didn't feel like a home at all, more like a hotel suite. The walls were mostly bare as if he had just moved in. A few commercial paintings had sports themes—sailing, golf, tennis. The small kitchen was clean and she knew without looking there was no food in the refrigerator that would be safe to eat. One door led to a dark bedroom and inside another room she saw the outline of a desk, computer, and fax machine. The proverbial home office.

He was taking down two champagne glasses when she said, "You know what? I've had enough for one night." When he looked at her significantly she added, "Enough to drink."

"It'll help you relax," he said.

"What makes you so sure I'm not relaxed?"

"Comments like that."

"Dash." She couldn't help playing off his words. "There's only one thing that could really relax me."

He leaned back against the refrigerator and put one hand on his hip, saying: "Yeah? What's that?"

They had both played this game before. But it had been a while for her and she felt the old excitement in a dirty kind of way.

She turned away and wandered out onto the balcony, feeling the ocean moisture in the night air. Lighting a cigarette (damn, it was her last one—they forgot to stop on the way here) she looked down at the boats in the marina, thinking each one was worth at least thirty grand. Sell one boat and it would bail her out—so to speak. Pay off some debts, get Joe underground, give him a decent headstone.

Give her a chance to get back on her feet again. Just one boat. And there were hundreds out there. Probably some hadn't been out of the harbor for months.

Dash moved in behind her, standing half a head taller. She liked that. She'd met a lot of good men that were just too damn short. He put his hands on her waist. She felt his body pressing into her, his breath in her hair, and wondered how it would start. *Get ready, 'cause here it comes,* she thought, remembering the old song, flipping the cigarette and seeing the glow tumble end over end into darkness. She enjoyed the anticipation and decided to let it happen on its own rather than forcing things like she did that afternoon with Harold when she made such a fool out of herself. Why the hell did she act that way? Maybe it was seeing Joe like that, or being so goddamned desperate for money all the time.

A night wind ran through the marina, making ropes clang against masts as the boats swayed. She said, "All the pretty little white boats. I'd like to get on one, get the hell out of here."

Then he was kneeling behind her. She forced herself not to turn. He had his hand on the inside of her bare leg at the ankle. He slowly rose, his hand sliding up the inside of her leg until he was standing, his hand on the inside of her thigh. Involuntarily she spread her legs to give his hand room to move up in between them. He continued up as high as his hand could go, then reached forward, cupping her. She felt herself going all liquid, and leaned back into his arms.

Sometime later they moved into his bedroom and lay naked on cool sheets with an ocean breeze coming through the window, and she finished what she started that afternoon. With the skill of a surgeon removing a tumor, he extracted an orgasm that had been building since Joe disappeared. But when the incredible waves of pleasure subsided she found she felt strangely empty, shell-like, because she still lacked the one thing that she really needed, the only thing she had been after from Harold, and that was the feeling of being with another living breathing human being who was as tortured and guilt-ridden as she was.

Christ, I really need a cigarette, she thought, leaving the bed and moving toward her purse, lying on the floor next to her crumpled clothes. She had the purse open and was rummaging around inside when she remembered: She'd finished the pack on the balcony. And she had even flipped the butt away, robbing her of a relight, an emergency nicotine fix.

"I need a cigarette," she said to the still form in the bed. Then, "Hey, Dash—"

Breathing. Deep breathing, as if he had just surfaced from the bottom of the ocean.

She had moved around to his side of the king-sized bed, ready to shake him awake, when she kicked his pants and heard a muffled jingle of keys. Let him sleep, she thought, fishing his keys out of his pants, I'll run out and get my own smokes.

Inside the Rover she saw condensation misting the windows and thought, *That's strange.* She found the seat lever and rolled it forward closer to the wheel. She readjusted the mirrors and fired it up. It was strange being in Dash's car, kind of like going through his underwear drawer. But it didn't stop her from taking a look around: car phone between the seats, radar warning device above the rearview mirror. The upholstery held the memory of his cologne. And then there was the pack of gum and a hairbrush in the door panel. The car revealed no other clues about its owner other than the fact that he was meticulously neat; a sheen of Armor All coated the dashboard and the glass was so clean it seemed to disappear.

Vikki backed out, then dropped the shift lever in D and rolled forward, hearing the tires squeaking on the concrete floor. An automatic opener lifted the huge garage door and she pulled out into the late-night deserted streets of Newport Beach. Which way?

She thought she remembered seeing a strip mall just after they got off the freeway so she took a right, giving it a little pedal, feeling solid acceleration and thinking, A *car this big, it must have a* V-8. Taking another right onto the main drag, she felt the tail swing out, surprised that the expensive machine handled so poorly, like it was carrying a load of concrete bricks or had low tire pressure in the rear. Still, it was fun to be up high in the four-by-four after years of driving at street-level in the low-slung Healey.

All the stores in the strip mall were closed. Damn. She continued on down the street, looking for a place to double back, took another right, and found herself on the freeway ramp. Oh, well, take the first exit and pull a U-ie. The freeway carried her up and out of Newport, passing a string of cheap hotels and fast food restaurants, all closed now. Ahead, billboards for airlines flying out of John Wayne Airport were dark too.

Her mind drifting, feeling the responsiveness of the strange car, she found herself thinking, *This is the way Dash commutes every morning.* She was picturing him behind the wheel, neatly dressed, carefully shaved, heading for a day at the office when—*Wait a second!*— it suddenly hit her. Reaching below the ignition, she felt the heavy cluster of keys and realized that his office key was probably on the ring too. *Why not?* she thought. *Why the hell not*? Then, if she went to Joe Covo Matsura to buy a car, and decided to insure it with Dash, she'd know what she was walking into.

She put her foot down, driving with purpose now, and for the first time since she had had sex with Dash, she stopped craving a cigarette.

Harold had always known public transportation in LA was lousy, but today he got a chance to experience it firsthand. It took him *eight friggin' hours* to get back to the South Bay after Vikki ditched him at the motel. Eight hours of waiting for buses, then waiting *on* buses, all the time surrounded by lowlifes, drunks, and screaming high school maniacs with orange hair and pierced bodies. As soon as he got back to his room over the Club Cheri, he was going to soak in the shower, wash this shitty day off his skin and out of his mind.

The cab pulled into the lot on Harbor, almost empty now that it was past midnight, and stopped at the entrance to Denny's. He paid off the driver, who was so obese the steering wheel disappeared into his mounding flesh. Another ten-dollar expense draining his already depleted reserve. And that operating money he dreamed of seemed more distant than ever. Could things get any worse?

Heading for his car, past the restaurant, Harold walked through a hot blast of exhaust from the restaurant smelling of fried food. His stomach was grinding on acid. The vision of a juicy patty melt rose in his mind but he pushed it back. He'd closed his wallet for the day and he wasn't going to open it again. Still, he couldn't stop thinking of how good the burger would taste, smothered in salsa with a little Tabasco to pep it up.

Harold walked into the parking lot, absentmindedly looking for his dad's Impala, reviewing the day again in his mind.
The lights of the LA sprawl reflected orange off the underside
of dirty ocean clouds parked over the land. The air was cold
and heavy, the pavement glazed with a cruddy smaze of
engine oil and smog.

One good thing, now Vikki knew where Joe was. And he
had led her there. Of course, they couldn't get the insurance
money until the investigation was done. And the investigation wouldn't be done until they dragged him over the coals
again. They were using Joe to get at Harold. And, Harold
realized with a sickening lump in his stomach, Vikki was
paying the price.

Harold stood at the edge of the parking lot looking around,
thinking, *How'd I miss Dad's Chevy?* He started back, working
his way up and down the rows of cars, his mind fully on the
problem now, thinking, *It's not like anyone would want to steal
it. . . .* But still he didn't see his dad's cream puff, the car he
learned to drive in, the one that reminded him of being a
teenager, in love with cars—a dorky kid, sure, but filled with
some reasonable hope for the future. Not like now. Living
from day to day, always afraid of going flat broke, falling on
his face and dropping through the cracks forever.

He was back at Denny's now, kind of half laughing, saying
to himself, *No one would steal it, not a car that old,* and expecting
at any time to see it and go, *Oh, yeah, there it is!* and go home
to his awful little room and soak in the shower until he got a
brilliant idea that would breathe life back into this scheme.

But the Impala wasn't there, he realized ten minutes later,
after checking every damn car in the lot. And now he wasn't
laughing or even half laughing because his worst nightmare
was realized—he was in LA, without wheels. He was
grounded. Big time.

It just kept getting worse and worse, he thought, remembering something else, something even worse than having his dad's car ripped off. Joe's folder, the one Vikki gave him yesterday, was lying on the front seat of the Impala, wherever it was. It was too much, he thought, standing under low orange clouds, with the moist exhaust smell of fried foods engulfing him. He felt dizzy and weak-kneed, like he might dissolve and blend into the cruddy smaze coating the asphalt under his feet, and he realized he had just lost his final hope for staying connected to Vikki.

He went into Denny's to call the cops, report his car missing. Maybe someone had just taken it for a joy ride and the cops had already found it, Joe's folder lying where he left it. Sure, the battery might be missing, or something else easy to replace, but the car would be intact, the folder lying right there on the seat. Yeah, that was possible.

As he reached for the phone, the beeper on his hip moved. He checked the display, hoping it was a certain number in Palos Verdes, a 310 area code number he had forced himself to memorize. But it wasn't, of course. It was 714—Orange County—then 433—Huntington Beach maybe? Wrong number probably, he thought, dialing the cops and hoping—almost praying—that they had already found his dad's car.

The big yellow Denny's sign glowed in the night like a beacon, guiding Vikki off Harbor Boulevard and into the lot, where she parked by Dash's second-floor office. Climbing the stairs, she found the glass door with *TransPacific Insurance— Life, Auto, Home*. Her heartbeat kicked up a notch as she tried the keys until the door opened on a still, empty space. She locked the door behind her, instinctively moving out of the light that angled in from outside. Two desks faced her, where she had seen the two women sitting yesterday when she and Harold arrived here. If she was going to find anything it wouldn't be here. She moved down the hall and into his office.

Standing in front of his desk, Vikki had a delicious sense of expectation. Maybe there was something here that would tell her what Joe was up to, where to look for his money. And maybe it would even explain the big man in the Suburban who had been following her. What if they were all linked somehow?

LIGHTS!

Her pulse went through the ceiling. But looking through the front window, she saw it was only a cab pulling into the parking lot, stopping at the entrance to Denny's.

Time to get to work.

She turned on a small tungsten lamp, which threw a warm circle on the polished wood desktop. She sat in Dash's desk chair, smelling his cologne again, and heard the leather creak as it took her weight. She swiveled, scanning the desk, which had been cleaned since she was here last. This boy has good work habits, she thought, looking at the computer, still humming in the quiet office, the fax machine and paper shredder with a trash bucket of curling paper strips below it.

In the top desk drawer she found neatly sorted pens, pencils, and erasers laying in a plastic tray. She lifted the tray, thinking, *What's this*? and found the small Baggie of pills. She picked one up and read the writing on the capsule: *Roche* 2. What had she read about them? *Roofies, the Forget-It Pill.* They're used in date rapes or something. . . . What did Dash need them for?

Another slip of paper contained a handwritten list of first names and telephone numbers. Most of the names sounded Hispanic and had 310 area codes. Dash's handwriting (she assumed it was his) was excruciatingly small and perfectly formed, like a typewriter.

Then she found the keys she had been looking for, noted their exact location, and opened the filing cabinet beside the desk.

The top file drawer held hanging folders labeled with what looked like case numbers. Each folder held computer-generated printouts of accident reports and insurance claims. He had written notes on each case. Everything was orderly and looked legitimate.

She rolled the top file drawer shut and opened the lower drawer. The numbers on these folders were much longer and she realized they were the VIN numbers of various cars. In each folder was a single sheet that held dates, car models, initials, and prices. This could be how Dash tracked cars as they were sold, stolen, recovered and—she couldn't figure out the final price, which was always bigger than the purchase price.

Vikki paused, staring at the sheet in front of her, and felt a chill run up the back of her neck. Looking again, she saw that Dash had written the initials JCM in front of some transactions. Joe Covo Matsura? She leafed through the files and pulled more out until she had a half dozen with the initials JCM. Maybe the VIN numbers on these cars matched the ones in Joe's files. She'd have to see if Dash's handwriting on these files matched the records she found in Joe's wall safe.

The records that she had given to Harold yesterday.

She picked up Dash's desk phone and dialed Harold's beeper number, left Dash's office number for the return call, and went back to the records, sorting and pulling out more files. A half hour later she still hadn't gotten a return call from Harold. She called again, and left the office number a second time.

Time to pull things together. Now, if she only had a copier.

She thought about firing up the old beast she had seen in the front office. But then she saw the fax machine. That'd work. She ran the reports through the fax machine to make copies, then refiled the originals.

Standing at the window, she looked down at the parking lot and saw a lone figure moving between parked cars, and wondered again what she hoped to prove. Find out what Dash was into and turn him in to the cops? That wouldn't help her. No, it might be better to exploit her knowledge to take control of what she wanted all along: her stake in Joe's dealership.

But maybe Dash was in deeper than just auto theft and insurance fraud. Why did she think that? Because there was something about him that didn't fit. He had the clean-cut exterior, sure, but that smile . . . It seemed to say that he liked to walk on the wild side. She flashed on the scene at the restaurant, that big guy showing up, chewing on his napkin, and looking at Dash like he would eat him alive. Where had she seen him before? They left together, and when Dash returned he was smiling, proud of himself. She shuddered, feeling a wave of disgust sweep over her as she remembered being with Dash in bed only hours before, turning in his arms, his long dangerous body reaching deep inside her and extracting an evil pleasure.

Yes, knowledge is power. But what did she know? She had never spent any time at the dealership. She didn't know how to read these records she'd found. But Harold would. If he ever called her back.

Standing in the strange office in the middle of the night, she thought of Harold as she had last seen him, leaving the hotel room to go get a beer. Where was he now? Had he even made it back from Santa Barbara yet? Or was he heading back to—

Harold!

He was right in front of her, walking across the parking lot toward a pay phone by the entrance of Denny's. He must have come back from Santa Barbara to pick up his car. Gathering up her papers, she realized that the sight of him made something jump inside her. It was probably because he would know how to read these papers. That was all. But first she would apologize for leaving him stranded like that. He'll understand, she thought, checking the desktop once more, making sure everything was exactly as she found it, then heading into the outer office.

"Lose something?"

It was a woman's voice, familiar, calling to him across the parking lot. Harold turned, hoping to find—yes, it was Vikki, standing there on the wet pavement holding rolled-up papers in her hands, the smile on her face saying all sorts of things he wanted to know more about.

"You look like you lost your best friend," she said, moving toward him. He was about to apologize when he realized, by her tone, that he didn't need to. In fact, maybe he could get away with being just a little bit pissed off. I mean, he was the one who had to take the slow boat back from Santa Barbara.

He stood there taking it all in, wondering what she was doing there, how she had found him, and realized that he hadn't gotten a word out. Finally, he just said, "Man, what a day."

"Yeah. Look, I'm sorry about all that." By *all that* Harold guessed she meant their wrestling match in the motel. "I don't know what I expected to prove by—"

"It's all right. All right? I mean, basically, you were right."

"About?"

"Using you. I thought I could get in and out, make the identification and clear things up for you. Man, was I wrong. But I'm gonna call that cop, set up a meeting. I'll—I'll give him my statement."

"But you said they'd arrest you."

"I'm working on a way to get around that. I.e., I might try to work a trade."

"Trade what?"

"That's what I'm working on." He hoped it sounded mysterious and important. But it came out kind of pathetic. He quickly changed gears. "And now I've got another crisis— my damn car just got ripped off."

"What?" She stopped slapping the roll of papers into the palm of her hand.

"Well, not my car. My dad's, actually." Admitting it made him sick to his stomach. "But the cops recovered it this morning. They got a tip—found it in a driveway up on Gaviota in Long Beach. A driveway? Wouldn't you think that would make the cops just a little suspicious?"

She was staring at him, mouth open, jaw cocked, connecting what he said with whatever she knew.

"I don't believe this."

"Neither do I. I'm thinking, 'Who'd steal a car that old?'"

"No. I mean, I was just—" She pointed the rolled-up papers at Dash's office. "Listen, I bet Dash had it stolen."

"Dash?"

"Yeah. Look, I found this—" She unrolled the papers but it was too dark out here. And besides, he didn't look too excited about hearing her theory.

"Wait, wait a second. You were in Dash's office? That's what you're doing here?"

"Yeah, see, I was out of cigarettes and—" She thought of

something and changed course again. "It's a long story. Look, I'll tell you on the way to get your car. I'll give you a ride."

She gave him a come-along wave and they began walking toward what he assumed was her car. But he didn't see the hot little two-seater anywhere.

"Where's your car?"

"Over there." She pointed at the Rover. "Actually, I'm borrowing a friend's."

Harold stopped. "That's not Dash's."

"Actually, it is."

"And where is he?"

"At home, sound asleep." Her giggle built into a throaty laugh.

"Why is that funny?"

"Don't look so worried, Harold. I'm just borrowing his car, for Christ's sake."

"And searching his office."

"Yeah, well . . ." Her laughter bubbled up again.

"Look. Could you not do that, please?"

"Why?

"I'm just a little bit nervous."

"You know, for the past nine months, the bastards have kept me in the dark. About Joe, the dealership. And Dash—however he plugs into all this. Now I'm the one in the driver's seat. And I like that. I like it a lot."

She began moving forward again. Harold hung back, his eagerness to get a free ride somewhat diminished. Finally, he said, "You've had a busy night."

The chirp of the car alarm echoed off the buildings as she pressed the remote on Dash's key ring. Harold heard a car motor behind them and turned, jumpy. A cab was pulling into the lot, the one Harold had called to take him home, and he saw it was the same driver, the obese man in the baseball cap. Harold picked up the pace again and climbed into the Rover.

"**D'ya** feel that?" Vikki asked.

They were rolling down Fourth Street in Long Beach, heading for Harold's room above the Club Cheri, where he would raid his dwindling stash of traveler's checks to retrieve his car from the pound.

"Feel what?"

"The car moved."

"Moved? Of course it moved. We're moving."

"No. I mean—There! Like that."

"Maybe it was a little shaker. Earthquake comes, people think they have a flat tire or—" He left the sentence hanging as he reached for the beeper on his hip that was vibrating.

"This thing handles like shit." Vikki began cutting the wheel experimentally, feeling the way the Rover responded.

"Cop sees that he'll think you're loaded."

He struggled to read the display on his beeper, saw it in a passing streetlight and said, "Oh, man." A cold hand clutched his heart. Why was his father paging him in the middle of the night?

Harold looked up from the beeper and saw the neon sign: *Club Cheri*. "Pull in here. I've gotta make a quick call, get some money, then we'll be on our way."

Vikki turned into the parking lot of a liquor store. As Harold stepped out, he heard music leaking out the front door of the Club Cheri across the street. Upstairs was his room with his suitcase and the wad of traveler's checks stuffed into one of his socks. Christ, it was tempting just to pack it in for the night, tell Vikki to come up for a nightcap, and . . . But he didn't want her to see the dump he was crashing in. Besides, he had to see why his dad had paged him.

Harold moved toward the phone, a steel box on a square post, claimed by the signatures of graffiti taggers. A guy was talking on the phone holding a steel chain that led to a sleeping pit bull. He was shirtless under a silk Raiders jacket and a tattoo ringed his neck like a collar.

"Gonna be long? I got an emergency," Harold said to the guy. The pit bull looked up and growled.

"Come any closer, he'll take your fuckin' leg off," the guy said. He turned back to his phone call, blowing smoke all over the receiver as he said, "No, you listen to me, okay? The bitch is lying. I ain't seen her since—" The dog lay back down and began licking his crotch. This might be a long call.

A rolling, scraping noise drowned out the jukebox. Around the corner came a kid on a skateboard, thirteen, fourteen years old, scrawny and pale, stringy brown hair in his face. He jumped the curb and went tumbling to the sidewalk.

Harold looked at a Budweiser clock in the liquor store window. Almost two. "Kind of late to be out, isn't it?" he said to the kid.

"They don't care what I do."

Harold couldn't tell if he was bragging or felt sad about it.

The kid began rolling around the parking lot, the sound echoing in the night, a lonely sound, Harold thought, a neglected boy, the age his own son would be if he and Linda had kids, if they hadn't split up. If his life hadn't gone to hell.

He glanced back at the Rover. Vikki was looking at something in the backseat. He had to get moving.

"That's bullshit, okay?" the guy was yelling into the phone. He gestured angrily as if the person he was talking to could see him. "Want to come down here now, say that to my face? Or are you too much of a—" He looked at the receiver, dead in his hand. He slammed it back on the hook. He kicked the phone, grunting obscenities, pounding it with his fist. The dog watched, unamazed.

"Hey, come on!" Harold yelled.

The guy whirled around.

"I need the phone, okay?"

"Bite me." The guy flicked his cigarette at Harold. It hit the ground and showered sparks across the pavement. He yanked the dog to his feet and walked away.

Harold looked at the skateboarder. The kid giggled, a goofy teenage laugh, his face hidden by stringy hair. He pictured him in school, giggling about girls, horsing around in class, typical teenage stuff.

The receiver was still disgustingly warm, glazed with pit bull breath. It reminded Harold of using a public toilet too soon after the previous customer. He held the receiver away from his ear as it rang. The hospital operator connected Harold and he heard his father's voice, weak and almost unrecognizable.

"Harry? Randy said the cops called the house. Something about my car."

"Yeah, Dad. It, ah—it got towed."

"Towed?"

"I parked it in the wrong place." That much was true. "I'm going to pick it up now."

"Is it okay?"

"I wouldn't let anything happen to your car, Dad."

"'Cause you're gonna need to give me a ride home soon."

"Really? You feelin' better?"

"They say there's nothin' else they can do."

Harold pictured his father, alone in the hospital with tubes stuck in him, and hated himself for not being there with him.

He felt that cold hand grip his heart again, the hand that carries away the people you love, then returns to get you.

"Dad, you know, I was remembering that time, a while ago, when you worked at that filling station, up by the traffic circle."

His father said nothing.

"Remember how the place got robbed and those two maniacs came at you with hatchets. Dad, you there?"

"Yeah."

"And you ran 'em out of there—they didn't get a dime. You remember that?"

"The 76 station?"

"Yeah, by the traffic circle. Two guys against you. And they couldn't put you down. You remember that?"

"I don't know . . ."

Harold's prized memory was suddenly as thin as tissue paper, dissolving in the rain.

"That's the way I remember you, Dad. You were a tough son-of-a-bitch."

"It mighta been a Shell station."

"Whatever. The point is, that's how I remember you. Okay?"

His father said nothing.

"So, Dad, call me when you want to go. I'll come get you, we'll head up to the airport, catch a plane to Chile."

"Sure. Okay."

Harold hung up feeling like he'd just gotten the wind knocked out of him. He looked at Vikki, who was stepping out of the Rover now, moving to the rear of the car. He had to squeeze in one more call. He had to talk to Marianna. He'd tell her that Dad was coming back with him. That was something. A little thing. But it was a beginning.

But Marianna wasn't there. Or she wasn't picking up. She did that sometimes, just ignored the phone if she didn't feel like talking. Lucky thing, too, because Vikki was staring into the cargo area of the Rover, backing up in amazement, looking around for Harold, then back to the trunk.

Harold hung up. He was crossing the parking lot, moving toward Vikki, when he saw the skateboarding kid again, looking at him as if he needed help, too.

"Go home," he said, trying to make it a joke. The kid smiled weakly, put his foot on his board, pushed off, and rolled down the street. A lonely sound in the middle of the night. So much loneliness, Harold thought, reaching the Rover.

Vikki was facing him now, waiting for him to look into the back of the car, saying, "I knew I'd seen him before."

The big man was curled up like a baby. He looked happy enough, except for the blood-soaked newspaper under his head. Then he heard Vikki say, "He was the guy in the Suburban following me."

"Then you better say hello," Harold told her. "Because it looks like he's waking up."

Vikki turned back to the car and found herself looking into the open eyes of the big man who had no name.

Marianna had the door locked and was heading for the taxi when she heard the phone inside ringing. *Harold.* Who else could it be? She'd never reach the phone in time, and besides, what would she tell him? She continued toward the taxi and worked her way into the backseat.

Watching the Chilean countryside glide by, seeing the dawn bring light to rolling fields and grazing cattle, Marianna couldn't suppress the rising excitement she felt about what she was going to do. Even in the last week, since Harold left, she had made amazing progress with the braces. They looked like hell, sure, but at least she was out of that damn wheelchair. And to think it all started when she visited that doctor in Santiago, the one where she finally got a second opinion, an opinion that was very different than what the doctor told her nine months ago in LA, just after she was shot in the back by Vito in the park near the airport.

She could remember that first doctor, in Los Angeles, holding up the X-ray and pointing to the faint white line where he thought the nerve was severed.

"Nerves grow," he said. "But they grow very slowly." His face was red as he leaned over her and spoke slowly, as if to a second-grader.

Marianna wanted to say, *Thanks for that, you quack.* But in her good girl voice, which she learned to use when talking to doctors and other figures of authority, like cops and lawyers, she said, "You're saying months?"

"More like years. Unless . . ." Then he described the operation she could have, how they could use synthetic tissue and laser surgery. But there were no guarantees, of course. They wouldn't know for sure if she could walk again until they "got in there."

Great. And of course they couldn't "get in there" until someone shelled out ten grand for the operation. She didn't have ten grand. And, after she wound up with Harold in Chile, she found that he didn't either. At first they both felt lucky to be free, not in some hellhole of a prison, or even on death row. But as the months passed it made Harold angry that he couldn't help her, even though their new life in Chile progressed pleasantly in every other way.

One morning, she woke up in an empty bed and found Harold in the kitchen, a cup of coffee at his elbow and steam rising up into the overhead light, his left hand hooked around, writing on three-by-five index cards. Later she found where he had hidden the index cards and read them. *Secure*

I.D., one note said. *Tell Z to check computer warrants*, read
another. And finally, *Transfer moneys out of country*. He was
scheming again, planning how to recover the insurance
money for Vikki Covo. And as he continued to scheme, it
brought a different mood to this house at the end of the dirt
road. Sure, he was still tender and attentive to her. But part of
him had wandered off—was somewhere north of here, ready
to do business.

She had known it would come to this eventually, and part
of her was glad it finally had. Some days she was bored and
restless. But other days she was happier than she had ever
been. In her wheelchair she could roll around the house and
garden, where Harold had put down planks and ramps until it
looked like a skateboard track in an Orange County rec
center. If she wanted to venture farther she had to go with
Harold.

Their favorite outing was to have Harold push her down the
dirt road to the path through the pine trees. Then she
abandoned the chair for Harold's arms and he carried her,
feet slipping in the sand, his breath hot on her cheek. He
would finally collapse on the top of a dune, the sound of the
surf gradually replacing their breathing.

They lay there, not even talking, gazing out at the ocean
that connected them to North America, and Marianna had a
hard time imagining that Los Angeles still existed, the
snarled freeways, the razor-wire-topped road signs spattered
with graffiti, the gunshots at night, the layoffs and riots and
fires. It seemed impossible that this world could coexist with
Chile, where each day had a slow rhythm, dreamlike and
narcotic. Sometimes, not a damn thing happened all day.
And that was just fine.

The third morning she awoke alone, she decided to
confront Harold about his plans. She wrestled her way into
the chair parked next to the bed. It was a maneuver that had

taken her a month to perfect. But it meant she could get up without bellowing for Harold and having him baby her. She fished the brush from the pouch on the chair's arm and dragged it through her thick hair before starting for the kitchen, the wheel *squeak squeaking* in the dark hallway.

Harold looked up, the warm light on his big face, his gray-green eyes sparkling happily as she approached. She poured herself some coffee, then watched as he worked, tracing words until they became thick and black and drawing arrows beside key phrases.

She finally said, "You're going after the money."

He seemed to consider denying it, but instead just said, "Thinking about it."

"Thinking pretty hard," she said, pointing at his notes.

"We're just about broke, you know."

"No, I didn't. You don't tell me these things."

"I don't want to worry you."

"Being broke doesn't worry me. I've been there before."

"I'd say this is a little different, i.e., how're we going to make anything down here?"

She shrugged. "So you figure you'll go after the insurance money?"

"Yeah. We get a part of that, we'll be set for a while." He looked at the figures in his notes in front of him and added, "A long while."

"When do we leave?" She watched him carefully as she asked it and saw it surprise him. He started to answer several times, his mouth opening but no words coming.

"I'm leaving next week," he finally said.

"What about me?"

She knew what the answer would be. And she thought that Harold might even be right to leave her behind. It wouldn't be easy dragging a gimper around. But while Harold was out getting his tickets for his big trip north, she visited the doctor that Tina, the maid, recommended. This doctor looked at the X-ray and the reconstructed vertebrae and said in formal Spanish, "I see no physical evidence that you can't walk."

He threw it out there, playing those psychological games doctors think they are so good at. It took her a second—then she was pissed.

"You're saying I'm faking it."

He looked at her impassively and said, "I'm saying there is no *physical* reason you can't walk."

At first she hated the pompous bastard for that remark. But then, she realized what he was saying—maybe she was fully wired after all. She let the doctor probe the nerves in her spine with electric shock and, sure enough, she felt a tingling. It wasn't much, but at least the feeling was moving south, down the side of her right hip and into her leg. Could she walk on one leg? Stroke victims did. They wore a brace on one leg so it was rigid—nothing more than support—while they used the other to propel them. Slowly, of course, but at least they were standing, moving under their own steam.

The doctor rigged her with braces and when Harold returned to pick her up, she was walking. Jesus, what a relief it was to look people in the eye, to move, one leg after another in that easy rolling way you always took for granted. The doctor told Harold that surgery would speed things up, get her out of braces. But at least she could say *adios* to the wheelchair. And staring at people's belt buckles. This new development only increased Harold's enthusiasm for the trip and he left two days later.

Then there was his phone call from the motel, the motel where he stayed with Vikki. *We're in separate rooms.* Why did he volunteer that? Men were soooo obvious. And she could read Harold like a book. Her mind began to throw up pictures of them together, Harold touching Vikki the way he touched her, caressing Vikki's perfect breasts with his big hands, which could be so strong and so gentle at the same time. Maybe they had already recovered the insurance money, and they took off on a spending spree somewhere. Maybe he wouldn't ever come back.

Marianna surfaced from her dark thoughts and, through the cab windows, saw the sun was almost up now. Ahead were road signs for the airport. It was morning in Chile, still night in LA. She thought of Harold up there. And Vikki. And then Harold again. She had to make sure Harold didn't get pulled down into that whirlpool of slime. Harold was a strange one. But he was her man. And he needed her.

"Which terminal?" the driver asked over his shoulder.

"International," Marianna said, the word raising her excitement to a new level.

From the back of the Rover came the sound of snoring as Vikki drove west on Fourth to the auto pound. The snoring was their signal that the monster was unconscious again, rocked asleep by the moving car.

"So what's our move?" Vikki asked. "Or are we just going to drive around until he wakes up?"

Harold was busy looking back at the thin vinyl covering pulled over the cargo area like a window shade. And it offered about that much protection too. They stopped at a light, holding their breath, waiting for him to wake up and come roaring out of the tight space like a bull from a rodeo chute.

The light changed and she pulled out. Harold breathed easier now that they were moving again. "So you think this was the guy at the restaurant?"

"Yeah. When he showed up he looked familiar but I

couldn't place him. When I saw him just now it hit me—he was the guy in the black Suburban, following me. Maybe he was the guy on the phone too, telling me to drop the suit. Coulda been—the guy sounded big and scary."

"So you're saying Dash took him out, konked him over the head, and stuffed him in the back there?"

"Well . . ." Vikki let the question hang there as she stared at the string of green lights leading them toward the auto pound. The lights of the harbor were showing now on the other side of the Long Beach Freeway.

"You know what?" Vikki said, the realization breaking over her. "I think Dash drugged him. I saw some pills in his office. He bought him a beer and slipped something in his drink. That's why he told me to stall him—to let the pills work."

"Okay, so he's drugged. So he's not, like, knocked unconscious or something. So that gives us some time."

"Maybe. I don't know. What do you have in mind?"

"Take the car back to Dash. Let him deal with the guy."

Vikki looked at Harold. She said nothing.

"Here's the pound. Let me off, I'll get my car. Follow you back to Dash's place."

Vikki pulled over. Christ, he wished she wouldn't do that. All it took was a couple of cops, bored on the night shift. *Everything okay, folks?* Then: *Hey. What's that snoring sound coming from your trunk?*

Vikki was staring at Harold, her eyes crackling with anger.

"You're going to have to do a little better than that, Harold."

"It's the safest thing, all way 'round."

"*Safest?* Listen, safe ain't gonna work. We need a class move here."

"Like what?"

"I don't know. You're the genius that ducked four homicides and skipped the country. You're the pro, you're the Bird

9 4

Dog. That's why I asked you to help me get the insurance money. That's why I wanted you on my side. Now you better dig a little deeper here because—because I think what we've got is a great opportunity here."

"A great opportunity to get my ass thrown in jail."

"Harold, we're talkin' big bucks here. Not that nickel and dime shit you usually go after. This is for all the marbles. You said you wanted in. Now you're wimping out on me."

A loud snort came from the back and the car began bucking on its springs as the monster seemed to be waking.

"Go!"

Vikki floored it and the car shot forward. The gates of the auto pound were straight ahead. So was the ramp to the freeway.

Vikki looked at him, wanting an answer.

"The freeway," Harold said. "Take the freeway."

She blew by the pound and climbed the ramp.

"Okay," he said. "You're right. There's a connection here. Just give me time."

The cutoff to the 405 Freeway was looming ahead.

"Go south," he said. He was remembering his days as a troubleshooter at Aerodyne, where he worked for years as a chemical engineer. He loved tackling problems, making notes, drawing graphs, sometimes sketching a diagram on a napkin in a restaurant, listing options on three-by-five index cards. The first step was always to define the problem.

Q: *What should I do with the monster in my car?*

See? This was just a problem, like many others he'd solved before. Well, not exactly like the others, he thought, his heart beating wildly. Christ, he wished he had some paper and a pencil, a cup of coffee maybe. But Vikki wanted answers now.

"We need to get rid of this guy," he began.

"That's what I'm thinking. We take him out in the desert, find a big rock and—"

"*I.e., temporarily.*" Harold wanted to stop that line of thought right away.

"Why? Anyone investigates, they'll think it was Dash."

"We don't want Dash in trouble either. He's our link to the insurance money."

"You're right," she admitted.

Great, he thought. I finally scored a point. He was on a roll now.

"The question is, why would the same guy threatening you be after Dash?"

"He was squeezing Dash for money. I heard them talking."

"Money they made together. Stealing cars maybe."

"Maybe."

"But where's this guy fit in?"

"I don't know. I don't even know who he is."

"Dash didn't introduce you?"

Vikki thought back on the scene. "Fabian something."

"Fabian *what*?"

"I can't remember. I was trying so hard to think where I saw him. . . ."

Harold felt like he was gaining ground, giving Vikki something she couldn't do on her own. But he was still smarting from her speech. CHICK-*en*! It was like being a kid again. How many times had he been goaded into a fight with those words? CHICK-*en*! It was no different now. I *dare you*, Vikki seemed to be saying, and now, here he was trying to show her he was a real man. How could he do that?

"I'm gonna get his wallet."

"Now?"

"How else are we gonna find out who he is? Wake him up and ask him?"

"Yeah. Okay. Good."

But he didn't move, just looked around at late-night traffic on the 405 as they headed south, passing through the

Orange curtain. The cops down here in Orange County were a bunch of Nazis. If they got pulled over . . .

"You gonna get his wallet or what?"

There it was again. That tone. *Scared? Come on*, CHICK-*en!*

"Just making sure the coast is clear. Hold the speed down."

Harold took off his seat belt and struggled into the backseat like an overgrown kid. The snoring was louder back here. He found the release and slowly rolled back the vinyl cover over the cargo area. The big man was revealed below him, lying on his left side. And Harold could smell him, his sweat, and the bad breath of sleep.

If the man was right-handed his wallet would be on his right hip. Harold, left-handed, carried his on his left side. It was an unwritten guy thing—that and wearing your watch on your opposite wrist.

He reached into the man's right hip pocket and touched a thick object. But his pants were pulled tight. Harold wormed his fingers in and closed around the wallet. Man, the thing was as thick as a double cheeseburger. Was it better to inch it out? Or do it fast?

"Got it?"

"No."

"What's the problem?"

"Nothing just—" Okay, okay. He'd do it fast. Then get away from the stinking breath.

Harold snatched the wallet out of the pocket, then froze, waiting for the man's eyes to open, his hands to reach up and close around his throat. . . . But the big man slept on. Harold pulled the cover back in place and joined Vikki in the front seat.

In the dome light Harold saw the man's photo on his license, smiling, satisfied, like he'd just eaten something tasty. And underneath, his name.

"*Fabian Skura.*"

"Skura. That was it."

"Jesus. He's got a lot of dough in here."

"How much?"

"Coupla hundred."

"Let's split it."

"What?"

"Split the money. After we dump him."

"I don't think so."

"Why not?"

"I just don't want to. You want it, go ahead."

She said nothing.

"Here's his card: *Fabian Skura, Auto Export, Salvage &
Dismantling.* In Wilmington. That means it's probably a chop
shop."

"Why?"

"Wilmington is loaded with 'em. Cop I knew told me that.
There's an area there they call the Third World—the place
has completely gone to hell."

Harold was feeling much better. He was doing his job.
Giving her answers. But there was still one small problem. The
monster wouldn't sleep forever. And Harold wanted to
volunteer a plan before Vikki used that tone again. Christ, he
wished he had paper and pencil. And time. Then he could
come up with a plan that would knock her socks off.

"Okay. So we need this guy out of the picture. And we
don't want him coming after Dash either."

"You already said that."

"I'm thinking out loud. It helps me, okay? So we need to
park him somewhere."

"You said that already too. But if we dump him in the
desert, he'll be back tomorrow."

"But we've got his money. His ID."

"Big deal. He phones home, says come pick me up. Or they wire him money."

"It's not that easy."

"Why?"

Harold felt the tingle of a good idea. A solution. It was somewhere in his mind, rising like a bubble in a lake, ready to reveal a way out of this mess.

"Listen, we're, what, an hour from the border? We take him down to Baja, dump him in Mexico. Without his ID how's he going to make it back across the border? They'll think he's an illegal. By the time he gets it straightened out, Dash will get us the insurance money and you'll own the dealership."

"But the border guards—"

"They never stop you going south. Just coming back."

"Then—"

"Then you take the car back to Dash before he even wakes up."

They were both picturing the whole thing.

"And no one gets hurt," Harold added. "That's the beauty of it."

Vikki was still running it through her mind. Softly, then building, she began to laugh.

"I love it." She turned to Harold, her face beautifully alive. And Harold knew then that, whenever he could, he would always try to be her hero.

When they were south of Rosarito Beach, Vikki turned the Rover onto Mexico Highway 1. They passed a string of hotels facing the beach, their signs gaudy in the headlights, and she noticed one where she had stayed with Joe called La Fonda. The two-lane highway abruptly left the ocean, then turned east, climbing into the mountains. As the road switched back and forth Harold could see the coastline below dotted with the lights of hotels and restaurants. The glow in the distance would be Ensenada with its harbor and the fishing boats that would leave long before the first light came.

Ahead was a turnoff onto a crossroad.

"Here?" Vikki's voice was tired and strained.

"Yeah. Here."

She cut the wheel and they bumped over a cattle guard. In the lights, they saw a rutted pair of tracks climb a steep rise, then fade to nothing among the tumbleweeds and cactus. She stopped, shifting the short stick into four-wheel drive. The jeep bucked forward again on firm footing. They topped the rise and a wall of brush appeared in their headlights, branches waving in the wind.

Vikki stopped the car, set the brake, and got out.

Harold got out of the Rover thinking, *All I have to do is drag him out of the car. What's so hard about that?* But he was jumpy and his hands were slick. The cold wind felt good on his face.

Vikki came around the other way and Harold noticed her purse was still slung over her shoulder. *So I'm not the only one who's just a little nervous*, he thought.

They stood there, looking at the back of the Rover, then looking at each other, faces red in the taillights, the cold night wind moving around them.

"Well—" said Harold and he stepped toward the trunk. He yanked up on the lever, pulled, ready to step back. It was locked.

"Need the key."

"What?"

"I need the key. To unlock the—the thing—here."

"Oh." She dug in the purse, stepped forward, and un-locked the tailgate. She swung it open. And as she stepped

100

back Harold saw she was holding a gun—the one he'd seen in Joe's wall safe.

"Hey," he said.

"Watch it," she said, stepping back, pointing.

Harold turned and saw Fabian's eyes were open. His massive arms were groping around, looking for a way to pull himself out of the small space.

Harold turned to Vikki.

"Put the gun away."

"Watch him! Watch him!"

The man was hauling himself forward, grotesquely straining, trying to form words with his mouth, words that sounded like, "Ma . . . ma . . . my . . ."

Vikki was still pointing the gun into the back of the Rover.

"I said put the gun away."

She didn't seem to hear him. "These fucking bastards," she said, pointing the gun into the car.

"Ma . . . ma . . . my legs . . . ," the man was saying. "My legs . . . my legs . . ."

Harold surrounded Vikki's gun with his hands and steered the barrel so it pointed west of the Rover. She tried to shake him off and the little gun suddenly exploded, Bam! Bam! jumping in their hands like a snapping dog. She dropped the gun and it went off again, Bam!

Harold stooped to get the gun when he heard a roar, turned, and saw the big man launch himself from the Rover with his arms. He hit the ground and lurched forward, stumbling on rubbery legs, diving for Harold, catching his ankle and pulling him down. Harold dug at Fabian's hands, trying to pry loose a finger and break it back. Fabian's thick fingers were like steel cables. Harold struggled to stand on one leg, kicking with the other to get free. He saw Vikki scrambling for the gun and shouted, "No!"

Harold fell again and felt the man reeling him in, hand over hand. He had to break his hold. He got back up on his one leg again, looked down at the man's straining face, and hit him hard in the nose. It made a mushy sound, like slugging a drunk. Harold laced his fingers in the man's hair, pried his head back, and punched him in the throat. Instantly, the death grip on his leg relaxed. Harold scrambled free, then found his feet and stood.

Fabian's fingers clawed at his throat. The night was filled with his tortured breathing.

Vikki was beside Harold. "Jesus. Is he dying?"

"Let's get out of here—"

"But if he ever—"

"*Come on! Let's go!*"

Fabian was recovering again, looking around at them. He dragged himself forward on his hands, torso raised like a sea lion. They ran around him and into the Rover. Pulling away, Harold looked back and saw him bellowing in rage, his bloodied face raised to the sky.

He was returning from a great distance now, from the mysterious place we go when we sleep, like he was rising through deep water, carrying some urgent message, something that was screaming for his attention. NOW!

Dash awoke in the predawn darkness of his room with the horrible feeling that he had forgotten something absolutely essential. He awoke panting and sweaty, looked at the glow of the clock radio and saw it was 4:56. Beside him, Vikki slept on, her face and blond hair a warm glow in the feeble light.

That's why he'd slept so deeply, he realized. You don't get great sex like that every night. And it had been a while since he'd gotten any. It was a week, at least, since he went home with Dixie and—

It was coming back now, with redoubled urgency. He remembered sitting on the patio with Vikki, teasing her with promises of money, hatching the plan to buy a car from Joe Covo. And then he remembered Fabian showing up and—

FABIAN!

Minutes later, Dash was approaching the Rover in his garage, walking slowly, holding a carving knife he'd taken from his kitchen drawer. This was what he had planned to do last night, if he hadn't passed out after getting done with Vikki. He planned to drive Fabian out to the desert, roll him out of the car, and plunge the knife in. Once, twice . . . Whatever it took.

Dash listened at the tailgate of the Rover. Nothing. Good. Fabian was still knocked out. How long did that stuff last? He opened the driver's door and slid the knife under the seat. Sitting behind the wheel in the ultraquiet car, he put the key in the ignition. But first he listened, listened for breathing. Nothing. Why did the car feel empty?

Holding the knife in front of him, Dash returned to the tailgate. He quietly unlocked the door, then slowly swung it open . . .

In the weak light of the parking garage he saw the bloodied newspaper. But nothing else indicated that Fabian had ever been in there.

So somehow Fabian woke up and got out. So okay. So now what?

Still holding the knife, Dash did something he would do a lot of in the next few days: He turned and looked behind him. Scanning the garage filled with cars, the concrete pillars, the dumpsters, he thought how there were a lot of places a man could hide in here. Even a man as big as Fabian.

The inch-thick bullet-proof glass, pasted with signs saying you had to pay in cash, made it hard for Harold to hear the black lady inside the office of the auto pound as she shouted, "Your *vee*-hicle! Where'd the cops pick up your *vee*-hicle?"

Lotta pissed-off people came in here, Harold thought, trying to be sympathetic. Still, you should be able to hear what the hell she was saying. I mean, that seemed like a minimum requirement.

Harold looked at the police report. "Gaviota and Seventeenth!" he said, leaning down to speak through the slit in the glass.

Man, he hated dealing with people with glass between them. Of course, if the glass wasn't there, he might strangle her. Nothing personal. It was just that kind of day. He had a gazillion things to do—meet Vikki at the dealership, call Wycoff in Santa Barbara, visit his dad in the hospital—and here he was schlepping around trying to get his car back. He really didn't need this.

The lady checked a list on a clipboard. "Down the end of the lot! Under the freeway!" She was getting frustrated with him now, pointing and waving out the window across the sea of cars. "Down the end! It's—oh—go outside. The driver'll take you!"

He followed her pointing finger, nodding and feeling like an idiot and stumbled outside into the morning light. No June gloom today. It was baking hot. Sun glinting off about fifty million smashed and broken cars surrounded by a chain-link fence topped with razor wire.

He heard the knocking of a diesel engine, like marbles in a tin can, and a gigantic tow truck hit its brakes in front of him. The door swung open, a bald black man with a cigar jammed in the corner of his mouth leaned across the seats and called down to him to climb up.

" '64 Impala," the driver said as he read the carbon copy of the police report Harold handed him. "I 'member that one. Hauled it in myself."

He rammed the stick in gear, revved the diesel, and they surged forward toward an arching freeway ramp that soared above a distant corner of the auto pound. From his perch, Harold could see the jumble of car roofs all around him, once shining proud cars, now twisted and smashed, with spider-webbed windshields and bloodied interiors, stripped and gutted, burned out and unrecognizable as something that was once loved by someone.

They were crossing a rutted dirt road now and hissing to a stop under the freeway ramp, where the cars lay rusting like lepers in a cave, in the shadow of their former glory, the freeway, which soared above them throbbing with cars and trucks still in their prime.

His hope dissolving, Harold's eye searched among the shapes in the gloom and finally found it, or—*oh, Christ*— what was left of it. The chassis rested on the ground, wheels gone, not even blocked up to protect the tailpipe, the driveshaft, the Powerglide transmission. Hood up, doors open. Make that *doors stolen*. Both of them gone, leaving the interior open to the rain and fog and the endless dust that sifted down from the freeway above.

It had been a real cream puff. Now it was stripped. No question about it. Stripped and parted out.

"Jesus, you could have at least blocked it up," Harold said.

The driver said nothing. Harold became aware of the man's hoarse breathing for the first time.

"They totally stripped it," Harold said, his energy going, not looking at the driver, and feeling apologetic for accusing him.

"Damn shame," the driver grunted.

"Cops found it in someone's driveway, for Christ's sake."

The driver shrugged. "It wasn't really a driveway. More like an alley kind of a deal."

"It said *driveway* on the police report."

Harold climbed down from the truck and moved toward the Impala, tasting the dust in the hot air, the smell of crankcase oil and seeping gasoline.

"You can't touch nothin'," the driver yelled after him. "Got to pay first."

"Yeah, yeah."

Closer now, Harold noticed they'd taken the chrome horn ring too, the one that boasted *Super Sport* with 1964 pride.

And the folder that had been on the seat. Gone.

"Shit," he muttered, feeling the bottom completely dropping out now.

Dark visions suddenly invaded Harold's mind, shadowy forms, gangbangers maybe, crawling over the car, stripping it, using the parts for lowriders they cut and chopped with blowtorches in the backs of blackened garages. He had to stop. It was making him sick to his stomach.

He climbed back up next to the driver as the diesel engine idled in that rough way they always do.

The driver pushed the big shift lever into first and eased the clutch out. He slowly U-turned, then punched it out, heading for the cinder block office visible across the tops of cars roofs, under their coats of rain-spattered dust. Before they were halfway there Harold knew what he had to do.

The black lady in the shitty little office, with the hostile signs about only paying in cash, seemed surprised when he asked for the number of a towing company. She started to say, "For *that*?" but then saw the look on Harold's face and just handed him the phone book.

Harold paid the eighty dollar release fee (another unexpected expense) and signed the forms she pushed across to him. Then he dialed the towing company, pushing away the vision of his car under the freeway, stripped and broken, and instead remembering how it had looked when his dad drove it home from the dealership on that Disney-perfect day, the tranny shifting as smooth as silk, motor whispering, the chrome horn ring with *Super Sport* catching the light. Dad was right, Harold thought. You find a cream puff like that, you never let it go. Never.

Besides that, whoever had stripped his car probably had Joe's folder. One would lead him to the other.

Still waiting for the towing company to answer, Harold took the three-by-five index card out of his pocket, the one with the to-do list, and added one more item: *Recover stolen parts*.

Blow and glow. Glass and chrome and paint jobs so shiny you could comb your hair in the hood of a car. Balloons and plastic banners snapping in the wind. Rows of sedans and pickups and cute little coupes with their hatchbacks popped open, ready and waiting. And above it all, a huge inflatable gorilla stood on the showroom roof holding a banner that read MONSTER SAVINGS, hoping to lure motorists off the 405 Freeway.

Vikki was having a hell of a time hearing the salesman over the roar of the pump that inflated King Kong. Tacky, she thought. Real tacky. Joe would never have done something like that. But Joe was gone and Eddie Fallon was running the shop now, and so the giant black ape swayed in the wind looking like it could fall over and crush them both.

"*What?*" she shouted for about the tenth time.

The salesman (Jeff something, sandy-haired twerp who laughed after everything he said) shouted back: "Too hard to hear!" and waved her into the showroom. Following him, she thought how strange it was to be back in Joe's dealership because, when it came right down to it, she felt that she owned the place. But here she was, being treated like any other walk-on, a hot prospect, a sucker to be softened up by the greeters and floor whores, then handed off to the closers in F&I. If this was the way Joe did business, she understood now why he never talked about it. Not something to be real proud of.

Couple of times she brought the subject up with Joe. Things she had heard from people she knew that bought a car from his dealership. She remembered the way he got quiet and stared at her, finally saying, "You like this house? Like the setup you got here? This is America. Last time I checked it was still legal to make a buck. Why do you care where the money comes from?"

She didn't care where the money came from back then. But then he was alive and the money was pouring in like someone turned on a tap and it was flowing all over the house. When he disappeared last year the river of money dried up. Or was it flowing somewhere else, making someone else rich? She wanted to find the tap again so she could get just enough to keep going. Until she figured out what to do with her life. Or how to get the dealership and run it her way.

Harold was supposed to meet her here. But she got sick of waiting for him, left the Healey parked on a side street and walked onto the lot alone, began browsing among all that glass and chrome until Jeff appeared in his crisp white shirt and tie with his friendly manner and his probing questions. He kept bragging about the SHO cars he customized for the track. She had to stop herself from talking cars with him.

That'd be a tip-off. She wanted him to think she was a virgin. That way she might learn more about how this deal worked.

Once they got inside the dealership Dash had warned her to watch her step. She would use her maiden name: Victoria Pearlman, so no one would make the connection between her and Joe. Dash had said just to flow with the salesman, make any kind of a deal so the papers would be walked into the Finance and Insurance room. And at that point, she thought, once she understood how it worked, she would simply leave the contract unsigned and walk out.

"There's a closer in F&I named Eddie Fallon," Dash explained that morning over breakfast at a coffee shop near the Mardi Gras, when he took her to get her Healey from the lot where she left it last night. *Eddie Fallon*. Vikki had heard Joe once on the phone, laughing with someone about Fallon and the stunts he pulled just to get customers to sign the sales contract.

"When he tries to sell you insurance, tell him you already have an excellent agent who can take care of—well—all your needs," Dash said, spreading his hands and smiling to avoid stating the obvious.

"I mention your name—that's the tip-off?"

"Basically."

She sipped her coffee, hoping it would kick start her system after getting basically no sleep.

"So I take possession of the car immediately, drive off, and then it's stolen."

"Correct."

"And the insurance pays me the full value of the car."

"Correct."

"I pay off my loan from the dealership."

"In thirty days. Then I give you ten grand. Nice, huh?"

"Where's the ten grand come from?"

"What?"

"The ten grand. Where's that come from?"

"Believe me, Vik, you don't want to know."

"Why?"

"It's not necessary. What's necessary for you to know is Dash is gonna take care of you." He covered her hand with his and added, "You trust me, don't you, babe?"

Babe. There it was again. Why was it the guys she got involved with always called her *babe*? But she didn't mind it too much coming from him. It felt like he was caressing her.

"Of course I trust you. But I don't know about this."

"About what?"

"This whole deal. I want to think about it for a few days."

"Why?"

"What if your Eddie Fallon recognizes me?"

"So what if he does."

"I'm in the middle of a hostile lawsuit with the dealership. You think Fallon wants me to know he's a crook?"

"Ever met him?"

"Not that I can recall, but . . ."

"Then don't worry about it."

"I just want to think about it."

He kept smiling, but his words had an edge. "Sure. And while you're thinking about it, the sheriff changes the locks on your house. Hey, I told you it's a no-brainer."

No-brainer. Yeah, sure, Vikki thought, being yanked back to the present as Jeff got her settled in the salesroom while he took her offer into the sales manager. A few minutes later he reappeared.

"Good news!" Jeff said laughing. "Looks like we've got a deal. Easy, huh?"

Jeff stacked the sales sheets. "I'll take you into F&I now to draw up the contracts. Ten minutes from now you'll be driving off in one hot piece of machinery. Man, those Accells are *soooo* awesome," he said, laughing again. She felt like slapping him.

They walked out into the long hallway and through a heavy wooden door into what Vikki realized used to be Joe's office. Joe's stuff was still here, his oriental rugs, even his wedding pictures (with a much younger picture of her), but someone new was at his desk. She saw the top of a man's head, fingers of greasy hair combed over a bald dome. The head turned up and became a wide face with small black eyes behind half glasses. She breathed easier; she couldn't recall ever meeting him.

"Is this the lucky new owner of that silver Accell?" Fallon said, extending his hand. His ring dug into her hand as she clasped it. She imagined that he was looking at her closely. But any good salesman would, try to read her and see how to work this prospect.

Jeff introduced them and left. They sat across the desk from each other and he looked down through his half glasses at the contract in front of him.

"Victoria Pearlman," he read, then looked up. "Your friends call you Vikki?"

"I like to be called Torrey."

"As in Torrey Pines? You a golfer?" Typical salesman looking for common ground.

"Tried it. But the bug never bit me."

"Buddy and me go down to Torrey Pines a coupla times a year. He kicks my butt but we have a good time."

"Your buddy Joe Covo?" She just threw it out there to see what he would do.

"No," he answered slowly. "Why do you ask?"

"I heard he was a big golfer."

"You know him?"

"Friend of a friend." Vikki wondered if Dash had told Fallon that Joe's body had been found in the morgue in Santa

Barbara. Judging from his manner, she doubted he knew Joe was officially dead. That was the kind of news that would ruin his day.

Fallon took off his glasses, folded them, and set them on top of the contracts. Silence. He let it build, pretending to be deep in thought.

"Torrey, everything looks in great shape. And I must say, you are getting one fantastic deal."

"Am I?"

"You must have really beat up on Jeff."

"I don't think I hurt him any."

"There's not much left in the deal for his commission. But anyway . . ." He tapped the contract with his glasses. "You're getting a damn good price on a hot piece of machinery. Now we like to believe we are doing more than just selling cars. We believe we are protecting our customers. Now, since you've saved so much on the purchase price of a car, I *highly* recommend you buy the best insurance possible."

"Let me guess," she said. "You can give me a good deal on the right insurance."

"How did you know?" He smiled, playing along.

"Mr. Fallon, I'd like to take you up on your generous offer but I'm already working very closely with an excellent agent. His name is Dash Schaffner."

Long pause. Slow smile.

"I see. Okay. Yes. He is an excellent agent, no doubt about it. And did he send you in to see me?"

"He said you could arrange everything."

"I certainly can." He glanced down at the contract again. "But if Dash sent you over, why'd you grind so long on the price?"

"Force of habit."

"You in the business?"

"I just like to stand up for myself."

He looked at her very directly, then finally said: "There's nothing left to do but sign." He layered one contract on top of the others. His arm covered the page as he extended a pen to her and said, "Sign here, here, and here."

Vikki grasped the contracts thinking she would pull them to her side of the desk and read them. Then, when she knew what they had done with the numbers, she would stand up and walk out. But Eddie wasn't letting go. She pulled a little harder. He still wouldn't let go. She looked up.

And their eyes met above the contract.

"I'd like to read it, please."

"Why? We both know the drill."

"Tell me about it."

"Honey, why don't you ask Dash to fill you in."

She pulled on the contract again, thinking, *Okay, just walk out. Walk out now.* But she couldn't seem to stand up.

Fallon's voice was firm in the quiet room. "Sign here, here, and here."

She stared into his eyes, finding them flat and hard. She saw her hand accept the pen.

She signed there, there, and there.

Fallon drew the contracts back into his possession with a satisfied look. He began looking them over, then stopped, looking closer. His expression hardened. He pressed the intercom.

"Jeff? Get Gary in your office. I'll be right in."

He looked up at her and softly said, "Be right back."

He left her there in the empty room wondering what had gone wrong. She began to get a very bad feeling and stepped out into the hallway. Looking through a glass-fronted office she saw Fallon, Jeff, and another man leaning over the contracts. Jeff looked up, saw her, and nodded to Fallon. The three men stepped out into the hall, filling it.

"Everything all right?" she asked as they came toward her.

"There's one little detail . . ." Fallon gestured toward his office and she stepped back inside.

Fallon looked at her with his flat eyes and said, "Torrey. You need to work on your signature."

"What do you mean?"

"You signed these contracts as Victoria Covo."

She said nothing.

"You're Joe's wife."

"What if I am?"

"You're not working with Dash."

"Sure I am. Call him."

"What're you doing here?"

"You don't want to make a deal? Fine. Tear up the contract and I'll leave."

She stood up.

"You ain't going nowhere."

She saw now that Jeff and the other guy were standing in the doorway.

"Vikki, we have a very big problem here."

"And what is that?"

"You came in here under false pretenses."

"I came in here to buy a car. What's false about that? Now if you're not interested—"

"You know goddamn well why you're here."

She heard the big guy at the door mutter, *Lying bitch.* This was getting ugly.

"I don't have to take this."

She started toward the door. The big guy smiled down at her, arms folded across his chest. They weren't letting her out.

"Excuse me, please."

From behind her Fallon said. "We want to know what you intend to do."

The intercom clicked on. A woman's voice said, "Mr. Fallon, do you have Vikki Pearlman with you?"

Vikki had used her maiden name with the receptionist.

"Yeah."

"Her attorney is here."

"*What*?"

"A Mr. Dodge."

"A fuckin' attorney?" Fallon said, looking at Vikki. "You brought your attorney?"

Relief flooded Vikki's system. Relief and a sudden desire to laugh. She looked down the hallway and saw Harold moving across the showroom, between the gleaming new cars, wearing that old suit of his. He was smiling, in control, as if anticipating something satisfying that might happen soon, and she realized that, for the first time, she was seeing him in his element.

When Harold reached the door, he looked around and said, "Gentlemen," and smiled again as if he was laughing inside. He saw the contract in Fallon's hand.

"Have you signed?" he asked Vikki.

"Yes."

"Do you want the car?"

It seemed the best way to get back at these bastards. Evidence of what they were doing and how they were doing it.

"Of course I do."

"Then it's yours."

Fallon started to speak but Harold's voice overrode him.

"California Consumer's Protection Act, 1984: 'When the contract prepared by the seller is signed by the buyer, the ownership of the vehicle is immediately transferred.'"

"Who the fuck're you?" Fallon looked like he was going to have a seizure.

1 1 5

"You don't believe me, read it in here." Harold said, waving a paperback book at them. She knew without looking it was *How to Buy a Cream Puff.*

No one said anything. Finally Harold said, "I'm a witness. This contract has been executed. The car belongs to her."

Fallon slowly extended the keys to Vikki.

"Enjoy your new car, Mrs. Covo."

"Pull over. I'm gettin' out."

"You're not serious."

"I'm just gonna take a closer look."

Vikki looked at Harold and saw that he really wanted to do it, so she eased the new silver Accell to the curb in front of the address on Gaviota where the police report had said they found his stolen Impala.

Harold stepped out onto the street.

Right off Harold realized that standing street level was different than seeing it through tinted glass while they circled the block in air-conditioned comfort (for a rice burner, that Accell was a *nice* set of wheels). For one thing it was blazing hot here in North Long Beach. And it was loud too; the crazy thumping came from an Econoline van in a back garage, the rear doors open and the huge speakers lofting noise into the air like moist explosives.

Harold moved down the long driveway (or was it an alley?) toward the noise, noticing three punks watching him from the porch of a nearby bungalow, sitting on propped-up car seats as they downed tall boys and threw the empties into the yard that was covered with purple flowers that gave off a funky rotting smell.

The long driveway led to a two-car garage on the right,

then to an open dirt strip where Harold knew the trolleys once ran bringing tourists to Rainbow Pier to ride the Cyclone Racer and stroll along the ocean. That was before they bulldozed all that to rubble and downtown Long Beach began dying. Now the trolley right-of-way was a no-man's land of weeds and bottles and a broken-down fence claimed by some tagger named *Chakko*. As he watched, a pack of kids chased a cat. Harold didn't want to see what they would do with it when they caught it.

Harold was halfway down the driveway now and he could see into part of the wooden two-car **garage**. It was filled with car parts and tools. He stood there in the bright sun trying to see past the van and the huge speakers they were wrestling into place like slaves building the Pyramids. The van was propped up on jack stands and he could see a pair of legs sticking out. But there was another car in there too, an old car, three taillights on each side. It looked like—

Staring into the darkness, Harold was suddenly convinced that his Impala parts were in there. As he stared, and became more sure, he saw the legs moving out from under the car.

Behind him, a horn blared and he turned toward Vikki's car but didn't see it because the three men were off the porch now and coming toward him, their shorts bagging down around their calves, hair oiled back or heads shaved in a dark stubble. The biggest one wore a sleeveless undershirt and wasn't twenty years old. But the faded tattoo on his shoulder—Mi *Vida Loca*—let everyone know he had done time. He was a *veterano*.

"What you lookin' at?" the tattooed one asked, hands on his hips.

"My car got ripped off," Harold said. "Cops found it in this driveway."

"Driveway? This ain't no driveway. It's a alley."

"It leads to that garage."

"That don't make it no driveway."

It was futile, but Harold had to ask: "You see my car here? A green '64 Impala."

"Let me tell you something, man." He jabbed a finger at Harold. "Anyone fucks with my car, I'd kill 'em."

Harold nodded at the garage with the car parts and the back end of the jacked-up Econoline.

"Whose garage is that?"

"Shit, man." The tattooed guy laughed and looked at the others. Harold looked past them and saw the Accell was gone. *Caught behind enemy lines*, Harold thought, his self-destructive forces fully operational now.

"You don't get it, do you?" The guy stepped forward.

"I just asked—"

"You don't come in here, start talkin' shit about whose garage is that and—"

A new voice came from behind them. "Whassup, homes? Whassup?"

Harold turned toward the garage and saw a skinny kid with grease up to his elbows swaggering toward them.

"Neto, man, this here guy's talkin' all kinds of shit about who's garage is that and shit like that."

The kid squinted at Harold, laughing. Then asked: "Do I know you?"

"Hey, look," Harold said. "My car was ripped off and dumped in this driveway here and—"

"Driveway?" Neto said. "This ain't no driveway. This here's an alley."

"It looks like a driveway to me."

"That's cuz you're confused in your head, man. That's your problem. Cuz this ain't no driveway and I don't know shit about no Impala anyway."

I didn't say anything to him about an Impala, Harold thought.

"The cops found it here, in this driveway," he said. "And you're saying you didn't see *anything*?"

"Man, you didn't listen so good," the tattooed one was saying again, laughing in an amazed way. "Neto, you want me to jam this piece of shit?"

Neto spit, then looked at Harold, smiled and said, "Kick his bitch ass."

But then the blast of a car horn turned them all and Harold saw the silver Accell had slid up behind the gangbangers. Vikki pulled right up next to him so he got in. She plowed through them, making them jump aside as they pounded on the hood and roof, then threw their beer cans after them, rattling in the street as she accelerated away.

"You trying to get yourself killed?" she said when they reached PCH.

Harold was still breathing hard, adjusting to the fact that he hadn't gotten his head beat in like he thought he would.

"They're the ones stripped my car," he said.

Vikki stared at him, reappraising him. "You just stood there. They were going to kill you and you just stood there." She suddenly laughed. "Like in the dealership. You got me out of there."

He was relieved now. Relieved and proud. He couldn't help boasting: "Hey, I told you I'd do it all. From womb to tomb— that's me."

She laughed some more and said, "I've never known anyone like you," shaking her head. Harold felt the energy between them rising. She was looking at him with new eyes— a man who could deal with people and come out on top, a man who could stand up to other men, someone who could get answers, dammit.

They were almost through downtown Long Beach, climbing the Vincent Thomas Bridge to Terminal Island. Palos Verdes was a knob of land in the distance, rising above the cranes and freighters in the harbor.

"Where're we heading?"

"I need to swing by the dealership and pick up the Healey. Then let's head back to my place. I need a shower, clean clothes."

The implication was suddenly heavy in the car. She turned to him. "Don't worry. I won't go off on you again, if that's what you were thinking."

"I wasn't thinking that. Just—"

"What?"

"You said you got some files from Dash's office . . ."

"Copies. I want to check them against Joe's files. You got those files?"

"Sure," Harold said, keeping his voice casual. "They're in the Impala. I'm having it towed to my dad's house. Lend me a car and I'll go pick them up."

They were almost to the Healey now, they could see it ahead, under a tree dropping purple flowers on the dark green hood. Vikki slowed and pulled up beside it. Harold was trying to think how to handle this—he couldn't tell her Joe's files were unaccounted for.

"Look, why don't I follow you back to your place."

Idling, she turned to him, her quick eyes probing him.

"I won't go off on you," he said, and she smiled. "I got an idea what might be in Dash's files, something I could check out while you grab a few Z's."

She nodded, gave him the keys to the Healey. "I don't have to ask if you can drive a stick."

He was out of the car and crossing the street when he heard the power window whirring behind him and turned to see the glass sliding down revealing her face, a face he could stare at all day if she let him.

"You call that cop in Santa Barbara yet?"

"Call 'em from your place," he answered cheerfully, hoping that when he got there, she'd forget what he said. "See you there."

"I've only got one question at this point," Jim said in his emotionless way. "Where do the cars go after they're stolen?"

Sitting in his office, listening to Jim Shields lay it all out, describing how the cars went from Covo's dealership to his insurance agency to Bobby Skura's body shops around the South Bay, Dash realized he had been sold out. Things were coming unraveled and someone was going down. Bobby must have seen it coming and handed him to Shields. That was the problem with this kind of a scheme—the insurance guy was always the man in the middle. Dash took a bigger risk for a bigger profit. And here he was paying the price.

As Shields continued, Dash realized that, unless he did something fast, this could mean the closure of the agency and his arrest. Of course, he could avoid prison with another midnight departure. That had worked in Atlanta, in Dallas, and Las Vegas. But it would be tough to set up shop again somewhere else. His past would catch up with him again just as it was catching up with him now.

What really amazed Dash was the way the guy came straight at him. He seemed like a real wimp the first time he came to his office. Now he'd changed. And all the proof of Dash's crimes was right here in this room, under Jim's control. It hadn't bled out into the rest of the world yet, bringing with it the inevitable string of tedious auditors, investigators, and district attorneys. There was something decent and old-fashioned to this one-on-one they were having. Give him a chance to refute the charges before blowing the whistle on him.

Dash stood up and turned toward the window, where a shaft of sunlight glinted off a car windshield in the parking lot next door. A teenage couple came out of Denny's still sucking on their drinks. He said something to tease her and she playfully punched him. Young love.

"So where do they go?" Jim asked again. "The cars, after they're stolen. What do you do with them?"

"I don't want to spoil your fun," Dash said, still watching the couple, wondering if he had ever been like that and suddenly realizing he never had.

"Pardon?"

"You've put together an entertaining scenario so far. I'd love to see what else you can come up with."

"I know this isn't easy. But I've actually had cases where the agent I was investigating thanked me."

"For what?"

"They were professionals who had gotten off the track along the way and it troubled their conscience."

"This *won't* be one of those cases."

Jim was silent. Dash turned from the window and stood behind his chair looking down at Jim.

"In fact, for the record, I deny all of what you've laid out here."

"That's your right. Then I'll present these documents to our fraud division. If they think there is just cause they'll turn it over to the State Insurance Commission."

"And close me down while they look into it."

"Probably."

"Not *probably*. Definitely. And you know it."

Jim didn't say anything. Dash's voice softened as he said.

"Why do all that?"

"Pardon?"

"I don't see why you want to do all that."

Jim blinked at him, amazed—or as amazed as the deadpan guy ever got.

"Because what you're doing is illegal. It's fraud."

Dash took a seat and folded his hands in front of him. *Use the client voice*, he thought. *Reasonable. Reassuring. Find this guy's buttons and push them.*

"Jim, what would happen if you went back to your claims manager and said, 'Hey, I checked the guy out and it's all on the up and up.'"

"I don't see what this has to do with—"

"Theoretically. I'm just talking theoretically now."

"It would be dropped. But—"

"So this is all up to you right now."

"No. It's up to what I find."

Dash licked his lips. His mouth was dry. He was talking too fast. Slow down. Slow down. He took a deep breath, leaned back, and waved his hand at the papers Jim had laid out.

"This—this fraud you've outlined here. If it was true, that would mean I'd have a lot of money somewhere, wouldn't it?"

"Possibly."

"It might even mean that there was extra money for another person."

Jim said nothing.

"Look at it this way: The investigator in a case like this might get ten grand in cash for telling his claims manager he looked into it and found nothing. And you know that ten grand in cash is worth about fourteen, fifteen grand in the real world. Well, I don't have to tell you the value of money. Right?"

Jim looked down.

"Think of what you could do with that cash, Jim." For one

thing, Dash thought, he could get a new sport coat. The thing he's wearing looks like shit.

Jim began to gather up his papers and pack his briefcase. "There might even be twenty grand if you could wait a week or two."

The documents were back in the briefcase now and Jim snapped it shut. Dash noticed that the leatherette covering on the briefcase was worn at the edges, exposing the cardboard core. It filled him with disgust that this pathetic little man with his worn sport coat and battered briefcase was trying to destroy him.

"Mr. Schaffner, I'm going to do you a very big favor."

"What's that?"

"I won't mention this in my report."

"Mention what?"

"That you tried to bribe me."

Dash laughed. "Man, what planet are you from? This is how business is done."

Jim stood up.

"Oh, so that's it then?"

"What?"

"You come in here, fuckin' ruin me, then just walk out?"

Jim turned away, walked through the door and down the hallway.

Dash followed.

"Hey, come on, Jim," he said, hating himself for pleading with the guy. "Let's take a look at the numbers again and I'll show you how the policies were—"

They were in the outer office now and he saw Dixie look up at him, maybe guessing what was happening and probably afraid for her job. Another thing to worry about.

Jim kept moving out the door and down the stairs. Dash ran after him and caught him in the parking garage under the building as he approached an old yellow Camero. He put his hand on Jim's shoulder saying, "Hold it!" and Jim turned, a sliver of fear in his eyes.

They faced each other in the quiet garage with the smell of damp cement around them.

Finally, Dash smiled his slow easy smile, the one that always got him what he wanted, and said, "Come on, man. Let's work something out."

Jim's eyes blinked behind the thick glasses.

"I mean, there's gotta be a way."

"I'm sorry. It's out of my hands now." Jim turned, unlocked the driver's side door, and threw his briefcase across the seats. He fired up the Camero and the engine began bucking under the hood like a bad heart. Blue smoke poured out of the exhaust pipe as he backed out.

Dash stood there with his hands in his pockets, jingling his car keys. Unexpectedly he thought: *No, Mr. Shields. it's not completely out of your hands. Not yet, anyway.*

"Dash?"

"That's me."

"Hey. It's Bobby."

"Hey, Bob. How ya doin', man?"

"Great. Couldn't get you at the office so I thought I'd try you on your car phone. Where are you?"

"Out and about. What's up?"

"I guess I need to ask you that. I call your office, everyone's gone. What's happenin'?"

"I let Dixie go early today. Boost her morale, you know?"

"Sure, I'm concerned with the morale of my guys too. Fridays for lunch, I take 'em over to Angel's. We watch the girls jump around on stage, shaking their tits, the guys come back and work like bastards all afternoon."

"Bob, for the record, I just want you to know, I think you're a beautiful person."

"Thanks, man. Hey, where are you?"

"In my car."

"I knew that."

"I'm trying to catch up with a friend of mine."

"Catch up where?"

"Oh, lemme see . . . I'm on Ocean in Long Beach. Let me tell you, traffic's a bitch."

"You're not far. I want you to swing by the shop."

"Love to, Bob, but I've really got to catch this friend of mine."

"Anyone I know?"

"Just a colleague."

"Hey, Dash, you happen to see Fabian?"

"Fabian?"

"Yeah, you know, my little brother. Big dumb guy, gets real upset when people owe him money."

"Saw him last night, as a matter of fact."

"Really? Where?"

"Mardi Gras."

"Where? You're breakin' up. You in a tunnel or something?"

"High tension wires."

"When I go over the bridge my cell phone sounds just like that."

"Is that right?"

"Yeah. So how'd it go with Fabian?"

"We had a few beers, watched the Bulls get their butts spanked."

"Subject of money come up?"

"We got that all worked out."

"Really?"

"Sure."

"You know, Dash. When I saw Fabian, he told me if you didn't have the money he was gonna rip your fuckin' head off."

"It's still on my shoulders, Bob."

"My point is, either you paid him or . . . Or you did something to him."

"Like what?"

"I don't know. But first thing this morning I get a call from Bernette. She's ape shit cause the big bastard never came home. Kids are cryin' *Where's Daddy?* Cops call her a couple hours later. They found his Suburban. Guess where it was parked?"

"I don't like where this is leading, Bob."

"*Don't call me Bob! All right? My name is Bobby!* Look, I want you to come by the shop, now, and tell me exactly what happened."

"Sorry, I've got some priorities right now."

"Make this your A-Number-One fucking priority. Okay? I'll tell you why. I got this kid works for me. He's one of these kids you read about in the paper has no regard for human life. You following me?"

"I'm breathless."

"He wants his associates on the street to respect him. You know how he gets respect in his neighborhood?"

"Through hard work and personal initiative?"

"Wrong. By taking the life of another man. It's sad, I know, but he has chosen his destiny."

"As have we all."

"True, Dash, very true. Now this young man I speak of is here with me in my office right now. I'm looking into his eyes right now. If you see him coming, it will be the last thing you see. . . . Dash, you there?"

"You know what, Bobby? Something just came to me."
"No kidding."
"I'm just guessing here, but I bet Fabian went fishing."
"*Fishing?*"
"You know how he loves that yellowtail."
"Then what's his car doing in the lot at the Mardi Gras?"
"Maybe he took that deep-sea fishing boat leaves off the end of the pier there."
"Bullshit."
"Seriously. He'll turn up in a day or two. By then I'll have your money for you. And then we'll all be friends again. . . . Bob? You still there, Bob? What do you think of that?"
"I think you're lying."
"That's your choice."
"Here's the deal: You come into my shop now. You look me in the eye and tell me my brother's alive. Or I'm comin' after you."
"I didn't get that, Bob, you're breakin' up too much."
"Dash! Dash, don't—"
"Gonna have to call you back later, Bob. Bye."

There was a certain irony to the fact that, as an insurance adjuster, Jim Shields had investigated thousands of auto accidents, and he could tell you everything about what caused them, but he had never been in a bad wreck himself. Seeing the carnage and destruction firsthand made him a very defensive driver, like a city cop who moves to the country and still sleeps with a gun under his pillow.

This irony might have been in Jim's mind when it began, when his car started moving in a direction it shouldn't and he began to experience the awful *tumbling* feeling. Yes, he might have described it as a tumbling sensation—not just the car as it left the road, but it was like everything had come loose inside him and was tumbling around in a sickening way.

Jim's own inattention might have been a major cause of the accident, as was so often true in these cases. He was busy telling himself he had done the right thing by confronting Dash. He had thought the man would react differently, come clean and give him the final piece in the package so he could lay it all out in front of Howard in the TransPacific offices high above Wilshire Boulevard.

The idea of delivering a complete package had led him to his favorite daydream as he headed up the steep slope of the Vincent Thomas Bridge over the Los Angeles Harbor with the hammerhead cranes and freighters and oil tankers below. He thought Howard might be so impressed with his investigation that he would bring him back inside.

Jim had stopped at the TransPacific offices before going to see Dash. He wanted to tell Howard how well the investigation was going. Howard was tied up in a meeting. Jim waited, then left a copy of his report with his secretary. It was incomplete but he wanted Howard to see that this was much bigger than they had thought. It involved a network of body shops and car thieves across the South Bay. Howard would like that because he had told Jim the State Insurance Commissioner wanted to crack down on this kind of fraud. It was just this kind of expense that was driving business out of California.

Jim pictured Howard reviewing the file and realizing that Jim would be perfect for the claim's manager slot he heard was opening up. He imagined getting the call from Howard, pausing as the offer was made, maybe even bumping them up on the salary. As he started down the long descent on the other side of the bridge, the Camero picking up speed, the V-8 throbbing, he saw himself hanging up the phone in his home office and casually turning to his wife.

"Howard needs me downtown," he'd say. He pictured Terry's amazed expression as she rewrote her image of him.

Jim was brought back to the present by headlights in his rearview mirror, coming fast, and the shuddering impact as he was rammed in the left rear quarter panel. The back end of his car was shoved out into the fast lane, and he had the feeling that he had broken loose inside, the membrane that held him in place was torn and he began tumbling.

Something signaled his brain that he was in extreme danger—cars coming head-on at 60 mph, screaming tires, breaking glass—and the events took on a clarity he'd never experienced.

His car was sliding sideways now and through the windshield he saw bridge suspension cables and nothing else. He turned the wheel—don't lock up the brakes!—but he couldn't stop the car from 360-ing on the slick bridge pavement. He wasn't sure if he was heading with traffic or back into it. He cut the wheel once more and saw the guardrail coming up fast and beyond it the pale evening sky.

BOOM!

Through the guardrailing and airborne for a second, waiting for the lights to go out but amazed when—

BOOM!

He landed, slid, then started rolling, shreds of ice plant alternating with the sky and the grinding and crushing of his car as he was ripped from his belt and began rolling around inside the car along with all the other junk from under the seats and in the door panels.

Then everything stopped moving.

Silence.

His body systems began checking in: head, arms, legs. But something hot and wet was on his face. Spattering like rain inside the car. Where was it coming from? He got an arm free and wiped the liquid from his eyes. Oil? No.

Slowly, he realized his car was on its roof in the ice plant off the bridge embankment. Feet appeared outside the window. Help was coming. Thank God. They would get him out of here and he'd be all right. He might even make that meeting with Howard. Show him what he found and see his amazed face.

He tried to call out but his voice was garbled. A silhouetted face appeared upside down and then a hand reached into the car. He wanted to touch that hand. To let someone know he was alive. But the hand was groping for something else. His briefcase began to slide away and disappeared from view. Nothing moved as it should. Everything was angled and floating. The membrane was torn and he couldn't put it back in place. He wanted his feet on the ground again, the sky over his head. And he wanted this hot rain to stop falling on his face.

The person was back in the window again, an arm reaching inside holding something long and thin with a rounded end to it. The thing swung through the air and an awful thud shook what was left of his world. Then another thud. And another.

Then there was a rushing feeling as if he was flying away from himself through a world of images of his life. Each image held Terry's face and he was surrounded by a beautiful sadness as he realized he would never see her again. And he realized, with a tiny spark of relief, that the awful tumbling was about to stop.

Fabian was riding in the back of a pickup truck, bouncing down a dirt road, looking at his hands and trying to remember how they got scraped up so bad. He had woken up, baking like a piece of meat in the hot sun, with no idea where he was or how he got there. He wandered for a while in the desert, then some farmers in a pickup carrying crates of fruit stopped for him and he climbed in the back.

Defense wounds. The phrase jumped into his mind, emerging from the drifting toxic clouds of confusion. The scratches on his hands, the blood on his face were what the cops called defense wounds. He remembered being questioned by two cops in the back of a cruiser once. They pulled out eight-by-ten glossies of some guy got hacked to pieces.

"See the cuts on his hands," they said. "Guy tried to take the knife from you. Right? You came at him, he tried to take the knife. He got the blade, you got the handle." He hadn't cut up that guy, and he told them so. He never hurt anyone. Unless they deserved it.

The truck stopped as the dirt road reached a paved highway. The glass panel at the back of the cab slid open. One guy stuck his head out and said, "*Mexicano?*" Fabian stared back at him. There were words in his head but they didn't come out. It was like he was hearing them in his brain but they couldn't find their way to his mouth.

The glass panel slid shut and the truck pulled out onto the paved road. Christ, he was thirsty. And his hands were killing him; he could feel his heartbeat in the gashes. Fabian closed his eyes and slumped back against the cab, his head bouncing as the truck bumped along.

Pictures began coming back from the night before. Lying in a cramped dark space. Driving in some car. Bright lights. Laughter. Darkness again. Then a lonely wind and a flash of a gunshot. He was fighting with someone—was that Dash?— grunts and curses and the feeling of death circling above.

Seagulls. He woke up, still in the pickup truck, hearing seagulls and feeling cool ocean air and smelling rotten food. The motor stopped and he opened his eyes. A row of buildings with red tile roofs overlooked a beach. The truck was parked at the back of a restaurant. The farmers were talking to another man and they were all looking at him. The new man came toward him.

This man had the broadest shoulders Fabian had ever seen. His thinning sandy hair was combed forward and his nose had been broken.

"You okay, fella?" the man said. He had an accent of some kind.

Fabian wanted to say, "Yeah, except for these friggin' cuts on my hands." But he wasn't able to speak.

"Who are you?"

Fabian tried to give him his name, but couldn't form the word. He reached into his hip pocket for his wallet. Gone.

"Whyn't you come inside." The man turned toward the others and said something in Spanish. They helped Fabian out of the truck and led him into a restaurant with a red tiled floor. It was cool in here and smelled of ammonia. A big woman appeared in front of him wearing an apron blotched with stains. She held out a glass of water. It was cold and the glass was beaded with moisture. It was the most beautiful sight Fabian had ever seen. He took the glass of water and tossed it down. The woman laughed and said, "*Thirsty.*"

The man with the accent said to her, "Maybe he's just dehydrated. I used to get that way when I was still playing. Even on the ice I'd get so dehydrated I could hardly talk."

The woman brought him another glass of water and watched as he drank that down too. She laughed again, appreciating his appetite. The water and the cool shade inside the restaurant made him feel better. He looked up at the woman and saw her smiling at him. He smiled back.

"Sophia, let him rest for a while," the man said. "I'll be in my office."

He started to turn away when Fabian suddenly heard himself say, "I ain't no Mexican." The man turned and waited.

Fabian said: "I'm Armenian, for Christ's sake."

They were standing in Vikki's kitchen, looking at copies of Dash's files, their heads close together. Whenever their shoulders touched Harold felt like about two thousand volts jumped between them.

"If Dash had my Impala stolen, like you said, then the parts might be in one of the shops he used. Or—" Harold paused, putting it together in his mind. "What was the name of that body shop Fabian ran?"

She looked up from the page, her quick eyes considering what he said. The house around them was quiet, the wind moaning occasionally.

"You're saying Dash was involved with a chop shop."

"A car's worth more parted out that it is whole."

"What about the Accell? Dash said it would be stolen."

"There're lots of car rip-offs around. Could be he had a couple of things going."

"But how could he sell a brand-new car without the title?"

"Shave the VIN numbers, forge a pink slip. It's not hard to do."

She lapsed into thought, her eyes still on him. Slowly the intensity drained and Harold saw the exhaustion take over. She forgot about chop shops and stolen cars and touched his arm.

"Sorry, I'm asleep on my feet. I got to take a shower, get some sleep."

But she didn't leave. Just stood there close to him, looking at him, worried and excited at the same time. Her face suddenly showed her age, but Harold found it easy to be understanding. Hell, even dead tired she still looked great. He sensed Vikki's pain and wanted to make it better, wanted to stroke her hair and, yes, take her upstairs into the bed where they would make love (not like the wrestling match they had yesterday). Then they would sleep and with fresh energy they would solve all their problems and talk about cars and see what there was between them.

But what about Marianna?

Harold needed a little time to think that through. He still loved Marianna. But was she his type? Was Vikki? What a stupid question—Harold had never met a good-looking woman who wasn't his type. *Damn!* These questions were tying him in knots. He needed to do something simple and straightforward, like get his dad's Impala back on the road. Yeah, he could handle that kind of a problem. These other questions would have to wait.

Vikki turned and started down the hallway to the stairs and the shower and the bed. She stopped and looked back at him.

"Take the Accell if you want. Just don't disappear on me."

"Disappear?"

"Don't start hunting around for your Marianna."

"That comes after we're done with this."

"Womb to tomb. Sure."

She smiled and Harold saw that her face was natural for the first time, no tough girl act, no anger, no sarcasm.

"Harold . . ." God, he could listen to her say that all day. She couldn't finish what she was going to say. Instead, she thought of something else and the energy came back into her eyes. "When you get Joe's folder, let's cross-check the numbers."

Joe's folder! He'd almost forgot about that.

"And when you get back, if I'm asleep, wake me up. Okay?"

"Sure."

"So long."

"So long."

Later, he remembered her standing there like that, in the hallway, her face finally natural. Then she disappeared up the stairs. There was no particular reason he should remember that moment. But he did.

It was late afternoon when Harold reached the bridge and drove east toward Wilmington in Vikki's silver Accell. The oncoming traffic from Long Beach was streaming back over the bridge to Palos Verdes. All the fat cats had made their money in the trenches in Long Beach, in Orange County, and were returning to the safety of their Palos Verdes mansions and their manicured lawns and ocean views. And beautiful wives.

Harold pictured Joe heading home from the dealership, looking forward to seeing Vikki after a hard day. Or did he? The Joe Covo he remembered, from his short stint as a salesman at the dealership, took it all for granted. He was that kind of a guy—he felt the world owed him everything—easy money, expensive cars, and beautiful women. And wouldn't you know it, the bastard got it all. That seemed to be the way it worked.

Harold glanced down at the card they took off Fabian, saw the address. He consulted his *Thomas Guide*, then, as he cleared the Vincent Thomas Bridge he took the first exit north on the Terminal Island Freeway. Then he exited and turned off onto side streets.

For a second Harold thought he had wound up in Tijuana. The road was potholed and the buildings around him were pieced together from sheets of corrugated tin. Stray dogs ran in the street and he saw a vacant lot with two sick-looking cows in it. A circle of men squatted on a street corner around a caged pit bull. In the distance a bulldozer labored, working its way up a yellow mountain of sulfur.

He checked the address once more, looked up and saw it, the chain-link fence and a sign, AUTO EXPORT, SALVAGE & DISMANTLING. The huge warehouse and surrounding junk-yard lay under the girders of the bridge to Palos Verdes. He parked in front of the gaping doors and went in.

Steel shelves climbed to the ceiling, overflowing with distributors, water pumps, and cylinder heads, their wires and hoses hanging loose like severed arteries. To his right was a machine shop with lathes and drill presses, open tubs of solvents and cleaners beside drums of chemicals. Deep in the gloom, a welding torch sputtered, stroboscopically illuminating a figure bent over the chassis of a car like a butcher over a side of beef.

Harold waited, expecting someone to appear—or maybe a pack of junkyard dogs to descend on him. Instead he heard a voice from a corner of the warehouse. He looked down a row of shelves and saw light coming from a cramped office.

"Will you relax?" the voice was saying. "There's a million places he could be . . . How should I know where? You know the crazy shit my brother's capable of."

Harold moved closer and saw the man attached to the voice. He was slumped in a grimy vinyl chair, turned to the wall, the back of his head showing a pale bald spot growing in thick black hair. He spun the knotted phone cord around his finger as he talked.

"Just 'cause his Suburban was there doesn't mean—" He

looked up and rolled his eyes at someone else in the room. Harold could see a pair of Nike cross-trainers propped up on the desk. He moved closer and saw a boy, a teenager maybe, bent over a pad of paper, drawing cartoon figures. "I know what the cops said. I—Look, Bernette, I'll call you as soon as—Okay. Okay? Then don't! See if I give a—"

He slammed the phone down. "The woman's crazy," he said to the kid. "Out of her fuckin' gourd."

Harold realized they might turn and see him there eavesdropping so he cleared his throat, moving forward, scuffing his feet on the rough floor, ready to ask them to show him the Impala parts they had in stock to see if they matched his. They didn't look around.

"Here's what I want you to do," the man said, fingering the perimeter of the bald spot as if to see if it was spreading. Harold could see the kid, and—Jesus—he looked familiar. Familiar in a bad way, Harold thought, waiting to draw a match with recent entries for time and place.

The man was standing now, head jutting forward between broad shoulders as he shoved his arms into a leather jacket, saying, "Take the cell phone. You find him at his condo, call me. I'm goin' to his office just in case that bitch lied to me when she said—"

The man turned and saw Harold. His face darkened.

"We're closed. Okay?"

"Okay." Harold started backpedaling. The man looked at him, wondering how long he had been there. "Whaddaya want?"

"I'll come back later," Harold said, feeling his feet moving him quickly away. He would come back later, but only when he was sure that the kid wasn't there, because his memory had finally given him a match: He was the punk from the garage on Gaviota, the garage where he now knew he would find some or all the parts stolen from his car.

But, as Harold put these realizations together, moving out into the open air again, climbing into the silver Accell, he realized he wouldn't be heading back to Palos Verdes anytime soon. Traffic was jammed in both directions as a swarm of emergency equipment, lights flashing, surrounded a yellow car, wheels up, in the ice plant below a broken section of railing.

Vikki was lying on her bed listening to the radio and reading the contracts she took from Dash's office, thinking Harold would be back soon with the Accell, when she must have dozed off. She was falling deeper into sleep, approaching that point of no return, completely wasted from last night and the craziness of today, when she heard a *click* below her bedroom window. Not loud, but distinct. *Click.* There it was again.

She climbed out of the pit she had been falling into and stumbled to the window. The outside lights illuminated the lawn and the darkness beyond as the cliff dropped away toward the ocean. Someone was down there, but she couldn't see who it was or what they were doing.

Click.

She moved downstairs, still in that drug sleep of an evening nap, not knowing what she'd find, and stepped outside and saw it was Dash, standing over a golf ball, his long body both relaxed and braced for violent motion. He swung the driver back, paused at the top, swept down into the ball, and *click.* The ball hissed off into space, finally disappearing from the lights as it fell into blackness.

"What're you doing?"

"Trying to hit a low draw," he said, not looking around, just teeing up another ball and—slow backswing, and—*click*. She couldn't help enjoying how he moved.

"Fade the ball, it rises up and lands soft. Good if you want to stick the greens. Draw the ball and it bores through the air. When it hits it runs. Gives you ten, twenty extra yards easy."

She saw that he had all his clubs laid out on the grass. A white golf towel lay nearby with dark stains on it.

"I keep it low, I might be able to reach the ocean."

"No way."

"Yes way." He smiled—it wasn't how he talked. As usual, he was imitating someone else. "I got close a few times."

"It's dark. You can't see where it goes."

"I can tell by the feel."

He swung again. The *click* was clean and crisp. She rubbed her forearms, feeling the gooseflesh.

"How'd that one feel?"

He smiled that slow easy smile that made her turn inside. "As pure as mother's love."

"How would you know?"

"I had a mother once." He held out the driver to her. "I bet you have a beautiful swing."

"Oh, yeah?"

"You've got fantastic rhythm." When she reached for the club he caught her hand and pulled her in close. Her stomach jumped. Turned on, or afraid? Why couldn't she tell the difference?

She twisted free. "Golf's a stupid game."

Dash pulled out a wedge and began hitting shots off the grass, taking huge divots, the ball jumping into the air like it had been fired from a mortar.

"Jesus! Take it easy on my lawn."

"So get the gardener to lay new turf. And tell him to put in a putting green for me over there."

"Yeah, *right*."

"Don't worry, babe. You'll have plenty of money soon." He said it casually, cutting off her response by swinging again. *Click.* The ball climbed out of the lights, then fell back through them like a meteor. He had cut a row of identical divots, the soil black and wet underneath.

"What are you saying?" She tried to keep her feelings out of her voice.

"Talked to Santa Barbara P.D. today. Worked out a deal with them."

She felt something rising inside her. He was feeding her all the words she wanted to hear and part of her knew it could all be lies, pushing her buttons to get what he wanted. Now he was quiet again, making her ask for the details.

"Okay. What did they say?" Her voice was tight. She wanted to believe him. God, she wanted to believe him.

"Just a matter of days now." *Click.* "It gets better."

He waited, making her beg for it.

"Okay."

"If they rule homicide, your policy pays double."

It was too good to be true, almost. But she had had her share of bad breaks. Maybe her luck was finally turning.

"What about Harold's statement?"

"Who? Oh, the Dodge Charger." He laughed. "The cops said they have a line on him."

"A line on him . . . ?"

"That's what they said."

He was watching her face, smiling. "Long-term forecast is looking up for this girl," he said, his face close to hers.

"What about the short term?"

"You want an advance on the settlement, that's not a problem."

She wanted to ask, *How much of an advance,* but stopped herself. He turned his back on her and began hitting balls again.

"I heard you knocked 'em dead at the dealership. But why'd you bring your attorney?"

She took the driver out of his hand and teed up a ball. Dash was behind her, arms around her arms, positioning her above the ball. His hips pressed into her like they had last night on his balcony.

"It was Dodge, wasn't it?" he breathed in her ear.

"Huh?"

"Your *lawyer*. It was this Dodge."

"What if it was?"

"Word of advice, Vik. Steer clear of Dodge."

"Why?"

"He's going down. You don't want to go with him." He ran a finger down her spine. "Tension. I feel tension all the way down here." She shivered. "Let it go, babe. Let it go."

He stepped away and she was suddenly cool where he had held her. She swung and felt solid contact all the way up her arms and into her shoulders. *You hit that one on the screws.* That's what Joe used to say to her.

"Pure as mother's love," he said.

"Golf's a stupid game." She tossed the driver onto the lawn. He picked it up and began lovingly rubbing the head with the golf towel.

"How'd you get over the bridge?" she asked him. "I heard there was a sig-alert. Someone went into the ice plant."

"I was ahead of the wave. Look—" He dropped the towel into her garbage can by the back door. "Let's celebrate. Take me out in your brand-new car. We go to some pricey little seafood place, ocean view, we spend the whole time trying to figure out how to spend all your money. That sound like a good use of our time?"

Why was spending her money suddenly his job?

"We can even do the paperwork by candlelight."

"Paperwork?"

"You're about to get the best coverage money can buy. You're gonna pray that new car of yours is stolen."

"Oh, yeah. Look, what if I want to just keep it?"

"Keep what?" His voice and smile hadn't changed. But something behind it was cold now. She rubbed her arms again.

"My car."

"Why would you want to do that?"

"I changed my mind. You know how women are."

"Do I?"

"Based on your performance last night, I'd say you know a lot about women."

He was quiet for a moment, still smiling at her but distant, thinking thoughts she could only guess at. He might be furious, he might be thinking about where to go for dinner. She had no idea. And this frightened her because she knew her powers to resist him were very low.

He started speaking slowly. "You like the car so much, you can buy another one just like it in a couple of weeks—cash."

"It's not just that."

"What is it then?"

"I'm—" She didn't want it to come out this way, but: "I'm scared."

"Scared of what?"

Of you, she thought, but she couldn't tell him the truth so she said, "I don't want to get caught."

He laughed, relieved, and his smile was real again. "Babe, we're talkin' white-collar crime here. No one gives a shit. And let's say, worst-case scenario, we're busted. We get sent to Club Fed. A little time to work on your swing, catch up on your reading, network with some like-minded folks."

He was there holding her again and she realized she was turned on. Afraid, sure. But that was part of it. He kissed her lightly. His voice caressed her ear.

"Dash ain't gonna let you get in trouble. I'm here to bring back the good times." He kissed her again. "Let's roll. I'm starvin'. Maybe you'll let me drive your new car."

Vikki suddenly remembered about Harold. "I let a friend borrow my car."

Dash stepped back, surprised.

"Yeah, he had an emergency so I let him take it. He'll be back soon."

"This isn't, by any chance, the Dodge Charger again?"

"Yes, it is." Then she thought of something and watched him closely as she said, "His car was stolen."

He smiled, like they were sharing a joke. "What's this world coming to? Tell you what. Why don't we send out for something? You make the call, I'll get the insurance papers out of my car."

He started to move around the corner of the house, carrying his clubs. He turned back, "Oh, and Vikki? While you're on the phone, I'll fix the drinks."

Then he left her there and she thought how glad she was that Harold would be back soon.

Sometimes things worked out just right, Harold thought, loading one of his stolen Impala doors into the trunk of the Accell, which was parked in the shadows on the old trolley right-of-way. Some things seemed easy but were tough—like Vikki and that insurance deal—and other things looked tough but were a piece of cake. Who'd have thought he could just waltz in here and retrieve his stolen doors like this?

There was only one little problem. He had only found one of the doors they had stripped off the Impala. He pictured himself driving the Impala with the passenger door missing. Kinda windy. Naw, that wouldn't work. So he decided to head back into the garage for one more look-see. Besides, there was still a chance he would find some of the other parts they had taken. And the folder from Joe's wall safe.

Harold started back through the darkness to the garage near where he had confronted the gangbangers that afternoon. He had had a hunch his car had been stripped there and he was right. When he saw that skinny little shit (did they call him *Neto*?) at that body shop in Wilmington, it all fell into place—he stripped cars and took what he needed for his own purposes, sold the rest to Auto Export. Maybe that was where Dash had stolen cars shaved and resold. Maybe this was what Harold could trade to the cops to stay out of jail? But he'd need documentation of some sort. Like Joe's files. Where the hell were they?

The flashlight swung heavy by his side but Harold didn't turn it on. Better not use it until he had to. Someone looked out and saw a flashlight beam moving around, they might call the cops. In this neighborhood they would call the cops for anything. But would the cops come? That made him think of a bumper sticker he just saw: *If you dial 911 and no one comes, try .357*. Not a comforting thought.

He turned up the driveway (*not* an alley) and stood in front of the wooden garage at the back of the long narrow lot behind the bungalow. The side door on the garage was a black rectangle, still open from when he broke the hasp and shoved inside on his earlier trip.

Harold hesitated before stepping inside, enjoying the cool night air, listening to the city around him: a siren, dogs barking, car alarms, TV voices spilling out of a nearby house. He looked up to Signal Hill and saw the red lights of the radio towers flashing, just like they had when he parked up there in high school, telling girls they were there to watch the submarine races out in the ocean. It was a funny line and it relaxed them. That was back in the days when a good hot kiss could blow your socks right off. Because you never knew how far it would go. You might get lucky and wind up in the backseat and make it all the way around the bases. You might stay on first base all night, making out until you felt you were going to explode.

Now he knew where all that led. He'd been to the end of a couple of relationships and he knew that kissing in a car at night under a flashing radio tower beat the hell out of anything he'd done since. He stood there, his current women cycling through his mind. He pictured himself in a car with Marianna, kissing until his lips were raw. She could tease him to death and he would thank her with his dying breath. That's why he was here, risking his life in gang territory, for Marianna and their life together.

Of course, Vikki was still an open file, too. He felt that, given the right set of circumstances (or maybe the wrong ones) he could end up in the sack with her again. Without meaning to he traced a series of events that could take him there tonight. After he got his doors, he would stash them in his room above the Club Cheri, then head up to her house. She might still be asleep. He could lie down next to her, say, "Want to hear something funny?" and tell her what he had done. Together they would laugh, picturing the car thieves discovering how they'd been ripped off. She'd get a kick out of that. Then, as their laughter died . . .

Back to business.

He stepped through the doorway and into darkness. The garage was tight around him, smelling of warm timber the way the attics in old houses do, and gasoline and the sharper smells of solvent and paint. A window was straight ahead now. Through it he could see the back of the bungalow and a bluish TV light though the rear window.

He moved along the side of the Impala lowered almost to the ground. And probably shaved, too—serial numbers shaved off the engine block and all the major parts. Now, where was that door? He slid his feet along the floor, touching tools and odd metal shapes that might be auto parts, or heavier objects like toolboxes or pans of engine oil.

With his hand over the flashlight, Harold turned it on, the blood in his fingers glowing red. He leaked out a sliver of light and it fell on the floor, catching a disembodied headlight, lying there like an eyeball out of its socket. He stepped over it and stood at the trunk. It was closed but not locked. He curled his fingers around the cool metal of the trunk lid and lifted. He heard a sliding noise, silence, then—

SMASH! Glass breaking.

Damn! Something had been on the trunk.

The flashlight fell out of Harold's hand and rolled around on the floor, throwing light crazily on the walls. He dropped to his knees and recaptured the flashlight, turned it off, then froze, breathing like he was having a cardiac, waiting for a swarm of gangbangers to rush in and kill him.

But nothing happened. Dogs were still barking. The TV voices continued faintly. He was okay. Harold stood up and looked through the window at the house. No change.

He turned on the flashlight again and looked in the trunk. There was another door. But it wasn't his. It was a candy apple red, like the body of this car. They only needed one of his doors so they took two and sold the other one to Auto Export. For a second Harold considered taking this door anyway. But that would be stealing and he was no thief. They deserved it. But he wasn't about to stoop to their level.

No, he would take what belonged to him and nothing

more. That reminded him. He shoved the door aside and saw some papers . . . he strained forward, reaching . . . Was it Joe's folder? He touched the file and it slid away . . . then finally into his grasp. It felt right but—

Light angled into the garage. A floodlight lit up the backyard. Out of time, he thought, moving toward the door, tripping over tools lying all over the floor. Out of time, but hopefully not out of luck, he thought, stuffing the file folder into his shirt and stepping back out into the night.

The Crown Victoria pulled to the curb on Gaviota in front of the Spanish-style bungalow and the headlights died. Inside the car, Bobby Skura scanned the street to see if Neto and Oscar had come back yet. He looked for Oscar's blue metal-flake customized Econoline van, lowered to the ground, with the doors he'd open so twin speakers, the size of orange crates, could send blasts of pulsing bass through whatever neighborhood they happened to be terrorizing at the moment.

Bobby didn't see the van so he settled back in the driver's seat, his leather jacket creaking against the leather seats and, against his will, he thought of his younger brother. His mind touched the possibility that Fabian might be lying dead in a field somewhere, then pushed it away because it was too terrifying to face. Instead, he tried to keep his mind on Dash Schaffner and think where he could find the son-of-a-bitch.

It was crazy but, when Dash said Fabian was down in Mexico fishing, Bobby almost believed him. It was just the kind of whacked-out thing his brother was capable of doing. But then, Dash was probably blowing smoke up his ass while he ran and hid somewhere. But somehow it had the ring of truth. He passed it along to Bernette, to show her he was working on the problem, then cruised down to Dash's office in Huntington, while Neto and Oscar paid a little visit to his condo in Newport. The office was locked up tight, like he figured it would be. But still, you couldn't rule out anything for sure. Dash was a crazy motherfucker. He might just be sitting there at his desk smiling, waiting for Bobby to walk in.

What really had Bobby spooked about all this was that, when he was a kid, and long before Fabian became a three-hundred-pound monster, he used to have these dreams about his little brother dying. It was always the same. In the dream, Fabian would come up to Bobby and say, ''I have to go now,'' something simple like that, and then he'd walk away, and Bobby knew he was going to die, and he would wake up with an ache in his gut. That's how he felt now, empty inside.

Most of the time the big ape pissed him off, doing stupid things Bobby had to make right. Like when they were kids hanging around their old man's machine shop in Glendale, he had to try to keep his little brother in line or his father would blow his stack and beat hell out of both of them. No matter how he tried, Fabian still got into things around the machine shop and Bobby got smacked for it.

So why did he even care what happened to him? Because Fabian was his brother, that's why—his only brother. It wasn't like in these Mexican families with fifty million kids running around. Fabian was the only brother he had. And if Dash had killed him Bobby would never see him again. Never.

Eddie Fallon.

The named jumped into Bobby's head. He might know where to find Dash. He grabbed the cell phone and dialed, the number ringing just as the Econoline pulled up behind him and he saw Neto and Oscar climb out.

"Eddie? Hey, it's Bobby."

"Hey, Bobby! What's happenin' man?"

"Lookin' for Dash. You seen him?"

Bobby got out of his car, phone to his ear, and stood in the dark street. Neto came toward him with Oscar and said, "Hey, Bobby, I checked his—"

"I'm on the phone! Can't you see I'm on the phone? Jesus. Sorry, Eddie. What was that?"

"Dash said he was comin' by with some insurance docs. But he never showed. I kinda want to talk to him too."

"Oh, yeah?"

Now Bobby saw Neto was walking down the driveway alongside the house.

"He sent this girl over to us today, sold her an Accell."

"Anyone I know?"

"Vikki Covo."

"Joe's wife? Why the hell'd he do that?"

"That's what I'm gonna ask him."

Neto was running back up to him, telling him something. Bobby pulled the phone away from his ear.

"How many times I got to tell you? I'm on the phone here."

"Get in the car, man! It's him."

"*Him* who?"

"Get in the car!"

Neto said something to Oscar in Spanish and ran back down the alley.

"Eddie? I got a situation here," Bobby said, sliding into the Crown Victoria, Oscar getting in the back. "Dash comes by, tell him to call me. No—listen. Don't tell him nothin'. But find out where I can find him. Then call me. Okay?"

Bobby was pulling out, turning down the driveway to the garage in the rear and Neto was there in the headlights, waving his arms.

"Hey, Eddie, it'll be worth a few bills, okay?"

"You got it."

Bobby cut off the cell phone and threw it on the seat. "What the hell's going on?"

"Some asshole ripped him off," Oscar said from the backseat.

Bobby pulled up next to Neto and Neto jumped in, breathing hard.

"That way!" Neto pointed down the alley.

Bobby angled around the corner, then hit the brakes. In his headlights was the dirt strip grown up with weeds and strewn with rocks and broken bottles.

"I'm not drivin' on that shit!"

"Go around, man! He's gettin' away."

Bobby threw it in reverse and palmed the big wheel around. His lights swept fences, garages, and a house. Then he was back on the street, tires squealing as he rounded the corner, the silver Accell growing larger in the headlights as Bobby pulled up behind it, right on the bumper, and he could see the guy's head turn, looking in the mirror and thinking, *Who's climbing up my tailpipe?*

"So who is this guy?" Bobby said.

From the backseat Oscar said: "A thief, man. Fucker ripped off Neto."

"What're you talking about? You're a thief."

"This asshole broke into my garage."

"Just now?"

"That's what I'm tellin' you, man. He took shit out of my garage."

Bobby laughed. "Why would a guy take shit out of your garage?"

"It was shit we took off his car! That's what I'm tryin' to tell you."

"Wait. Just wait a second. Okay? You stripped his car. Now he's stealing the shit out of your garage."

"That's what I been tryin' to tell you if you'd just listen to me."

"What'd he take?"

"A door."

Bobby eased back on the gas and put some space between him and the Accell. "This is so fucked up. He's not stealing nothin'. The door was his."

"The guy's a thief," Oscar said.

"And this guy was at your shop this afternoon, Bobby. Don't you remember nothin'?"

"At my shop?"

"You were on the phone and when you hung up the guy was there, like, listening and shit. You remember now?"

"That's *this* guy?"

"That's what I'm tryin' to tell you."

"Wait, wait now. Why would this guy who was at my shop be here takin' stuff out of your garage?"

"Listen, Bobby. I think Dash fucked us up, man."

"Dash?"

"He told you to get me to boost this guy's car down in Huntington."

"So Dash knows this guy."

"That's what I'm trying to tell you, man."

Dash. The name burned in Bobby's gut. He seemed to be everywhere, messing with his life.

Oscar was talking from the backseat again: "And it's the same guy came to your house today, Neto. 'Member? Comes on saying, 'My car was in your driveway.'"

"He was *where*?"

"In my driveway," Neto said.

"What'd he want?"

"I don't know."

Bobby thought it over, then said: "I don't like this."

The Accell stopped for the light at Seventh and they pulled in behind him. The Ford's V-8 was so quiet they could hear the higher-pitched four-cylinder Accell engine in front of them, ticking over as they waited for the light.

"Nice car, man," Oscar said, feeling the Ford's leather upholstery. "What'd it cost you, Bobby?"

"Thirty-two and change."

"I'm gonna get me one. Maybe pick up a dealer repo or something."

"I always buy new," Bobby said.

"You can save a lotta money buyin' used."

"Yeah. But I want to be the first one to fart on the seat."

Neto laughed that crazy laugh of his, then he said, "Oscar'll buy one of these cars, put lifters and Daytons on it."

"Fuck you."

"And fuzzy dice and all that shit like you got in your van."

"Just fuck you. Okay?"

The light changed and the Accell pulled out. They moved after it.

"Think he's got your door in the trunk?"

"It ain't in the garage no more. I looked. And the papers are gone too."

"What papers?"

"The papers I was gonna show you. With numbers of cars we stole. Why would he have that in his car 'less he wanted to fuck with us?"

Bobby was quiet again. Then he said, "Oh, man. I really don't like this."

They were on Cherry now, heading south on the narrow street under low trees with houses tight on either side. The sidewalks were crammed with people. The Accell was in front of him, guy still checking the mirror. For a second Bobby felt like this guy *was* Dash. He knew Dash somehow, so maybe he

knew where Dash was and what he did to Fabian. Bobby
pulled in a little tighter to the Accell. Didn't want to lose him.

"So, Neto, what're you gonna do about this guy steals
from you?" Bobby asked.

"No one steals from me. You understand what I'm saying?"

Oscar said: "Let's jam him."

Bobby: "What? Here?"

Oscar: "I don't know. Wait till he stops, then me and Neto
get out, go like, 'Surprise motherfucker,' and give him a
beatin'."

Neto had been very quiet, staring through the windshield
at the guy in the Accell. But then he said: "I'm gonna kill
him."

Bobby felt a thrill go through his system.

"Don't kill him. Here's what you do, okay? Stomp the guy,
then ask him where Dash is. Okay?"

Neto thought it over. "Yeah, cool."

"Hey, hey. Look!"

The Accell's signal was flashing, the car pulling to the curb.

They cruised past him and stopped a half block down.
Bobby turned and looked back. The guy was out of his car,
going to a phone in the corner of a liquor store parking lot.
He looked around. Drunks were staggering out of a place
called the Club Cheri. Next door was a pizza parlor with two
cops walking out, working toothpicks in their mouths.

"Hold it! Cops!"

They were silent, waiting in the car. They watched as the
cops took off their night sticks, slid them onto the seats of
the cruiser, and climbed in. They heard the cruiser's engine
start and it pulled out down the street.

The guy was still on the phone. Bobby was aware of Neto
taking something out of his pocket.

"Okay. Go!"

Harold was checking his mirror, wondering if someone had followed him from the garage on Gaviota, but decided the Crown Victoria didn't look like a gangster's car, when his beeper moved on his hip and he saw Vikki was calling, so he forgot about the Crown Victoria and pulled to the curb in front of a liquor store across from the Club Cheri.

As he got out he took Joe's folder with him, thinking he would have something to write on, and saw the skateboarding kid was there, jumping the curb again, stringy hair hanging in his face.

"Go home," Harold said to the kid, playing with him, the kid smiling, remembering Harold.

The pay phone was free so Harold called Vikki's house and didn't get an answer. He started to panic and quickly dialed his voice mail and waited for the message wondering what the hell could have happened since he left her asleep there this afternoon.

"Harold . . ." Her voice was low and intimate. He loved it. "Where are you . . . ? You said you'd be back after—"

Footsteps behind him. Coming fast. *Real fast.*

He turned and saw two punks closing in on him—saw one was Neto, the punk from Auto Export—and knew this was trouble. Neto swung a pistol at him and he saw it coming and tried to duck but—

Crunch!

His vision exploded like pieces of burning glass shooting into his brain.

He fell back, catching hold of the phone, trying to stay on his feet, rolling away from thudding blows on his back and shoulders, the side of his head. They were on him. He brought his knee up hard, felt contact, and heard a grunt, then broke free, trying to get clear but they had his arm, wrenching it back, turning him until he saw Neto swing the gun—

Crunch! His vision broke up again and he saw the pavement tilting up toward him, thinking, *That's really strange,* and saw he was falling next to a pickup truck so he hit the ground and rolled under the truck where they couldn't get him.

The skateboarding kid saw them swarming Harold and yelled, "Hey!" like he was going to do something about it, but Neto pointed the gun at him so the kid ran to the liquor store entrance yelling, "Hey!" to a guy in a cowboy hat buying a pint of Old Grand-Dad from the Korean owner behind the counter.

Harold rolled under the truck, his consciousness shrunk to a needle point, and watched hands reaching in to grab for his legs and distorted faces screaming at him. He tasted blood in his mouth and felt hands on his legs now, sliding him back out into the open so he kicked up, crushing a hand against a hot tailpipe, and he heard a shout of pain and the hand let go.

But the second one had slid under the other side and was kicking him in the face, lying there on the pavement next to him pounding his head with his shoes and cursing him, driving him out where the second one could get him again, and they had his legs now and he was being pulled out into the open again, and when he looked around for help he saw a guy with a goatee in a leather jacket standing across the street laughing. *Laughing!* Who was this guy?

Footsteps were coming now and a voice yelled, "The fuck you doin' to my truck?" The guy in the cowboy hat grabbed one punk and spun him around, then saw the gun coming up and yelled, "Whoa!" and swiped the gun out of his hand. The pistol flew across the parking lot and into the street. Neto ran for it as the Korean stepped out of his store with a short-barreled shotgun, racking a shell into the chamber. He aimed the gun at Neto, in the street, and said, "GO!"

Everyone stood there under the yellow lights of the liquor store sign and finally Neto looked at the other punk, giggled, and said, *Unbelievable.* He picked up the gun and they both took off down the street as a cruiser came flying into the parking lot. Two young cops jumped out and the Korean pointed to where the punks had taken off. The cops pulled their guns and ran after them.

Time for the old disappearing act, Harold thought. *Got to go before the cops come back.* He stood up and took a step but— here comes the pavement again. It kept tilting up toward him, like he was on the deck of a ship in a storm. He crawled a little, then lurched forward, pulling himself up on the Accell hood.

Siren. More cops were coming. Paramedics.

They would find his wallet and run his name through the computer, maybe find his outstanding warrant. The point was, it was time to hit the road.

He opened the Accell door and fell across the front seats, hoping he wouldn't bleed on the upholstery. He dug his wallet out of his hip pocket and slipped it under the floor mats, just in case he got stopped. Better not to have an I.D. than have one that landed his ass in jail.

Joe's folder! He'd dropped it during the fight.

Harold looked out and saw it lying in the parking lot like a piece of trash. He struggled out of the car and let the door slam shut behind him. The parking lot was really rolling now. Must be a big storm. And here came another wave because the deck was right in his face. He lay there, feeling the pavement cool on his cheek.

Now a sound was building in his ears, splitting his head in two, a paramedic van pulling into the parking lot, siren trailing off. Someone knelt beside him, holding him down saying, "Easy, sir. Take it easy now."

But *the file! Where was it?*

Another paramedic was next to him. He felt something stiff wrapped around his neck. Lights in his eyes. Crackling radio voices. Heads bent over him, backlit by the yellow liquor store sign looming above like a rectangular moon.

Harold felt himself being strapped down now, then lifted, moving somewhere, heading for the meat wagon maybe. The gurney paused at the doors and he felt something being pushed into his hand. *Joe's folder!* He looked over and saw the skateboarder stepping away, the scrawny kid with stringy hair, saying, "It's his—he dropped it," to one of the paramedics.

Harold held the folder like a life preserver, wanting to thank the kid, hoping he was at least smiling at him, but when he opened his mouth, he heard himself say: "Go home now, okay?"

It was a good thing he had pulled his Rover into Vikki's garage, Dash thought as he saw the headlights starting up the drive. He was in the garage getting his briefcase with the insurance docs in it when he turned and saw the car and thought it was the Dodge Charger returning the Accell and he planned to have a few words with him. But then he saw the car was a Crown Victoria so he hit the button and the door rumbled down, leaving him in the quiet garage. Outside he heard the car pull up and then Bobby's voice telling someone to get their ass out of the car and come with him.

He moved quickly into the house, upstairs and into Vikki's bedroom, where a small TV was showing a news clip of an overturned car taken from a helicopter (check that out later, he thought). Vikki was on the phone talking softly but she hung up when she saw him and the guilty look on her face made him wonder who she'd been talking to. He noticed that the drink he fixed her was untouched beside her.

"I'm not here," he said.

"I find that hard to believe."

"No, I mean, tell them I'm not here."

"Who?" She picked up a brush and began stroking her hair.

"The guy who just drove up. Tell them I'm not here."

"*Them?*"

"He's got two guys with him."

She turned with the brush still raised. "Dash. What the hell's going on?"

But then the doorbell rang and he said, "I'll tell you once you get rid of them."

"Everything?"

"Babe, I'll tell you my whole life story, if you want."

Dash followed her to the top of the stairs and watched her go down to the front door. He didn't like sending her down alone. But he knew that Neto might just shoot him on sight, so he figured this was his only option.

"Hello, Mrs. Covo," he heard Bobby saying.

"Who're you?"

"Bobby Skura. Friend of Joe's. You probably heard him mention my name."

"No."

Dash smiled, imagining Bobby's eggshell ego getting crushed under her heel.

"Mrs. Covo, could we step inside for a second? There's something I'd like to ask you."

"Ask me here."

Pause. Then Dash heard the anger in Bobby's voice.

"I'm looking for a guy named Dash Schaffner. Is he here?"

"Why should he be?"

"He's your fuckin' insurance agent." The anger was leaking out. "Look, is he here or not?"

"It's none of your business if he is."

"What if we come inside and look for ourselves?"

"I'll call the cops and have you arrested."

"It'll take them a while to get here. We could be in and out by then."

"And you'll feel pretty stupid if he's not here, won't you?"

Jesus, Vikki, Dash thought, make it easy on yourself. Just tell them I'm not here.

Dash moved to an upstairs window and looked down. He couldn't see Bobby, but he could see Neto and the other guy, the one they called Oscar. They were looking at each other, smiling and swinging their arms. Oscar had a bandage on one hand.

"You're shit out of luck," Vikki said, "And if you're not out of here in thirty seconds, I'm calling the cops."

The door slammed.

Dash watched as Bobby turned and said something to Neto. They talked for a few minutes, standing on the front lawn looking back at the door.

Vikki was beside him now, saying, "How'd I do?"

"You were beautiful." He pulled her to him and kissed her. "But why didn't you just tell them I wasn't here?"

"I don't like to lie."

Dash stroked her hair, thinking, It's the color of summer, and wondering if he heard that in a song somewhere. He was feeling all sorts of good things, one of which was the anticipation of going back down the hallway to Vikki's bed, when he looked out the window. Bobby took a last look at the house and he and Oscar got into the car.

Neto just stood there on the front lawn smiling and looking up at the house. Then he pulled out a large black gun, pointed it at the house, and began firing.

Sometime in the middle of the night, Vikki found herself naked, stumbling down the dark hallway of her empty house, without any idea where she was going or how she got there. All she knew was that something terrible was happening to her.

She leaned against the wall, shivering, feeling she might collapse any second. Her mouth was parched and pictures were in her head. She'd been drinking, with Dash. And she kept thinking Harold would come back and make things right and—

That's where she was going! To call Harold!

She groped her way down the hall and into the kitchen. She picked up the receiver and dialed the number she had written by the phone. She heard the recording of Harold's voice, and she was leaving him a message when the door from the garage opened. Dash stepped into the dark kitchen. What was he doing in the garage? He took the phone from her and hung it up.

"Where'd you take him?" His voice was low and threatening. "Fabian. You took him somewhere. Where'd you take him?"

"I don't know what you're talking about."

"You borrow someone's car, you don't want them to know about it, I suggest you fill up the tank. You drove a long way, dumped Fabian. What'd you do with him?"

"I'm so confused."

"I gotta know. Where is he?" His anger scared her. "You kill him? You and that *Dodge*?"

"No. I . . ." Her voice was weak and faraway and belonged to someone else. She felt she was shrinking, getting smaller and smaller until she would disappear.

"You better remember what you did with him. It's my ass they're after."

She knew the memory of what happened was there somewhere. But she didn't have the strength to find it. She didn't even have the strength to stay on her feet, she thought, clawing at the last scraps of consciousness.

Then it came to her, passing like a road sign in the night, and she heard herself say, "Baja."

"*Baja?* Baja, Mexico?"

Words floated in her head but she couldn't seem to grab any of them.

"Where in Baja? I've gotta find him." He shook her violently, her head flopping from side to side.

And then she was moving through darkness, remembering their drive south of the border. She was passing another road sign. And somehow she knew this would be her last.

"La Fonda," she said.

"La Fonda," he repeated, as if memorizing it.

Then she realized she really was shrinking, collapsing on the cold, hard kitchen floor. And Dash didn't even help her break the fall.

Fabian was sitting in the back of the restaurant, eating a plate of rice and refried beans and thinking of ways to kill Dash, when everything changed.

He had spent the afternoon with two Mexicans digging out a busted water main behind the restaurant, his hands sliding on the smooth pick handle. One of the Mexicans he worked with spoke a little English and told Fabian where he was, which turned out to be somewhere between Rosarito and Ensenada in a hotel named La Fonda. It was owned by Paul, the guy with the big shoulders who played pro hockey in Canada. He told Fabian if he dug out the water main he could have dinner and a place to stay.

Fabian enjoyed the work. His muscles seemed to remember the loading and unloading from his meat-cutting days and the routine filled the immediate now while his mind drifted to the pleasant future, which he hoped included finding Dash and killing that son-of-a-bitch with his bare hands. He could feel Dash in his grip and imagined the bones snapping as his arms tightened around him, squeezing him so hard his guts would come out his mouth.

But now he was feeling more mellow, the platter of rice and beans filling a stomach made hungry by honest work. He was sitting alone at the rear of the patio listening to a little fat guy play the guitar while roaming among people eating dinner, mainly drunk Americans from LA, the ocean close by, the sky black over the water. Fabian might have dozed off because, when the singing started, he opened his eyes and forgot where he was.

It was the big woman, the one they called Sophia, who had taken care of him in the kitchen that afternoon. She was singing Violetta's aria, "Sempre Libera" from La Traviata, the music flowing through her like a heavenly river and surrounding Fabian with visions of a life he could live away from the scum and filth of Los Angeles, his brother's evil world that had trapped him and turned him into a monster.

As Sophia sang her face looked like an angel to Fabian, an angel who was opening a door to a new life and, without thinking, he rose on cue and sang, "Amor, amor è palpito dell'universo, dell'universo interno, misterioso, misterioso."

His voice boomed out across the patio and silenced even the surf, and she turned to him, as if she had expected him to be there, answering: "Amor è palpito dell'universo!" And as the song crescendoed, their voices calling and answering, they met in the middle of the patio with everyone watching (even the cook came out to see what the hell was going on) and before the final words were sung, and the applause exploded throughout the restaurant, Fabian knew he would try to forget all about his previous life in the hellhole to the north and settle here where he could work like a peasant and sing with this angel.

Harold woke up in a cool dark room, a hospital room, he realized, looking around. And, although he couldn't see anyone, he was aware that someone else was in here with him.

He had been out for a long time. It could have been an hour or two, or a day or more. But it was night now, he realized, looking through the large windows and across the city to the top of a high rise with searchlights pointing straight up in the air, illuminating the underside of orange clouds.

Breathing. Someone was breathing nearby. No, they were crying. He tried to turn his head to see but something was wrapped around his neck. He touched it: a neck brace. He always thought these things looked geeky so he tore open the Velcro fasteners and took it off.

Pain shot through his neck and head, bringing with it the memory of what had happened: stopping to use the phone at the liquor store, getting pistol-whipped, dragged out from under the truck. And after that? He remembered sliding down a bright tunnel, machinery whirring around him. Then, the painful tugging on the skin of his forehead. And through it all someone kept calling a name, as if it was his name, but it wasn't. What did they call him? The answer disappeared in his memory, like something dropped into dirty water.

And now, here he was, waking up in this cool dark room with the ventilation whispering around him and someone nearby. He rolled onto his side and looked into the gloom of the hospital room. Someone was in the corner. A woman. Long black hair, her olive face a warm oval in the darkness. It almost looked like—

The woman moved toward him, walking slowly and awkwardly but with enormous determination, as if she could push mountains aside with her willpower. There was only one woman he knew with that strength.

Marianna.

Harold almost felt he was dreaming. But he wasn't. She was there in front of him, walking slowly across the dark room now, her leg braces clicking. She looked down at him, her eyes both sad and angry, and said, "Harold, what have they done to you?"

"I—"

"It's okay now," she said, leaning over him, a tear falling on his face and running off his cheek as if it were his own. She kissed him and laid her lovely cool hand on his forehead. Her touch was magical—knitting the torn flesh, healing the swollen tissue.

"I'm here now, Harold. And I'm going to help you." She kissed him again, her hair hanging fragrant around him, bringing memories of their months together in Chile, how they sometimes spent all morning together in bed. But he felt his guilt rising too, guilt for even considering a relationship with Vikki.

"Who did this to you?" She lightly fingered the stitches on his forehead.

"Some punk."

"Who?"

"This kid stole my car and I—"

"I'll kill him."

"You don't understand. He—"

"He did this to you, I'll kill him." Her voice was cold. "Just tell me one thing."

"What?"

"Have you been faithful?"

"You mean, *to you*?"

"Who else is there?"

He started to answer but—*Panic!* Memories of Vikki in various states of undress gushed into his head like blood at a murder scene. He couldn't lie to Marianna. That was almost worse than betraying her.

"Come on now, Harold, you don't have to think about it, do you? I'm asking a simple question: Did you fuck her?"

"No."

"Did she want you to?"

"Yes. But I—I got away," he blurted out.

She kissed him, not saying anything, her eyes crystallizing into cold points of hatred. She was putting Vikki on the hit list along with the punk that bashed Harold.

"Where is she now?"

"I don't know. I left her at her house and—"

"I'll go talk to her. I'm here to help you, Harold. We'll finish this together."

"*What are you doing here?*" A nurse stood in the doorway, silhouetted by the hall lights.

"Taking care of my husband," Marianna lied. But still, it gave Harold a thrill to hear her say it so naturally like that: *my husband*. "No one else around here seems to be doing a damn thing for him."

Marianna smiled at Harold as if to say, *let's have some fun with her.*

"It's after visiting hours. *Way* after visiting hours. You'll have to wait in the lounge."

Marianna stood, moving carefully.

"My husband has just regained consciousness, and you're kicking me out?"

"You should have come when I first called you."

"Called me?"

"I left you a message—hours ago." Marianna looked at Harold, puzzled. The nurse continued, "This is a very sensitive time for your husband. You'll have to wait in the lobby."

Marianna bent and kissed Harold once more, whispering, "What have you been telling them?"

"I don't know," Harold said, sitting up in bed but—*damn, that hurt!*

"Where are you staying?" he said, clinging to Marianna's hand.

"Nova's. In San Pedro." She pronounced it San *Pee*-dro, the way the locals did.

"Ma'am, do I have to get security?"

Marianna began walking toward the nurse, putting weight on the braced leg, then swinging the other leg around. It was awkward, but she did it with great dignity and the effect was impressive. The nurse watched her approaching uneasily, losing her nerve. As Marianna passed her and proceeded down the hallway, Harold heard Marianna say, *Bitch*, under her breath.

The nurse picked up a phone on the wall, punched a few buttons, and said, "It's Karen in 519. Page Dr. Kumar. And see if the officers are still in the lounge."

The nurse hung up and came toward Harold carrying a clipboard.

Here we go, Harold thought. Doctors, cops, questions. The hospital would turn him over to LA homicide—Gammon and Torres—or Wycoff up in Santa Barbara. Or they'd find the outstanding warrant from last year and . . . This was going to be bad.

"How are you feeling?" The nurse held the clipboard like a shield against her chest.

"Really lousy."

"When they found you you didn't have any identification."

Harold was ready for that. "They got my wallet, those punks."

"What's your name?"

"My name?" Harold asked, scrambling for a good alias.

"Yes."

"Ah, Joe." *Joe? Where did that come from?* Then he remembered the voice calling to him in unconsciousness *Joe . . . Mr. Covo . . .* Sure, that would work. Joe was dead, but that news probably hadn't reached the records department yet.

"Joe?"

"Yes," Harold continued with more conviction. "Joe Covo."

The nurse nodded, smiling. "That's what I told them."

"You did?"

"This was with you when they found you." She held up Joe's file. "Your wallet was gone but we got your wife's number from this. But it doesn't have your insurance information. Who's your prime carrier?"

Need a diversion, Harold thought. "Man, I'm thirsty. Could you get me a drink? Two glasses, please: one with ice and one with just water."

"You have to see the doctor first," the nurse said. "We'll call your employer in the morning for your policy number."

Employer? Joe Covo Matsura. That would let Fallon and the boys know where he was. Harold didn't like the thought of them showing up here. He saw a telephone on his bedside table. He'd better call Vikki and let her know what was happening. It would be a hell of a jolt to get a message that

Joe was alive in the hospital after she had just seen him in the morgue in Santa Barbara.

The sound of a police radio crackled in the hallway. Two officers entered the room, a guy and a lady cop, adjusting the volume on their radios and looking down at Harold.

"It is him, Joe Covo," the nurse said. "I told you it was him."

"I'm Officer Pavlick," said the first cop. She was pretty in an ordinary way, her chest flattened by body armor, sandy hair pinned up. Harold saw her muscled arms were tanned and covered with fine golden hairs.

"My partner and I would like to ask you a few questions."

Harold waited.

In the background the nurse picked up the phone again, saying, "It's Karen in 519. Where's Dr. Kumar?"

"Do you recall the events that lead up to the assault?" the lady cop asked.

"Somewhat . . ."

"Did you know your assailant?"

"The asshole that attacked me?"

"Right."

"Yes," Harold caught himself. "Well, no."

The other cop, the guy, looked at him and said, " 'Yes . . . no?' What's it gonna be?" Harold took an instant dislike to this cop with his narrow face, red hair cut in a flattop.

"I'd seen him before. But I didn't know his name, is what I meant."

"Okay. We'll need a description. But first, can you tell us what prompted this incident?"

Harold started to speak, then laughed. "You're not going to believe this."

"I've been a cop for ten years," Officer Pavlick said, taking out a notepad and pencil from her breast pocket. "I think I've seen just about everything."

"Okay," Harold said. "But it's really bizarre." He noticed the nurse was leaning against the wall listening. He had an audience. He'd better make this good.

"Couple of days ago my car was stolen. The police found it in a driveway up on Gaviota and Seventeenth. In a *driveway*, okay? Now, you'd think that would make the cops just a tiny little bit suspicious, right?"

The two cops looked at each other. The red-haired cop said, "Sir, do you have any idea how many cars are stolen in this city every day?"

Harold ignored him and said, "Anyway. I decided to go there myself, check it out."

"This was a police matter, sir. You shouldn't have taken things into your own hands."

"I had no choice, i.e., the cops wouldn't do it so . . . See, I'm in the car business. And my car's a real cream puff—'64 Impala SS—"

Officer Pavlick snapped her fingers. "You're Joe Covo. Joe Covo Matsura. On the 405 in Torrance. Right?"

Harold nodded casually.

Pavlick looked at her partner. "I knew I knew the name."

Harold felt her attitude changing. He wasn't some crackpot vigilante. He was a man of substance. Hell, he had his name on a big sign by the Freeway. That had to count for something.

"Hey, do you sell any used cars?" she asked.

"We have a huge selection of new and used cars."

"I need a new car. Not a new new car. Just a good used car. Something dependable, you know, something to rat around in."

Harold nodded as if mentally reviewing the cars on his lot.

"This piece of crap I drive," she continued, animated, "it leaks brake fluid on my foot. Eats up my shoes, makes the pedal slippery."

"What're you drivin'?"

"Ford Escort."

Harold nodded. Escorts held a bad connotation for him.

"Why don't you come down to the lot? I'll get you into something for little money down. I'd give you my card but those punks took my wallet." Harold was amazed how easily the sales talk came back; it was a part of his past he just couldn't leave behind him.

"I'd like a two-door. Maybe a hatchback with a moon roof."

The other cop scowled. "Can we get back to this situation? What did you do next, sir?"

"So they stripped my Impala and I knew the parts were in the garage there."

"And how did you know that?" he asked.

"It was real complicated, I looked in there and saw them." Harold felt it was safe to increase his level of sarcasm. "That's when I saw this kid, that attacked me."

"Okay, so you saw him in this garage up on Gaviota and then he followed you and assaulted you."

"There's more," Harold said, realizing he was onto something here; maybe he could get the cops to do some legwork for him. The two cops waited. The nurse was smiling, shaking her head.

"The doors were missing off my car so I thought maybe they'd parted it out. That means they strip it and—"

"I know what it means," the red-haired cop said. "What I don't get is: Why all this for an older beater?"

"If you knew anything about cars you'd know a '64 Impala SS is one of the best cars Detroit ever made. It's a damn collector's item. So anyway, I went to this junkyard in Wilmington—they're all chop shops over there and—"

"And you found the doors?"

"No. That's when I saw this punk."

"What's the name of the place?"

"Auto Export."

Officer Pavlick muttered, "The Third World." The other cop laughed.

"So you gonna bust these guys?" Harold asked.

"Who?"

"Auto Export. It's a chop shop."

"We'll look into it," the other cop said.

" 'Look into it.' What does that mean?"

"It means, we'll look into it. Okay?"

"No. It's not okay. I want my car in one piece again. If you don't do it, I will."

"Sir, I wouldn't advise that," Pavlick said. "We'll take care of this."

Harold knew he should probably be playing good citizen right now. But he had every right to be pissed. He had gotten his head broken because the cops weren't doing their job.

"Officers, please," a doctor said, entering the room. He was a spiffy little guy, Indian or something, with a coffee stain on his white jacket. "Would you please be so kind as to give us a moment before you continue?"

"We got what we need," the red-haired cop said. "Let's go." He walked out.

Officer Pavlick put her pad and pencil away. She handed Harold a card. "Remember about the car. Just something dependable, you know, something to rat around in."

"I'll see what I can do."

She smiled at Harold and left.

The doctor sat on the bed next to Harold, saying, "How are you feeling, Mr. Covo?" The doctor's hands were already moving over his body, probing him here and there, touching the stitches on his forehead, shining that damn light in his eyes again. Why did they do that?

The doctor was listening to his heart and lungs now. Harold lay back, relaxing, enjoying the attention, thinking about his new identity as Joe Covo. Could it backfire on Vikki? Not likely. The nurse would say the woman she had seen in room 519 didn't look at all like the real Vikki Covo. Just another insurance rip-off. Everyone knew insurance fraud was rampant in Southern California.

Then he remembered something else.

"Excuse me, Doctor. What hospital is this?"

"St. Mary's."

Stroke of luck, Harold thought, settling back, thinking of his dad downstairs somewhere. Once he got on his feet again, he'd have to drop in for a little visit, let him know he was working on a plan to get him out of here, move him down to Chile. Once he was there, it would lift his spirits, brighten his final days. Who knows, maybe he'd make a comeback. It's happened before.

Maybe things weren't as bad as they first seemed. Marianna was back, and maybe she could find Vikki. Harold's new identity as Mr. Covo would give him a little freedom to move around. And maybe those two cops might put some heat on the Skuras.

There was just one thing little thing he still had to figure out: How could Mr. Covo disappear before they found out he was actually dead?

When Marianna stood in the living room of Vikki's house she could see light coming through the bullet holes in the wall. Right through the wood and plaster and everything. Anyone that had been standing here would be history, she thought, looking around for some clue about what happened to Vikki and whoever else had been here with her. She knew someone else was here because of the tequila bottle on the kitchen counter and two glasses in the sink.

But the house was empty and the rooms were vacant, just like Harold had said, with all the stuff sold off as if everyone had left for good. She moved from room to room, hearing the unsteady tread of her feet in the still house. The stairs were tough, she had to drag herself up using the banister (pulling her leg up by the cloth of her pants) but it was worth it because she had to see for herself whether maybe Vikki was lying dead up here, hit by one of the bullets.

But she wasn't. The bedroom was as empty as a motel room at checkout time, just the king-sized mattress on the floor with the stained sheets on it, and the walk-in closet with all the expensive clothes and a pile of dirty undies in the corner.

She turned back to the king-sized bed and imagined Harold on it, making love to Vikki in the slow and strong way he had. He said he didn't sleep with Vikki and Marianna mostly believed him. But still she fed this image to her mind because it gave her energy. This bimbo, this dumb blond, fucking her man and doing god knows what other dirty acts with him here in this room. She took a deep breath as if there might be residual odors from their carnal lust. But the air held only the smell of emptiness.

She turned away, thinking how Harold might try to hide things from her, or distort what happened, but he would never lie. That's why she stayed with him. He was playing this game for a higher purpose and, although she thought he was crazy to do it that way, she had to respect him. He was like the kind of man you might dream about having when you were a girl and didn't know jack about the world yet and what pigs men really were. Harold was a man who put you on a pedestal, gave you little gifts, and worshipped you till you wanted to say, *Enough, okay*?

The floor started shaking. *Earthquake*! No, it was the door to the garage below rolling up. She looked out the window and saw a big green Rover coming through the gates at the bottom of the drive and passing Nova's car, where she'd parked it on the street. The Rover came up the hill and disappeared from view into the garage below.

Must be Vikki, Marianna thought, moving through the house, expecting to see her come in at any time. But she didn't, so when Marianna got to the kitchen she pushed open the inside door to the garage and saw a man she didn't recognize leaning into the back of the big Jeep and scrubbing something with a rag. She stood in the open doorway to the kitchen, watching as he put a set of golf clubs inside the rear of the Rover and slammed the door. Then he came around and stood looking at something—a crumpled right front fender. He picked at something. A piece of yellow paint flew off.

The man sensed her standing there and turned.

"Hi there," Marianna said.

He looked at her, wondering how long she had been watching him.

"Didn't see you there," he said, sweeping his blond hair back, then resting his hands on his hips. Marianna saw that he was very thin, the crisp white shirt tucked into a pair of expensive pleated pants, nicely defining his hips.

"I'm looking for Vikki." Marianna's eyes wandered to the crunched fender. Why did that seem significant?

"She's not here right now."

"I see that. Where is she?"

"She went out." A wise-ass smile slowly spread across his face as if they were playing a game they both enjoyed. But then he thought of something and said, "You know, I might see her later. I could give her a message."

"No. I'll come back."

There was silence in the garage, each sensing the other had much more to say.

"I'm sorry, I didn't get your name?" he said, knowing goddamned well she never gave it to him. His smile stretched until it turned crooked at the edges.

"Marianna Perado," she said, watching to see if this meant anything to him.

"I'm Dash." He came forward, extending a hand. She balanced herself carefully as she reached for him, feeling his light grip, a handshake he used to charm the ladies.

He was still standing on the garage floor, two steps below Marianna, but he was as tall as she was. She never trusted very tall men and that rule applied to this snake too. He thought he was so good-looking, he was probably used to having women fall all over him.

"So you're Vikki's husband?" she asked, playing dumb.

"No. No, I'm . . . Actually, she's my client. I'm an insurance agent."

"Is that right?"

"Yes. And how, may I ask, do you know Vikki?"

"Friend of a friend."

"Who's the friend?"

"My, you're nosy for an insurance agent."

He laughed, liking her spunk. "I guess you could say Vikki's more than a client. She's a very close personal friend. I'm investigating a claim for her. So, who's your friend that knows Vikki?"

Nothing ventured, nothing gained, Marianna thought. "Harold Dodge."

"Ah." The name plugged into something Dash needed,

something Marianna knew was important but didn't know why and in what way.

"You know," he said, smiling a big white smile and smoothing his hair back, "this is funny."

"Really. In what way?"

"You're looking for Vikki. I'm looking for Harold Dodge."

"You're right. That is funny. Why do you want Harold?"

"Well, actually, it's confidential."

"I see. Official insurance business."

"Something like that." He liked her messing with him.

"Can I ask if this claim involves Harold?"

"In an indirect way, yes, it does."

They smiled at each other, thinking of possible next steps. Finally, Dash shook his head and laughed quietly, saying, "This is even funnier than I thought."

"How so?"

"I think we both know what we're both talking about."

Quite true, she thought, but I also remember a certain story from last night's news, an item about a driver leaving the scene of a fatal accident, driving away in a green Rover with front end damage. That's a little factoid that is bound to be useful before all this is over.

Total darkness.

She awoke and opened her eyes but couldn't see. Where was she? With great effort she moved her hand, exploring, touching glass, something round—a steering wheel. With her other hand she touched a gear shift knob, one that felt familiar in her hand. She was in her Healey.

The last thing Vikki remembered was being at her house with Dash, drinking tequila and talking and having him push some insurance documents at her. Then drinking and getting crazy on the mattress in her bedroom. Her body felt loose and open. Incredibly loose, to the point where she could hardly move. She stumbled to the phone in the kitchen, but Dash was there, stopping her, asking her questions about Fabian. He carried her back to the mattress, where it all started over again and the incredible pleasure swept over her body like a wave burying her under black water.

Her fingers crept along the armrest until she found the door handle. She opened it and leaned her weight against the door. It moved a few inches, then hit something and stopped. Cool air came in through the door and with it, a stale smell of rust and dirt. *Get out and see where you are.* But she was too weak. Too apathetic. Lie back and rest.

Sometime later (had she slept or passed out?) she awoke and found it was hot and stuffy, the rust smell mixed now with that of fresh-cut lumber she remembered from when Joe added the deck behind their house. The heat built and her throat craved water. Reaching around, she found a glass of water on the dashboard, as if it had been left there for her. It tasted bitter. But it was liquid and the heat was suffocating. So she drank it.

And the darkness rose up and buried her again.

Harold had the phone to his ear, propped up in the hospital bed, checking his voice mail. As he waited for the messages to play, he looked out the window at low clouds that had oozed in from the ocean during the night.

"First message, sent 7:25 P.M.," said the computerized voice. Then Vikki's voice came on the line: "Harold . . . Where are you . . . ?" This was the message he was listening to when they attacked him last night. "You said you'd be back after you got the folder. Look, Dash is here now so don't bring out the files I got from his place. I don't think it'd be too cool if he knew I went through his stuff. Okay? See you soon, I hope."

Dash? What the hell was Dash doing at Vikki's place?

"Second message, sent 9:30 P.M.: "Harold." Her voice sounded excited. "Look, Bobby Skura showed up looking for Dash. I think he thinks Dash did something with Fabian. We've got to make sure—" The phone cut off suddenly.

Harold waited for the last message, hearing his own breath in the receiver, feeling his panic building.

Third message, sent 1:55 A.M.: "Harold . . ." Vikki's voice was slurred, confused. "Harold . . . Where are you?" She was almost crying. "I—He's got me. He's taking me away. I want you here . . . now . . ." Then a man's voice in the background: "Who ya talkin' to, babe?" and the line went dead.

Harold kept listening, hoping somehow he'd missed a message, one that would say everything was all right again. But the line hissed, then cut off. The phone was a dead piece of plastic in his hand. He looked out the window again with that familiar feeling that everything was falling apart. Sunlight was overdue. Maybe it was out there somewhere. But it was seeming more and more like an impossibility.

"We spoke with your employer," said an unyielding voice.

Harold turned and found a new nurse by his bed. Her name tag read *Grace, Rn.*

Harold waited, still thinking of Vikki, out there somewhere.

"We spoke to a Mr. Fallon. He told us you've been missing for some time."

"*Missing*? In what way?" It was all he could think of at the moment.

"*Missing*, as in, you disappeared. He said there was a police investigation—they thought you had been murdered."

"Murdered? Oh, you talked to Fallon, right? Eddie Fallon?" Harold laughed, as if that explained it all.

"Yes."

"Is he at the office yet?"

"We reached him at home. But he said he was going to his office to get the records."

"Lemme give him a call." Harold reached for the phone with an I'll-get-this-cleared-up tone of voice. The nurse kept standing there so he added: "I'll ring you when I get an answer."

She slowly left the room.

Checkout time, Harold thought, pulling the I.V. out of his arm and sticking it into the mattress below him. Harold quietly moved past his sleeping roommate in the circled curtains and closed the door on early morning hospital sounds and the approaching smell of another mushy meal. He found his clothes in a paper bag on the closet shelf. Everything was there, even his beeper. But as he put on his shirt he found the collar and shoulders were covered with his blood. That might be a tip-off that he was leaving a little earlier than his health care practitioner advised.

Looking through a gap in the curtains, Harold saw his roommate was a heavyset man, maybe sixty, and he might be roughly his height. Not a bad fit, he thought, slipping on the man's shirt. Little tight in the shoulders maybe, but it would do. Harold's nose rebelled at the man's strong odor but he knew that, with the day he had planned, his own scent would soon be the dominant smell.

Digging deeper into the man's possessions he found a baseball hat with a Caterpillar logo on the front. Opening the plastic snap on the back of the hat, Harold found he could pull the hat down to hide the bandages on his head. Harold stuffed a ten dollar bill in the man's pants pocket for the things he was taking.

All set to go. Better disappear before Fallon came down to the hospital to see if Joe was really alive.

Wait a second, Harold thought. There might be a nice opportunity here. One he didn't see at first. Fallon and Dash were in this together—with Fabian and Bobby. That meant Fallon might know where Dash was and that would lead him to Vikki. Hell, he might even know where the missing door for the Impala was. There were a lot of things Fallon knew. And he would damn sure tell them to his boss, Joe Covo. The same Joe Covo who had made a surprising reappearance, showing up in St. Mary's Hospital, Room 519, with only a minor head injury.

Harold sat on the edge of his bed and opened Joe's file. Here was the number for Joe Covo Matsura. He dialed. *Recording, damn!* They weren't open yet. Harold was about to hang up when the recording was interrupted. A man's voice came on the line.

"Eddie?"

"Who's this?"

"Joe." Harold lowered his voice and made it gruff, the way he remembered Joe from his days working there.

"Joe? *Joe Covo?*"

"Right."

"Jesus, Joe. They called me from the hospital but I couldn't believe it."

"Believe it, Eddie." He felt a little silly doing this. But it seemed to be working.

"Where you been? I still can't believe—"

"I'll explain when I see you."

"You don't sound too good."

"I'm not too good. I'm in the hospital, remember?"

"Hey, well, welcome back, okay?" Fallon wasted no time sucking up to the boss again. What a kiss-ass.

"Eddie, listen. Dash fucked us up—royally. Okay?"

"How do you mean?"

"We still runnin' cars through Auto Export?" Harold was guessing now.

"Yeah . . ."

"Now listen to me. Dash is the one, okay? Where is he?"

"I don't know, Joe. I heard Bobby's lookin' for him too."

"Bobby?"

"Bobby Skura. He thinks Dash took out Fabian."

"Do something for me, okay, Eddie?"

"Name it."

"Find out where I can get Dash."

"*Get* him?"

"You heard me."

"He's comin' in with some papers later. He sent—" Fallon stopped, thinking of something. "Joe, did you know Dash is hooked up with—with Vikki?"

"Why the fuck you think I'm looking for him?"

"Oh. Right." Fallon was still putting it together. "Joe, I don't know if Dash is the one. I think maybe it's this guy Dodge."

"*What?*" Harold almost forgot to make his voice sound like Joe.

"He came in with Vikki. I called this buddy of mine, a cop. He said Dodge is bad news—they want him for two homicides last year up by the airport."

"Know where to find him? This Dodge?"

"I got some guys looking for him now."

Harold saw the door opening. Was Grace Rn getting impatient waiting for him?

"Gotta go." But Harold couldn't stop himself from adding, "Hey, Eddie, get your shit out of my office, okay?"

"You got it, Joe."

Harold hung up, backing out of sight behind the curtain as a nurse entered pushing a cart.

The smell of overcooked food invaded the room and he heard the nurse saying to his roommate, "Ready for a little breakfast, Mr. Gomes?" in that singsong voice they think cheers people up. The sleeping man gurgled, then began coughing.

Harold checked to make sure the nurse was still occupied with Mr. Gomes. He slipped past her and headed out into the corridor.

It was one of those attitude things, Harold thought. If you believed something strongly, people would pick up on that, and leave you alone. Like now, he thought, stepping off the elevator and walking toward his father's room. He was just a patient visiting another patient he'd made friends with. Nothing unusual about that.

Ahead, down the long hallway, Harold saw a nurse wheeling a laundry basket out of his father's room. For some reason the sight made him feel panicky. He reached the room and stepped through the door now, moving inside, his alarm building. The bed where his father had been was empty. The curtains were open and the flat light of an overcast day illuminated the room.

Harold's legs felt shaky and he thought they might give out. And it was then he realized how much he wanted to see his father. And how he wasn't ready to say good-bye.

"Can I help you?" A nurse stood beside him, looking at him strangely.

"The guy in this room, Sam Dodge. What happened to him?"

The nurse looked at Harold, seeing how pale he was. "Sir, are you all right?"

"Did he go home? The guy who was in here. Did he go home, or—?"

"Are you family?"

"Just, just a friend." It felt lame when he said it, and it must have sounded that way to the nurse too. The nurse reached for the phone. He backed out saying, "I'll check again later . . ."

He ducked into the elevator, trying to get the attitude back, trying not to think of that empty bed and what it might mean. Maybe his brother, Randy, took him home. Or an ambulance. They do that sometimes, bring medical junk into the house, get it all set up.

He found himself on the ground floor, outside the emergency room. That was fortunate. He'd blend in with all the other bandaged gimpers here. He found a pay phone on a wall and dialed his father's number. No answer. But that didn't mean anything, either. If they were just cleaning his hospital room, that means he just left. He'd call later.

To distract himself he worked on his attitude again. He began thinking about the miracle of modern medicine, about how even a person as seriously injured as himself could be treated on an out-patient basis and released. Thinking this, he wandered out onto the loading dock outside ER and stood there for a few moments, seeing the sun was breaking through, the wind was moving in the palm trees. He nodded to a paramedic team loading a gurney into the back of an ambulance. Looking around, as if waiting for a ride, he slowly wandered away, and Joe Covo was last seen walking south on Atlantic Boulevard.

Several blocks later, Harold realized he was no longer thinking like Joe Covo. He'd left him behind at the hospital. He was thinking like Harold Dodge again, and Harold Dodge was in a hell of a jam. But he had the beginning of a good idea. He'd call Sergeant Wycoff in Santa Barbara and offer him the chance to bust a major auto theft and insurance fraud ring. All he had to do was come down and take Harold's statement—without arresting him. It might work. And if it did, he would have all sorts of good news for Vikki—once he found her.

Dash opted for street parking and moved through the new cars on the lot and into the showroom of Joe Covo Matsura. He moved past salesmen bullshitting about the NBA playoffs, past the receptionist doing the Jumble in the morning paper, past the demos and floor models, down the long hallway and through to the heavy wooden door.

Eddie Fallon was standing at the big desk putting his things in a cardboard box.

"Finally shit-canned you?"

Fallon looked up: "Dash! No. Never felt right in this office."

"Ghosts?"

Fallon looked at him, startled. "Something like that."

"Got the papers on that Accell." Dash settled into a chair.

"Outstanding." Fallon crossed behind Dash and closed the door, then returned to sit at the desk. His salesman eyes read Dash like a prospect.

"Lookin' a little rough there, Dash. You goin' native?"

Dash stroked his chin. He'd forgotten to shave. "Yah. Goin' native, mon. Goin' back to de islands."

Fallon laughed, then let it die, studying Dash, tapping his half glasses on the desk.

"You know, Dash, your name's been comin' up a lot lately."

"In what context?"

"Bobby's lookin' for you."

"He's got this thing about people owe him money."

"I heard there was more to it. I heard he thinks you took out Fabian." He watched Dash closely as he laid it out there.

"I took out Fabian?" Dash laughed. "Get real. Me? You don't believe that, do you?"

"Doesn't matter what I believe. That's what Bobby thinks. He keeps calling me, says, 'Dash was the last one to see him.' Now he tells me the cops found Fabian's Suburban in the parking lot of the Mardi Gras. What's he supposed to think?"

"This is so bizarre." Dash laughed as if it was just one of those weird things that was hard to understand but actually happened. Vikki had told him she dumped Fabian down in Baja. But how could he explain all that? Then he remembered Fabian standing there, watching the fishing boat head out into the dark. He remembered how Bobby had paused when he said Fabian went fishing, like he'd really swallow that story. Maybe it would work again, with a little ad-libbing thrown in to make it believable.

"Okay. You want to know what happened? I'll tell you. I'm havin' a few beers, watching the playoffs, and Fabian shows up. He goes, *Can you give me a ride*? I go, *Sure*. We get underway, turns out he wants to go down to Baja, okay? Fishin'. You know how he loves that yellowtail. And he doesn't want anyone to know where he is. On the drive down he's goin'. *I'm sick of LA, I'm sick of Bobby shoving me around, I'm sick of my wife*. And I'm, like, not listening, you know, just going, like, *yeah, okay, whatever*, not thinking how it could backfire on me. I get back and, suddenly I'm like this killer or something."

"What're you goin' do about this situation?"

"Go down and find Fabian. Tell him, 'Come on, man, give your brother a call, get him off my back.' "

"When?"

"Just cleanin' up a little business before I head out."

Fallon was tapping his glasses again. "Ya know, Dash, I might be able to help smooth things over with Bobby. Let me tell him I talked to you and you're workin' on the problem."

"'preciate it, Eddie."

"When I get Bobby back in his kennel, I'll give you a call. Where can I reach you?" Fallon picked up a pen, held it poised.

"Cell phone, beeper. You got my numbers."

"Know where you'll be stayin' down there?"

"In Baja?"

"Yeah. In Baja."

Dash paused, reading Fallon the way Fallon was reading him. And as he did, images of the night before flickered through his tired brain, images of Vikki in front of him, groping in her jumbled memory as he questioned her in the kitchen, asking her where Fabian was.

It took Dash about ten seconds to assess the situation, assess the impact of giving and receiving information, who would be hurt and who would profit from the knowledge he held like a good poker hand, and finally he reached a conclusion and said, "La Fonda. I always go to La Fonda. Place between Rosarito Beach and Ensenada, forty miles south of the border."

Smiling, Fallon wrote the name on the blotter. Without looking up he said, "What you know about this Harold Dodge character?"

"Harold Dodge?"

"He was in here with Vikki Covo yesterday. Figured you must know him."

"Met him a few times. Don't know much about him. Why?"

"Know where I can find him?"

"No." Dash thought about it. "But I might be able to find out for you."

"Do that. It'd be worth a few bills."

Fallon picked up the Accell papers, waved them at Dash, and looked over the tops of his glasses. "When's Bobby's crew gonna pick up this car?"

"To be arranged." Dash stood up. "Thanks for your help, man. Talk to you soon."

Fallon watched Dash disappear down the hallway, then out into the showroom. He picked up the phone and punched a button on his speed dialer. A man's voice answered.

"Got some intelligence concerning our friend."

"Where is he?"

"Leaving the dealership. But I thought you might like to know where he's heading."

"Yeah, I would." Eddie imagined Bobby's face, a predatory smile slowly growing. "I'd like that very much."

Leaning on the adult video rack in the air-conditioned liquor store, Harold looked out the window, watching for a car to pull into the parking lot, a car he assumed would be one of those boaty unmarked sedans the cops drove. At the wheel would be Sergeant Wycoff from the Santa Barbara Coroner's office. He was due any minute. But before then, Harold hoped to squeeze in a quick phone call. Only problem was, some three-hundred-pound lady in a housecoat was hogging the phone.

Harold moved his eyes between the fat lady on the pay phone and Vikki's silver Accell, still parked at the curb, the sinking sun reflecting in the windshield. He was thinking of getting his wallet from under the floor mats and buying a nice cold drink, a beer maybe, and pouring it down onto a handful of aspirins, see if he could stop the pounding in his head.

But there was a problem with retrieving his wallet. He couldn't forget Fallon's ugly voice: "It's this Dodge . . . I got a couple guys lookin' for him."

Who were these *guys lookin' for him*? Bobby Skura and his Boy Scout troop? They knew the Accell was parked here by the liquor store. They might be watching it right now. From the Club Cheri maybe . . . ? A parked car . . . ?

Harold remembered how Bobby looked last night, standing nearby, hands on his hips, laughing as he watched Harold get the shit beat out of him in a little two-on-one action. Recalling this, Harold felt the anger working in his gut, making his cracked skull throb like it might explode.

Harold toyed with the idea of heading over to Auto Export, his identity concealed by the Caterpillar hat and those old-guy sunglasses that covered most of your face. He'd innocently inquire about some junker in a remote part of the yard, then head over there with Bobby, and when Bobby was looking down into the engine, Harold would nail him right on the bald spot with a half-inch-drive torque wrench.

Harold came back from the scene, finding himself still in the liquor store leaning on an XXX video called *2 Hot 2 Handle* and watching the pay phone and thinking, yeah, that would be a cheap shot, but it sure would be fun. But he had to look at the big picture. He had a number of problems here, and they were all wound up in his dad's stolen Chevy. When they went to see Dash about Joe's life insurance policy, and his car was stolen, everything started to unravel. So he figured if he could put his dad's cream puff back together, he could work some magic on the other fronts too. That's why he had called Santa Barbara P.D. and convinced Wycoff to come down to take his statement.

And Wycoff was due any minute. Wycoff had agreed to hear what Harold had learned about a major auto theft and insurance fraud ring. What Harold didn't tell Wycoff was that he intended to prove his allegations by retrieving his last remaining car door from Auto Export. He would get his parts, clear the arrest warrants, and, with luck, wreak havoc on the punks that beat him up—all in one class move, as Vikki might say.

"And you won't arrest me," Harold said to Wycoff when they talked on the phone that morning. "That's part of the deal."

"I won't arrest you," Wycoff answered slowly. "If this tip on the chop shop pans out, I'll tell the D.A. you're playing ball with us. Beyond that, I can't promise anything."

"But you won't arrest me," Harold repeated.

"I won't arrest you," the cop said, choosing his words carefully.

The fat lady finally hung up the phone and shuffled away in her slippers, hands deep in her housecoat pockets, back to whatever nightmare apartment she crawled out of. Time to make one more call, Harold thought, moving out into the glare, crossing the parking lot, walking across the very spot where the paramedics worked on him last night, seeing the wrappers for the bandages underfoot, a discarded needle, the dark stains in the asphalt, remembering the beating and feeling his anger feeding him what he needed to pick up the phone and—

Who should he call first?

He dialed his father's number. Still no answer. He might be in bed. Couldn't get to the phone. Harold started getting that shaky feeling again. He quickly dialed again.

Seconds later: "Eddie Fallon."

"Get what I need?"

"Joe . . . That you?"

"Yeah. Find Dash?"

"I said I would, didn't I? But first, you got to tell me what the hell this is—"

"Later, okay? Now just give it to me. Where is he?"

"Headin' down to Baja."

"Baja?"

"Place called La Fonda. South of Rosarito. And let me tell you, it wasn't easy gettin' it out of him."

"What about the other?"

"Other what?"

"Dodge. What about him?"

"All I know is, couple of Bobby's guys caught him last night, stomped him pretty good. Bobby's checkin' hospitals now to see if—Hang on, this is him. Gotta put you on hold."

Click. Hold music. Think fast, Harold told himself. Think of something in case they know who you are. Or just hang up if it looks like—

Eddie' voice came back on the line. "Uh, Joe?" His voice was different, not kiss-ass anymore. Did he know? "Bobby's got something to tell you."

"What?"

"Can't tell you on the phone."

"Tell me, Eddie."

"Sorry."

Fallon knew. He wasn't dead sure, but he was damn suspicious.

"Look, Joe," he said *Joe* like it was a joke now, "we gotta meet. You name it, we'll be there. We'll take care of Dash, get everything straightened out."

"What about Dodge? Bobby find him?"

"No word on him yet."

Harold thought of Wycoff, thought of their little mission

over to Auto Export. It would go easier if Bobby wasn't around. Maybe this was a chance to send him off on a bogus meeting, get them out of the picture.

"Okay, Eddie. But it better be good. Signal Hill. Right under the radio towers. Be there in an hour." Harold hung up, turned, and saw a dark green sedan signaling for a turn into the parking lot. Big Chrysler Le Baron, the kind cops use for unmarked cars. The fiery sunset was bright on the windshield as it pulled into the lot and Harold couldn't see inside. Could be Wycoff. Could even be Bobby. Time to find out.

Harold moved toward the car and opened the door.

Marianna was parked across from the Lighthouse Motel in Huntington Beach when she saw the big green Rover pull out of the parking lot, find an opening in traffic, and head north on PCH. Dash was alone in the Rover. That meant he had left Vikki in the room. Time to go and get her. See if she was okay (see if she was even alive). After what Marianna had seen earlier, she wasn't sure what the hell she was going to find.

Marianna had been following Dash all afternoon, trying to find out where Vikki was. And right away she saw that Dash was one busy boy, running errands all over town. And they weren't the sort of errands that a legit insurance agent would be doing.

First stop: Joe Covo Matsura. Dash glided into the dealership and disappeared down the long hallway toward Joe's office. That meant he was paying a visit to the head honcho—whoever it was now.

Sitting across from the dealership in the car she borrowed from Nova, she realized she had returned to the source of the problem. This is where it all started nine months ago, where she innocently came to buy a good reliable car and soon found her life was spinning out of control, as if she had opened a door that released evil into her world. She wasn't a bad person, a criminal, but she had been on the dark side of the law ever since she bought that car last year.

After Dash left the dealership he headed for the harbor. She watched from a distance as the Rover disappeared behind a stack of those big boxes—what do they call them—cargo containers? The kind they unload from ships, then put on tractor trailer trucks. When he drove out a few minutes later, he had a passenger, a flash of yellow hair catching the last rays of the day.

It was Vikki. And Vikki didn't look so hot. Dash kept trying to prop her head up on the headrest but it would flop over and bump on the window as they pulled out of the dirt lot and got back on the Terminal Island Freeway. Marianna guessed that Dash was controlling Vikki for the same reason Harold was after her—he wanted all that dough she was coming into. But he was taking a more direct approach, keeping her prisoner somehow, stashing her one place, then finally moving her to this hotel on PCH.

And now that Dash was gone off on yet another errand it was time for Marianna to find out what was going on. She found a parking space and stepped out of her car. Nearby, a maid was pushing a cart loaded with towels and sheets.

"Señora? I have a question for you," Marianna said, approaching the maid. The woman turned, confused, shaking her head to show she didn't speak English.

Marianna began again in Spanish, saying, "I'm trying to help a friend who is staying here." She paused dramatically, then said, "I believe she may be in danger."

"Danger? What kind of danger?" It sounded like the woman was from Mexico City. Marianna adjusted her accent accordingly.

"Domestic abuse. Her husband is a pig—beats her all day. You might have seen her come in. She's blond."

The maid's eyes lit up. "Very light? Very blond?"

"Yes. Probably dyed."

"Oh, yes, I saw them. She could not walk without help."

Marianna nodded. "What room are they in?"

The maid hesitated, nervous, but said, "Room 39, I think."

"Take me there please, Señora," Marianna said. Moments later, they stood in front of the door. Marianna knocked. No answer.

"Open it please, Señora," Marianna said firmly.

The woman shook her head and moaned. "Ohhhh. I could get in so much trouble."

"She can't go to the police. The last time she did that her husband tortured her with a cigarette."

The woman moaned again, shaking her head. But she reached into her housekeeping coat pocket and pulled out the key. The door slowly opened.

It was dark inside. Marianna moved into the room, sweeping a hand along the wall and turning on a dim hallway light. She listened and felt for movement. TV sounds came through the walls. PCH was a rushing river of traffic in the distance and, yes, she could hear surf across the beach.

Two white blocks took shape in the gloom—double beds. Both were empty. Marianna turned on a lamp on a bedside table. Protruding from behind the beds were legs—legs in blue jeans. The legs were motionless.

Marianna cautiously moved toward the end of the room and stood looking down at Vikki Covo, the beauty, the bimbo, the killer blonde, sprawled on the floor, her golden hair spilled around her. And she was startled to see that Vikki's eyes were open and they were staring at her. It was as if she were both dead and alive at the same time.

"What are you doing?" Marianna asked.

"Trying to leave." Her voice was as dead as ashes. A moment of silence, then Vikki added: "You're Marianna Perado."

"Are you hurt?"

"I try to walk, I keep falling down. He drugged me."

Looking down at this former beauty, more helpless than even herself on her treacherous legs, Marianna actually felt a flicker of sympathy, which was completely unexpected. This woman was no competition now. She was debased and humiliated and nearly destroyed. Another victim in this sad parade of misery.

"I've come to help you," Marianna said. She remembered the maid was still there and said, "Help me get her on the bed."

They bent over her, smelling urine and earthy moisture. When they got her on the bed Marianna said to the maid, "You have been very helpful and I thank you. But you must go now."

The maid protested, but Marianna backed her out the door. She returned and sat beside Vikki on the bed. They looked at each other for a long time in silence.

"Do you really want to help me?" Vikki asked.

"No, but I will."

"Why? The money?"

"Yes."

A terrible look filled Vikki's eyes and she turned her head away. It was the first movement she had made, showing Marianna how limited her ability for motion was. She could barely turn her head, let alone stand and walk out to the car or hide in an adjacent room where Dash wouldn't find her. No, Marianna would have to come back with Harold to get her.

"I'm so thirsty," Vikki said.

Marianna found a glass of water on the beside table and was about to help her drink it. She sniffed the water. She held it up and saw sediment. In the bathroom she refilled the glass, noticing a man's shaving kit on the back of the toilet tank. When she returned to the bed, she was carrying a hairbrush. She helped Vikki drink. Then she took Vikki's blond hair in her hands and began brushing it. It was thick and full and silky, like the tassel on an ear of corn.

"When I was a girl," Vikki began, "I wanted black hair, like yours."

Marianna kept brushing, trying to decide if she believed her.

"Everyone in my family had blond hair and I wanted to be different."

Marianna thought there might be some truth to what she said.

"What's this asshole going to do with you?"

"Take me to Baja."

"Why?"

"Says he's looking for someone down there."

Marianna thought about that as she kept brushing. She had most of the tangles out and there was a glossy look to her hair that caught the light of the weak lamp. Looking down at this woman, like a life-sized doll, Marianna saw that she had made her beautiful again, although she was broken. A gorgeous corpse.

"Harold is mine."

Vikki didn't answer at first, then her expression clouded and she said, "Where is Harold?"

Marianna ignored that. She was feeling in control again with each new piece of information she got.

"I know what you tried to do to Harold."

Vikki looked confused.

"You wanted to fuck him."

She seemed to recall that, distantly.

"That was a mistake on your part. A very big mistake." The brush was caught on a stubborn tangle. She pulled hard. Vikki's eyes closed in pain.

"Harold is a good man. But even a good man can be unfaithful without wanting to. Touch him again, I'll kill you." There, that tangle was finally gone. Marianna removed a big clump of hair from the brush.

There was something like anger in Vikki's eyes as she thought all this through from her point of view, perhaps thinking how, if it hadn't been for Marianna, walking into her husband's dealership, she would still be a trophy wife, living in a mansion on a hill. But times had changed, Joe Covo had been killed, and a cloud had settled over sunny Los Angeles.

They were silent so long Marianna began to realize Dash might return. She got to her feet, trying not to let Vikki see how she struggled to stand.

"Don't leave." Vikki had that lost little girl look again.

"I'll be back soon. And I'll help you."

Marianna stood looking down at the face lying in golden silk on the pillow.

Vikki's eyes held something like sadness and dread, but disconnected, as if the sadness was for someone else, or for the self she had once been.

"He's going to take me down there . . ."

"Where?"

"Baja. He says he's looking for someone down there. But I know why he's really taking me there."

Marianna felt a chill, a sudden physical chill, and wondered if she were under an air-conditioning vent. Or was it that door opening again, the one that brought so much death into her life?

"What's he going to do?" Marianna asked, not wanting to hear the answer. Because she already knew it.

"Kill me."

Marianna stood, thinking, *Get me out of here.*

But she couldn't stop looking in Vikki's eyes, wide now with horror as she said, "I have these pictures in my head—I see myself by the road, lying there dead. I have these pictures in my head . . ."

Marianna was backing away from her, shaking her head, wanting to say something, but feeling the cold all around her, in the room, filling the world.

"Get me away from him . . . please," Vikki moaned lifelessly. "I'll never come back from Baja."

"**A** car door? You got me down here to help you find a car door?"

"That's right," Harold told Wycoff, riding south on Orange Street. "But it's not just any door." *For one thing it's my door,* Harold thought. "It was stolen off my car and I know where it is. That'll prove the place I'm talking about is a chop shop. Here, turn right here."

They came around the corner onto Ocean and saw the long boulevard open up in front of them with palm trees and glass office buildings and the bridge in the distance ready to carry them over into the harbor.

"I'm glad you called me," Wycoff was saying, splitting his attention between the road and Harold, his cop eyes taking in his hat, the bandages, his bloodshot eyes. "I'm anxious to clear this thing up. So I arranged to have two detectives meet us there."

Harold's heart jumped. "There? Where?"

"The address you gave me—Auto Export."

"You said you wouldn't arrest me."

"I won't. But I'm not walking into some chop shop alone. These guys want to hear what you have to say. Maybe you can make a deal with them."

"My deal's with you."

"Listen, Harold, I'll be quite frank with you. I know you had some serious problems last year in LA. Now I'm gonna do everything I can to help you. But if you're dirty, and you try to hold out on me, that's it, I'm done with you."

Harold sunk down in his seat. *Detectives.* Who were these cops they were meeting? And how believable a witness would he make, dressed in Mr. Gomes's hat and shirt, bandages holding his cracked skull together? He had thought Wycoff would be the easy route. Now he seemed like any other hard-assed cop. He even had on his gun and badge, not like when he had seen him in the coroner's office three days ago.

It was time to take action, Harold thought. He tried to assume a new attitude, like he was a tax-paying citizen who knew his rights and had nothing to hide. He would try to throw this whole thing back on Wycoff.

"You closed the investigation on Covo yet?"

Wycoff sneered. "How could we? We got no witnesses to the shooting. We don't know how his body got there."

"But you can rule out suicide—i.e., there was no gun next to the body."

"He was washed downstream. Maybe there's a gun near where he pulled the trigger. I mean, he's not exactly going to blow his brains out, then put the gun back in his pocket. That's not how it works, Harold." He laughed at the impossibility of what he said.

Harold looked over at Wycoff and hated him deeply. Hated him for making it all so difficult, hated him most of all for showing him what he had become: a cheap criminal, mixing lies and truths until he could hardly remember what had really happened.

They were on the Vincent Thomas Bridge now, the Le Baron moving easily up the steep slope, their view of the South Bay enlarging by the second until, yes, there were the buildings of downtown LA, shadowy in the hazy dusk.

"I got a very simple question for you, Harold. And I want you to answer it truthfully. Will you do that for me?"

Harold's attempt to turn the tables on Wycoff was losing steam.

"Why wouldn't I?"

"Did you dump Covo's body there by the stream, Harold?"

This was easier than he thought: "No."

"Then who did? That's the person we're after."

Marianna.

The name jumped into his mind so loudly he was worried Wycoff could hear it. To make matters worse he realized that Marianna was now in danger. When he started all this she was safely tucked away in Chile. Now she was up here, in the thick of things.

They were coming over the top of the bridge now and starting down. The Terminal Island Freeway was visible ahead. Five minutes from Auto Export now.

"Let's get this done first," Harold said. "Then I'll tell you everything."

"Will you, Harold?"

"That's the deal. You get me my car parts—I'll tell you what I know."

Wycoff was looking around now, suddenly quiet, sobered by what he saw, the desolate landscape of corrugated tin shacks, junkyards, the underside of freeway ramps, and now, moving into the Third World, the chain-link-fenced yards of cargo containers. And, living among this chaos, broken human beings crawling like worms through garbage, ragged men and women sleeping in drainpipes and sharing bottles in paper bags.

At the end of the block he saw the big gates of Auto Export, the stacked, stripped cars, the massive warehouse, and the yellow mountain of sulfur looming behind, the bulldozer, as always, struggling up the slope, moving forward, then sliding back, never really getting anywhere.

"What're we getting into here, Harold?" Wycoff's voice was tight.

"Little different than Santa Barbara." Harold couldn't resist needling him.

They were bumping forward on the rutted road, the dirt baked hard as cement, the big Chrysler rocking on its springs.

Moving through the chain-link gates now and into the parking lot, the black rectangle of the warehouse door like an open mouth pulling them in. Three cars were parked in the lot. What did Bobby drive? Did he take the bait and run off to meet Joe Covo on Signal Hill? Or was he inside waiting for them?

Wycoff killed the ignition, looked around saying, "So we're looking for doors. Is that it?"

"Yeah. For a '64 Impala."

They got out, Wycoff muttering, I *can't believe this* . . . , as he pulled on a dark sport coat, letting it fall down and cover the gun on his hip in the worn leather holster.

Starting toward the dark interior of the warehouse now, Harold tried to keep in his mind the picture of his '64 Impala SS the way he had first seen it—showroom perfect, the new car smell, paint job waxed and buffed, the engine purring under the hood with solid power. It could be like that again soon, Harold thought. But then he looked up and saw the sun was down behind the Palos Verdes Peninsula to the west, where Vikki's house was, and it reminded him how many things that had started so well, had gone so wrong.

When Gammon exited off the Terminal Island Freeway and they hit the streets, he looked around and said, "Jesus, what a cesspool. You'd think we were in Mexico or something."

There was a cold silence in the car and Gammon looked at his partner, Torres, and added, "Sorry, Richard. You know what I mean."

They looked around at the scrap metal yards and rusted auto bodies and the groups of men on the street corners who looked away sensing they were cops. Gammon said, "I see why they call it the 'Third World.' "

Torres had the *Thomas Guide* open on the seat and said, "Who patrols this? Wilmington?"

"Which is to say no one patrols it." Gammon's big laugh filled the car, then he added, "I guess the Sheriff's in charge here."

"Shall we call them?"

"For what?"

"Backup."

"That kind of backup we don't need. Besides, we're just here for a meet, right? Bird Dog's got some story about stolen cars and chop shops and we're here to listen."

Torres put on his gimme-a-break expression.

"The judge said we could use the Remy warrant if we had to."

"*Had to?*"

"If we couldn't talk him in."

"You think the Bird Dog's gonna let himself get talked in?"

Gammon swore, then laughed. "I just thought of something. The Bird Dog's gonna sing. Get it? Bird dog? Sings?"

"Here it is."

But Gammon missed the turn through the chain-link fence into Auto Export.

"I'll circle the block."

They scanned the lot as they cruised by. Pickup truck, Crown Victoria, a couple of Toyotas.

"What's Bird Dog driving these days?"

"Wycoff's bringing him over. He's in a green Chrysler."

Turning the corner they saw an enormous pile of something yellow with a conveyor belt piling on more yellow all the time. The sun was low over the Palos Verdes Peninsula and the flat light made the yellow mountain stand out unnaturally against the darkening sky.

"The natural wonders of Los Angeles," Gammon said. "Shit."

They watched as a bulldozer climbed the yellow mountain, the diesel laboring.

Torres would never admit it to Gammon, but the area did make him feel he was back in Mexico, along Via del Pacifico as it climbed into the mountains above Tijuana. He lived there till he was ten, then moved north across the border to Boyle Heights in LA to be with his mother. He still had a brother in TJ somewhere. Every once in a while he thought of trying to find him, bring him up here, get him set up in some kind of a job—maybe painting houses, landscaping. . . .

Torres found himself retracing the coincidences that brought him to this place. Chance. Fate. Was it just chance that he was a cop in LA while his brother was a junkie living in a shack in TJ? Or was there something more to all this?

They came around the block and saw a green Chrysler rolling through the chain-link fence, two guys inside.

"Hey, really, let's get some backup."

"You want some deputies riding in on their horses and spooking him? All we got's this bogus Remy so we're gonna have to talk him in. Besides, the Bureau knows where we are."

"Gammon, you always were, and always will be, nothing more than a fuckin' cowboy."

They were watching the Chrysler now, a guy getting out, hat and a loose shirt.

Gammon laughed. "There's our man, in disguise as usual. Let's go hear the Bird Dog sing."

Bobby was on the phone in his office when Harold came through the door with Wycoff.

Bobby said, "Hang on," cupped the receiver and said to them: "Yeah? What do you want?" Recognition was showing in his eyes as he looked at Harold but with the hat pulled low he didn't place him.

"You can start by giving me my damn car parts back," Harold said, seeing Bobby was actually here, not on top of Signal Hill like he thought he'd be, but suddenly glad he was here because something was rising inside him, seeing the smug asshole again, remembering his stripped car and the beating he took in the liquor store parking lot. And the pain. The pain that was still splitting his head apart. *Cool down*, he thought. He knew he had to handle this carefully. What he really felt like doing was cutting the guy apart with a welding torch.

He heard Wycoff say, "Easy, Harold. Wait for the others."

Bobby put the phone on the desk and moved toward them, hands on his hips, belligerent, saying, "Do I know you?"

"You should by now. You stole my damn car. And did this to me." Harold lifted his hat and pointed to his bandaged skull, which was beginning to pound again with the pressure building inside him. Maybe the top of his head would blow right off.

Bobby looked at Wycoff and said, "What the hell's he talking about?"

Wycoff started to say something but Harold rolled over him saying, "I want to see all the parts you have for a '64 Impala four-door automatic. And I want to see them right fucking *now*."

His hands still on his hips, Bobby laughed and said, "You're nuts. Get out of my shop."

"Maybe I'm nuts," Harold said. "But you're gonna have cops crawling all over your ass in about two seconds."

Bobby stepped in, saying to Wycoff: "You better get your pal out of here before I kick his ass."

Wycoff held up his shield: "Police officer."

Harold loved the way Bobby reacted, stepping back slightly and making little sputtering noises as he tried to get out a question.

Someone was approaching. Harold turned and saw a guy in a grimy jumpsuit beside him. Other workers were coming out of the darkness around them, welding masks tilted up, body hammers and pry bars in their hands.

A booming voice behind them said, "All right!" and Harold turned to see a big man coming in out of the dark, in through the open garage door wearing a flannel shirt and cowboy boots. He thought he knew the voice and then, as light fell on his face, he saw he knew the man. It was Gammon with Torres behind him.

"Oh, Jesus," Harold said turning to Wycoff. "You screwed me, didn't you?"

"They're gonna listen to you. They said they'd listen. You want to get this cleared up, don't you?"

"Who're you?" Bobby was saying, looking up at the big man.

"Gammon, LAPD. This is Detective Torres." He looked around at the audience, then back to Bobby. "You in charge here?"

"I own this place, yeah."

"Can we step into your office please, sir?"

"Why?"

"We have something to straighten out between you and Mr. Dodge here. And it would be best to do that in private."

Maybe they're really here to get to the bottom of this, Harold hoped for one brief shining moment, but almost immediately discarded the idea. They'd give his gripe lip service, then pull out the cuffs.

"This doesn't have anything to do with me." Bobby said, acting tough in front of his guys.

"Mr. Dodge says otherwise." He turned to Harold. "Isn't that right, Chief?"

"They stole my damn car and stripped it."

"Bullshit," Bobby said.

"Then he followed me and did this—" Harold lifted the hat again.

Bobby stepped toward Harold. "You're out of your fuckin' mind."

Torres moved between them, saying, "Okay . . . That's enough."

The workers pressed in tighter.

Gammon looked around at the circle of men. "Got any work to do?"

"They're my guys. They do what I say. And I want them to hear this police harassment bullshit."

"We're giving you a chance to cooperate," Torres said to Bobby, his voice even. Very smooth. "Want us to come back with a warrant for all your records? Maybe we run the numbers on these cars, see if you got pink slips for all of them. You want that?"

"We run a clean shop here," Bobby said backing down a little.

"Run the numbers!" Harold said to Gammon, hoping to get Bobby as agitated as possible. "I'll tell you what they do—steal cars and part 'em out."

"Do I have to listen to this?"

"As a matter of fact you do," Gammon said. He seemed to be enjoying himself.

Harold continued. "Or they buy a car through a dealership, insure it, and—"

Bobby lunged at Harold again. Torres caught him.

"Hands on the wall. Both of you." Gammon was taking his handcuffs off his belt.

Torres was trying to turn Bobby and get the cuffs on him but Bobby shook him off saying, "You're not puttin' those things on me."

Wycoff looked at Gammon. "Get a couple of cars in here. Let's take 'em out."

"Right," Torres said, reaching for his radio. "Let's go."

Then Harold heard feet moving, heels on the dirty cement floor. Torres spun around. Then everyone started running.

Torres and Gammon pulled their guns.

A face appeared around the corner of a row of shelves and he saw the punk that hit him last night and saw the gun in his hands and the look in his eyes as he saw Torres with his weapon pointing now at Bobby. Harold moved for the kid, trying to knock the gun down, but then there was the explosion and he saw fire pour out of the barrel and felt solid impact behind him, turned and saw Torres falling and the incredible rush of blood from his throat as he thrashed on the floor.

Everyone was shouting and there were more explosions,

Boom, Boom, Boom, like hammer blows on his ears in the tight space, and Gammon kneeling beside Torres shouting into his radio, "Officer down! Officer down!"

Harold saw the open door and ran out into the night, sprinting down rows of junked cars, crazy and desperate, then climbing stacked cars, onto their hoods and roofs until he was up and over a chain-link fence and then falling into darkness. He hit hard and his knees came up into his chin and he bit his lip and tasted blood.

Up and running again he skirted a fence with junkyard dogs leaping at him, his senses exploding, nerves raw. His feet slipped in something loose and heavy and he looked down and saw he was in the sulfur mountain and he caught his foot and went face first into it, smelling the rotten egg stench and clawing it from his eyes as he tried to keep moving, almost blind now, wanting to get as far away from what happened as possible.

Sirens filled the night air, wailing from all directions. A helicopter thumped in low over the Vincent Thomas Bridge, its cone of light reaching down and rippling over the ground. All the forces of the law were converging on the Third World, all searching this desolate landscape, for a cop killer.

How did it happen? What went wrong? Harold pictured fire pouring from the gun barrel and saw Torres falling. *Just get me the hell out of here. Disappear. Crawl into the ground. They catch you, you're dead.*

The helicopter was overhead now. Harold threw himself under the bulldozer, still hot and stinking of diesel from its day of futile labor on the yellow mountain. The light roved the yard, outlining the bulldozer cab spinning shadows on the ground. The helicopter circled away and Harold saw its light flickering over a vast field of oil pumps crosshatched by gas lines.

They'll get me here, said a voice in his head as he ran. *Move! Move!*

But where? He had to get back to his neighborhood, to the Accell parked by the liquor store. And that was a couple of miles away.

He got to his feet and looked back at the warehouse. Cop cars were bouncing down the rutted dirt roads of the Third World, emergency lights sparking off walls of corrugated tin. The sound of an air horn rose above the sirens drowning them out. A paramedic van and fire truck fought the traffic on the bridge.

Harold looked around—chain-link fences topped with razor wire, and beyond, that desolate oil field of pipes and valves. Then darkness and moving headlights on the 405 Freeway elevated in the distance and finally, the lights of the refinery.

A Jeep Cherokee was speeding up to the warehouse now. The doors flew open and three German shepherds leapt out, surging against their chains, cops struggling to hold them back. A voice shouted: "Turn 'em loose!" and the dogs took off, unrestrained.

Harold ran along the fence, his heart slamming in his chest, searching for a way out. The dogs were bounding toward him now, ready to tear him apart. And the cops behind them— would they call the dogs off? Not a chance.

You're finally getting what you deserve. You thought you could come up here, make a quick score. What happens? You screw up everything, as usual.

He found a section of the fence that was curled up and broken loose from steel poles. Harold pulled up hard and slid under. The oil field lay ahead. The helicopter was to the south now, over the bridge. Maybe he could make it to the freeway, or even better, to the refinery beyond. If he got in that maze of catwalks and power lines they'd never find him.

He began running again. Tripping, falling, jumping over gas lines, the freeway embankment rising ahead.

The helicopter was returning now, sweeping in low out of the sky, its noise flattening him to the ground, its circle of light sweeping the field. Almost to the freeway. Almost there. But the helicopter was closing on him, the light ready to pin him to the ground so—

He threw himself under a jumble of pipes and valves. Eight lanes of traffic were a steady roar above him. The light from the helicopter held him down, blinding him with its intensity as if the sky had opened and the light of justice was examining him.

Shadows spun crazily around him. The helicopter hovered, beating the air. He could feel each thump of the blades in his gut. *Have they spotted me?* He looked back across the field and saw the dogs coming. They'd get him now, first the dogs, then the cops. He'd never stand trial. He'd die alone in a basement lockup, his own belt around his neck.

The helicopter was circling again, the light coming from different angles, and over the pulsing blades he heard the German shepherds, closer now, yelping and crazy like dogs on a scent.

Only one way out. He climbed the embankment, slipping and fighting his way through ice plant until he stood in the breakdown lane feeling the steady wind from the river of cars and trucks hurtling past at 70 miles an hour. Headlights in his eyes. His brain filled with light and noise.

He looked back at the dogs. The cops were right behind them, guns out, flashlight beams sweeping the way ahead of them. They looked up and saw Harold, pointed at him, shouting something he couldn't hear.

Unexpectedly, he pictured himself as if he were looking down from above. He looked tiny and pathetic, a man running in terror, and he realized that, in the eyes of time, he was only a speck of dust, among billions of other specks of nothingness, blowing randomly through this dark universe.

Harold looked back and saw the dogs bounding up the embankment. Then he looked into the oncoming traffic, into the solid wall of light, and he decided he wouldn't run to his death in a blind panic. He would do it calmly because he knew that a man who had reached the bottom and was ready to die had nothing left to fear.

Moments later, the cops reached the top of the freeway embankment and stood in the breakdown lane breathing hard, watching the man they were chasing moving into the river of speeding cars. And as they watched they felt something inside them pull up tight, waiting for the impact, watching the man's head moving among the cars passing at terrible speeds, tires screeching and cars swerving, still waiting for the impact, thinking at any second they would see it, see something they could never forget. But when they saw him vault the center barrier, and continue across the oncoming lanes, they realized there was a chance, a very good chance, that he would make it alive. And escape.

Nova's bungalow was high on a bluff in San Pedro overlooking the harbor. From the deck in the back Marianna could see helicopters circling and it gave her a feeling of dread she couldn't explain. She moved back inside and sat in a leather recliner, her legs throbbing. The nerve endings were waking up after nine months and screaming about all the damage she was doing to them.

Marianna was alone in the house now that Nova had left to spend the night with her boyfriend. Nova also took her car so Marianna was grounded, no wheels, with only a few scraps of information that didn't add up to much and no game plan other than to hope Vikki didn't disappear into Mexico before Harold returned.

Marianna pulled her legs up onto the footrest, killed the reading light next to her, and closed her eyes. Cool air played over her from the open sliding glass door to the deck. The pulsing of the helicopter swelled and then suddenly died. She heard a train whistle somewhere. A car passed in the street.

Descending into sleep now she began to feel disoriented, unsure where she was and what she was doing. It felt as if she had been dropped into someone else's body and she knew nothing of the life she inhabited. She was falling, falling deeper into a terrifying state of sleep filled with twisted images from the day: Harold's battered face on the hospital pillow, Dash roaming the South Bay, Vikki lying on the motel floor. These memories circled in her mind like the helicopters she had been watching and she found she was cold and hot at the same time, writhing in the leather chair.

Then the dreams broke and she was filled with a sense of calm. She lay back and wanted to sleep forever.

Except someone was holding her hand.

She was surprised it didn't alarm her. She awoke with the smell of sweat and the earth in her nostrils. A man was kneeling beside her, holding her hand, his face mottled by dirt, his clothes torn and filthy.

"Don't turn on the light," a voice said. "I.e., someone might be watching the house."

It could only be Harold. She heard herself say, "They were looking for you, weren't they? The helicopters."

He nodded.

"Harold, what did you do?"

"Nothing."

"Of course not. But what did you do?"

"A cop got shot."

"Jesus," her breath hissed in her throat. "Do they think you—"

"I don't know." Then he continued in a strange voice: "They chased me—cops and dogs—and cornered me, by the freeway. I knew they'd get me unless—" He paused, then as if he still couldn't believe it: "I ran for it—across eight lanes of traffic. Every second I thought I'd get hit. But I made it somehow. I made it . . ."

He laughed, amazed, reliving it.

A rectangle of light appeared on the wall as a car slowly drove down the street. The light slid along the wall revealing pictures, a mirror, a bookcase. Harold was quiet, waiting for it to pass, and Marianna knew he was afraid it was the cops. It rounded the corner and disappeared.

She tenderly touched the stitches that seemed to have zipped his head back together and said, "I know where she is."

He was very still, waiting.

"I followed him back to a motel in Huntington. He's got her drugged in there. I got into the room but I couldn't move her. When I got back to the hospital you were gone. He's taking her down to Baja." Marianna didn't want to say it. But she had to: "She thinks he's going to kill her down there."

Harold nodded, understanding what Fallon had said to him that afternoon. "La Fonda. That's where he's taking her." Then starting to rise: "Better get movin'."

She pulled him back to her and clung to him, feeling a terrible loneliness sweep over her as if he really had been killed out there on the freeway, and then thinking of the bed in the other room, wanting to clean him up, to wash the dirt from his torn flesh, feed him something simple, then to sleep with him beside her. Tomorrow they could leave. But not tonight. Please, not tonight.

"Will it always be like this?" her voice only a whisper.

"What do you mean?"

"Leaving in the middle of the night. Chasing someone else's money."

"We make it back to Chile, we'll never leave again. I don't care how broke we are."

She was thinking of that bed again. Maybe he read her mind because his voice broke a little as he said, "Christ, I need you."

"Less than you think you do."

"No. I really do."

Harold stood up, still holding her hand. "I'll help you off the deck. The back stairs are tricky."

"The hell you will."

"What?"

"You drag me out of here in the middle of the night, I'm leaving by the front door."

"But the cops could be—"

"Front door. Or I'm not going."

They stared at each other in the dark strange room.

"I'll pull the car up, come back in and get you."

"I'll be ready," she said, settling back in the recliner. A few more moments of peace, she thought, as he slid out of the room and disappeared.

A weak orange light oozed through the gauzy curtains of the motel room showing her vague outlines of the objects around her. Vikki's legs were weak and unsteady so she moved slowly, listening to Dash's heavy, rhythmic breathing.

The dark regions of her mind, which work even in sleep and especially under drugs, had been searching for the cause of her current confused state of mind, sliding aside panels of her memory, looking in dusty corners and picking up long discarded snapshots that her eyes had taken and connecting them with new information. She had a lot of time to think, flat on her back and still as death, trying to remember even basic information about herself and the faces hovering over her, asking questions.

Then, finally, her brain connected two memories and she remembered the pills she had seen in his desk, Roche 2. *Roofies. The forget-it pill, date rape drug.* Knocked you out, then made you forget what happened while you were out. Dash was using them to control her. But, in one shining idea, she realized how she could turn the tables on him. If he slept through this.

Step one: Find her purse. It was on the bureau next to a small suitcase she recognized as her own. But she hadn't packed it. Dash did it for her; he'd been busy while she slept.

She stepped into the bathroom, still humid from his shower, and flipped on the light. She waited, listening to see if he had awakened. Didn't want to blow it since she'd only get one chance.

Unzipping her jeans, she sat on the toilet. It was then that she smelled her own urine soaking her clothes. And it filled her with hatred for this man who had made her foul herself like a hopeless drunk. The rage was distant, slowed by drugs, but she could feel it making its way back to her brain, firing the familiar nerve endings. Once it arrived, it would help her with what she had to do.

She rose, thinking how much she wanted to shower and change. But she was far too weak. And besides, she had to find them first if she wanted to get out of this alive. Problem was, there wasn't much to search. They were either in his shaving kit, as she had guessed, or she was out of luck.

His large black leather shaving kit squatted on the sink counter. She nursed the zipper open and looked inside.

Razor, travel-size shaving cream, hand lotion, cologne, styptic pencil, brush, shampoo. No pill bottles. No baggies. Nothing. *Damn.*

But it had to be here. The idea had come to her with certainty, pushed to the surface with urgency through the clouds of her drug storm.

She removed his razor, shaving cream, and all the other things, her heart coming alive, her hands slick with cold sweat, body shivering. She spread the empty kit open wide and found a small inside pocket, just the place for, *yes,* a small silver pillbox. She opened it up and saw seven tiny round pills, *Roche* 2 printed on them.

She opened her purse, found her plastic birth control pillbox, and counted out seven pills. She placed them side by side on the sink counter for a comparison. Close enough. She smiled, thinking that now, when he slipped her a pill, he'd actually be helping her periods stay nice and regular.

She put the birth control pills in the silver box and put the box back in his shaving kit. Then she put the roofies deep in her purse. *Hey, what's this?* she wondered, finding a wadded bundle of papers in her purse. Spreading them flat, she saw the copies she had taken from Dash's office, the copies that held the evidence of his crimes. Better not let him see them. She considered flushing them down the toilet. But she would need them later. She folded them in a tight wad and stuffed them back in her purse. He'll never look there. Guys hate looking in women's purses—afraid they'd see tampons and makeup and all that stuff.

Back in bed she began thinking how the remaining hours of the night would metabolize the residual drug in her system. Then, on the edge of sleep again, a troubling thought occurred to her: What if, when she was fully recovered, she forgot everything that Dash had done to her?

The light on the dashboard of the Accell glowed 4:03 A.M. when they neared the Lighthouse Motel in Huntington Beach. A car was pulling out. They saw headlights, then the Rover moving out onto the deserted street, and Harold said, "Too late."

"Don't lose them!" Marianna said, seeing the Rover accelerate away. "Go! Go! What're you waiting for?"

The streets were empty and Harold risked it, putting his foot down, feeling the Accell engine kick into a lower gear, and flying through the intersection as the light turned red, a hundred yards behind the big Rover.

"That what you want? Get us arrested for driving crazy."

"There's no one around, Harold."

"That's when the cops stop you. They got nothing else to do so—"

"I'd think you'd want to stick with her. Or are you going to tell me you're just doing all this for the money?"

He laughed, wanting to change the mood, wanting to stop arguing like some old married couple. He let her question hang there for a while, then smiled at her. "Of course it's the money. What else would it be?"

"Yeah, right." She pulled her collar up around her neck and said, "I saw her, you know."

"So you said."

"She's beautiful." Pause. "In a slutty kind of a way."

He was carefully quiet, knowing she was probing him.

"But she's the type guys go for," Marianna said, as if the concept was beyond her grasp.

"Not this guy."

He felt her eyes on him so he kept everything neutral,

concentrated on driving, tried not to think of Vikki naked in that motel room, tried not to feel anything at all for Vikki, even though he couldn't get her desperate voice out of his head, that awful phone message saying, "I want you here now. *Please.*"

They were silent, following the Rover through the night, onto Interstate 5 heading south to San Diego, past the INS check station in the northbound lanes, border patrol agents checking vans and trucks for illegals. Sometime later two huge yellow signs appeared in their headlights on either side of the freeway with silhouettes of a family running, holding a child by the hand. Underneath it said: *Por Amor de Dios, No Cruces las Autopistas. Mas de 135 han muerto.*

It took him a moment to unscramble the Spanish. Then he said, " *'For the love of God, don't cross the freeway'* . . . You'd think they'd know that."

"Where they come from, there aren't freeways," she said, an edge in her voice he hadn't heard for some time. Everything he said seemed to lead to an argument. "Besides, lots of them are carrying things. Like babies."

A mile passed in silence. They both watched the back end of the Rover moving ahead of them through the night. They could see Dash's head, above the headrest. But Vikki was slumped to the side, leaning against the door panel.

"How much you think she's worth?"

"Who?"

"Princess up there in the Yuppie-mobile."

"Insurance could be worth a million. The dealership is worth a lot more than that."

"And we might get five percent of that?" Her voice was no longer sleepy.

"I figure we might walk away with a hundred grand."

She rested her head on his shoulder and her lips were close

to his ear when she said, "We could really use that money, Harold."

"That's what I'm thinking."

"I mean, we get enough, we won't have to come back here again. For a very long time."

"If ever. Tell you what, I wouldn't mind saying adios to LA—permanently."

Ahead, the Rover's turn signal throbbed in the moist ocean air.

"Okay then," she said, her voice decisive, "let's rescue the bitch."

Gammon sat on the toilet lid in the bathroom of his Culver City one-bedroom apartment and began undressing. As his left boot came free in his hand he saw the darkness on the tanned leather and realized he was touching a small part of Richard Torres. He looked at the bloodstain, recalling the way his partner died on the cold concrete floor. Then, by an act of will, he replaced that awful picture, with a composite portrait of Richard built from the thousands of days they had spent working together: a quiet man, tough and sharp, someone he never really knew, but someone he always respected.

He wouldn't sleep, of course, but after his shower, he'd lie down for a while. Right now, there was nothing else he could do to catch his partner's killer. He had been up for over twenty-four hours and the world was taking on that thin look, like a faded B-movie that stopped making sense just after the opening credits.

Grief was out there somewhere and Gammon knew it would punish him with sledge-hammer blows of self-incrimination, and later, bouts of gnawing depression. But for now he held it at arm's length, processing the information about the shooting in the methodical way he had developed over the years.

He reviewed that moment in the chop shop when the tension broke and everyone started moving. He was trying to cuff Bobby Skura when he saw Dodge take off, moving, and someone else rounding the corner. A kid, Hispanic—a gangbanger? Then he saw the muzzle flash, and Richard fell beside him. Did Dodge pull the trigger? In his gut, he didn't think Bird Dog would shoot a cop, or anyone, for that matter. It wasn't his style. Who did it then? The Hispanic kid? But they never caught him. And the dozen or so guys they rounded up, after chasing them through all that shit in the Third World, knew nothing about him either. No one saw nothing. No one knew nothing.

He stepped into the shower, hoping it would relax him, or at least remove the film of dirt encasing him after hours in the interrogation room listening to Bobby Skura's lies. Finally, they released him knowing they could get him again, squeeze him after dismantling his chop shop and running the VIN numbers on his cars. They could nail him on a G-Ride at the very least. If he didn't give up the one who pulled the trigger on his partner.

Under the hot water Gammon's thinking changed to a more basic mode. He was a cop and it was his job to find people, gather evidence, and build a case for the D.A. True, he was now on house rest following the shooting, and he would be sent to head shrinkers who didn't know squat about how he felt. That's what the department required and he would play along even though, like most cops, he felt all that touchie-feelie horseshit only made things worse. The best therapy was work; and a detective without a case is a cop ready to take the pipe.

So, Gammon decided, he would assign himself a case.

He'd do it for himself. For Richard. And he would begin by using the most basic theory of investigation: the 36/36 rule. It stated that the roots of most crimes lay in the events thirty-six hours prior to the crime. And the solution had the greatest likelihood of being solved thirty-six hours after the crime.

That was the beauty of having Bobby Skura on the streets. A stupid scumbag like that didn't realize the tools the police had at their disposal. There was a good chance that Skura was—at this very moment—using his cellular phone and, thus, revealing his whereabouts by the way the calls were routed from one microwave tower to the next. Gammon was sure that Skura would lead him to Richard's killer, might even lead him to Harold Dodge and show him what the connection was—if any—between these two men.

Gammon knew the technician that did the phone tracking and had already placed a call to him. The techie had known Richard too. And he knew what it meant to Gammon to follow through on this case. He might even guess that Gammon, in his present state of house rest, had more freedom to follow this case to the end and secure a measure of justice the courts could never obtain.

Vikki woke up with a dry wind on her cheek and sunlight on her face. Crows cawed nearby and when she opened her eyes she saw orange sky and the kind of cactus that always comes to life in cartoons and dances around. A barbed wire fence ran along beside this dirt road and black mountains were in the distance.

Dash was standing next to her open car door watching her. He bent down and kissed her forehead, smiling and saying in his rich deep voice: "Hey, babe."

On the floor of the car was a paper bag and from it he took out two cartons of orange juice. They were still cold and she watched him open one and hand it to her. It tasted incredibly good. She finished it all at once.

"How ya feelin'?"

She ran her fingers through her hair. Snarled. Her face felt puffy and dead.

"Where's my purse? I must look like hell."

He picked her purse up off the car floor and set it in her lap. She opened it, looking for a brush as she stepped out of the car and tried to stand. She wobbled and he caught her, saying, "Whoa. Easy."

She put her purse on the hood, leaned against the car with Dash still holding her. His arm felt good around her waist and he nuzzled her hair, kissing her again. She heard a drone in the desert stillness. A silver car moved slowly along the road in the distance. Dash was quiet, watching the car.

"Where are we?"

He took his eyes off the car. "Near Campo. That's Mexico over there." He pointed at the black mountains.

Vikki was waking up now, finding pieces of the past few days lying all over the surface of her brain.

"What's wrong with me? Everything's . . ."

"Too much of a good thing."

She waited for more.

Dash shrugged. "Everyone celebrates when they come into money."

"I've been hungover before. This ain't hungover."

"You never know what's gonna happen when you start mixing."

"*Mixing*?"

"I found them in your medicine cabinet. You should have told me. Scared me to death when you passed out like that."

"Found what?"

"Ludes."

"Ludes?" She laughed. "Those were from way back. Joe had back spasms and . . ."

His smile seemed to say, *Denial, denial . . .*

"No big deal. It was just bad timing, that's all."

He took two coffees from the paper bag and pried the lids off. The smell came to her in the dry desert air and reminded her of how good it felt to be alive. She watched him set the white cups on the hood as she thought about his last words: *Bad timing?*

"Look, Dash, just tell me what's going on. And no bullshit. Please."

He was squinting at the car in the distance. He took a deep breath and focused on her, saying, "The gist of it is this: Someone's trying to kill you."

He waited to see how she'd take it. She hesitated, then laughed, and laughed again, trying to fit what he said with the broken pieces she found scattered in her memory.

"Kill *me*? Those guys that shot up the house were after you. I remember that much."

"Lot's happened since then. They came back looking for you. They found out you dumped Fabian in Baja. But don't worry—" He smiled and purred. "I handled it. Dash ain't gonna let nothin' happen to you."

"I'm sorry. It's just not coming together for me."

"Me too. But while you were, ah, incapacitated, I checked around. I know some people that know some people."

"Yeah?"

"With you pushing the lawsuit, Fallon sees he could get cut out of everything. You disappear, the suit goes away."

"The suit's been around for months. Why's he doing this now?"

"He heard Dodge told you where to find Joe's body. With Joe officially dead, he knows you could get the dealership."

She sipped her coffee hoping the caffeine would jump-start

her system. Dash was stroking her hair, watching her face with his lazy eyes.

"Okay . . . I remember now. . . . You said Joe's policy was going to pay out. If we could get Harold to give a statement to the cops."

"All taken care of."

"*What*?"

"Why're you so amazed. I said I'd handle it, so I handled it."

"So where's my money?"

He reached into his breast pocket and drew out a check, folded in half, and handed it to her. She saw her hands were shaking as she unfolded it. It was for $100,000. And it was drawn from his agency's account.

"The policy is going to pay off in increments," he said. "You'll be getting ten more checks, just like this."

She felt light-headed, the weight of the last nine months suddenly lifted from her shoulders.

He laughed, enjoying her reaction. "Let the good times roll, right, babe?"

She laughed too, looking around as if the world was all new to her. "Well, let's get back. I've got to pay off the house. I've—" She laughed again. "I've got a lot to do."

"Not so fast. We still got Eddie Fallon and his guys to deal with."

That stopped her.

"We got to find Fabian."

"Fabian?"

"You remember, the opera wanna-be."

"I remember but, I mean, he's, like, a killer."

"I'll turn him around—he can deal with Fallon for us."

"So where we headed?"

"You're going to show me where you dumped Fabian. In Baja."

Baja. The word connected to something inside Vikki and she felt a wave of dread. She searched Dash's face. She wanted to believe him but her bullshit meter was still sounding the alarm. Maybe once her head cleared, she thought, sipping coffee and taking her purse off the hood. She rummaged for a hairbrush and, as she lifted it out, a wad of papers fell onto the desert sand. A breeze fanned the pages apart as Dash stooped to pick them up for her.

"I'll get them—" Vikki said. But she wasn't fast enough.

Dash had seen the rows of numbers, car names, and locations, all written in his excessively neat handwriting.

"Where'd you get these?" His voice was cold.

She thought of a thousand answers, but none of them would sound right so she said: "Your office."

"I keep my files locked."

"I found the key."

"What'd you plan to do with them?"

"Ask you about them."

He nodded, not buying it.

"Vikki, maybe our relationship would be stronger if you would learn to trust me."

"And maybe I'd trust you if you stopped lying to me." It was out before she could stop it. A lot of anger was inside her, and she didn't fully understand where it was coming from.

"I'm sorry I had to keep you in the dark," he said, making her think, *In the dark?* "But, see, I was protecting you."

He reached out to touch her. She flinched. He slowly put his hand on her shoulder, around her neck, then drew her to him. She shuddered inside, feeling that sick thrill again.

"Trust me, babe," he breathed in her ear. "You mean a lot to me."

Of all the things he said, she found that the hardest to believe.

Dash stepped back, the papers still in his hand. He put them back in her purse.

"From here on in, no secrets."

She watched him carefully. "You gonna fill me in now?"

"On the road. Let's get rollin'."

He pointed to the black mountains to the south. "We'll cross at Tecate, cut down to the coast. I know a little hotel down there you'll love, right on the beach and everything. You can catch some rays while I look for Fabian."

She couldn't help wondering how in hell finding Fabian was going to solve all her problems. But then she thought of the check Dash had given her with the promise of more. Maybe she could learn to trust him after all.

"What's he doing now?" Harold asked, cruising past the strip mall in Campo, the one they saw the Rover pull into a few minutes ago. It was a mangy collection of storefronts baking in the desert sun, most of them selling insurance for tourists venturing into Mexico. Insure your car, yourself, and your friends for twenty-four hours, for only ten bucks.

"He's—yeah—he's getting out," Marianna said, looking back. "Pull a U-ie."

"Where's Vikki?"

"Still in the car. Let's get her."

"What?"

"Get her! This is our chance."

Harold was about to cut the wheel around when he saw a green border patrol van barreling down the road in the other direction.

"Pull a U-ie, Harold!"

"I will, but look—"

"They don't give a shit. Come on! Come on!"

Harold steered into a dirt parking lot, turned a tight circle, kicking up dust, and bumped back up onto the pavement.

"In there." Marianna pointed to the strip mall. "There's his car. Park over there."

Harold pulled up in front of a convenience store. He craned his neck around and saw Vikki sitting alone in the Rover. He could see Dash through the glass front of the insurance office.

"Go get her."

"Okay." But he couldn't make himself go. He wanted to think it through first.

"GO, HAROLD!"

"All right! Jesus!"

He opened the door and stepped out. There was a wooden sidewalk like in the old Westerns and he heard his heels hitting the boards moving him toward her. How long did it take to fill out those insurance forms?

Looking into the store, Harold saw Dash bent over the counter, writing. He stepped over to the Rover and tried to open the passenger door. Locked. Through the window Vikki's face looked out at him, alarmed, like he was some maniac trying to break in. Then Harold remembered the hat he was wearing.

"It's me, Harold," he said, lifting off the hat, revealing the shaved section of his scalp, the stitches. Shit, that just made it worse.

Vikki opened the door, stepped out.

"Harold!"

"*Let's go.*"

"What are you doing here?"

"Let's go. I got your car over there." He pointed. "Quick. Before he comes back."

"Why?"

Harold took her arm, trying to get her walking. She shook him off.

"Harold! What're you doing?"

"Tell you later. *Come on.*"

A lady with two kids stopped on the sidewalk, watching them.

"Dash told me what you did," Vikki said. "It's all been settled."

"What I did?"

"The policy has paid off so—"

A low voice from behind them: "It's the Dodge Charger."

Dash stood on the sidewalk above them, tapping an insurance folder into the palm of his hand.

"She's coming with us," Harold said.

"She doesn't look like she wants to," Dash said. Then to Vikki: "Back in the car, babe."

Vikki hesitated, confused. She said to Dash: "You said he gave his statement to the cops. Right? I mean the policy paid off, right?"

"Vikki, we've been through all this."

The lady with the kids was still watching them. A man stepped out of the insurance office saying, "Is there a problem here?"

Harold took Vikki's arm. "Come on, Vikki. Now."

Dash tore Harold's hand off her arm and shoved him back against the Rover. "Don't touch her!"

Harold saw the man duck back into his insurance office.

"Vikki, look, I don't know what he told you, but—"

"It's over between you two. Now stop harassing her. Understand?" Dash was playing up to the bystanders, making Harold seem like a jilted lover. To Vikki he said: "He's crazy. Come on, babe, back in the car."

She slid into the Rover and he closed the door. Then he

turned on Harold, backing him up, saying. "I don't want to see you around her again. Got it?" He circled the Rover and jumped in, starting it up and revving the big V-8, almost drowning out Harold's voice as he yelled to Vikki through the window: "He's lying to you!"

Then Vikki was torn away from him and the Rover was flying out of the lot.

Harold walked back toward the Accell, moving as fast as he could without seeming suspicious, just in case that guy had called the cops and they pulled in here any second. He saw the Accell backing up toward him, Marianna driving. When he climbed inside she said, "Nice work, Harold."

"I don't need this right now," he said, looking around for the Rover and seeing it down at the end of the street, being waved through the border by the guards and disappearing underneath the huge sign that read: MEXICO.

They drove into Mexico, hoping to see the big green Rover appear in front of them as they rounded each bend in the road. But all Harold saw were black mountains, tiny villages, boys on horses, old men on bicycles, and finally, the Pacific. They had no map and little hope of finding Vikki down here. All they had were two words that weren't on any map and no one seemed to recognize: "La Fonda."

Then, late in the afternoon, in an Ensenada souvenir store, Marianna found a young woman who nodded her head and began speaking in rapid Spanish that Harold couldn't follow. When she was done Marianna said, "La Fonda's not a town. It's the name of a hotel. Twenty miles north of here."

A half hour later they turned off Mexico Highway 1-D and found a cluster of stucco buildings on sandy cliffs looking like cardboard boxes in a roadside dump. Out front was a hand-painted sign: "Welcome to La Fonda Hotel." And in smaller letters: "Charming ocean-view rooms!" They drove through stone gates and into a cobblestone courtyard filled with parked cars.

And there was the dark green Rover.

The waiter on the patio at La Fonda was just telling Dash about a big guy who showed up last week and sang opera for the dinner crowd, when Dash looked inside and saw Bobby at the bar, Neto beside him on a tall wicker bar stool, drawing on a napkin with a felt-tipped pen. They would turn now and see Dash so he reassessed the situation very quickly and decided it was best to be proactive. He started toward Bobby, shifting the pieces in his mind as he moved out of the sunlight of the patio into the dark bar with the low ceiling made of straw or some shit that hung down in your face.

He reached Bobby as the man turned and saw him coming, eyebrows like thunderclouds, and Dash said, "Amigos! Welcome to Mexico! Any problem finding the place?"

Dash was aware that Neto was giggling, shifting on the wicker stool and watching Bobby, who was very still, staring at him in disbelief.

"Were my directions okay?" Dash continued.

"Your directions?"

"You got my message, right? I found Fabian and called your machine. I told you he was fine." Fabian's name had the desired effect so Dash pushed on. "I mean, that's why you're here, right? Or is this just, like, some incredible coincidence?"

"I'm here because your buddy Fallon told me you were here."

"Whatever," Dash said. "The point is, Fabian's here and everything is okay now, so you can call off the killer Chihuahua." He pointed at Neto. Neto suddenly stopped laughing and got off the stool.

Bobby held the kid back, saying, "Fabian's here? I don't see him?"

"He'll be here tonight."

"You seen him?"

"Look, the waiter here guarantees he's here every night. He sings here, for Christ's sake. People get drunk, they get sentimental, and out comes Fabian singing 'Moon River.' " Maybe if he kept talking it would be all right. "Listen, man, everything is coming together. I've got this whole thing wired."

"Really?"

"Want me to lay it out for you?"

"Definitely," Bobby said in such a way as to make Neto start giggling again.

The bartender set two clear bottles of Corona on the bar for Bobby and Neto and hung back waiting for his money.

"Una mas," Bobby said to the bartender. Then to Dash: "So you got it wired?"

"Si."

"A way to pay me what you owe me?"

"Right."

"A way to get that Covo bitch off Fallon's ass?"

"Right again."

The bartender brought the third bottle. Bobby paid him off and handed the frosted bottle to Dash. He clinked his bottle against Dash's saying, "To my brother."

"To Fabian," Dash said.

They all raised their beers and when Dash's first swallow was on its way down the hatch Bobby stepped in and drove his fist up into Dash's solar plexus. A geyser of beer shot through Dash's mouth and nose and he dropped to the floor choking. Two big Mexicans appeared out of nowhere but

Bobby backed off saying, "He's okay. It just went down the wrong way. Neto, help me with him."

They dragged Dash to his feet and shoved him out into the parking lot, where the wind was kicking up, banana plants waving long whippy branches at them, and a guy stood nearby trying to sell a bunch of cheap-looking oil paintings. Dash's face was blood red and he still couldn't stop coughing. Bobby reached into Dash's pocket and lifted out his car keys.

"See you at dinner, *amigo*. If I don't hear my brother sing, you and me're goin' for a walk on the beach. *Comprende?*"

When Harold opened the flimsy door of Room 10 at the La Fonda Hotel he saw this was no Holiday Inn. No telephone and no TV. And nothing was sanitized for anyone's protection. The paintings looked like something left behind after a Tijuana swap meet. The king-sized bed had a canopy over it and two hanging plants were carefully positioned so you banged your head on them getting in and out of bed.

Pushing aside the sliding glass door, Harold stepped out onto the balcony, leaving Marianna inside, and scanned the balconies of the upper rooms, thinking he might see Vikki or Dash and figure out what room they were in. No trace of them. Below, there was a patio, then a swath of jungly foliage, then the beach, across which long lines of white breakers eternally rolled toward land. The ocean, so beautiful, so pure in Chile, was depressing here. Perhaps it was because of the musty odor of sewage blending with the smell of wood smoke from the hotel's bar and restaurant. The wind was whipping up now, bringing a chill off the desert mountains behind them.

Back inside, Harold ducked the hanging plants and gratefully lay on the saggy bed. Looking up he saw that there was a painting of a rainbow beside the bed with the inscription, "Today, may everything be beautiful." The painting swarmed with the signatures of couples who had slept in the room and the date of their stay. Harold couldn't stop looking at all the names; it was as if those couples were still in the room, whispering to him, pleading with him to think positively despite the seedy surroundings and the terrible jam he was in.

The last thing he remembered was Marianna looking down at him. "Poor Harold. You've been through hell."

He didn't say anything.

"All for me."

"For us, really," he admitted, settling his weight, feeling incredibly comfortable after two days with no sleep.

"You did it for me, Harold. So I could walk."

"No, no," he said, thinking he would explain, but he couldn't make his mouth move any longer. He fell asleep with the sound of the surf in his ears.

When he woke up, Harold couldn't remember where he was. There was a balcony beside the bed, the door open, and the smell of the ocean blowing in. The sky was almost dark and Marianna was sitting on the bed beside him as if she'd never left. But her hair was wind-blown, her face reddened as if she'd just come in.

"What time is it?"

"Close to nine."

Marianna lay down beside him, watching him. He was waking up now. He started to ask Marianna where she had been and what she had been doing, when he felt her hand inside his shirt, stroking the hair on his chest. It seemed like a century since she had touched him and, despite his exhaustion, he was instantly aroused. He turned toward her and her lips were there kissing him.

She bit his ear and whispered, "Been a while, Harold. I've missed you."

She unbuttoned his shirt, then bent down and began kissing his chest. He lay back and noticed the rainbow painting again, the one signed by all the couples, realizing they were now doing what the owners off all those signatures had done in this same room, on this broken bed.

"I'm going to undress you now," Marianna said, her voice soft and feline. "Then I'm going to make love to you."

"I'm filthy and I probably stink."

"It's your smell, Harold. It doesn't stink."

She pulled off his shoes and socks and dropped them on the floor. She unbuckled his pants and slid them off, murmuring approvingly at his erection. Then, precariously, holding the canopy bed for support, she stood and shed her clothes, revealing the braces. She slowly unbuckled the braces and pulled them off.

"You're the only woman I know who could make that look sexy."

She looked up, smiled. "You say the sweetest things, Harold. Maybe, soon, I won't need them. After we get the money. After my operation. I want to walk again."

"You're doing pretty good."

"I feel like a freak. I want to walk like I used to, easy, without even thinking. To walk like that I'm going to have to go under the knife."

She was naked now and Harold noticed the still-purple scars crisscrossing her thighs where the bullets had entered, and higher, the scar above her buttocks in the small of her back. She held his eyes as he enjoyed seeing her naked again, as if for the first time, surprised, as he always was, at how delicate she was for such a tough broad. And when she straddled him, guiding him into her, her eyes finally slid away from his and her face got that pleasure-pain look that drove him crazy.

She began talking as if she didn't know where it was coming from.

"I found them, Harold."

"Them?" His voice was nothing more than a croak.

"Vikki and Dash. They're in the next building. The room on one side is empty—they're remodeling in there so the door's open. I went in and listened through the wall."

She was riding him lightly, a mermaid bobbing in the surf he heard through the balcony door. He watched, barely aware of what she was saying, entranced by the way the blood rose and blushed first her beautiful neck, then her breasts and shoulders, turning ivory to rouge.

"It's going to be easy if you're willing to follow through."

"Follow through?" He wasn't really listening because, oh man, did it feel good.

"I've been doing a lot of thinking," she breathed, savoring him inside her. "On the drive here, then watching the waves while you were asleep, wondering where it's all leading and what's the right thing to do, and how to bring some justice to all this."

"We have to think of that. We really do."

"We have Vikki to think of too. We owe her, Harold."

"I feel guilty as hell about her. We've got to help her."

She stopped moving, settled her weight on him, and studied his expression. "Well, don't lose any sleep about it. She's a big girl. She knows you get burned when you play with fire."

He felt like a dog pulled up tight on his chain. She did that to him, gave him slack, then yanked him in. But part of him loved it.

"She's the key. We've got to get her away from Dash because he's working a scheme of his own. And he's not going to let her go easy. So you're gonna have to deal with him. And that means—"

He suddenly realized where this was going and didn't like it.

"Can we not talk for a minute here?"

"Why?"

"I just want to enjoy this."

"It helps me think. My thoughts just come out without wondering if I should say them or not."

"That's my point."

She slapped him playfully and he turned away from her hand as she tried to hit him again. Her raven hair swinging loose around her face, falling onto her breasts, her throat a fiery red and he knew she was—like him—very close to something sudden and wonderful.

She smiled at him and began to work her hips again, stroking deeper with a little turn to it, a playful twist at the end of each beat and he watched it all rise up through her, as if it came from the earth itself, arching her back and closing her eyes and bringing the breathy pain/pleasure moans from somewhere deep inside her.

She collapsed onto the bed next to him. He closed his eyes and felt he might fall, back into the pit of exhaustion dug by days of fear and pain, where he would be powerless to answer, to refuse, to contradict, and he heard her talking again. "I'll call Dash on his cell phone. He gave me the number when I saw him back at Vikki's. He's looking for you. I'll tell him you'll meet him up on the cliffs. I found a spot that's just right. It'll be dark. It'll be easy to do. You'll come out of the darkness before he knows what's happening. They'll find him on the beach in the morning. But we'll be back in LA with Vikki, buying first-class tickets back to Chile. Right after they rewire my legs."

There was a pause that might have lasted two seconds or thirty minutes. "It'll be so beautiful, Harold. We're gonna help her collect on what's coming to her. That's justice, isn't it, Harold? Harold?"

"Be back in an hour, babe," Dash said, kissing Vikki on the top of her head, right where her blond hair parted and the oil in her scalp gave off her special smell. She was sitting on the balcony watching the sun torch the clouds and turn the ocean a knurled gold. She looked tired and sad and he couldn't tell at all what she was thinking.

She turned her beautiful face up to him, eyes searching for answers, and said, "Why was Harold there, at the border?"

"Probably lookin' for a cut of your dough. What a pathetic guy."

"He went to the cops, though, didn't he? Gave his statement. That's all taken care of?"

"You got the check, didn't you? Now relax."

"But I thought I heard him say—"

"Forget about him, babe. He's out of the picture." He stroked her hair. "I tell you I found Fabian?"

She looked up, surprised. "Turns out he's singing in the bar downstairs. I'm gonna go down and square things with him. Be back in an hour. Okay?"

She looked out the window without answering, lost in her own thoughts.

He headed out the door and followed the walkways to the restaurant, under waving tropical foliage. Now he was passing the bar, the bartender popping an olive into his mouth, nodding to him, and emerged onto the patio, where the umbrellas were waving in the wind and palm fronds rustled overhead.

When he saw Bobby and Neto waiting for him a raw hatred rose in his gut, remembering how he writhed on the floor coughing beer from every pore in his body. But he knew that wouldn't help him now so he focused on Bobby's weakness: greed. It would be Bobby's greed he could play on and Bobby's greed would save him. He could talk his way out of this the way he had everything in his past, a past that lay buried for long periods but that was now, oddly, pushing to the surface of his mind for a reason he didn't understand.

"*Qué pasa*?" Dash said, shaking with Bobby, then nodding to Neto and saying, "Y *tú*?"

He would pretend the incident in the bar never happened, pretend until the moment he would get his satisfaction.

"How the hell'd you find this dump?" Bobby stabbed a thick Dorito into watery salsa. A shot and beer was at his elbow. Neto sucked Coke through a long straw. He had his felt-tip out and he was scrawling on the place mat. No sexy ladies this time—knives, guns, and death's heads poured from his pen.

"Client of mine comes down here for the fishing. Says the yellowtail are phenomenal. We're talkin' two, three feet."

Bobby looked out at the ocean and nodded appreciatively.

"When Fabian told me he needed some R&R, I offered to drop him off at Ensenada."

"You're still sticking to that story, huh?"

"Hey, ask him when he gets here."

"I'll do that." Bobby tossed the shot down. A waiter came and Bobby ordered another round. Dash got a margarita. He wanted to get that taste of beer out of his sinuses.

The patio was filling up now so Bobby leaned closer to Dash and said, "You said you had a plan."

"I do, indeed."

"Care to share it with us?"

"Bobby, I've got a plan that's so awesome, you're gonna sit there with your fuckin' mouth hangin' open and say, 'Dash, you're a genius, man.'"

"Nothin' would make me happier."

Dash licked his lips, leaning forward. "I owe you guys—what?—ten grand, right?"

"Correct."

"I don't have the money."

"I already figured that out, Dash. I mean, that's kinda why we're here."

"First, let me explain what happened to it—to show you what kind of a guy I am. Buddy of mine, securities analyst, gets an inside tip on a junk bond. Three weeks, he says, it'll go through the roof. Okay? I had the cash, your cash, from those premiums, ready to pay you, and I figured, Bobby will *thank* me for turning his ten grand into twenty. You'd like that, wouldn't you?"

"I never play the market."

"But this was an inside tip."

"I *never* play the market."

"It was a sure thing is what I'm telling you."

"Then why didn't it pay off?"

"Reason I bring it up is to show you how I was thinking on your behalf. Okay?"

"Do me a favor, Dash. Don't do me any more favors."

The drinks arrived and Dash watched Bobby knock back the shot and sink his teeth into a lime. Neto kept drawing, hideous creations interwoven on the place mat. On the other side of the patio a short guy came out with a guitar on a strap around his neck and began singing "*Celito Linda*" for a table of drunk Americans who bellowed, "A*y yay yay yay!*" when it came to the chorus.

Bobby leaned in close to Dash, his face flushed from the booze, and said, "I'm ready to hear this brilliant plan of yours. And it better wind up with how you're going to pay me every penny you owe me."

Dash didn't like the look in Bobby's eyes so he decided a simple, direct approach would work best.

"Tomorrow at dawn, we get in our cars. Me and Vikki in one car. You and the Chihuahua over there in another." Neto's gaze fell heavy on Dash.

"Look at him. He hates my guts."

Neto smiled.

"Hey, Neto, here's a joke for you: Try to say Chihuahua without barking. W*ow!* W*ow!* Get it?" Dash laughed for them both, then jerked his thumb at Neto, saying to Bobby, "He wants to kill me."

Bobby said, "You were saying, about Vikki."

"Me and Vikki in one car. You and the boy wonder in the other. I tell her we've chartered a boat out of San Felipe for some deep-sea fishing. Somewhere on a lonely mountain road, between here and San Felipe, I fall asleep at the wheel. Vikki's not wearing her seat belt and she dies of head injuries."

In the silence Dash noticed the wind was coming on stronger, flattening the smoke that poured from the chimney above the patio.

"You're saying you're gonna kill her."

"I told you, she dies of head injuries in the crash."

"Uh-huh. Maybe I'm stupid, but how does killing Vikki Covo help me?"

"Insurance is a wonderful thing, Bobby. For ten bucks at

the border, I bought a half million life insurance policy on Vikki."

Bobby looked at Neto, then back at Dash, and said, "You're sick."

"True."

Bobby smiled at Neto, then turned back to Dash, impressed.

Dash continued: "Let me point out something else, Bobby. Fallon's your contact at the dealership, no? If Vikki wins her suit against him, she gets the dealership. And if that happens, I guarantee you your business is gonna dry up, pronto, cause she's one straight shooter. So what we're talking about here is solving two big problems with one small accident."

The guitar guy was gesturing to someone in the bar and he saw a tall bosomy woman emerge as the first chords of a familiar song began. Once she started singing, he knew conversation would be difficult so he sat back, hoping the awful beer taste would be replaced by honest Mexican tequila. But his feeling of control evaporated immediately when he felt a pair of huge hands on his shoulders, hands that were scabbed with ugly scratches, and heard a booming voice that he had last heard groaning in pain.

But it ain't over till the fat lady sings, he thought, realizing, with mixed emotions, that Fabian was back.

When Fabian was done singing he turned his back on Bobby and just walked into the restaurant. Just like that. Guy disappears for five days without a word, then treats me like shit, Bobby thought, shoving back in his chair, following him, getting more pissed off with each step, and finally catching him by the kitchen, next to this glass case with a dead fish on

PHILIP REED

ice looking up at them. By this point he was so mad he was ready to kill him.

It was a brother thing, Bobby thought, remembering again how he used to catch hell from his father in the dingy machine shop in Glendale, seeing his father's thick arm raised above him and dreading the painful blows he knew would follow. All because Fabian wouldn't listen to him then, and he wasn't listening to him now, either.

Fabian was looking down at the dead fish in the case and said, "Hey, Bobby, he's givin' us the fish eye."

"Oh, it's a joke to you, is it?"

"Yeah. Life's a joke, Bobby. See me laughing?"

"Bernette ain't laughing. The cops found your car at the pier. She thinks you're dead."

"I don't care what that bitch thinks. I'm done with all that."

"All *what*? Your girls? They're cryin' their eyes out. *Where's Daddy*? You don't care about them?"

Fabian looked away, not wanting to think of that, not wanting to get drawn back into all that shit again.

"And what about me? You don't care what trouble you caused me."

Fabian's voice was a low growl. "Bobby, you been on my ass my whole life."

"On your ass? O*n your ass*? Is that how you see it?"

"Yes. On my ass. All the shit you got me into—it was a lie. Okay?"

Bobby couldn't fuckin' believe it. He stood there, hands on his hips, as Fabian added: "I found something better here, okay, something I've always wanted."

"*Something better*? What's that mean?"

"It's very simple, Bobby. Maybe even you can understand it. Ready? I *ain't comin' back*."

The music started up on the patio again and Fabian turned away. Bobby grabbed his sleeve and when Fabian turned

242

back, his face had that ferocious look, teeth exposed, ready to explode.

Time to take a different slant, Bobby thought, dropping his sleeve, lowering his voice.

"Listen, man. Dash is tellin' everyone he got the best of you. Tellin' them he cheated you out of ten grand. He's *laughing* at you. You understand what I'm saying? *Laughing*! You gonna let him do that?"

Something terrible rose behind Fabian's eyes.

"We gotta do away with the guy, is what I'm saying," Bobby continued. "I figured you'd want to be the one. I mean, you want the satisfaction. Right? Am I right?"

The look in Fabian's eyes frightened even Bobby. But then it subsided, dropping back into his dark interior.

"You're doing it again, ain't ya?" Fabian shook his head.

"What?"

"Exploiting me. You always did that. But you exploited me for *your* good, not mine. But that's behind me now, Bobby. I'm done with all that."

The music had started again and it seemed to be calling to Fabian. The big fleshy woman was belting out some opera song that sounded vaguely familiar to Bobby and she looked over at Fabian and extended her arm to him, and Bobby suddenly thought how this was just like those dreams he had of his brother leaving him. But this was no dream and he was going to stop him.

Bobby caught Fabian's arm once more.

"Fabian. I'm your only brother. You can't turn your back on me."

"Is that right?" Fabian said. "Watch me."

Fabian began singing, his voice filling the restaurant, silencing everyone, and as he moved toward the woman, and took her hand, Bobby finally realized what this was all about.

The only pay phone was located out by the front entrance to the restaurant, near the guy selling cheesy oil paintings, and when Marianna was done talking to Dash, she hung up and turned to Harold and said, "He went for it. He'll be there in fifteen minutes."

"Was he in his room?"

She thought it over. "I could hear singing in the background so, no, I guess he was in the restaurant. Why?"

"Just wondering where he'd be coming from. I.e., I don't want any surprises."

"It's going to be easy, Harold. I told you that already. Now you better get going. I'll go up and get Vikki."

"Look, after you get Vikki, go straight to the car. I'll come back, we'll take off, be back in LA before dawn."

She looked at him closely, as if he was trying to pull a fast one on her.

"Harold, you got to finish him. You don't, he'll be on us before we get a mile down the road."

"Don't worry."

She moved toward the stairs leading to Vikki's room, then stopped and looked back at him.

"See you soon," she said, as if he were going to get a six-pack of beer and rent a video, instead of leaving to kill a man. "It's the only way, Harold," she said and disappeared up the stairs.

Harold left the lights of the hotel behind and moved into the wind and the darkness, walking toward the spot Marianna had found on the cliffs, just below the southbound lanes of Mexico Highway 1-D and near the tall green sign that said, ENSENADA 50 K. He walked along the dirt road past a row of condos on the bluff. Then the road petered out without warning, as roads do in Mexico, turning into a footpath that climbed a hundred feet, then ended in a circle of boulders that formed a scenic overlook spot above the ocean. The highway and the enormous road sign loomed above him, throwing a greenish light on the scene.

Finish him, Marianna said. This would be the second time he had killed for her. Last year, he ran down Vito Fiorre with his pickup truck, sent him flying into the LA night sky, and then falling dead to the ground. But that was a crime of passion; he killed without deliberation, to defend Marianna, the woman he loved.

What was so different about this? He was defending Vikki. He didn't expect to build his life around her. Still, they had a lot in common—i.e., cars. Lately it seemed he had more in common with Vikki than he did with Marianna, who had sniped at him all day long, never pleased with what he did, pushing him in directions he didn't want to take. It was never that way in Chile. It forced him to admit that now, back on her own two feet, things had changed.

On the highway above, a truck suddenly snarled, bringing him back to the present.

Pick a spot and be ready, he thought, looking over the edge and seeing the surf on the rocks two hundred feet below. It was steep, but not a sheer drop. He moved around, trying to pick a place where he would be in the darkness, Dash would be in the light from the road sign and traffic on the highway. How was he going to do it?

Thinking it through, Harold began to feel that it wouldn't be as easy as Marianna thought. He needed something extra, a weapon maybe. He looking around on the ground for a rock or a stick or—light glinted off a wine bottle. Holding it by the neck, it was heavy in his hand, and he felt his confidence returning.

He wanted Dash to have his back to the ocean. Then he'd lean against this rock, his left hand with the bottle would be out of the light. He would wait for the right second, or make a diversion of some kind, then swing up the wine bottle and—

Could he really do it? Kill another man in cold blood?

If only he was driven by emotions like he was when he ran down Vito. Anger, hatred. That's what he felt for Dash, this man who had drugged and used Vikki, had him beaten by gangbangers, had stolen and stripped his Impala.

Recalling these events, a flame sparked to life in Harold's gut and grew. Dash's smug face, smiling, cool, seemed to be at the intersection of all the bad luck he'd had in the past few days. If it weren't for Dash, this thing would have been a piece of cake, a quick score, and he would right now be converting his share of the insurance money into a cargo container bound for Chile, filled with TVs he could easily move for a nice profit.

Harold gripped the bottle neck tighter, thinking how good the hatred felt as it grew and burned inside him, giving him energy and determination, making him sure he could *finish him*. Yes, *finish him*. And these thoughts came to him just in time because he saw a figure coming toward him, a tall man, moving easily up the slope with long powerful strides.

As Marianna struggled up the stairs to Vikki's room, a kid passed her, taking the steps two at a time, and right off she knew he was going to be trouble.

Sure enough, when she got to the top of the stairs, she saw the kid was tapping on Vikki's door. Marianna stepped into the vacant room, the one where two-by-fours had been nailed across the open doorway. She slowly crossed the dark room and moved out onto the balcony, hearing the voices next door growing louder in anger. She looked around the partition to the next balcony and into Vikki's room, which was dimly lit by a hanging bulb in a wicker shade.

Vikki stood beside the bed facing the kid in the open doorway.

"So what're you sayin'? I can't leave?" Vikki had her hands on her hips.

The kid said something she didn't catch.

"Well fuck you, pal," she said. "And you can tell Bobby Skura to fuck himself, too."

Vikki moved toward him, as if to push past him and out into the hallway, but she stopped when he pulled his hand out from under his baggy flannel shirt and pointed the big handgun at her. The gun was dull blue in the weak light and it stopped Vikki, backing her up a step or two. The kid moved into the room, and as he did so, a few rays fell on his face and Marianna saw how young he was—barely even sixteen.

Someone else came into the room now, a short powerful man with black hair and goatee, forcing his way into the room and looking at Vikki, then moving toward the balcony.

Marianna drew back, thinking of Harold out there in the darkness somewhere. He was expecting to find her waiting with Vikki in the car. Better get back down there and let him know that Vikki was in deeper trouble than they had imagined. Still, with Dash out of the way, these two jokers would be a whole lot easier to deal with.

But now the two guys had stepped out into the hallway, blocking her exit. They closed the door to Vikki's room and talked in low voices. She moved closer, thinking that if she couldn't free Vikki, at least she might overhear something that would help her figure out what their next move was. If they had one.

"**Just** you." Dash said to Harold, walking into the circle of stones high on the bluff above the ocean, the light reflecting from the highway sign making his face a hideous greenish color.

"Just me," Harold echoed, getting ready, his left hand out of sight.

"Where's your sidekick? The lady with the sexy walk."

A black wave of anger rose inside Harold, swelling and blinding him. *Easy*, he told himself, just add it to the rest and use it. He'd need it because, now, with Dash here, he saw it would be harder than he thought. He was much taller than he remembered, and he seemed balanced, hands hanging easily by his sides, as if ready to spring.

Harold was standing near the opening of the circle, and Dash had his back to the ocean. Perfect position. Now, he'd look for the right moment. He'd need a little distraction, something little so he could get one good shot in, then over the cliff.

"Your sidekick said you wanted to talk to me," Dash said.

"That's right," winging it, waiting for him maybe to settle back against the boulder, fold his arms . . . look away for a split second.

"I put the cops onto Bobby Skura's chop shop."

"Chop shop? I'm not interested in chop shops."

"It's the one you had my car taken to."

"I'm not with you."

"My Impala. You had them steal it out of the lot by your office."

"Oh, right. I remember that piece of shit."

"Keep working your mouth, your ass'll be on the way to jail."

"Jail?"

"That's right. My deal's this: Maybe I can keep the cops off you. I'm going to give them Bobby Skura, Eddie Fallon, the whole bunch. I'll even give them you if I have to."

"Oh, please, what can I do to save myself?"

"Tell me where my door is."

"Your door?"

"My door and the horn ring off my Impala."

"That's what you want?"

"That's it."

Dash's laughter cut Harold like a dull knife. "You know, as soon as I saw you drive up in that old beater, wearing that old suit, it told me everything I needed to know about you. I said to myself, this old guy's a real loser."

Loser . . . old guy. Okay, Harold knew he could do it. He had everything he needed now—except for the little distraction.

Harold forced himself to keep talking. "I'm not the one losing. I got my car back. And in a few minutes I'm taking Vikki with me back to LA. The only think I lack is the door to my Impala. You get it for me, maybe I'll keep the cops off you. What do you say?"

Dash laughed his low easy laugh, shaking his head. "You're either crazy, or very stupid."

"Maybe I'm both," Harold said, realizing it didn't make sense, but saying it with conviction anyway, getting ready. "What I want to know is, have we got a deal?"

"I don't deal with losers like you."

"Then why'd you come here?"

"To kill you."

So calm. So matter of fact. *To kill you.* Harold felt the sweat break out. Here he was looking for the right moment to kill Dash, and Dash was doing the same thing to him. So Harold knew the time had finally arrived. But he still needed just that little distraction.

Harold laughed, as if he weren't taking the threat seriously. At the same time he said, "Listen. Do we have a deal or not?" and extended his right hand for a deal-clinching handshake. But Dash didn't know that Harold was left-handed, and when he glanced down at Harold's right hand, a nonthreatening move, Harold brought his left arm out of darkness, moving fast, the bottle swinging in a tight arch.

Dash rolled away from the blow and the bottle caught him behind the right ear, not breaking but giving off a hollow *pong*.

Dash staggered back and Harold moved in, swinging as hard as he could, like a street fighter trying to land as many blows as fast as possible, looking for an opening, grunting, and putting everything into it, wanting to see Dash fold, so he could bring the bottle down from above, crushing his skull. But Dash was too tall, backing up, out of range, cursing and growling, beginning to fight back, so Harold ran at him, hit him low in the chest, drove him back against the waist-high rock. Suddenly, Dash wasn't there anymore.

Harold heard a crashing and rolling. His held his breath, waiting for a splash.

Just surf and wind. And the traffic up above.

He stood there, breathing hard, then looking at the bottle in his hand, still unbroken, seeing light glint off wetness and wondering how bad he'd hurt him.

Then happiness rose up inside him. He won! He'd gotten the better of this slick asshole. This monster. It was over now. He'd go back to Vikki and Marianna and they would drive back to LA.

One last look over the edge of the cliff and then he'd be on his way.

Ten feet below he saw Dash, the greenish light on his contorted face, hands clinging to a root, teeth bared with the exertion, a grunting noise coming from low in his chest.

Finish him! Harold could hear Marianna's voice in his ears. *Finish him!*

He raised the bottle, leaning down, picking a spot on Dash's forehead.

Dash's face looked up at him, pleading—if he raised his arm to shield the blow he would drop into the ocean. He was at Harold's mercy.

Finish him! Marianna's voice shrieked at him. But Harold wasn't a cold-blooded killer. And in that small moment of mercy he heard Dash's voice over the sound of the surf, "Help me. Please help me."

I'll help you, all right, Harold thought, *Help you by not bashing your brains in.*

Harold threw the bottle over the cliff and headed back to the lights of the hotel. Halfway there, Marianna's voice was in his head again: *If you don't finish him he'll be on us a mile down the road.* He broke into a run, looking back over his shoulder.

When he got to the parking lot, Marianna was waiting for him. No Vikki, just Marianna, arms folded impatiently, trying to read Harold's face.

"Where's Vikki?" Harold was breathing hard, sensing trouble.

"In her room."

"In *her room!* You were supposed to get her! We've gotta go!"

"We're not going anywhere, Harold. They're here. The two guys who beat you up. And they're holding Vikki in her room."

"Jesus."

"How'd *you* do?"

"What?"

"With Dash. How'd you do?"

"I—I did it."

"So what happened?"

"I threw him over the cliff."

She thought about it, the wind blowing black hair across her face. "Okay, but did you finish him?"

"I threw him over the damn cliff. What more do you want?"

She didn't answer. But her expression said it all.

Gammon got the first call at 6:30 P.M. His buddy, the tech guy in phone surveillance, told him Bobby Skura was on the move. He'd placed a series of calls on his cellular phone on a line with Interstate 5 heading south toward San Diego. Then, at seven o'clock he made several calls from a place in Baja, a point halfway between Rosarito and Ensenada.

Time to get moving.

Gammon threw his gear into a leather duffel bag along with a change of clothes. He headed down to the parking garage of his Culver City apartment and cranked up his '87 Chevy Caprice, and headed along the same route Bobby Skura had taken.

Before he crossed the border he checked with his buddy one more time. Skura had made two more calls from the same location. Gammon checked the map. There were a string of hotels along the coast in that area. He'd have to check them all and hope he'd find Skura's Ford Crown Victoria.

Maybe he could spot the Ford and call the plate in. If it was Skura's car, then he could alert the border patrol or the San Diego P.D. Maybe the kid he'd seen in the chop shop would be with Skura when he headed north. Maybe the kid would be dumb enough to still have the gun on him. Maybe ballistics would match the bullet that went through Richard's throat. And maybe the D.A. would try him as an adult and give him the death penalty.

Was that why he was down here on his own? For a lot of maybes? No, he was here looking for *closure*. That's what the counselor had called it. Thing was, they were talking about two different kinds of closure.

Sometime after midnight Gammon turned the Caprice onto the frontage road off Mexico Highway 1-D south of Rosarito Beach. It was a dirt road, deeply rutted. The duffel bag jumped off the seat beside him as he hit a pothole. He hauled the heavy bag up onto the seat next to him, feeling the barrel of the shotgun poke into his leg.

Ahead was a new hotel with a bank of lights on the roof, illuminating the surf on the beach below. He got out and walked the length of the parking lot, scanning the cars, feeling the bite of the cold wind and smelling salt in the air. From the hotel he heard loud music, Mexican trumpets wailing, and it made him think of the time, ten years ago, when he went down to TJ with some guys from Vice. They got polluted, wound up at some bizarre strip joint where the girl they were drooling over turned out to be a guy—whipped off the old G-string and there it was, big as a *burrito grande*. They staggered out into the street laughing their asses off.

Wait a second, he thought, stopping in the parking lot, Richard had been with him on that little jaunt. It was the first time they met. Two months later Richard transferred to Homicide and they were partnered. So that's how it happened, Gammon thought, I'd almost forgotten that.

He was at the edge of the parking lot now and he still hadn't found the Crown Victoria. There was another hotel to the south, within walking distance. He was out of the car and it felt good to be walking in the cold night air, so he decided to continue on foot. Ten minutes later the heels of his cowboy boots turned unsteadily on the cobblestones of the courtyard parking lot, but his eyes rested on the license plate of a late-model Ford Crown Victoria.

It was a good thing he had come on foot. He would scout the place out now, maybe check with the manager, then pick the best place to wait for them to make a move. Only problem was, his duffel bag was back in the Caprice.

Harold walked along the base of the cliffs below where he had struggled with Dash, looking for his body. On the one hand, he hoped he found it. That would mean Dash was out of the picture. On the other hand, if he found it, that would make him a murderer. And he didn't want another death on his conscience.

Moonlight fell around him like watery milk, and his eye kept jumping from one odd shape to the next, examining it, sorting it, moving on. Harold walked close to the crumbling sandy cliff weaving among boulders humped in the sand like partly buried cars, bending to look closely at dark shapes, prodding rotting piles of kelp. Once he found a dead sea lion, partly decayed; the drying hide pulled the lips back, exposing sharp teeth. He gave the carcass a wide berth.

As he searched he thought of Vikki, imprisoned up in her room, thought of how she had trusted him to help her, thought of her voice on the answering machine, terrified, pleading, saying, "He's got me. He's taking me away. I want you here . . . now . . . I want you here now."

Then a picture of Dash rose in Harold's mind, tall and dangerous, methodically planning to kill Vikki in his smooth way, smiling as he killed her, his voice not even rising in passion. And it was with these thoughts in his mind that he began to hope he would find Dash dead here in the sand. He imagined probing the corpse with his foot, then regretfully removing his wallet and anything from his pockets. Sad, but it had to be done, even if it made him a murderer.

But he had reached the end of the cliffs and his search found nothing. He turned and looked back at the buildings of La Fonda, dark blocks in the weak moonlight, and saw that all the lights were out now, even in Bobby's room next to Vikki's. Dark and quiet and—yes, almost peaceful-looking. Eventually, even killers have to sleep, he thought.

Harold walked back toward the hotel, telling himself he would make one more pass for Dash's body, then he would have to consider him a living threat. And he would have to add him to the deadly mix he would face in the morning.

Harold's mind now turned to Marianna, finding the frustration still hovering in his mind from their day together, sniping at each other, feeling her resisting him, doubting him, criticizing him at every turn. What had happened to the relationship they shared in Chile? Those long afternoons on the sand dunes, sleeping in each other's arms, sitting quietly on the patio with a glass of beer as the sun went down? Assuming they survived this, and escaped the law too, would they find their love waiting for them in Chile, as if they had parked it there before leaving for Southern California?

But then, what would happen if Harold got Vikki out of this and helped her score on the insurance deal? Was there a chance she would want him, not for a quickie in a cheap motel, but want him as her husband, a man to share a new life with, the one into which she was growing now that these scumbags—Joe and Dash—were out of the way.

Harold paused, reeling as he imagined living with a dream woman—a goddess—like Vikki. Me, Harold, an *old guy*, a *loser*. Was it possible she could love me? Maybe. She had seen Harold in action, had seen him get the better of younger men, stronger men—yes, even smarter men. Maybe there was a chance for him. If they made it out of this alive.

But now, reaching the smooth flat sand without finding a

corpse, Harold realized that Dash had hauled himself back up the cliff and was alive. His fantasy relationship with Vikki was dynamited into oblivion and left him feeling, as he so often did, like a complete idiot. Here he was dreaming of living with a blond goddess in a mansion on the hill when Dash was still out there somewhere, knowing he had everything it took to make Vikki do what he wanted.

No, Harold Dodge wasn't Vikki's type. He *was* an old guy, a loser driving a car with only three doors, a has-been living with a cripple, a guy who couldn't even put together a simple export deal of old TV sets. How the hell did he expect to go up against Dash and win?

Harold couldn't help remembering Marianna's instructions: *Finish him, Harold!* He had had Dash at his mercy, recalling his hideous green face, looking up, saying, "Help me. Help me, please." He had the bottle in his hand. He could have closed him out then. But no, he walked away. And now he was paying the price.

As these thoughts tore at him, like the waves eating the cliffs above, Harold found a new surge of determination. He knew Dash was alive. And Marianna had overheard them saying they would make their move at dawn. So he knew he would follow Vikki wherever they took her and try once more to be her hero.

Vikki was lying in bed listening to the wind banging the screen door to the balcony and the noise of the surf, and the shouting in the next room—Bobby and Fabian fighting, swearing, crashing into the walls, and a third voice, younger, that punk that pulled a gun on her, giggling, a crazy falsetto that cracked and ran all over two octaves.

She guessed it was way after midnight, and Dash had been gone for hours now. She had just about given up on him when she heard a new voice in the next room, his low voice, and her heart jumped. Dash was back. And maybe he could get her out of this mess.

The door opened and she saw Dash's tall frame slide into the room.

"Dash?"

"Yeah, babe."

"Where the hell've you been?"

She reached for the bedside lamp but he said, "No."

She lay back and heard water running in the bathroom, saw him washing his face. He was in there a long time. Then he was lying down beside her, groaning slightly as if in pain.

"What happened?"

"Ran into a little trouble."

"Fabian?"

He didn't answer. Instead he found her hand, then pulled her to him. Their faces were an inch apart, she could see his eyes in the moonlight that fell between the pulled curtains, stretched across the French doors to the balcony.

She said: "Dash, let's get the fuck out of this place. It's getting too crazy. Let's just get out of here."

"I would, but they took my car keys."

He rolled onto his back and his voice had an edge of self-loathing she'd never heard before, and which she knew would only be there in the dark hours of the night. During the day he'd be smiling and cool, impossible to read.

"I owe them money," he said. "A lot of money."

"For what?"

"Their cut on a bunch of phony claims."

"Hot cars?"

"And staged accidents. Medical claims. You name it."

"How much did Joe know?"

"Nothing. Fallon and I set up the whole thing."

"But I found some files in his safe."

"Fallon said Joe was getting suspicious, starting to ask questions, but then Joe disappeared so . . ."

Vikki thought it over.

"And the check you gave me—for a hundred grand?"

"It's no good. I just gave it to you so you'd stay with me." His voice was filled with disgust. "I've made a real mess of things."

She felt he was revealing something real about himself for the first time. His guard was down and he was just another poor jerk in over his head. Either that or he was playing another role.

"I haven't exactly been a nun myself," she said.

He kissed her and his voice was finally natural when he said, "Thanks, babe."

Then, suddenly, it was quiet. No wind, no drunken voices from the next room. Even the surf sounded quieter. Out in the parking lot, a car started up, backed out, and pulled away, accelerating hard.

Dash got out of bed saying, "Maybe a nightcap would help us."

He produced a bottle of wine from his bag, cut the lead, and pulled the cork. She turned on the light, but he said, "Better not. We don't want any visitors." She turned it off again and as he poured he spilled some and said, "Damn." He took her glass into the bathroom and she could see him using the single threadbare towel. He appeared again and handed her the glass as he sat on the side of the bed.

"Tomorrow, things could get kind of crazy," he said slowly. She was holding the glass, not drinking any. "But I think I can pull it out. If you give me one more chance."

"What do you want me to do?"

"Trust me. There's no reason you should—after what I put you through. But I'm asking you to give me one last shot."

His face was in the shadow but she knew he was smiling that crooked little-boy smile of his, the one that always made her do what he wanted her to do.

"What's going to happen?"

"You and me are heading over to San Felipe, like we're going to do some fishing. You and me in one car, Bobby and Neto in the other."

"Yeah . . ."

"On the way there, we're going to lose them."

"Lose them."

"It'll be easy. I've got four-wheel drive and there's a lot of desert out there. How's that sound?" He held the glass out to her for a toast.

She thought it over.

"What was supposed to happen if we got to San Felipe?"

"There would be an accident."

"Me or you?"

"You."

"Why?"

"Bobby told Fallon he's going to take care of you—so Fallon can run the dealership. Vikki, I want you to know—" He struggled to continue. "I can't do it. They wanted me in on it because they think you trust me. I can't hurt you."

She thought it over and said, "I like your plan better. Let's put it in four-wheel drive and take the detour."

He touched her glass again and waited for her to take a drink. She hesitated, a vague memory of paralysis and darkness flickering across her mind. But then she remembered her own cleverness, switching the pills. She was safe, even if he tried to drug her. In fact, this might make an interesting test. Dash held his glass up, inviting her to drink and, as he moved his head slightly the moonlight fell on his face. She was right, he was smiling that crooked little-boy smile. The wine was cold and crisp and very dry. She took another big sip and lay back.

"When this is over," he said, "I'm thinking maybe we deserve a little getaway trip."

"What've you got in mind?"

"Ever been to Kauai?"

"The garden island. No."

"They've got a resort there you wouldn't believe. You're playing this par five, and the fairway goes straight out to the ocean. Like a big green ramp, right out into the ocean. And the air there—it's warm and full, like someone's touching your face, telling you everything's going to be okay now. How's that sound?"

"I could get used to it."

"Me too, babe."

"Tell me some more, Dash."

He began talking again as she took another sip of the wine. His voice was in her mind, the words coming loose and floating around pleasantly, taking her across the ocean to a place where it was always sunny. And she realized then that the nightcap was beginning to have the desired affect.

A pounding noise penetrated Dash's sleep and he knew it wasn't the wind slamming the screen shut anymore, so he got up and opened the door and found Bobby standing there with Neto next to him. Dash figured Bobby hadn't slept at all, boozing and fighting all night, and sure enough, his eyes were like two little piss holes in the sand.

"You want to go fishing or not?" Bobby said, his voice too loud, looking past Dash to the sleeping form in the bed.

Dash stepped out the door and lowered his voice. "What's the deal?"

"Goin' fishin' just like you planned," Bobby answered.

Dash looked at Bobby and saw his face was set. So Dash smiled and held out his hand. "Need my car keys."

"You get 'em when we go. Get your shit together and come on down."

Dash got Vikki on her feet and she dressed automatically in the cold dark room, putting on her clothes from yesterday and not saying a word, just responding to the sound of his voice. Dash helped her straighten her simple white top like he was a good dad helping his sleepy girl get ready for school. Then he brushed her hair, thinking, *It's the color of summer*, and feeling a hollow dread. But he had made his choice and he'd stick to it.

Vikki stood by the door staring at the floor as he put their things in the duffel bag. He rechecked the room, as he always did in hotels, then took her hand, and they stepped outside into the new day. It was dawn now, the sun rising somewhere behind the mountains to the east. Although it was still cold, there was the smell of a warm day in the air.

Bobby and Neto were standing in the cobblestone courtyard below, jingling car keys and talking in low voices.

"Ready, babe?" Dash said before they started down the stairs.

Vikki looked at him with empty eyes and said nothing. He kissed her cheek and they went down.

"Morning, Vik." Bobby was chewing gum now and as he smiled at her his lips pulled back, showing his teeth.

Vikki didn't answer. Bobby looked at Dash and nodded at Vikki. "Don't say much, does she? You two have a rough night?"

"Yeah, the guys next door wouldn't shut up."

"My, my. What the hell kind of a place is this?"

Neto giggled.

"Let's roll. Ship pulls out at seven." Bobby said jingling a set of car keys. "Here's Dash's keys," he handed them to Neto. "Why don't you drive Vikki? Looks like she needs more sleep. Dash and I will follow you. We need to talk."

Dash reacted. "Hang on—she's going with me."

"Change of plans, Dash. We got a lot to cover."

"So we talk on the boat."

"It's best this way—for everyone." Bobby fake-winked at Dash and smiled.

Dash looked at Vikki and saw something moving in her eyes. He held out his hand to Neto. "Come on, man. Give me the keys."

Neto stared back at him.

"Hey, Neto's a safe driver," Bobby said. "He might even get his license some day."

Neto and Bobby thought that was very funny.

"We agreed," Dash said.

"We agreed on shit." Bobby turned to Neto. "Take her in the Accell. We'll follow you."

"Those keys are to the Rover."

Bobby squinted at him, confused. "You drove the Accell down here."

"I drove my Rover." Dash pointed at the big green four-by-four at the end of the row.

"What's that doing here?" He nodded at the parked silver Accell.

"You got me."

"Whatever," Bobby said. "Vik and Neto—in the Rover. Let's go."

Vikki just stood there. She was looking at Dash, her eyes no longer hollow but filled with regret as she spoke for the first time that morning. She simply said, "Dash?"

Dash looked away, saying, "See you there, babe."

When Neto rammed the stick in reverse and almost backed into a wall, Vikki said, "Why don't you let me take the wheel?"

He looked at her funny, surprised to hear her speaking so clearly. He pulled out and the tires spun in loose gravel, then hit pavement and they shot forward.

"Go back to sleep," he said, and giggled.

She felt like slapping that giggle back down his throat, knocking that shit-eating grin off his face. If it came to it, she'd do just that. The point was that it was all up to her now—now she knew she couldn't trust Dash.

Watching the road climb ahead of them into the mountains, they shot past a sign that said "*Curva Peligrosa 500 M*" and she thought, *When're you gonna learn about men? You're almost thirty-five years old, you keep going for these head cases*, picturing Joe dead on the slab in Santa Barbara. And *killers*, she added, thinking of Dash behind her somewhere, ready to move in as soon as the smoke cleared.

Last night she must have been nuts to get suckered into believing Dash. Luckily, her little switcheroo with the pills had worked. The wine gave her a few hours of sleep and she woke up sensing that she should act drugged, see what Dash did. It seemed like that's what he expected from her so she kept it up. And when they met Bobby in the parking lot, she thought if she played along with Dash they might lose them in the mountains, like he said he would. Instead, Dash buckled when Bobby leaned on him. And now here she was riding in the death seat on a collision course with a fixed object. But they had another name for this seating arrangement—*riding shotgun*. That sounded a little more active. She didn't have a shotgun, but she knew more about driving than this baby gangster. And if she couldn't get away, she would make sure they were involved in the accident of her choice, not his.

The Rover leaned heavily in the *curva peligrosa* and she saw that the road narrowed ahead, then snaked down into the valley, where a cluster of farms was strung along a muddy river. Neto was checking his mirror, flashing his lights. She leaned forward until she could see into the right wing mirror and she caught the reflection of the Crown Victoria a quarter mile back, the silhouette of two men inside. And once they piled up, who would be there to help her? One thing at a time, she thought grimly.

Then she remembered her Accell was there at the hotel, the Accell she loaned to Harold. Was it possible . . . ? Maybe he had followed her after Dash brushed him off at the border. *Womb to tomb*, he said. Is this what he meant when he said that? And so far, he had been there when she really needed him. But men were a constant disappointment. Better not expect anything from them, even from Harold, she thought, checking the mirror again.

Wait a second, another car was gaining on the Crown Victoria. A compact. Couldn't see what it was. And here goes Neto with the lights again.

Better get ready, take stock. Front air bag. Seat belt low and tight across her hips. Seat belt release between the seats within easy reach. Now, what could she use for a fixed object? A head-on collision would ram the steering shaft right through Neto's pimply chest. Maybe that would stop that annoying giggle.

Harold had heard the voices below in the courtyard in the quiet of the dawn and had been watching them through the window of the hotel room with Marianna asleep behind him in the bed. Then he saw them step away and heard car engines starting up, and car doors slamming, and he knew he had run out of time for anything other than a desperation move. He grabbed the Accell keys and ran to the car, watching as the Crown Victoria and the Rover crossed the coast highway and disappeared up a mountain road.

The Accell's speedometer was touching eighty when Harold came over the rise and saw the two cars and realized there was a mile or so of straight road ahead of them before it dropped out of sight again. Pedal to the metal time. His foot on the deck now, he heard the engine roar and felt his speed steadily building. He watched Bobby's silhouette ahead of him and realized his radar hadn't picked him up yet. Why should he? No reason to check the rearview—at 5 A.M. most honest citizens are home in bed.

The Accell had more guts than he thought. Now if he could only pass the Crown Victoria before they saw him. Then he'd be between Bobby Skura and the Rover with Vikki in it. Then they would know he was here and they wouldn't pull anything.

Or maybe they would kill him too. Neto had a gun and Harold had seen him use it. He had seen Bobby laughing while they beat his head in at the liquor store parking lot. But none of that would happen if they were still moving. While they were still moving, Harold thought, they still had a chance.

Coming up fast now on Bobby's Ford, wind roaring in the

vent window, the car weaving unsteadily, Harold pulled into the left lane, needle touching the century mark and still climbing. Christ, where was the top end on this thing?

The Crown Victoria went by in a flash on his right, so fast he only caught a glimpse of Bobby's face coming around, mouth falling open in a classic, "What the . . . ?" expression. But he recovered quickly. Couple of seconds later the big sedan was bearing down on him like a friggin' locomotive.

Harold had all this speed now and he figured he might just as well pass the Rover too. No such luck. The little gangbanger saw him coming and floored it. And those Rover's had plenty of power, big V-8, they passed everything on the road except a gas station.

But at least he was in the picture now, distracting them, letting Vikki know he was here now and, at least for a few microseconds, that might be comforting.

Here comes the Crown Victoria again, Harold realized, looking in his wing mirror and seeing the big car's high beams flashing. He couldn't hold his position on the straightaway. But he might do better in the curves than that land yacht Bobby was driving. *Curva Peligrosa 500 m.* If he could just hang on until he got there. He jammed his foot into the floorboards but there was nothing left. Time for some fancy driving.

Bobby was closing fast, about to come around him, when Harold pulled into the left lane and blocked him. The Crown Victoria's tires screamed and smoked as he tried to reign it in, tried to shed some speed. He pulled right to pass Harold on the other side but Harold pulled back in, seeing that the curves were coming up faster than he thought and realizing that he had a new problem—ahead was thin blue air, the road cutting sharp to his left and dropping out of sight. Below lay a broad valley and a scattering of farms. Maybe he'd just take off and try to fly this thing.

Accelerate in the curve. It came back to Harold from the old days, when he was a teenager running Chevys through hairpin turns up on Mulholland Drive on Saturday nights. If you want to hold the road at 80 miles an hour, the hotshot drivers told him there was only one way to make it—keep your foot off the brake and floor it halfway through the curve. A *power turn.*

Funny how he never suspected that bit of advice would be useful later in life. It worked then. It might work now. If it didn't, he hoped the end was clean and fast.

Gammon had the binoculars to his eyes, watching the group in the courtyard, trying to get a good look at the Hispanic kid. But the kid seemed to sense he was there and kept his back facing him. Yeah, he looked like he was the right height and build. But he had to see his face.

Turn around, you little prick, Gammon thought. *Let me get one good look at you and I'll be on your ass in a second.*

What the hell were they talking about? Gammon wondered. He recognized the blonde, Vikki Covo, and Bobby Skura from the chop shop. But the kid. If he was a kid. Was he the one?

Turn around, you little son of a bitch!

The figures walked out of the twin circles of his vision. He took down the binoculars and saw them splitting up, heading toward the cars. The Rover came out of the gates first, pausing to check for traffic. He had the binos up but the sun reflected off the window and he couldn't see if . . . The Rover pulled out.

And Gammon saw the kid's face. It was him.

He'd only seen him for a second. But that was how long he had seen him in the chop shop. He saw his face come around

the corner. Saw Dodge moving toward him, then saw the
muzzle flash and felt Richard falling beside him.

Gammon fired up the Caprice and caught them as he
reached a plateau and saw the silver Accell blow off the
Crown Victoria. He checked his seat belt, then pulled out his
.45 automatic and lay it on the seat next to him.

Ahead the cars disappeared over the ridge as if they'd
never been there. But he had the feeling that, just out of
sight, over the crest of the mountain, all hell was breaking
loose. He felt a tightening in his chest, a feeling he used to
get as a street cop, arriving on a scene, bailing out and
starting to run—not knowing what you were running into but
knowing you better get there pretty damn fast.

He hadn't felt this way for a long time. And it was a good
feeling—that tightening. It reminded him he was alive. And it
reminded him that he was, as Richard used to say, *nothing but
a fuckin' cowboy.*

Lying sprawled across the bed after they made love, Sophia
looked at Fabian with her big dark eyes, like liquid pools of
emotion, and said, *Go to your brother. Give him the chance to
understand about us.*

No way, Fabian thought. She doesn't know what Bobby is
like. She doesn't know how the bastard controls me.

I'll go with you, she said. *I want to meet him, your brother. We'll
talk, drink coffee, forgive each other. He'll understand. He's your
brother, and he loves you.*

Loves me? Fabian didn't think so. They had fought for hours
last night until Bobby had said, fuck it, you do whatever you
want with that whore, I don't give a damn anymore.

Maybe Bobby had gone back to LA. Fabian hoped he was

gone because he didn't want anything to take him away from this woman. He was filled with emotions he didn't know he had. It was as if, overnight, he had become a different man, a man who was finally alive, not stumbling through life playing the role of Bobby's attack dog.

Fabian looked in Sophia's liquid eyes, into those pools of emotions, and felt that he was falling into her, becoming one with her, the way they were when they sang together. So he said yes, they would go talk to his older brother and try to make things right. They dressed together and headed outside into the stillness of dawn surrounding her ranch along the river on the valley floor and smelled the new day coming.

You'll see. Everything will be all right, she said, *he's your brother and he loves you.*

And when they got into her old VW bug and began driving back over the mountains to La Fonda, she grew afraid of his expression, so to cheer him up she sang the opening bars of "*Sempre Libera*"—the song that had brought them together— and, as they headed into the first turns on the climb up the mountain, his rich, powerful voice joined hers, singing: "Amor, amor, e' palpito dell'universo."

The Rover was up on two wheels in the first set of curves, leaning like it would scrape off its door handles, and Vikki knew it was time to take action or die scared. One thing was for sure, she didn't want to go over the edge, down into the river. That was certain death. So she would pick an inside curve. Strapped in tight, even if they rolled, the Rover probably had a reinforced passenger compartment. She just might make it.

One last check in the mirror: Harold was a quarter of a mile back and Bobby was right behind him, flashing his lights and trying to pass him. Neto had seen Harold coming and was pretending the Rover was an Indy car, not a top-heavy death trap ready to flip into the river below.

Vikki reached down between the seats and popped Neto's belt loose, then pulled the steering wheel so the Rover veered in toward the rock wall on her side of the road.

"Hey!" he yelled, looking at her, then tried to backhand her across the mouth as he fought the wheel, the Rover all over the place now.

Vikki threw an elbow, feeling the bony point hit him hard and heard him yell, Bitch! as they swung down into another curve, hairpinning around a huge boulder.

Neto groped under the seat with his free hand, coming up with a gun. She hit him again, not caring now what was happening to the car, only trying to keep him from getting the gun leveled at her.

BOOM!

The gun exploded the windshield, the glass blowing in all over them. She swung again and drove her fist into his eye. The gun flew from his hand, bounced off the car door, and fell under his feet.

Neto was drawing his arm back to fight her off when he saw the Crown Victoria pulling up beside them in the curve, looked over at Bobby, came out of the turn, and found a VW bug coming straight at them. Bobby locked up his brakes and cut the wheel, sliding sideways, glancing off the Rover, spinning back around, then hitting the VW head-on, crushing the little car and flying up and over it into the air, turning once, then landing across the road in front of the Rover.

The Crown Victoria appeared in front of the Rover for an instant, then—

Vikki's mind shut down.

During the second or two the accident lasted she was dimly aware of tearing muscles and tissue, the hideous sound of crushing metal and breaking glass. But, on another level, her mind was suspended, waiting only to find if, on the other side of this chaos, there would be any form of consciousness left waiting for her.

When the Rover finally came to a rest, and her mind returned from wherever it had been, she became aware of a terrible pressure on her chest. The seat had been torn off the floor, thrown forward, but her belt had held, pinning her chest and squeezing the life out of her. Seconds later the air bag deflated and she could again see, looked up and saw daylight through the driver's side door and realized they had rolled. The door was sprung open and Neto was gone. And the smell of gas was heavy in the air.

Then, in the sudden silence, during which she began to wonder who was left alive to come and help her, she heard, somewhere up the road, an inhuman cry of agony.

For one second Fabian thought Sophia was all right. Her beautiful face, her shoulders and dark hair, it was all just as he had last seen it, seconds before the impact, teeth flashing, that heavenly voice filling the car with happiness.

She's all right! he thought as he picked himself up from beside the road where he had been thrown. She's alive!

But then he saw that, while her face was untouched, the lower half of her body was gone; it had been torn away and lay somewhere inside the crushed VW, which was now engulfed in flames.

Fabian staggered backward, horrified, hands clawing his face, a strange cry gushing from inside him, and turned to see his brother, struggling toward him, his shirt torn open and blood on his face. Bobby stopped in the road, staring at him, and gasped, "Fabian . . . Jesus . . . Thank God."

But then Bobby turned to see Sophia lying there, looked back at Fabian as he rushed him, picked Bobby off his feet, and held him aloft for a moment before, with an animal roar, he hurled his brother over the side of the mountain and into the river below.

Gammon topped the rise and, as the scene unfolded in front of him, he slowed the Caprice and stopped beside the Accell. He took the .45 automatic from the seat next to him, climbed out, and stood in the road next to Dodge as they both stared at the wreckage without speaking.

Then they headed for the cars.

Somewhere inside all that metal was Richard's killer. The irony struck him that he might have to save the kid's life so he could extradite him, give him to the D.A., and put him on death row. He hoped it didn't come to that. That wasn't the closure he was looking for, the closure that would help him deal with his guilt and get on with his life. Maybe even go back to the department.

Coming around the VW Gammon saw the big man kneeling in the road beside something. He looked to see what it was—then quickly looked away and kept moving. Nothing he could do for either of them. Ahead, a man was struggling to get out of the Crown Victoria, his blond hair blackened by blood.

Dodge was looking into the Rover now and calling for him to come help. Gammon started toward him but then sensed motion to his right, over the edge of the road. He glanced down and realized he was looking at a kid, maybe fifteen years old, gangbanger garb with baggy pants and flannel shirt, crawling in the dirt, dragging his lower body like a sack filled with rocks.

Gammon scrambled down the slope, boots sliding in the loose gravel, and reached the kid, who looked up at him wincing, his face twisted by pain into something almost like a smile.

"It hurts bad. You gotta help me."

The gun was in Gammon's hand and he found his arm extending the weapon at this punk, this kid who seemed to be sneering up in his face.

"You gotta help me, man. I can't take the pain. Help me, please."

"You're the one, aren't you? You shot my partner." Gammon was surprised to see that the gun in his hand was absolutely steady.

"Fuck, man, don't you hear me? I'm hurtin'."

"The cop, in the body shop in Wilmington. You shot him."

"*Please.*"

"Just tell me what you did. Then I'll get you all fixed up."

The kid's expression broke and he started crying. And, as Gammon watched, the tears turned him back into a boy.

"You can't do this, man," he cried. "I know the law. I got rights."

"I am the law now. I can kick your ass off this cliff. I can blow your brains out if I want to. Now say it."

The kid started moving again, dragging himself like a dog hit by a car. And Gammon saw where he was headed. A gun lay in the dirt two feet away.

A strange wave of power swept over Gammon as he realized that, not only could he take this punk's life, but he could do it in a way that was entirely legal—even justifiable to himself. All he had to do was let him reach the gun.

Watching the kid inch his way toward the pistol, Gammon suddenly wondered if Richard was watching him now. He didn't usually have thoughts like this but there it was, and it made him wonder what Richard would want him to do. Would he want him to avenge his death by blowing away this barrio rat, a kid who might even look like Richard did at his age? Or should he go by the book?

Crouching next to the kid, Gammon spoke softly.

"I'm just asking you to admit what you did. That's not so hard."

The kid could pick up the gun now, if he wanted to. But he collapsed, exhausted, and said, "I thought it was a holdup, man. I come in, seen that dude with the gun on Bobby, and it was like, 'Whoa, these guys're jackin' us.'"

"So you shot him."

"I shot him! Yes, I shot him. Okay?"

"No, it's not okay." Gammon slowly stood up.

He looked down at this boy at his feet, the gun leveled at him, still feeling like he was a spectator observing himself, wondering what he would do next. And while he was wondering this, the kid's arm came up holding the gun and Gammon looked down into the barrel and could see the rounded dome of the lead slug waiting to be released.

Standing in the road, with the black smoke rising across the new sun, Harold felt the weight of this destruction on his shoulders and thought: Is there anyone left alive in all this?

As he moved toward the Rover he saw the back door had sprung open and luggage was spilled on the road. Brightly colored clothes and shiny golf clubs lay scattered across the pavement like broken promises.

Harold circled the Rover, turned on its side, gas leaking from the punctured tank. He crouched, looking through the blown-out windshield, bracing himself for what he might see, peering through the twisted steering wheel and the tangle of torn seats and broken glass and found Vikki's frightened eyes looking back at him as she said, "Harold. Oh, God, you're here."

The seat had torn loose and was thrown forward under the dashboard, her legs lost under there somewhere and Harold saw that the seat belt was crushing the life out of her, making her breathe in little puffs, *uh, uh, uh*.

"I'm gonna get you out," he said, kneeling beside the car, reaching through the windshield, "You're gonna be okay."

"You're here," she said, smiling against the pain. "I can't breathe, Harold. The belt release, push it."

He was half in the car now, the gas strong in his nostrils, groping for the release lever, their faces close, and he felt her breath on his cheek, thinking, *That's her life, I feel her life on my face.* He had found the lever now but it was jammed, frozen by the taut pressure on the belt. He pressed hard, his sweat-slick fingers slipping on the plastic lever.

"Get me out," she said again, her breath in his ear.

Then he heard her say, "No," her eyes locking on something behind him.

Harold turned and saw him coming—first his legs, then looking up to see the blond hair with blood running through it and dripping off his jaw. Dash was carrying a long steel rod at his side that looked almost like—

Harold backed out of the car and was scrambling to his feet when sunlight glinted off the steel shaft and he saw the golf club arching through the air.

THUMP!

The club slammed into his back, making him turn in pain, then, the flash of steel again as the club swung in over his raised arm and—

THUD!

The club crashed into Harold's skull and made him stagger

forward, stumbling and falling, then rolling onto his side, lying next to the Rover.

Daylight flickered and dimmed, the picture shrinking to a pinpoint like an old TV being switched off.

Black out now and you're gone.

It was a quiet voice inside him, speaking without alarm but with chilling conviction. He fought to keep the picture in front of his eyes because—

Black out, you'll be dead with your face in the road.

The voice spoke with a distant regret, as if coming from a separate source, with a sadness for this man who had come close to sorting out this mess he'd created, to being the hero, to finally doing something good.

Just keep breathing. Keep your eyes open. Then get up.

No, he wouldn't get up. Not yet anyway. He would lie there with the cool pavement on his cheek and look at the world sideways. He would lie here until it all went away. He couldn't get up again. He'd done that before and he just kept winding up on his ass.

Flicker. Flicker. Sorry, folks, we're losing the picture. Show's over.

He lay there, images sliding around in his vision—nothing connected to anything else. Nothing making sense. Like the voice he heard—Vikki's voice—saying, "Dash, please. Get me out of here."

And that low voice answering, "Hang in there, babe. I'm coming."

Now it looked like Dash had dropped the club and was slapping his pockets, looking for something he couldn't find.

"Careful, Dash," he heard Vikki say. "There's gas every-where."

"I know, babe. Just relax."

Now Dash went back to the VW, tearing loose a piece of burning fabric and, yes, he was coming back. Back where the smell of gas was strong in his nostrils.

Seeing Dash approach made Harold realize that, busted head or not, it was time to get his ass off the deck. Time to be a stand-up guy—a hero one more time before Dash turned out the lights on him for good.

But there just wasn't anything left. So Harold lay there, watching Dash coming, thinking of all the things that wouldn't get done if he died here, on this lonely Mexican road. He wouldn't save Vikki. And he wouldn't return with Marianna to their house in Chile, wouldn't take his dad there for one last taste of happiness.

His dad. When he thought of his father he heard the familiar words in his mind again, the words he'd kept close to him all his life: *Two of them came at me, Harry! But they couldn't put me down.* His father didn't remember that ever happening. But Harold was sure it had. In fact, he was absolutely positive.

Harold pushed himself to his knees, feeling the rough pavement under his palms. He rose to his feet. And he stood there, blocking Dash's path to the Rover.

Dash seemed a little surprised, still holding the flaming fabric. He looked at Harold, frowned, and said, "What do you think you're going to do?"

It was insane, but Harold thought he'd go out in style. So, just for the hell of it, he said, "I'm gonna kick your ass."

Dash laughed, shaking his head, saying, "The Dodge Charger . . ." He dropped the torch and picked up the golf club again, raised it above his head like he was driving a spike with a sledgehammer.

Here it comes, Harold thought. He had always wondered if he'd see his own death coming. And this is what it looked like: a tall man at dawn, his face dripping blood, swinging a club, ready to bring down the curtain on a life of pain and failure.

Harold waited for the downward stroke. And after that the film would break and they'd turn off the projector and the theater would be cold and dark again. And in that final moment, all Harold could think of was, *I'm so sorry, Vikki.*

BOOM!

There it was. It was over now.

But no! He was still alive. And Dash was turning, looking toward the edge of the road at someone coming.

Harold followed his gaze and saw a tall figure, Gammon, carrying Neto in his arms as if he were a child, the detective still holding his gun in his hand, the gun with which he had fired a warning to Dash.

And when Harold's vision finally cleared, and they got Vikki free, and loaded her in Gammon's car, they realized that at some point during all that confusion, the Accell had disappeared. And so had Dash.

Harold returned to his room at La Fonda looking for Marianna, ready to tell her about the whole bizarre series of events. But approaching their room, he sensed it was unnaturally quiet. And, as the door swung open on the empty space, he had a terrible sinking feeling, a feeling that deepened as he found that she hadn't left him a note to tell him where she had gone. In fact, there wasn't a trace to show that she had ever been there.

Staring at the empty room, and feeling the hollowness in his gut, he staggered forward, fell on the bed, and closed his eyes. Some time later he heard a voice: "You weren't thinking of leaving without saying good-bye?"

Harold looked up into Gammon's small eyes, his expression hidden by the wild beard.

"Time to get movin', Chief. We'll get your head put back together. Then the folks up in Santa Barbara have a few questions for you."

Two days later the door to Harold's cell opened and a Santa Barbara County Sheriff's Deputy said, "They want you again, Harold."

Harold had been lying on his cot in the clean stark cell thinking about what he would do during the sixty-day sentence he would probably be serving for the charge of Making False Statements. His book, How to Buy a Cream Puff, needed a revision. If he added some new material (an appendix on how to inspect a used car maybe?) he could call it a new edition and the bookstores would load up again. That would maybe put eight grand in his pocket. And making the revisions to the book would help to pass the time.

It really wasn't bad here, not like the jail he spent a night in last year in LA: six men in a cell. Guys screaming all the time until he thought his head would explode. No. It was a lucky thing he wound up back here. It was peaceful. Boring, really.

Harold stood up, feeling the too-small jumpsuit pulling tight across his chest, and followed the deputy down the freshly painted corridor. The door opened on the small interrogation room revealing Wycoff in his usual seat at the metal table. As Harold moved into the room he saw Gammon was also there, wearing a coat and tie, long legs crossed, smoking one of his black cigarettes.

"Hello, Harold," Wycoff said, his voice, as always, carrying sadness and regret.

Harold looked at Gammon, who said, "How ya doin', Chief?"

Wycoff leaned forward, folding his hands on the desk. "Harold, we're done with you." That didn't sound good. He waited for more. "We're turning you over to Detective Gammon."

"The time has come." Gammon smiled at Harold.

"What's that mean?"

"Means you're checkin' out of this country club and headin' back to the real world. I'm takin' you to County."

Harold didn't want to, but he had to say, "County?"

"Los Angeles County Jail. It was built for twelve hundred men but as of right now there's maybe five, six thousand guys in there. Mostly black and Hispanic. Half of them are gangbangers just waiting for some white guy like you to—"

"I get the picture, okay?"

"I don't think you do, Chief. Doesn't matter if you get convicted or not. Any time you serve in County is hard time. Guy I picked up last year on a G-Ride decided to be a little shitbird. Wouldn't plead. Waiting for his trial he wound up in County. White guy. Said something that offended a gentleman of color. They held him down, took turns jumpin' off the bunk beds onto his head. Want to know what he looked like when they finished with him?"

"No thanks."

Harold forced himself to hold Gammon's eyes, thinking, he's throwing the scare into me, then he'll make the offer. Wait for the offer, but don't beg for it. For a second Harold considered clamming up altogether, giving Zorich, his lawyer, a call. But then he remembered how he still owed the little weasel five grand in legal fees for his last bit of trouble.

"Now, you don't want to do County time, do you, Harold?"

"What do you think?"

Gammon stubbed out the black cigarette and leaned back in his chair, letting the images sink into Harold's imagination.

Wycoff took over, hunching forward again, lacing his fingers together in front of him, as if he had trapped a small animal in his hands.

"We searched the area where you found Covo's body. You

were right, we didn't find a gun. So we have to assume it wasn't a suicide, since his car was found in LA. We're proceeding on the assumption he was murdered somewhere else and dumped there." Pause. "However, I think you should know I've issued a new death certificate for Joe Covo. We changed the cause of death to homicide."

They all knew what that meant—with homicide as the cause of death, Vikki would get a million dollar payoff from the insurance policy. Harold tried not to show his relief, tried not to show any emotion at all to these two men who wanted to break him.

"So that part's settled," Wycoff continued. "But we still have to know who killed Covo, and how his body got there. You knew where to find the body—it would be logical to assume you dumped it there."

Harold was working hard to keep the images of County Jail out of his head. But Gammon's speech was taking its toll. He felt tired, disoriented. Over the past three days, Harold had answered so many question it was hard to keep track of what he had said.

"I didn't kill him."

"Then who did it? You must know."

"The same person that shot him, Vito Fiorre."

"And Vito's dead. Nice, Harold. Thanks a lot."

Gammon sighed, disgusted, losing his patience. "You think we're stupid. Is that it?"

Harold said nothing.

"I mean, you don't think we can figure it out? Okay, Covo was shot somewhere else and dumped by the rest area there. We know from the shape of the body that he was dumped sometime before a big rain storm hit October twenty-fourth. You found him October twenty-fifth. That means he was probably dumped the night of October twenty-second. Now, who drove him up here?"

"I told you, Vito Fiorre."

"I checked your story the first time you floated that one. Fiorre was in Harbor General with a busted skull October twenty-second. It couldn't have been him. So who did it?"

"If you're trying to put this on me, it won't work. I was in one of your lockups that night."

"I got enough on you, Chief. I'm giving the credit for this one to your girlfriend—Marianna Perado. She was pissed off about the way she was treated at Covo's dealership. She shot Covo, drove him up here, and dumped him."

Harold tried hard not to listen. Not to react. But the words got through anyway, and they were mostly true. He let his eyes slide off Gammon's face as if he was thinking of how to explain something that was really very simple.

"Marianna had nothing to do with this," he finally said, hoping it came across with more conviction than it sounded from the inside.

"That's just not true." Gammon leaned forward, his voice sympathetic. "Harold, Sergeant Wycoff and I have discussed this and come up with a solution that we think is very reasonable. Want to hear it?"

I do, I do, Harold thought, but suppressed the urge to speak.

"You don't want to take the fall for Perado, Chief. It's time to share the blame. And here's what you can do for us: Bring her in. We know she was with you down in Baja, you can probably find her in LA. You help us get her and we'll do the rest. You do that for Sergeant Wycoff here, and you'll only get sixty days. Sixty days, Harold! Up here, that's nothing. Half the time you'll be out there cuttin' grass with guys who got busted for jaywalking and spitting on the sidewalk."

Gammon was painting pictures in Harold's head again: Which do you want? A hellhole with cons jumping on your head, or mow the lawn with Ozzie and Harriet?

Now Wycoff leaned forward with one more little teaser.

"Harold, we think it's only fair to let you know that there's someone in the lobby right now, waiting to bond you out. Ten, fifteen minutes from now, you could be free."

Free. Harold's heart soared. Easy, he told himself, wait for the kicker. But he couldn't stop himself from looking at Wycoff and asking, "Who?" He hated himself instantly, knowing they wanted him to beg.

"What was her name again?" Wycoff asked Gammon, messing with Harold now, "Was it Virginia or something?"

"Vikki. It's Vikki Covo."

"She's a classy woman, Harold," Wycoff said, his sad eyes adding dignity to the moment. "And she's here to see you. But we've got a problem. See, the D.A. knows about your Failure to Appear down in LA last year. He's afraid you're gonna play rabbit again. But I'll tell you what I'll do for you. I'll vouch for you. I'll tell the D.A. you're working with me and Detective Gammon here."

Harold cleared his throat. "There's another way I could help you." They waited. "I could give you Dash Schaffner. He had this deal with Joe where—"

Gammon laughed. "Sorry, Chief, Schaffner was smart enough to cooperate. He put a wild hair up the State Insurance Commissioner's ass—now the fraud unit's busting chop shops all over LA. Tell you how helpful Schaffner was, he even claims Vikki Covo's not as clean as she looks. Says she's driving an Accell she bought with a bogus credit card. Turns out to be true, it could make a big dent in all that dough she just came into."

"So what's it gonna be, Harold?" Gammon asked. "Want to do your time here, nice and easy—or you want to do hard time—County time?"

It became quiet in the small room, and Harold tried to keep his mind from picturing Vikki out in the lobby. He tried to focus on the sounds around him, banging doors, a TV down in the day room. But his mind kept moving beyond these walls. He imagined being outside, with Vikki. He could be *free* if he said yes. *Free now*, with no threat of County hanging over him. He could walk out now if he said *yes*. It was easy. All he had to do was betray the woman he loved.

He looked first at Wycoff and then at Gammon, thinking how much he hated them both. Then he said it.

He said, "Yes."

Vikki had her back to Harold when he stepped into the lobby and when she turned he felt his breath catch in his throat. It was the first time he had seen her all fixed up: blond hair knotted in one of those fancy braids, white blouse and tan pants, makeup, the whole nine yards. And here he was in the clothes he was arrested in. Mr. Gomes's shirt and his incredibly wrinkled suit pants. He must look like a complete wreck.

But the biggest change to Vikki was the look on her face. She had pretty much dropped the attitude.

"Hello, Harold," she said, and he wondered if she was going to shake his hand or what, but before he knew it she gave him a kiss on the lips. She laughed, embarrassed, then suddenly hugged him tightly as if she had to express something she had felt for a long time. He hugged her back and felt her breasts press into his chest, swelling as she breathed.

"Come on out here." She took his arm and towed him outside, out into another knockout day, like the day they were at the coroner's office, with the same blue mountains hazy in the distance.

She kept towing him along, past rows of cars in the parking lot, saying, "Wait till you see."

"What? What?" Harold asked. He was having trouble putting together complete sentences because the feeling of being free, of Vikki looking so great (and hugging him like that), had completely overwhelmed him.

"Here it is!" Vikki said, gesturing at a really hot classic car—just like his father's. Wait a second, it *was* his father's car! The Bahama green '64 Chevy Impala SS with the 340-hp V-8 engine. And it had both doors. It had been painted, waxed and detailed, buffed and polished until it was as perfect as the day around them.

"What do you think?" She asked, studying his face.

"How did you—?"

"I went to your dad's house, convinced him to let me fix it up for you."

"My dad? You talked to my dad?"

"Yes. I told him I felt responsible for what happened. I took it to this guy Joe knew. He did the paint job: six coats, infrared heat lamp in between. Detroit couldn't do any better."

"And the door? Where did you—"

"Got it at Pick-a-Part. That's why I had to have it painted."

"So it's not my door?"

"No. But I mean—come on, don't you think it looks great?"

She was frowning now, worried about his reaction, showing her age just a little bit, small lines pulling in around her eyes and mouth. But hell, she still looked great. And his dad was alive. And the Impala was back in one piece. He felt dizzy, the day spinning around him.

Quietly, she asked: "What do you think, Harold?"

"I think it's a damn cream puff."

In the car now, Harold driving, heading south on PCH along the ocean, the V-8 purring under the hood, the windows down and stray pieces of Vikki's hair swirling around her face.

"They tell you why I'm out?" Harold asked.

"You gave them your statement. That's why the insurance paid off. I heard you might get a suspended sentence but . . . That's all, isn't it?"

"Not exactly."

"Well, what happened then?"

"They let me go so that I'd find Marianna."

"Uh-huh."

"I.e., *turn her in.*"

"Yeah?" she said, as if he hadn't told her the bad news yet. Then she quickly added, "You're going to do it, aren't you?"

He just kept driving.

"Oh, come on, Harold. For God's sake, do it!"

"You don't understand."

"You're right. I don't understand. I mean, that—that bitch is responsible for all this. Oh please, you've got to come to your senses."

"They'll put her away."

"Good! She deserves it. Harold, you're thinking with your little head again. And—" She thought of something else, "And let me tell you something, Mexican women, when they turn thirty—five years from now—forget it, el blimpo."

"Five years is a long time."

Harold shifted uncomfortably. Now that she was talking about Marianna she sounded like the old Vikki again. Major attitude.

"Listen. You tell me where she is. I'll tell the cops."

"I can't do it."

"Can't or won't?"

Pause, thinking. "Can't."

She was quiet, looking out the window, the light warm on her face, and Harold realized what a jam he was in. And how a woman, as beautiful as Vikki, stirred him deep inside.

She faced him, toning down the attitude. "I'm going to get the dealership. With the death certificate for Joe, and the insurance investigation, the other side backed out of the suit."

"You gonna run the place?"

"You bet." Pause, deep breath. "I called Fallon, said he could keep his job if he cooperated with me. So he's going to be the sales manager. So it looks like I need a new general manager—someone who knows cars."

"You know cars. I mean, for a—"

"Maybe. But I've seen you in action. You can handle anything. So what do you say?"

"You want *me* to be the general manager?"

"You, Harold."

"Go back to selling cars?" He laughed. But he also found he was excited somehow.

"It'll be different this time. I've got a new concept of how to sell cars—I worked the numbers—I think we can be fair and still make money. Real money. What do you say?"

Harold suddenly saw a whole new life open up in front of his eyes. He saw himself in a big office on a car lot, being smooth with customers, calling Fallon into his office and reaming him out just for the hell of it. But he would get to be around cars—new and used cars—and he loved cars. All cars. But there was only one problem: There was no room in this dream for Marianna.

"Give it some thought, Harold." She paused. "Then say yes."

She laughed and touched his shoulder and he found himself smiling, *Smiling like an idiot*, he couldn't help thinking.

Bait and switch. The phrase jumped into his head now that he was thinking about his car days. Hold out the bait, then switch the buyer to something else. Okay, he knew what the bait was that Vikki was offering. Now, he'd have to wait for the switch.

They went back to her place, a condo she had rented on the beach in Redondo. "The bank took the house," she said as they walked through the front door, "Besides, it would be really hard to live there now, after what happened."

It was a furnished apartment, one of those places that looks like it was decorated by a robot. Its only appeal, as far as Harold could see, was that it was clean and everything probably worked. She gave him a beer and they sat on the balcony and looked out at the ocean while the sun grew larger in the golden twilight, drifting down toward the horizon, in no particular hurry.

Vikki was quiet, staring into her glass of white wine like it was a crystal ball. Then she said, "He's still out there."

They both knew she meant Dash. Images of Dash had circled in Harold's mind during his stay in the Santa Barbara lockup. One picture haunted him: Dash with the club raised above his head, ready to end his life. Harold examined the memory, like a photo lying on the table in front of him, and kept wondering why it was so terrifying. Finally, he realized, it was the expression on Dash's face—a look of delicious expectancy at the thought of killing.

"He's making trouble for me," Vikki said, still looking away.

"So I heard." She looked at him, surprised. "The cops said Dash was feeding them information about you."

"He's telling them I was in on his car insurance rip-off deal. Said I came to him and asked to buy a car and then have it stolen. And he's got the Accell to prove it."

The sun was getting larger by the second, falling into the ocean. Vikki stood up and leaned on the railing, looking away from Harold as she spoke.

"I have an idea . . . But I need your help with it."

To Vikki he said, "Uh-huh." But inside he was thinking, yeah, I was right, it's the old bait and switch. Fix up my car, offer me a job, then reel me in. Then he got pissed at himself for being so suspicious, i.e., maybe she really did like him.

"We need to get Dash out of the way—it's that simple. And the Accell has to disappear too."

She turned to him and he saw that the attitude was back, the anger, the intensity. And he wondered which Vikki he liked best. He felt more at home with this Vikki because he knew he had one hell of an attitude too, one that followed him like a bad smell.

"Here's the deal," she said. "I've already talked to Fallon. I told him he could keep his job if he played ball with us. He went for it. I'm gonna get him to set up Dash."

Harold heard the need for revenge in her voice and found himself wanting a part of the action. He had fifteen stitches in his head to blame on Dash—that and five days of chasing all over hell.

"Fallon calls Dash and tells him I took some documents from his office—they're in his handwriting—and they show he was behind all this. He tells Dash these papers are in the safe, in the study, up at my old house. The bank owns the house now and they don't even know the papers are there."

Vikki continued, outlining the plan, her voice low and intense. And what she had in mind didn't fit at all with the sun setting behind her and the glass of white wine in her hand. When she was done speaking he saw the sun was finally down and felt the air moving restlessly now that the temperature was dropping. He didn't say anything, just let the dark images play in his head, thinking, *Did anyone deserve to die that way?*

Finally she turned and asked, "Will you help me, Harold?"

"You seem to think I'm like a bodyguard or a hit man or something. I told you in the beginning, I just know about cars."

She smiled, shaking her head. "You can tell yourself anything you want, Harold."

"What do you mean?"

"I've seen you in action. You're a scammer from way back."

"Sure, sometimes I have to cut corners a little . . ."

She laughed. "You don't know yourself at all. You're a scammer and a fighter and you love it. And I need you there with me. We can keep the dealership and make money and know that we gave that bastard just what he deserved. That's fair, isn't it, after what he did to us?"

"When're you gonna do this?"

"Tomorrow night. But I need you there. I—I don't trust myself around Dash."

Harold sucked down the last of the beer and jiggled the can.

"I'll get you another."

"I gotta get going." Harold stood up. "I gotta get back to my place, take a shower and . . ." He couldn't say it, but he had some heavy thinking to do about Marianna.

"Why don't you get your stuff and come back? I've got an extra bedroom or . . . But it's better than that dump you're staying in."

The dump he was staying in was calling loudly to Harold right now. Maybe, in the dump, he could stop his head from spinning and figure out what to do about all this.

"I got a lot to think about," he said. "But thanks."

She nodded, trying to understand, and finally, just trying to be a good sport.

They walked to the front door together, awkward, quiet in the bland hallway. When they got to the door she said, "Almost forgot!" and disappeared. She came back a few moments later with an envelope.

He cracked it open and saw a check. Twenty-five grand. He'd never held a check for that much with his name on it.

"When the insurance company heard what Dash did, they sent a guy over with a check. The insurance is coming through in two payments. That's five percent of the first check."

He didn't say anything.

"That's what we agreed on, isn't it? Five percent on the insurance?"

Harold nodded, looking into Vikki's eyes, earnest, eager to please him. A woman this gorgeous, this smart, had never tried to please him before. Hell, a woman like this had never even spit on him before, Harold thought, as he realized this whole thing just kept getting harder and harder.

It never rained in LA in June. But here it was, pouring buckets outside while he sat on a barstool at the Club Sheri the next day, watching bubbles rising in his beer and hearing the hiss of car tires in the wet street through the open door and wondering whether it would be his last alcoholic beverage before he checked into County.

Harold had spent most of last night in here, and—after the bartender helped him stagger up to his room upstairs—he returned and spent the morning here too. Most of the time he was parked right here on this stool. The rest of the time he was on the pay phone next to the cigarette machine. He made a call to Gammon to tell him he was still searching for Marianna. He also called Vikki to tell her he'd help her deal with Dash that night. Then he called Nova and anyone else he could think of that might know where Marianna was. Finally, he gave up calling and just sat on the barstool thinking that the time would finally run out and they would come and get him and cart him off to County where he'd get his head beat in. The way it was pounding right now, that would be a blessing.

Just when he was sure that Marianna had made a run for Chile, or had left town, or had finally given up on him, a hand reached into his blurred vision and took his glass. He turned to see Marianna sip his beer and say, "American beer sucks, doesn't it, Harold? I can't wait till we get back to Chile. They make the best beer in the world there."

It was a line he used on her last year, and he knew the comeback. In fact, it was all he could think of saying.

"The beer is so good in Chile you can even drink it warm," he said, feeling the happiness rising inside him, along with the anger at the decision he now had to make. And he thought how often anger and happiness were intertwined when it came to Marianna.

Harold flagged down the bartender and when Old Tommy arrived she said, "I'm in the mood for a fine light beer."

Tommy looked at her like she was crazy, but he drew a beer and set it on the bar in front of her.

After the first sip she said, "How'd you get out of jail?"

"Vikki put up the bail."

Harold waited for her to say something mean about Vikki. Hell, he wanted her to. Gimme a reason, he thought. Just gimme a reason. But all she said was: "So she got the dough from the insurance company?"

Harold nodded. When he looked at her, the sun was reflecting off the wet pavement outside, shining through her hair, and it looked like her head was on fire. He was so damned happy to see her. With the blood alcohol level in his system now, he decided not to be subtle, so he just said flat out: "I don't even know if you really love me."

"Harold, you're drunk."

"Of course I am. And I'm a bad drunk. When I get drunk I get sad and wonder why the world is so screwed up. And I always come up with answers that make me feel worse. But right now I'm just asking you if you really love me?"

"Now? At this moment?"

"No, more like *in general*, like over time. Do you love me and want to live with me? Would you even consider, like, having a couple of kids or something like that? I mean, give me a little help here—what do we have?"

She sipped her beer and answered in a voice filled with regret and wonder, as if she couldn't believe it, but had to admit it really was true.

"You never let me down. You get things really screwed up. But you always come through. I can't say that about any other man I've met."

The sun was very bright off the rain-slick street outside, and, shining through her hair, it now looked almost like a halo around her head. In Harold's mind something was settled, as if a switch was thrown. And he saw who he really was. He was a man who preferred living in a dump above a bar to a condo on the beach; he was a man who wanted a '64 Impala with the original paint job even if it wasn't as good as six infrared baked custom coats; and he was a man who loved a short woman with black hair who might be fat in five years over a blond goddess who would age gracefully and probably make a bundle in a new car dealership.

Harold took the check for twenty-five grand out of his pocket. He carefully laid it on a dry section of the bar and signed it over to Marianna. He handed it to her and watched her read the amount.

"Get the operation. Then go get my dad and take him with you back to Chile and wait for me there. Whatever you do, stay away from me for a while. If I call you, don't answer. And if you love me, take care of my dad and wait for me in Chile."

"Harold, come on. You're being a little melodramatic."

"The cops figured out you were the one that dumped Covo's body. If they pick you up you'd do time."

"What about you?"

"I might have to do a little stretch." *Stretch*? Shit, he was already talking like a con. "When I get out of jail I'll find you."

"So you're going to jail? For me?"

"For you. For me. For the mess I got us all into."

"Come on, there's gotta be another way. There's always another way. You said that yourself."

"Trust me. This time, there's only one way."

They sat there sipping their beers. And after a while Marianna said, "I've got to take Nova's car back."

She put her arm around Harold's shoulders and leaned her head against his. After a few minutes she slid off the stool.

When he looked up, she was walking out into the sunlight reflecting off the wet pavement. And it was raining again. Raining in LA in June. Shit.

When the thunderstorm finally moved out in the late afternoon it was like the air had been washed clean and the sky was so blue it made you ache inside.

They sat in Harold's Impala and looked up the hill through

the purple tunnel of flowering jacarandra trees and, farther up the hill, to the gates leading to Vikki's house. They sat silently in the parked car, watching the blossoms fall until the street was a purple carpet that flew into the air and swirled in the wake of passing cars. Shortly after dark, the moon rose above the Palos Verdes Peninsula and they could feel the ocean close by, over the edge of the cliff behind the big house.

Several hours earlier, after Marianna had left Harold in the bar, he knew he should sober up and pull himself together. But of course he ordered another beer, and then another, and another, thinking one or two or three more might make some kind of difference. Finally, he just ran out of time.

He carefully drove to Vikki's house. On the way he stopped at a grocery store and bought food and water and loaded it into the trunk, intending to transfer it into the Accell later. It wasn't part of Vikki's plan. It was his own idea because, if he had learned anything from all this, he learned that he was not a cold-blooded killer.

When Vikki climbed into the car she smelled the booze seeping out of Harold's body the way it does when you go on a bender. But she saw that he could still drive, and sensed his determination, so she said nothing and they drove up to her old house and parked on the side street down the hill, where he wouldn't see them as he drove up.

She spoke very little except to tell Harold that Fallon had warned Dash to get the papers out of the safe in the upstairs study of the deserted house. She told Harold she had been inside the house earlier that day and set everything up; everything they needed was in place.

There was a strained silence between them because there was a lingering question that was still unanswered. Then, knowing he would understand, she asked: "Find her?"

"Yeah."

"You going to turn her in?"

"No."

Vikki slowly breathed out, maybe trying hard to control her anger. "So you'll go to jail then—turn your back on my offer and go to jail. Just because you have a *thing* for that bitch."

"It's more than just her, i.e., I can't sell cars again. I'd screw up and make a mess out of things."

She wasn't used to having a man say no to her. "Yeah, I guess you would make a mess of it. That seems to be your way."

Time passed, during which they watched jacaranda blossoms fall on the quiet street and they both kept thinking about it and finally she said, her voice shaking a little, "I wanted you on my side, Harold. We could have done some good work together. We could have had fun and made some honest money. Beyond that, I'm not saying anything. But we could have worked well together."

An hour later they saw a silver Accell slowly pull up and park by the gates. The headlights died and a tall figure stepped out. He ducked through an opening in the bushes, skirting the gates. They saw him cross the lawn under the moonlight and head toward the house.

They climbed out of the Impala and followed at a distance, around the gates and up the shaggy grass slope in the darkness, Harold moving unsteadily, realizing he was still drunk. Then, as they got to the top of the rise, and stood there breathing hard, they saw the ocean spread out in front of them, so broad and pure, the moon casting a corridor of light on the water.

The house loomed ahead, dark and silent. Bullet holes still pocked the white clapboard siding and the front window was blown out and covered with plastic that was torn and snapped in the wind. The man pushed aside the yellow tape across the door and stepped inside.

The figure took the stairs to the room off the landing. They could hear footsteps and the floorboards creaking upstairs as he moved around. It was time to go up there now, into that same room where it all began only a week ago, with Harold's noble intention to "straighten things out." It had been a while since Harold had talked about straightening things out. Instead, it had come down to dividing the blame and eliminating the losers.

The carpeted stairs were silent under their feet and ahead, the flicker of a flashlight beam could be seen in the room. There was the rustling of paper and the shifting of weight—a quiet intensity that indicated the man was no longer measuring the noises around him but concentrating on something else. As they reached the doorway, the light from a page he was holding reflected up in his face and he quietly said, "Damn."

Harold moved to the doorway and saw that the moonlight was streaming through the window, illuminating the tall man as he groped deeper into the wall safe.

"We have the papers."

The man froze, then turned to face Harold.

"I heard you were in jail," his voice low and easy.

"I heard you made a deal with the cops to put Vikki out of business. We thought maybe you'd like to make a deal with us instead."

"Us?"

Vikki stepped into the room. Dash looked from Vikki to Harold, trying to understand their relationship and read her intentions.

"Hey, babe. How ya doin'?"

"Hey, Dash."

Harold said: "Here's the deal—we give you the papers Vikki took out of your office."

"In exchange for . . . ?"

"Two things. Vikki gets her Healey back."

"And?"

"We want the Accell shipped overseas—i.e., it's gotta disappear."

Dash thought about it, said, "I can make that happen."

Harold braced himself. Here comes the hard part. He reminded himself he was still drunk (even though he didn't feel it) and his emotions were all over the place.

"Will you give me your word on that?"

"You got it."

"You wouldn't let me down, would you, Dash?" Vikki's voice was even but Harold saw she was breathing hard. He felt the anger rising inside her.

"No, babe. I won't let you down."

"Then let's drink to it."

"What?"

Her voice came a little louder this time: "Drink to our deal." She pointed at three shot glasses. She had set them on the windowsill earlier that day. "Drink to it! That's not too hard to understand, is it?"

Dash looked at the glasses, realizing where this was going. "Tell you the truth, I'm really not thirsty."

Harold looked from Vikki to Dash. When he looked back at Vikki he saw she was holding the small black gun. He thought, *She was planning this the whole time. She's going to kill him now.*

"Jesus," Harold said.

She spoke to Dash: "When I took the papers out of the safe this afternoon, I found this gun Joe kept. It's one of those cheap things, a Saturday night special, the kind that goes off if you just bump it a little." She knocked the gun with her other hand. He flinched.

Vikki added, "When I picked it up I saw myself killing you with it."

"Remember what we planned?" Harold said to her. "It's better that way."

She said to Dash: "You used me, you bastard."

Then it all broke loose inside her and she started crying, crying and shaking, the tears glistening on her cheeks in the filtered moonlight streaming through the window.

Harold knew the gun would go off at any second and he didn't want to be in the same room when it did. So he said to Dash: "Want to die now? Or maybe take a chance? Pick up the glass and drink it."

"It's not hard to do," Vikki said. "It's good tequila. Here, here's how you do it."

She picked up the middle shot glass, just like she'd said she would, tossed it down, and swallowed. "See? It's easy."

The only sound in the room was her ragged breathing. Harold looked at the shot glasses on the windowsill, then down at the floor, seeing that Dash had tracked jacaranda blossoms onto the carpet. They were shriveling up and turning black in the moonlight.

He was thinking about those blossoms when he heard Dash's voice purr in the darkness, soft as velvet. "Don't hurt me, babe. Please don't hurt me."

Harold saw the effect of Dash's voice on her.

"I know you won't hurt me," he said to Vikki, confidence building in his voice. And Harold saw she wasn't going to pull the trigger. She couldn't. She shook the gun, banged it with her other hand, but she couldn't pull the trigger on him.

"Drink it!" Harold said to Dash.

"Shut up, ya loser," Dash said, and smiled at Harold.

Harold swung at that smile, hit him square in the face and knocked him back into the wall. Dash bumped down on his ass, sitting up against the wall, blood gushing from his nose and split lip.

Vikki leaned down, pressed the gun into the center of Dash's forehead. "You don't understand. I loved you, you bastard."

There it was, Harold thought. She loved this slick asshole, this killer. She'd only been interested in Harold to get things done she couldn't do herself. Harold crouched beside her, no longer afraid of the gun, maybe even wanting it to go off, wanting to see this man die in pain. And crouching there he saw jacaranda blossoms again and wondered why he kept thinking about them.

The confidence drained from Dash's voice as he pleaded with her, "Please, babe. Please don't hurt me."

Vikki handed him the shot glass. He hesitated.

"Don't worry. You won't feel a thing." She jabbed the gun barrel into his forehead, bumping it hard. Then again harder, bouncing his head off the wall behind.

"Go off," she said to the gun. "Please, just go off."

Dash threw down the shot, swallowed hard, looked up, and said, "Okay?"

Harold breathed out. It was over. They would keep him here, the gun on him, until he passed out. Then they'd put him into the Accell and load it into a cargo container. Fallon would get the container loaded onto a freighter to Japan. And all their troubles would sail out to sea. But it was over now. Over.

He saw Vikki relaxing. He looked out the window and saw the moonlight on the ocean. Then he saw there was still one shot glass on the windowsill. And it was still full. He could really use a drink.

He picked it up and drank the tequila. It burned all the way down. And as the tequila began glowing in his stomach, the thought came to him: Dash hadn't parked under the jacaranda tree. He had parked farther up the hill where he couldn't track in the blossoms that were now dying on the floor here. Someone else had tracked them in. Someone who was waiting in the next room.

When he finally awoke, he noticed the gentle swaying that, in another situation, would be pleasant and restful. But here it was combined with the deafening drone of machinery pounding away nearby and that trapped-air feeling like he had been buried alive.

His eyes were open but he couldn't see. And when he asked his brain for an explanation he got a dreamlike picture of two faces—a man and a woman—the taste of tequila in a moonlit room. He realized he should know who that woman was but her name just wouldn't come to the surface. And who was that guy? He had been in a lot of his dreams lately.

Feeling around him, he discovered he was in a car, in the passenger seat, and when he tried to open the door it banged into something close by and let in a smell of fresh-cut lumber. There was the feeling that he was in a tightly confined space, like a small garage, but everything was swaying as if—

HE WAS ON A BOAT!

But where was he going? And why was he here? This was the fate they had planned for Dash.

The knowledge of what was happening came crashing down on Harold. He was in a cargo container, deep in the hold of a freighter, buried under tons of cargo, sentenced to a lingering death.

Then he recalled the tequila, his drunkenness, and the confusion of the scene when Vikki drew the gun. Fallon had double-crossed them. He was in the room first. That was why those dead jacaranda blossoms were all over the place. He knew what their plan was. He saw the shot glasses and switched them, knowing either Harold or Vikki would get the spiked drink.

Then other pictures came to Harold—he remembered Fallon entering the room, how he had taken the gun from Vikki. And then the scene ended with Harold's apathy, paralysis, and unconsciousness.

He sat there in the car, feeling the throb of the freighter's engine, and wondered how long it would take to reach Japan. And, he wondered, was there a chance in hell he would be alive when the freighter finally got there?

Gammon had the binoculars to his eyes watching the two men climb out of a black Lexus with dealer plates parked along Pier 17 at the Los Angeles Harbor. They were exchanging words with the driver of a semi truck, a rust red cargo container on his truck. The three men opened the back of the container and peered inside. They seemed satisfied and slammed the doors.

Gammon picked up his radio and spoke into it: "Now."

Four cars pulled out of a nearby parking lot and moved toward the Lexus, kicking up dust as they went. Gammon threw his Caprice in gear and by the time he got there the two men were handcuffed over the hood of the Lexus, which was probably very hot in the noonday sun.

Dash turned, wrists handcuffed behind him, straining to look at Gammon. The bandage covering his nose flashed white in the sunlight. The other guy was bald, fiftyish. Gammon knew him to be Edward Fallon, general manager of Joe Covo Matsura.

"Sir, the State Insurance Commissioner's not going to be

pleased when he hears about this," Dash said. "I'm already giving him my full cooperation."

"That doesn't mean you can get away with murder."

"Murder?"

Gammon enjoyed the way Dash had to awkwardly turn to look at him, the cuffs nice and snug on his wrists, leaning on the baking hood of the black Lexus.

"The murder of James Shields. You ran him off that bridge—" He pointed at the Vincent Thomas Bridge, which loomed above him. "When the Insurance Commissioner found out Shields was working on a fraud case, he put up a nice reward."

"I have no idea what you're talking about."

"Maybe you'll remember when you see yourself on TV. Channel 7 got a nice shot of you reaching into his car, pulling out his briefcase."

Gammon thought about the phone tip he had received earlier that day. The caller sounded vaguely familiar: a young woman, faint Hispanic diction, a little like the way Richard spoke. The tipster said she had seen his Rover with damage to the front fender, the same damage described by a witness arriving on the scene of the fatal accident on the bridge. They called Tijuana and, sure enough, they still had the smashed-up Rover. They confirmed the front end damage and shipped it back to LA for evidence.

A whirring sound came from overhead. Gammon looked up and saw a huge crane dropping a cable toward the cargo container on the parked flatbed truck.

"Tell the crane op to stay the hell away from that container," Gammon said to another detective. "And get the photographer over here so we can open it up."

He already knew what they would find inside, since they saw Dash and Fallon loading it: the Accell under a load of furniture. And inside the Accell was Vikki Covo. Gammon felt this would prove Vikki had nothing to do with the insurance fraud Dash was working. He was relieved about this because he felt that enough bad shit had already happened to her.

Watching the crime lab guys opening the back of the cargo container, Gammon realized something else. Dodge had been out of touch now for thirty-six hours and he never came up with Marianna Perado's whereabouts. Vikki might be able to tell him where Dodge was. Maybe he got shipped out on an earlier boat. If so, Gammon doubted if he had the authority to turn the ship around. And frankly, he didn't want to even if he could. If he brought Dodge back, he'd just have to ship him off to County. One more burden for the taxpayers of California.

Wycoff ambled over to Gammon and together they watched the back doors of the cargo container being opened. Through the stacked furniture, they could see the taillights of the Accell inside.

"Where were they shipping it?" Wycoff asked.

"Japan."

"They don't have cars over there?"

Gammon turned to Wycoff. He had grown to like this man who carried the sadness of his job with him, but always with a certain dignity.

"They'll pay a bundle for a hot car, off the streets of LA. They think that's very cool. Ya know, it's weird but, half the world wants what we've got right here."

Wycoff pondered the statement. He nodded philosophically. "No shit."

"Excuse me, officer," Dash said. "Could you loosen these handcuffs? They're digging into my wrists."

"No," Gammon said. Then he added, "Listen up, Chief. I'm gonna read you your rights. Then, you're on your way to County."

Feeling around himself in the dark, Harold realized there was an upside to all this. He was seated behind the wheel of his '64 Chevy Impala SS, with the 340-horsepower V-8 engine. Now that was going in style. Besides, if someone on the other end was expecting a cream puff like this, they'd unload the container ASAP, pop the door open. No way he'd sit on the loading dock for long.

But that would be twelve days from now—twelve long days without water. Was there a chance in hell he could survive? Doubtful.

So the Impala would outlive both himself and his father. He pictured the Chevy cruising through the streets of Tokyo, Japanese teenagers checking out the car, nodding to each other, giving it the thumbs-up. That was immortality of a sort, he thought sadly.

Wait a second. His brain was clearing and something else was coming to the surface, floating above the drugs and booze.

Before he picked up Vikki that night, before they went to meet Dash, he had stopped at the supermarket and . . . Yes! It was coming back to him now. He had stopped at the store and loaded up on food and water. He put it in the trunk of his Impala, intending to transfer it to the Accell.

Now Harold realized, his compassion had saved his own life. All he had to do was worm his way through the stacked furniture and pop the trunk. He could also get his tool case out of the trunk and punch some air holes in the container wall. Then he'd sit back and enjoy the cruise. **Boring**, yes. But it beat the hell out of going to County, having minorities of all kinds jumping on his head.

Relaxing back into the tuck-n-roll upholstery Harold

thought how glad he was he hadn't turned Marianna in to the cops. This way he could hook up with her again. A few days of sightseeing in Tokyo, then he'd catch a ride back to Chile. And maybe—he was getting really excited now—maybe when he got back to their house, and walked in the door, Marianna would be standing there, beside his dad, with that knowing smile on her lips saying, "I knew you'd be back, Harold. You never let me down."

Harold was feeling much better now. So good, in fact, that he replayed his earlier fantasy of the Impala cruising the streets of Tokyo. But now he put himself behind the wheel, wearing shades, arm cocked out the window. The Japanese loved American things—our music, our movies, our cars. Hell, they even used a lot of American expressions.

Sitting there in his car, in the darkness, deep inside the freighter, Harold actually heard himself laugh out loud as he thought, "I wonder how they say 'cream puff' in Japanese?"